THE TURNING TIDE

Created: Helmsman Publications
www.helmsmanpublications.com

Published: Booklocker.com, Inc.
www.booklocker.com
2012

THE TURNING TIDE
Third Edition

HELMSMAN'S
WINGED COMET

Bill Baldwin

Other Novels by Bill Baldwin:

The Helmsman (Classic Edition: 1985) • (Director's Cut Edition: 2003)
Galactic Convoy (Classic Edition: 1987) • Director's Cut Edition: 2003)
The Trophy (Classic Edition: 1990) • (Director's Cut Edition: 2007)
The Mercenaries (Classic Edition 1991) • (Director's Cut Edition 2008)
The Defenders, 1992
The Siege, 1994
The Defiance 1996
"Last Ship to Haefdon" (nv) *Oceans of Space*, ed. Brian M. Thomsen & Martin H. Greenberg, DAW 2002
The Enigma Strategy 2009

NOTE: A Wilf Brim Glossary
especially for *The Turning Tide*
begins on page
347

The Galactic Almanac
(and handy encyclopedia)

Invasion of Emithrnéy/Bax (52014)
From the Edition for Standard Year 52016

General Information.

The main thrust of this raid into occupied Effer'wyck was to destroy the Gravity Dock near Eppeid City on Emithrnéy/Bax, a massive starship repair complex—vast enough to service the largest starships in the Known Universe and sufficiently impregnable to withstand poundings from the most powerful disruptors at the time. Before the invasion of Effer'wyck by The League of Dark Stars, the Effer'wyckean government had constructed the facility at enormous cost. Ironically, it was now serving as a furtherance to Nergol Triannic's ambition of conquering the entire Home Galaxy. Its destruction would deal a hard blow to The League.

The secondary objective of the raid was to capture a new BKAEW detection apparatus that League engineers had just finished installing on Lavenurb/Bax, next planet out from Emithrnéy/Bax. Because capture of this equipment was so important to the war effort, the Imperial Admiralty had decided to risk their new I.F.S. *Montroyal*, a brand-new medium transport starship. It was not enough to simply destroy this new leaguer equipment; Imperial research boffins on Proteus/Asturius needed to find out what made it tick. Doing that required *Montroyal* to bring it home.

Imperial Forces

For this effort, Combined Operations Command cobbled together a middling armada consisting of eight light cruisers, six Free Effer'wyckean disruptor monitors, 16 surface bombardment ships, two flotillas of tiny Electronic Warfare trawlers, and 25 of the latest armored landing craft—in addition to *Montroyal*. This force had been secretly assembled—along with nearly six thousand battle-ready commandos—on two uninhabited planets located less than a light year from the Imperial side of the 'Wyckean Void.

The entire operation was under direct command of Major General Megan Trafford, Imperial Army.

For overhead support, Fleet Command had likewise provided six squadrons, of 16 Starfury Mk 9 astroplanes each, to fight off defending starships—plus another four squadrons of WF Type-327 attack astroplanes, whose job it would be to smother defensive fire from the surface. Considering that a large percentage of the Starfuries were almost brand new and could therefore be depended to fly nearly any time they were needed, the numbers seemed adequate for the job—at least early in the mission, when the Imperials would face only local opposition.

However, when signaled by the Royal Engineers at Emithrnéy/Bax that the new Leaguer BKAEW had been loaded aboard I.F.S. *Montroyal*, two squadrons of Starfuries and two squadrons of WF Type-327s were to be diverted to this special operation for the remainder of the mission.

Both parts of this secondary operation were under direct command of Vice Admiral Wilf Brim, Imperial Fleet.

Preparations

On the surface, the attack appeared logical and well planned—an operation by, as well as for, the textbooks of interstellar warfare, carrying with it the potential for vast damage to the enemy and prodigious profit for the Empire and its Allies.

However, once the attack was underway, it was clearly understood the Imperials *could* encounter much unwelcome company in *very* short order. Fat Leaguer Marshal Hoth Orgoth commanded nearly fifteen hundred attack and killer astroplanes in Effer'wyck—and had never shown any shyness about using them. With all the myriad things that could go awry during such a large, complex operation, it was also clear that Operation Eppeid carried with it the quite-viable seeds of disaster.

Significantly, General Trafford was so certain of success she forbid talk of wasting resources on contingency plans, should the unexpected transpire.

The Attack

On D-Day, 25 Octad, 52014, the diverse ships of the Imperial assault flotilla slowed through Hyperspeed to arrive at an initial point off Emithrnéy/Bax within moments of zero metacycle—a genuine triumph of spacemanship in all respects and an excellent beginning to the operation.

Immediately, four Starfury squadrons fanned out to encircle the main target planet at Emithrnéy/Bax as a Combat Air Patrol. The remaining Starfuries and the four squadrons of WF Type-327 attack astroplanes headed toward the surface for an orbital holding pattern. At the same time, light cruisers and monitors were descending slowly through the atmosphere to secure the gravity-dock perimeter, should such be necessary.

Concurrently, while the raid commenced on Emithrnéy/Bax, a much smaller force of Special Services-Assault (SSA) commandos and Royal Engineers landed on Lavenurb/Bax, near the new BKAEW site. When the Commandos had the BKAEW site under control, Royal Engineers began to disassemble the BKAEW equipment (including all special antennae visible on the reconnaissance HoloPics). Subsequently, each piece would be loaded aboard *Montroyal,* which would withdraw as quickly as possible to the Imperial side of the 'Wyckean Void, with no regard to the larger operation.

At first, everything appeared as if it was proceeding perfectly.

The Anomaly

Then the anomaly occurred—one that immediately destroyed General Trafford's hope for surprise. One of the first two de-orbiting landing craft ran afoul of an escorted merchantman in the process of lifting for space. A furious fire fight erupted, and within clicks everyone was blasting away at anything that moved.

Suddenly, powerful disruptors on the surface went into operation, their blinding discharges fouling Hyperscreens on both sides. Two appeared to fire simultaneously, and Immediately, a tremendous explosion erupted in space that blasted the old heavy cruiser I.F.S. *Furious* completely out of the sky—with an immediate loss of its heavy disruptors on the ground— and nearly eight hundred Imperial Star Sailors

Quickly following this, another surface disruptor site exploded with a great burst of radiation fire, signaling that at least some of the Commando force must have made it to the surface and deployed. However, all hope for success on the surface faded when League battle crawlers appeared on the surface. The entire operation began to fall apart at that point.

General Trafford's Order to Withdraw

With the Eppeid Gravity-Dock operation now in dire straits, General Trafford reacted in great haste, ordering all astroplanes and starships to support an immediate exit for the ground forces. This order came before Admiral Brim could accomplish his secondary mission: supporting the capture of the League's powerful new BKAEW unit on Lavenurb/Bax. With the failure of the attack's main thrust, many League starships had already been freed to answer calls of help from the second front.

Admiral Brim's Partial Countermand

Moments after General Trafford issued her order to break off the attack and retreat across the Wyckean Void, Admiral, Brim made his fateful decision to support the operation on Lavenurb/Bax rather than to abandon that effort. Countermanding Trafford's orders, he ordered two squadrons each of Starfuries and WF Type-327s to report at highest priority to Lavenurb/Bax, then departed for that battle himself. In later testimony at his Court Marshal, Admiral Brim said his decision was based on the Imperial Fleet's acute need to counter the powerful new League BKAEW, which was already beginning to show results against Imperial shipping of all kinds.

Brim's actions saved the Lavenurb/Bax operation, but only barely. By the time he arrived, the Imperial Marines had nearly completed loading the disassembled BKAEW into I.F.S. *Montroyal*, but unknown to them, both Helmsmen for the big starship had been killed. Taking the situation into his own hands, Admiral Brim landed his Starfury near the big ship, set explosive charges to keep it from enemy hands, then boarded the big ship. Taking *Montroyal's* completely unfamiliar helm, he managed to pilot the big starship home.

Military Consequences

No major objectives of the raid were accomplished. A total of 3,623 of the 6,000 men (almost 60%) who made it to the surface were either killed, wounded, or captured. Fleet Command failed to lure the League astroplanes into open battle, losing 96 Imperial astroplanes (at least 32 to flak or accidents compared to 48 lost by the League), while the Imperial Fleet lost 33 landing craft and one destroyer

Personnel Consequences

Although General Trafford was generally cited for the failure, she retained her Imperial Army rank and commission. However, because Admiral Brim had countermanded her orders as senior commander of the failed operation, Trafford convened a court martial against the Admiral. Her testimony at this trial resulted in his being officially disciplined, then deprived of his commission in the Imperial Fleet.

Addenda

It should be noted that Admiralty's decision to relieve Admiral Brim of his commission was not unanimous throughout the Service, nor the Imperial Palace. Soon after Brim's court marshal, Emperor Onrad V announced the following decree:

> Know ye by these presents that I, Onrad the Fifth, Grand Galactic Emperor, Prince of the Reggio Star Cluster, and Rightful Protector of the Heavens do make and seal this proclamation by all powers and endowments vested in me at my coronation. From this day onward, Our loyal subject, Wilf Ansor Brim, shall be known throughout all the civilized Universe as Lord Brim, 1st Duke of Grayson. With this title, I also assign, from Royal Land Holdings, the five habitable planets and two non-habitable planets of the star Grayson,

and all properties, minerals, rents, leases, and income pertaining from them to his sole ownership. Decreed this first Standard Day of Decad in the Standard Imperial Year 5201

Prologue

. . .nearly two Standard Years later

GANTACLAR HARBOR, IMPERIAL PROVINCE OF
CARESCRIA, LINFARNE/NAVRON, 32 OCTAD, 52016

"Hands to stations for landfall!" buzzed the cabin loud speaker. "Hands to stations for landfall! All passengers to seats immediately."

The civilian packet ship was bumping down through remains of a huge storm that had rendered this whole region of Linfarne's surface white with snow. Through Wilf Brim's first-class stateroom Hyperscreen, the wintry landscape looked just as forbidding as he remembered from nearly 30 years in the past: *nasty*. Clusters of lights winked off here and there below while the star Navron brightened the Lightward horizon with a hazy brush strokes of pink and lavender.

Off to Starboard, he spotted the foreshortened outline of frozen Lake Kelton where wind-swept billows of steam signaled a runway melting for the packet's landfall. The gray sprawl of Gantaclar Wharves cluttered the near shore. Before the Farthington-291 asteroid mines had become unprofitable some years ago, those wharves had been of considerable importance to the Empire. From the lack of lights there, Brim gathered that little of its former activity remained. But, if his speculations about the upcoming conference was anything in the neighborhood of accurate, war was about to change all that. Radically.

They flew a quick circuit of the lake, then turned and descended rapidly toward the surface, the packet's Helmsman making constant— to Brim, *unnecessary*—corrections for what must have been a blustery wind. Back in '89 when Instructor-Helmsman Jim Payne taught Brim

1

to fly ore barges, he judged skill by the corrections people *didn't* make on final approach. Brim still made those judgments.

The packet flashed low over a familiar rocky shore, flared, then touched down on her gravity foot in cascades of spray: nicely enough; Brim allowed the Helmsman that, at least. As they slowed and the spray subsided below his cabin Hyperscreen, he could see a side channel had now melted ahead, curving off to a jetty where six optical bollards flashed on either side of a rusty brow. *Time to get going*, he told himself, snapping his fingers to attract the single portmanteau he'd packed. So far as he could tell, his was the only ticket to this destination—and little wonder. Gantaclar was *ugly*.

By the time they came abreast the brow, Brim was at the boarding-lobby Hyperscreens, watching tractor beams flash from the bollards to the packet's anchor ports, drawing her smoothly to the quay. He smiled to himself: perhaps he'd judged the Helmsman too harshly…

When the gravity engines ground to a halt somewhere beneath Brim's feet, the silence was half startling. "All hands and passengers prepare for local gravity. Repeat, prepare for local gravity."

Brim steadied myself; he'd never been good at gravity switchovers. Somehow they… *ugh* …he could taste his gorge….

"You all right, Sir?" a Steward inquired solicitously.

"Yes, …I'm fine," Brim choked, recovering as the local gravity took effect. It had always been that way with him; sometimes better, sometimes worse. He could never get used to the change—almost washed out of the Helmsman's Academy because of it.

"You sure you're okay, Sir?"

"Just open the hatch, please."

"Aye, Sir." Deftly, the Steward popped the hatch inward and carefully shoved it to one side. A blast of frigid air swept into the lobby along with the strong redolence of ozone. Brim heard a rasping screech outside as someone extended a poorly lubricated brow to the hatch. It connected with a CLANG; the Steward peered out to inspect with a professional aspect.

"Okay?" Brim asked, feeling impatient for some reason.

"Seems, safe, Sir," the Steward assured him, stepping aside.

2

Snapping his fingers for the portmanteau, Brim stepped out onto the small upper platform and paused for a moment, not quite ready for either the eerie silence or the half-familiar panorama of rusting gantry cranes, derelict holding bins, and abandoned C-97 ore barges beached in uneven rows along the snow-covered waterfront. His last view of Gantaclar had been a riot of clamorous, violent activity. Now, except for a small squadron of executive transports hovering on spanking-new gravity pads a thousand irals to Lightward, nothing except the packet on which he'd arrived seemed related to starflight at all. This wasn't the Gantaclar he'd known; this was the *ghost* of Gantaclar.

He carefully picked his way down half the steep, ice-speckled flight of stilled escalator treads—probably hadn't moved by themselves for decades. Below, a couple of military dock hands were talking with a cabby whose skimmer idled quietly a few irals from the brow. All three appeared to be staring up at him.

As he reached the bottom and stepped through the gate, a Chief Warrant Officer in the Imperial Carescrian Navy crunched forward through the crusted snow. He was heavy-set man with huge, grizzled hands and looked strangely familiar. "Admiral Brim," he said. "Welcome to Gantaclar, such as it is." With that, he clicked his heels and gave a military salute

Instinctively, Brim returned the salute before he could check himself. "Thanks, Chief," he muttered as his cheeks burned. "Except... I'm just Wilf Brim, these days. And I didn't catch....."

"Wouldn't expect you to recognize me, Admiral," the Warrant officer said. "We served together in Fleetport thirty durin' the Battle of Avalon. M' name's Blake, Chief Warrant Officer Harry Blake. I was a Systems Tech. aboard old Starfury sixty-five ninety-five the day that Gorn-Hoff got on our tail."

Brim shook his head. He'd been such a close acquaintance of death in the last few years, all the terrors of war seemed to blur together. He faked it. "Chief Blake, of course," he lied, extending his hand. "How could I forget?"

"Considering all you've gone through in the last couple o' Standard Years, Admiral," Blake said with a look of sympathy Brim didn't especially need, " I wouldn't be surprised if you couldn't remember your own name sometimes."

"Once in a while I can't," Brim quipped with a wry grin. Then he remembered the man's feelings. "But I deeply appreciate that *you* did."

"My pleasure," the Dock Master said, suddenly beaming.

"I recognized you, too, Admiral," the Cabby broke in. "Just tellin' the Spaceman First here about you."

Thinking rapidly, Brim blurted out, "Then I thank you, also," managing what he hoped was a grin. "And, er, where did *we* meet?"

"We didn't actually, Admiral" the man said. "But you were on the media a lot back, nearly two Standard Years ago when, ah...." He grimaced.

Brim felt his cheeks burn again. "It's all right," he said. "That, er, trouble doesn't much bother me much any more."

"Then you're a bigger man than I, Admiral," the Chief interrupted. "That was a put-up job if there ever was one—pure gorksroar, if you'll pardon the expression. Everyone pretty well figured what was really going on."

"Well, ...thanks," Brim mumbled. "But please, I haven't been an Admiral for quite a while, now. I'm simply Wilf Brim, now."

"Gotcha', Admiral," the Chief said, opening the cab door. "Whatever you're doin' here, we're wishin' you the best of luck." Suddenly, all three stepped back and saluted.

Brim managed another smile—funny how uncomfortable it felt after all the grief of his court martial. He returned the salute in spite of himself. "Thank you, friends," he said with real humility.

"I'll take you to Headquarters, now, Admiral," the Cabby said, directing Brim's portmanteau into the luggage compartment with a brief whistle.

Brim carefully stomped snow from his boots before he entered the cab. Then, before door closed, he had to ask, "Who sent you? I wasn't expecting anyone to meet me at the brow like this."

"Big guy, Admiral," the cabby replied. "A Master Chief in the Imperial Fleet—had a raft of campaign ribbons. He was with one of them Bears from Sodeskaya: an old fella'."

Somehow, Brim wasn't particularly surprised. "A big Chief and an old Bear, eh?" he repeated before he could stop himself. "You wouldn't remember the Chief's name, would you?"

"Ouch," the Cabby said, reddening, "Don't think I was supposed to mention him. Me and my big mouth."

"Well, now it's out, do you recall his name?" Brim asked, but he already knew. It couldn't be anyone else.

"Funny name," the Cabby said. "Something like…," he frowned with concentration.

"Something like *Barbousse*?"

"Yeah, *that's* it. Kinda' thought you might have heard of him before."

Brim had heard of him before, all right. "And just why weren't you supposed to mention his name?" he asked.

"Well, Admiral," the Cabby said with a frown, "I think he had the impression maybe you didn't want to see him."

"I understand," Brim mumbled with the deep sense of isolation that had plagued him since the final day at the military tribunal. How could he ever explain to…? "I'll keep it to myself that you mentioned anything," he mumbled.

"Thanks, Admiral. I don't like to rile Chiefs with that many hash marks."

Brim nodded. He understood *that* all too well: Master Chief Barbousse was not a man to cross. "You wouldn't remember the name of that Sodeskayan, would you?"

"Um, 'Borodon' or somethin' like that," the Cabby replied, sliding into the driver's compartment. "I think that's it—or somethin' close."

"How about *Borodov*?" Brim asked.

"Yeah, Admiral, that's it," the Cabbie said. "*Borodov*. Had a real gray muzzle and whiskers."

"Pretty well dressed?" Brim asked.

The Cabby hesitated. "Well, um… every one of them Sodeskayans looks kind of strange with their big, wooly hats and the boots and…."

"I understand," Brim said, leaning back in the seat as the Apprentice eased the passenger door closed. In a way, the Cabby had answered his questions. He smiled. "Let's go find those reticent gentlemen," he said. "I've kept both of them waiting a long time…."

— o — 0 — o —

A few hundred irals distant, a man known only as Covall the Wraith—a skeletal presence dressed in a dark cloak—concealed himself behind a rusting ore barge, watching through binoculars as Brim's cab started off. Before it was out of sight, he thumbed a HoloPhone and waited.

"Yes?"

"As you suspected, *he* arrived aboard the morning packet," Covall said, noting the phone's display was blank as always.

"You are certain is was *him*?"

"It was *him*."

"Return to the ship immediately, then stand by for further orders."

"Yes, Sir," Covall muttered into an already disconnected microphone, then trudged off toward the executive transport area, clutching the cloak around his scrawny neck. How he hated the cold!

BOOK I

RETURN OF THE NATIVE

Chapter 1

. . .a reckoning of sorts

GANTACLAR HARBOR, IMPERIAL PROVINCE OF
CARESCRIA, LINFARNE/NAVRON, 33 OCTAD, 52016

I n the morning light, deserted, snow-covered rail yards and stilled
forests of rusting gantry cranes fled past the cab window in bleak
tableaus out of a lonely dream—familiar somehow, yet so
disconcertingly strange. Brim couldn't say he was ready in any way
for what waited in the old headquarters building ahead.

There hadn't been much information in the terse set of Royal Travel
Orders commanding him to attend a secret meeting in this, one of the
most out-of-the-way spots he could imagine. He'd simply packed his
traveling case and hopped the first starship heading in the general
direction of Carescria. His orders might not have supplied much
information, but they did carry amazing travel priority.

All things considered, it was good to know Barbousse and Borodov
were there. Even though it would be a wrench dealing with them in
civilian clothes, he knew it was high time he faced the facts and got
back to living some sort of useful life. In the long months since his
court-martial, he'd been firm with his old friends: He wanted neither
kindness nor help, especially from Barbousse. Like so many of Brim's
friends, the Chief had been highly disconcerted about how things
turned out in court; he'd actually threatened to resign from the Fleet to
become Brim's private retainer. But immediately following the trial,
Brim had little idea what the future held for himself—much less
Barbousse—and his old friend at least retained a promising career in
the Imperial Fleet. Besides, at the time, the hoary old Empire needed
Barbousse a lot more than he did.

In the first two Standard Years of what was fast being dubbed the
Second Great War, Brim had watched star nation after star nation

9

across the 'Wyckean Void capitulate in the face of savage assaults by Nergol Triannic's League of Dark Stars: A'zurn, then Gannet, then Lamintir, then Korbu, then nearly half the planets of Fluvanna, followed by powerful Effer'wyck itself—the latter in concert with a final, humiliating retreat from the planet Aunkayr by General Hagbutt's battered Imperial Expeditionary Forces. When that particular debacle was concluded, nearly half the Known Galaxy lay prostrate beneath Triannic's jackbooted feet, with only the stubborn old Empire and a few of its dominions remaining in the way of the League's galactic mastery.

In subtle ways, however, the war was inexorably changing; the Imperials hadn't exactly been sitting on their collective hands watching civilization collapse around them. Project Sapphire—rebuilding the ancient space citadel at Gontor—had changed much of that. Now, Imperials had changed to fighting back aggressively. Their first offensive: Operation Spark—the invasion of Fluvanna from Gontor—had already begun, shortly after Brim had lost his commission in the trumped-up courts-martial.

He'd followed news of the simultaneous landings on two Fluvannian planets—then the breakout into the main planetary systems—as best he could while adjusting badly to his new status as a civilian. Being barred from the action was a terrible thing in wartime—especially for a dyed-in-the-wool Star Sailor. All the way across from Avalon to the sprawling Carescrian port of Caer Landria, where he'd hopped the packet for Gantaclar, he'd hoped against hope they'd have something in mind to get him back into the war—even though deep down he knew it would be a long time before anyone let him wear a Fleet Cloak again.

He pursed his lips and glanced out the cab window as he forced himself back to the present. With hard work and luck, much of Gantaclar's derelict heavy equipment might be restorable—some even operable now, like the landing pier where he'd arrived. But that would only serve as a starting place. If he'd learned anything about fighting Nergol Triannic, a meaningful attack on his League was going to require every resource the Empire could muster—from wherever it could be found. And because the old Empire had largely expended itself during the last war, a great deal of the present war's materiel would funnel through this very harbor—much more than it appeared capable of handling in its present condition.

In spite of himself, he shuddered. *Voot's beard* what a cold, ugly place this old spaceport was! Hard to believe he'd spent years here as a youth flying broken-down C-97 ore barges to and from the asteroid mines. At that long-ago juncture, he'd been so beggared that the place—awful as it was—seemed a big improvement over anything he'd known. Nevertheless, if it had been a ill-maintained junkyard *then*, well, after nearly two decades of utter neglect, it wasn't going to be transformed back into any kind of useful space harbor without requiring a lot of resources. And, of course, someone would be needed to manage the transformed Harbor Authority—perhaps even himself?

"We're here, Admiral," the Cabby said, breaking into Brim's reverie. As the cab crunched into the icy circular driveway this particular morning, the old headquarters building looked merely ugly. To a much younger Wilf Brim it had appeared more *threatening*: a place to which a summons often meant a lost job—or worse. At least *that* had changed.

— o — 0 — o —

Nearby, in the executive landing area, Count Tal Confisse Trafford, one of the most powerful civilians in the Empire, relaxed in the warm, perfumed salon of his magnificent starship yacht, *Princess Megan*, having final words of strategy over breakfast with his Cousin, Lord Daniel Cranwell. For all anyone at the conference knew, the Count had remained in Avalon, having lent Cranwell his yacht for the term of the conference. But Trafford had a keen personal interest in the outcome of this particular meeting. If all went well—and he had every hope it might—the next day or so would put in place the last of his preparations to bring about significant change in the Imperial Government.

Always careful to appear polite and sincere, the pudgy Trafford had collected his vast powers gradually in increments so tiny that often, potential opponents hardly noticed they had lost before they knew competition had even begun. Whenever sharing projects or activities with "partners," Trafford quickly did all the work, broadcasting news of his lonely struggle while damning his "partners" with faint praise by naming them in the credits. Perhaps his most clever strategies were downplaying others' creative ideas *just* long enough for the ideas to be forgotten—then "announcing" them as his own.

Trafford had a round, pink face, small eyes located much too near his sharp, beak-like nose, a balding head, and the tightly pursed lips of a bank auditor. But it was the eyes, round, and shiny with greed, that gave window to his soul—always shifting, always searching for the next small increment of gain, whatever that might be. It was the way rodents nibbled apart large buildings.

He sipped his cvc'eese thoughtfully. A wild card had appeared at the last moment: the dangerous nobody known as Wilf Brim. The man's unexpected presence here at the conference served yet again as a reminder that one can never take one's eyes off one's activities until they are complete. Even though the upstart Carescrian had many powerful friends—including Emperor Onrad, himself—it would be good to put him in his place early. Later, when the right chance appeared, he or Cranwell could arrange for the parvenu's death, thus insuring daughter Megan's continuing rise in the Imperial Army.

— o — 0 — o —

Brim hopped out of the cab and forced the fare on his protesting cabby—plus a generous tip—then led his portmanteau up the long, salt-stained staircase to the lobby doors. Something was making him uncomfortable. Nearly two years ago, as a working Rear Admiral in the Imperial Fleet, he'd have approached this conference with all the self-confidence a man can have—just another planning meeting at a reasonably high level. But now…. Now, he was a *civilian*—and worse, a civilian by reason of being convicted of incompetence by a military court martial. He grimaced touching the tarnished brass door activators. He *was* the same person he'd always been after all: same strengths, same flaws, same everything. Everything *else* seemed to have changed.

Inside the dark, musty-smelling lobby, he stomped salted slush from his boots—if the Harbor Authority could still heat landing and takeoff runs, why not heat the stupid *sidewalk*?—then stopped at a desk manned by two plain-clothes guards who appeared remarkably out of place in Gantaclar. Oddly, both would have looked more appropriate in the Imperial Palace back in Avalon than a backwoods Carescrian star harbor. These two were so *perfectly* civilian, they almost had to be Imperial Secret Service. In fact, more of these so-called *civilians* were stationed along the balcony girding the second story. Brim frowned. Definitely bodyguards. But *why*? Who here could warrant that kind of security? Certainly not Barbousse—and the Sodeskayan Knez in Gromcow would have sent a small army of his own secret service as protection for old Borodov. Briskly—*professionally*—one of the men examined his credentials, then raised an eyebrow and focused on his face. "Through those doors over there, er, Lord Brim," he said, nodding across the lobby as he deftly touched a sensor on his console. "They've been expecting you."

Brim glanced off toward a double set of doors that had just been opened by a massive, bald man dressed in the distinctive uniform of a Master Chief Warrant Officer in the Imperial Fleet. *Instant recognition!* Utrillo Barbousse: Powerful—well-nigh frightening—in every aspect. Keen, gentle eyes reflected the true substance of this man who had been Brim's fierce sustainer from the very first days of his military career. The two old friends met halfway across the floor.

Chapter 2

. . .old friends

HEADQUARTERS BUILDING, GANTACLAR, IMPERIAL
PROVINCE OF CARESCRIA, LINFARNE/NAVRON, 33 OCTAD,
52016

"Hullo, Chief," Brim said, uncomfortably, taking the giant's proffered hand. "It's… it's been a long time."

"Aye, that it has, er, Lord Brim," Barbousse said soberly. "Seven hundred ninety two days, exactly."

"Um, who're working for these days, Chief?"

"I'm, ah, assigned to Admiral Calhoun's Staff, M'Lord."

Abruptly, Brim noticed the Winged Comet above Barbousse's left breast pocket. "Chief!" he exclaimed. "You've become a Helmsman!"

"Aye, M'Lord," Barbousse said, blushing. "It's a long story, but, I, ah, found m'self sent to flight school right after your… ah…."

"My court martial," Brim filled in for him. "I'm all right about it now…, er, Chief; I've gotten over it. But *congratulations*. I always thought you ought to do something like that. I'll bet you were a natural."

Barbousse's blush deepened. "Well, M'Lord," he said, "they, um, did say I took to flyin' pretty well."

"Somehow, I'd have bet a milston of credits on that," Brim replied with a grin. "What are you checked out in, so far?"

"Aside from a lot of trainers, I-I've lately spent quite a bit of time in WF Type-327s, M'Lord."

Brim felt his eyebrows rise. "Those are *hot* starships, Chief. You really must be good."

"First in m' class, I guess," Barbousse said quietly, "...like you, M'Lord, if I remember correctly."

"That's been a zillion years ago, Chief," Brim said, feeling his cheeks burn. After that, he couldn't think of a thing to say, even though he had a lot of catching up to do. Clearly, neither could the Chief. Strange, Brim thought, how men have such a tough ride during times of emotion. Barbousse had been a close associate for most of Brim's career—saved his life more times than he wanted to remember. *So* much to say, yet....

Old Borodov broke the impasse. "Wilf Ansor!" he bellowed, exploding through the door like a furry battle crawler in Sodeskayan native costume.

His fur was chestnut in color and, though he was clearly bowed by his years, he still stood taller than Brim. Behind a pair of old-fashioned horn-rim spectacles, his eyes sparkled with youthful humor and prodigious intellect. And, although his graying muzzle was not nearly so intimidating as it must have been in his youth, enormous sideburns provided him with a most profoundly intellectual countenance. He was splendidly dressed in a handsome, ankle-length greatcoat of thick gray felt closed by two rows of massive brass buttons. From the open collar emerged a heavy vest of darker felt with high, embroidered collars fastened by a delicate necktie of golden rope. His boots were clearly made for riding, cobbled of stiff, shiny leather and equipped with unobtrusive spurs secured at the ankle by delicate belts. He wore a massive gray hat of curly wool—much wider at the top than at the headband—that gave his head the look of a wooly funnel. His left hand wore a delicately embroidered, six-fingered glove of ophet leather. "Is about time," he shouted breathlessly, "We have been waiting for you!"

Next thing Brim knew, he was engulfed in Borodov's embrace, a rib-cracking Sodeskayan Bear hug that smashed his cheek against the great brass buttons of the Bear's overcoat.

"Hey, Chief," Borodov chortled while Brim gasped for breath, "is good to see Wilf again, eh? When crag wolves slide in deep snow, Bear cubs play in tallest trees, as they say."

"As they say, yer honor," Barbousse replied resolutely.

15

"Anatole Anastas," Brim gasped, "you're killing me!"

"Pah! Humans so frail," the elderly Bear bubbled with glee, releasing Brim except for his hand, which he shook vigorously human style. Then, suddenly, he turned sober. "Is good you have decided to come back to war," he said. "We need your help."

"Wasn't me decided I should leave," Brim protested.

"All your friends—all who count—know that, Wilf Ansor," Borodov said with a deep growl. "Court martial was public travesty to save General Trafford."

"Travesty or not," Brim observed, "it still ended my service career."

"Temporary only," Borodov rumbled. "But all things even out with time." He winked at Barbousse. "Besides," he added, "who said one needs Fleet Cloak to serve? Old friends in conference see great need for your talents. Am I not correct, Chief?"

Barbousse nodded and pursed his lips. "Makes sense to me, Lord Brim," he said. "Can't imagine you'd be here for any other reason."

Brim ground his teeth. "Lord Brim" was even worse than the "Admiral" that no longer had any meaning. "You *really* comfortable calling me that?" he demanded.

"Aye, Sir," Barbousse replied solemnly.

"Well, Chief," Brim replied, "much as I appreciate your respect and esteem, I really don't like 'Lord Brim' coming from friends. How about, 'Skipper'? Can you live with that?"

"Aye, Skipper," Barbousse said with a big grin.

"Thanks, old friend," Brim said with relief. "I appreciate that."

"'Wilf Ansor' is still all right from me?" Borodov demanded with a rumbling, Bearish chuckle.

"Anything else, and I'll call *you* 'Your Grand Duke-ship.'" Brim warned.

"Hmm," Borodov murmured, stroking some of his long, white whiskers, "actually, *does* have certain ring, eh?"

Barbousse rolled his eyes skyward. "Gentlepersons," he said with a polite smile, "they've already started inside."

Borodov hesitated a moment, then turned to Barbousse. "Chief, need private words with Lord Brim for a moment. Would you mind?"

"Not at all, Your Grace," Barbousse said with a nod. He saluted Brim, then strode across the lobby.

Suddenly, all humor deserted Borodov's eyes. "Is time, Wilf," he rumbled solemnly. "War continues unabated. Next big operations need only establishment of reliable supply lines to start." He placed a bejeweled finger on Brim's chest. "We depended on your creative leadership of Project Sapphire to recreate great space fort Gontor from ancient asteroid—made Operation Spark possible. Now, we need that kind leadership again."

"B-but...." Brim stammered.

"No buts, Wilf Ansor," the Bear interrupted, raising a furry finger. "With or without Fleet Cloak, you are still same person commanded great Star Base at Atalanta and led raid on Otranto that destroyed most of Torond's Fleet—*while* masterminding and directing reconstruction of Gontor. *Do you understand?*"

"Do I understand what?" Brim demanded.

"You know exactly what, Wilf Ansor Brim," the Bear said, eyes boring into Brim's very soul. "I can only imagine how badly you are stung by this unfair court martial. But aside from fact that pride has understandably been injured, Emperor Onrad provided for you as best he could under circumstances by naming you Lord Brim of Grayson with all that came with title—including Grayson Castle *on its own planet*. You must admit, being one of wealthiest men in Empire can't be all *that* bad, can it?"

"Of course not," Brim said, feeling a little defensive, "but...."

"No 'buts," Borodov rumbled. "Is keeping in mind that some time while you are here, you may—or may not—receive next orders for waging war on enemies of both your Empire and my own Great Federation of Sodeskayan States. Is my guess whatever happens here will not be what you might have once expected—or particularly want now. But one thing I guarantee: meeting will be *important* to you. Are you ready to resume life again?"

"Well, of course...," Brim began, feeling his face begin to flush, but Borodov wasn't finished.

"Good," the Bear interrupted. "Now we have established you are once more among living, we can get down to important things, eh?"

"Yeah, Anatole Anastas," Brim admitted, "...with apologies. Guess I've been pretty much a crybaby."

"Had same befallen me," Borodov replied, "I'd have been worse off than you probably. But enough commiseration. Like Chief Barbousse and me, you have war to wage against minions of Nergol Triannic." He frowned for a moment, then nodded toward the conference room. "Inside, you will hear many assignments you could carry out better than those who receive them. But fact of life is you may well not receive yours until *after* conference is finished. And even then, job may disappoint, for it will likely not return beloved Fleet Cloak to shoulders. Nor," he added sternly, "will job regain any prestige associated with former rank of Admiral in Imperial Fleet." Smiling dolefully, he put a furry hand on Brim's shoulder. "But aside from obvious shortcomings, it will at least return you to important work. And, if I know old friend Wilf Brim, this may well be all is necessary." With a little smile on his gray muzzle, he flicked his whiskers and started across the lobby. "Is following," he ordered

— o — 0 — o —

As Brim and Borodov entered the darkened conference room, they were watched closely by a number of conferees, including Lord Daniel Cranwell, Imperial Minister of Commerce and blood relative of powerful Count Tal Confisse Trafford, whose blundering daughter, Major General Megan Trafford, had cost Brim his military career nearly two years previously.

Rude and uncouth by nature, Cranwell had a reputation for potent, independent action within Emperor Onrad's government. Presently married to the only heiress of a powerful family, he'd begun life as a low-level civil administrator, then used his latest wife's money to literally purchase his title. He was responsive only to those who could further his ambitions, and had little use for those whom he could not control. In another life, he might have been a slave master or a prison warden; either way, he would have been successful.

In his early fifties, the man had developed an unbridled passion for power and phenomenal talent for organization. He was short, powerfully built with the emotionless eyes and the rough demeanor of a policeman, appealing to persons who were more comfortable being led than leading.

Beside Cranwell at the conference table was Barnabas "Barny" Case, Director of the Interspace Transport Bureau. Until recently, the Bureau had been a backwater, nearly lost in the swollen bureaucracy Cranwell had made of The Ministry of Commerce. Then came the critical need for materiel to be transported over truly vast distances, and suddenly Case's little Bureau had great significance thrust upon it.

Wealthy son of the Industrialist H. Brandon Case, Barnabus was an intelligent, affable playboy—and little else. Gregarious and often drunk, he had been vetted in his position as payment for a number of favors accorded Cranwell by a father who wanted his son to occupy a position concomitant with his rank—but involving no political dangers that might reflect on the family. Short, squat, and powerfully built, young Case could always be counted on to remain under Cranwell's thumb.

"Who are *they*?" Case whispered to Cranwell as the two latecomers blundered through the half darkness, interrupting the briefer, who appeared to have just reached his stride.

"The Human is that troublesome Carescrian named Brim," Cranwell whispered, "— I had been warned he might show up at the conference. The Bear is a powerful Sodeskayan, the Grand Duke Anastas Borodov. You will keep your eye on the former at all times, Barnabas," Cranwell added. "Under the right circumstances, he can he dangerous to our interests."

"*Our* interests?" Demanded Case. "What does *that* mean?"

"Simply be careful if circumstances should find you dealing with him," Cranwell said, then held a finger to his lips to stifle further conversation.

Chapter 3

. . .big shots

HEADQUARTERS BUILDING, GANTACLAR, IMPERIAL
PROVINCE OF CARESCRIA, LINFARNE/NAVRON, 33 OCTAD,
52016

As Brim took his seat the conference room; he realized he and Borodov had blundered directly into the opening presentation. Some kind of summary, he supposed, nothing important in the grand scheme of things—but of course the speaker simply *had* to stop and stare, immediately drawing all eyes to the pair in a great yawning silence. *Thraggling WUN-der-ful way to begin!*

A long conference table filled the dusky room with groups of people seated around it two and three deep. Even in the relative dark he recognized a few of them and... Voot's Beard, *big shots*! No wonder the building was crawling with Onrad's Secret Service!

Seated at the near end of the table—presumably the head—was none other than Grand Admiral Baxter Calhoun, Supreme Chief of the Imperial Fleet—he turned and scowled at the interruption. Brim ground his teeth; even in formal uniform, Calhoun looked every thumb a Star Sailor, with the weather-beaten countenance of someone who'd squinted at a thousand different daylights on a thousand different worlds. No matter what lofty positions the Emperor called him to fulfill, he would always be, first and foremost, a starship's officer.

To Calhoun's right, General Harry Drummond managed to shoot a broad wink. It did more to calm Brim than a whole bottle of Logish Meem! Drummond's piercing gaze and prematurely white hair always gave him rather the look of a religious zealot, but everyone knew his only faith was the Empire herself. A true patriot, Harry Drummond. Brim was especially glad to see him there.

At Calhoun's left sat Vice Admiral Bosporus Gallsworthy, trying unsuccessfully to stifle a grin. Short and thin with a pockmarked face and bushy eyebrows, Gallsworthy had first surfaced in Brim's life as Principal Helmsman aboard his first ship, I.F.S. *Truculent*. Once considered the Fleet's greatest starship driver, he'd risen to the level of Vice Admiral and Chief of Defense Command, one of the highest offices in the Fleet, with a permanent position on Emperor Onrad's War Cabinet.

Among the other principals at the conference table, Brim recognized many notables in the Imperial government: Tazmir Adam, the improbably professorial Imperial Secret Service Chief; Cahil Hardinger, a bland, high-level official the Foreign Service sent to meetings like this when they didn't plan to participate, and— trouble!—the scowling face of Lord Daniel Cranwell, Imperial Minister of Commerce. Clearly Cranwell was an enemy at the conference, but other hostile frowns seated nearby gave clear indication that he was unwelcome to a significant coterie of the attendees. If nothing else, Brim considered, the meeting promised to be *interesting*, to say the very least.

"If ye Grand Duke an' Lord Brim hae' taken their seats," Calhoun growled in his broad, Carescrian brogue, "we shall attempt at resumin' the initial situation report."

"Aye Admiral," Brim mumbled with a grimace. At his left sat a slim, attractive blonde wearing a Fleet Cloak with a Commander's gold ribbons on its cuffs. Her name tag read, CMDR ANN HUNT I.F. She turned momentarily, smiled warmly from a face framed by straight golden hair rolled inward at the shoulders. In the moment their glances met, Brim caught the cosmopolitan warmth of someone whose keen intellect had seen and appreciated much of the Known Universe. He also detected the barest hint of perfume, forbidden by military code. He felt drawn to her immediately, but had no idea why.

The briefer was using a globular representation of the Home Galaxy that rotated freely in space beside his lectern. Its view had been peeled away to focus on the war zone: Stars of the Empire and her colonies outlined in Imperial Blue, then the 'Wyckean Void, separating Imperial Home Planets from the League of Dark Stars and its closest ally, The Torond, both outlined in black. Smaller star domains of Gannet, Lamintir, and Korbu huddled near their larger siblings: Effer'wyck, Fluvanna, and A'zurn, all subsumed by the terrible grinder of Nergol Triannic's jackbooted invaders. Brim could remember the day each nation had fallen. In the display, they were now outlined in the gray of occupied territory. Portions of the G.F.S.S., the embattled star nation of the Bears, covered half the view like a skein, but only a small portion actually was visible—and much of this was also outlined in deadly gray.

As the summary continued, it soon became clear to Brim the crux of the conference would be preparation for the coming invasion of The Torond.

Despotic leader, Baron Rogan LaKarn, had early on allied his palatinate with Nergol Triannic to form what was now termed the *Tarrott-Rudolpho Federation* for the capital planets of the two warlike star nations.

During the past Standard Year, LaKarn had considerably weakened his standing in the alliance by failure to repulse the recent Allied invasion of Free Fluvannian planets. This significant miscarry had also upset Triannic's long-range plans, when he'd been forced to "temporarily" shift League troops and equipment from active campaigns elsewhere into some of the occupied Fluvannian planets to help oppose the liberating forces presently nearing the Fluvannian capital of Magor.

Now, before either LaKarn *or* Triannic could recover from these setbacks, Imperial High Command hoped to take advantage of LaKarn's relative weakness by launching the first major attack of the war, Operation Beacon, against The Torond's home stars. However, three essential conditions had to be met *before* such an attack could be launched successfully—in Calhoun's own terms: these were *deal-breakers*.

First, a transportation stream resistant to *O-ships*, as the Leaguers called them, or benders—highly specialized attack starships capable of running invisibly in cloaked mode—must be established, permitting reasonably safe, reliable delivery of war materiel to invasion depots throughout Allied-held portions of the galaxy. From these, the cargoes could be staged not only to Imperial invasion forces but to beleaguered Sodeskayan allies as well.

Second, the campaign to liberate occupied Sodeskayan territories must become so successful—so *depleting* of the League's war resources—that an invasion of The Torond would ensue with only minimal interference from League minions. An additional benefit of this strategy: if the Leaguers sent no help to The Torond, they stood to lose a major ally. If, on the other hand, they *did* send the massive aid necessary to secure Rogan LaKarn's shaky empire, those resources would necessarily come from the Sodeskayan front, permitting the Bears to reclaim their vast star domain that much faster.

Third, the current Fluvannian campaign must be complete, or nearly so, in order it not dilute Allied efforts in the new campaign. Brim bristled at this announcement; the campaign had begun after his court martial, and he'd had no part in it.

Since much of the first prerequisite's material would flow from the burgeoning industrial base in Carescria, one of the first priorities clearly involved refurbishing the splendid, if sadly decrepit, space harbor at Gantaclar. Brim got his first disappointment of the day when he discovered someone else would be put in command of that job.

Chapter 4

. . .down to Hullmetal tacks

HEADQUARTERS BUILDING, GANTACLAR, IMPERIAL
PROVINCE OF CARESCRIA, LINFARNE/NAVRON, 33 OCTAD,
52016

Only after a long break did Calhoun steer the meeting onto a new subject. With issues concerning Gantaclar resolved, it was now time to address the vital subject of actually transporting material gathered at what would be known as the "Gantaclar Hub" to the war zones else where it would be put to its ultimate use.

This had been a topic of deep concern as long as anyone could remember: by fiat, the Imperial Fleet included very few merchantmen among its starships: specifically, those highly specialized for carrying specific, often unique, items. All other materiel moved aboard commercial starships, a policy beneficial both to the Imperial economy and the yearly budget of the Imperial Fleet.

In times of peace, this policy had worked quite well—so long as large items and bulk shipments could be planned reasonably well in advance. In wartime, however; this system quickly developed into a hindrance. As Brim recalled, Escort Command was known as a backwater in the Imperial Fleet, a career quicksand presently run by a group of senior Captains who operated conventional starships as escorts. Many of the Captains were facing retirement at the termination of the war, and were therefore under strong influence by ship owners who might provide postwar jobs. To handle truly large-scale operations, the whole command structure would very probably require a total overhaul—as well as some badly needed new technology.

Moreover, the tremendous—probably *historic*—number of passages necessary from Carescrian starports like Gantaclar to theater staging areas and the fighting fronts themselves would obviously require a great deal of overall coordination and control. With the predicted number of ships under way at the same time, there could be little question mere traffic control would be a problem—all onto itself. But even more critical would be grouping these assets in order to efficiently provide *protection*. Not even the shortest-sighted delegate could believe Nergol Triannic or his minion Rogan LaKarn would stand by and permit these merchant fleets to reach their destinations unimpeded. That's what benders were all about.

When the subject of ship management came up on the agenda, Brim wondered if perhaps *this* was why he'd been called to the conference. He was clearly one of the few delegates with enough actual shipboard experience to tackle that kind of problem, even though he'd spent a lot of time lately flying astroplanes instead of ordinary starships. *Still*, he wondered, *did he really want a job like that*? Certainly, he was a Star Sailor; it was really the only profession he knew. But it was warships he understood, not merchantmen! Ironically, he had a strong hunch that what he wanted, or even what he hoped, would prove of little importance in this conference.

Once Admiral Calhoun named the new position—Director of Transport Operations Underway, or DTOU—General Drummond glanced at Brim, winked, and immediately nominated him for the position. Admiral Galsworthy seconded, only just beating a number of other delegates who rushed to endorse the nomination themselves. Admiral Calhoun himself had already initiated the voting process when Lord Cranwell noisily pushed back his chair and jumped to his feet with an angry cry.

"Wait! How dare you attempt to appoint a mere astroplane Helmsman to deal with full-sized starships—especially this Brim? Everyone here knows the story of this no-account upstart, whose blunders—as well as inability to follow orders—were responsible for the 52014 debacle of Operation Eppeid, a military failure that nearly ruined the career of the Confisse Trafford's daughter, General Megan Trafford." Clearly, Cranwell had prepared himself for just such an eventuality; in mere moments, he was joined by other henchmen—and once delegates supporting Brim had joined the fray, it took the full power of Calhoun's voice and personality to bring the room back to order.

"Cranwell!" the Admiral thundered in the shocked silence following. "Yon outburst war' neither necessary nor particularly smart, Xaxtdamnit" He scowled. "I conven'd this conference to win a war, not to rehash General Trafford's failure to destroy yon Emithrney/Bax Gravity docks." He swept the room with his angry gaze. "Nae' one at this table can touch Brim's experience in ship handlin' *or* managin' delicate situations among people, *an','*" he added forcefully, "ew'eryone here ken it."

"I know nothing of the sort!" Cranwell exclaimed angrily—while other allies of Count Trafford joined in with boos and catcalls. Strangely enough to Brim, Barny Case seemed to be keeping out of the fray.

"It doesn't really matter what any o' ye *think*," Calhoun roared back, smashing his gavel on the table again and again. "Unless ye' can back up these allegations o' incompetence wi' facts, I intended to treat them for what they are—spurious hearsay." Then he corrected himself. "*Pernicious* hearsay is a better term."

In spite of Calhoun's obvious rage, arguments continued for nearly half a metacycle before Cranwell and his minions began to wear down.

In the end, however, Confisse Trafford's power was so far-reaching even Calhoun could not gain a clear victory. Brim recalled wishing a hole would open in the floor and somehow swallow him up. His face burned from the abuse heaped on him. Barbousse placed a hand over his eyes while Borodov ground his teeth in a great Bearish snarl. At last, Brim slowly got to his feet and held up his hands. "Enough!" he shouted over the discord, "Xaxtdamnit, *enough*!"

In the shocked silence that followed, Brim grasped the back of his chair and slowly turned to Calhoun. "Admiral," he said in a clear, angry voice, "I deeply appreciate the confidence you have shown in me this afternoon. But it has become quite clear the political adversaries presently arrayed against me would negate all chances for success in this venture. Therefore, I withdraw my name from further consideration."

"Ye canna' do tha', Xaxtdamnit," Calhoun roared in renewed anger. "I *order* ye to continue."

"With deepest respect, Admiral Calhoun," Brim replied quietly, "you cannot order me to do anything. I am a civilian." With that, he strode from the room with head held high.

— o — 0 — o —

That evening, Brim stepped to the end of a long queue for taxis at the Visitor's Quarters, prepared for a considerable wait. Unexpectedly, the man in front of him turned and extended his hand. "Barny Case," he said. His breath reeked of meem.

"Wilf Brim," Brim replied, instinctively gripping the man's hand.

"You're that Carescrian who came in late this morning with the Bear, aren't you?"

"That's me," Brim answered, trying to place the man at the conference. "And *you* were sitting with Lord Cranwell, weren't you?"

"Yeah, I was, "Case answered with a grin. "The old man sure had his sights on you today."

"Seemed that way," Brim said evenly.

"Well," Case said with a chuckle. "Wantcha' to know that up close, you don't seem half as bad as he makes you out to be."

Brim grinned in spite of himself. "Nice to know," he said. "I'll remember that next time I see you."

"Hope ya' do, Admiral," Case said, giving a parody of a military salute. Then the next cab pulled up, and the door opened. Without another word, Case lurched clumsily into the back seat.

Before Case's door slid closed, Brim heard him give orders for one of the new gravity pads he'd seen along the shore. Probably where Cranwell's ship was parked, he guessed, then laughed: they could have shared the cab: he was bound for one of the nearby pools himself, to join a private banquet aboard Calhoun's executive transport.

Abruptly, the next cab at the curb was Brim's; he gave no further thought to the man named Case....

Chapter 5

. . .various hangovers

LAKE KELTON, GANTACLAR, IMPERIAL PROVINCE OF
CARESCRIA, LINFARNE/NAVRON, 34 OCTAD, 52016

Next morning, long before dawn, sleeplessness forced Brim out of his room in the Visitor's Quarters where Borodov had dropped him after a long, meem-soaked reunion aboard Calhoun's executive transport. During the evening, he'd learned that the delegates eventually voted in Commander Ann Hunt as DTOU—the strangely interesting blond Commander sitting beside him—almost as if his opposition really hadn't cared who filled the position, just so long as it wasn't Wilf Brim.

Nursing a monumental hangover, he'd hiked until he was trudging aimlessly through ankle-deep snow in one of the old lakefront repair yards—attempting to sort out just how he'd come such a pass. If he'd had *any* idea what was in store for him at that meeting...!

Angrily, he skipped a rock out across Kelton's frozen surface. Nothing had turned out the way he'd hoped, and despite the warm reception he'd received aboard Calhoun's yacht, yesterday's noisy controversy in the old Headquarters Building had dampened much of his desire to get back into the war, at least in an official capacity. Grinding his teeth, he shrugged. No remedy for it; he'd turned down the job. Now, he had only one recourse: To find some alternate—even illegal—method of joining the war effort, then to do the best job he could under the circumstances. Unfortunately, he had absolutely no idea what that might be.

He plodded on among the snow-covered shapes of rusting, long-abandoned machinery while the star Navron attempted to penetrate thick layer of clouds occluding the horizon—clouds he'd flown through so many times he could hardly remember what it was like to come in all the way from space on visual flight rules. A Xaxt of a place, Linfarne/Navron —at least it had once been for Wilf Brim the young Helmsmen. For a much-older, recently court-martialed civilian Wilf Brim, it was turning out to be... well, *confounding* to put things in the mildest perspective.

He paused, absently picking up a shred of metal, again skipping it out onto the ice. There on the cold, windswept shore of Lake Kelton, it was still difficult remembering any part of the meeting without considerable rage—in spite of himself.

"Good morning, Wilf Ansor," a deep voice rumbled from behind.

Startled, Brim spun around to see old Borodov offering a cup of steaming cvc'eese.

"Is good for what chills insides this morning, Wilf Ansor," the Bear said. "Also contains small dollop of Sodeskayan hangover curative."

Brim gratefully took the cup and sipped, the hot, thick liquid burning his tongue and warming him all the way to his belly. "Good morning, Anastas Anatole," he said, breaking into a grin in spite of his best efforts to continue grumping.

Producing a vacuum bottle and a second cup from a pocket of his greatcoat, Borodov poured his own cvc'eese, sipped, then stepped forward and touched his cup to Brim's. "Is not look particularly happy, furless friend," he said.

"You know me well," Brim agreed. "I came all this way for what? I'm *certainly* not back in the war."

"Is truth," Borodov answered with a bleak aspect. "So what do you intend?"

Brim smiled. "Guess I'll just get back in the war on my own," he said. "Can't see much in the way of alternatives right now—and I Xaxtdamned well don't intend to sit out the hostilities while I've still got something to contribute." He held out his cup for a refill.

"Thought you might say that, Wilf Ansor," the Bear commented, carefully pouring Brim's cup full, then finishing the flask into his own.

"Is why Onrad personally wanted you to suffer what you suffered yesterday."

"Onrad *what*?" Brim demanded.

"Emperor Onrad felt you needed experience of what happened yesterday to fully understand that your most powerful friends—including Onrad himself—remain politically powerless to put you back in war, at least in official capacity."

"Anastas, you're talking about *Emperor* Onrad, right?"

"...Prince of Reggio Star Cluster and Rightful Protector of Heavens," Borodov said with a serious look.

Brim sipped his cvc'eese. "I don't understand," he protested. "Admiral Drummond just about had those zukeeds worn down when I called it quits. What if I hadn't? What if right now I *was* DTOU?"

"Then you would be DTOU, Wilfooshka" Borodov said, "—but you would also be very troubled DTOU who would need great deal help to carry out duties in even marginal way."

"That's what I mean," Brim remonstrated. "It would have been a disaster."

"But *was not*, Wilfooshka," Borodov said reassuringly. "Admiral Drummond and I counted on you to make decision you made. We also wanted Cranwell to show hand, and, well, he *did*, eh?"

Brim looked at his old friend and smiled. "Yeah," he said, "I guess he did."

"So," Borodov said with a phlegmatic shrug, "conference ends as is supposed to, eh?"

"If you say so," Brim replied wryly. "But where in Xaxt does that leave me?"

"Happens I know partial answer to question," Borodov said. He finished his cvc'eese, placed the cup in a pocket with the vacuum jar, then reached into his greatcoat again and this time produced a large blue envelope with a holograph of the Imperial seal shimmering in its center. "Is travel ticket for you, friend Wilf," he said.

"Travel tickets for me?" Brim demanded, "—in a pouch with the Imperial Seal?"

"Is what I have been told," Borodov said with a little smile.

"Where'd you get this, Anastas Anatole?" Brim demanded.

"Courier brought—must have arrived on early packet."

Frowning, Brim placed his thumbs side-by-side on the envelope's security seal and waited. In a moment, the envelope's flap fell open. Inside was… a one-way, first-class passage to Avalon issued by the Imperial Travel Service. Attached was a tiny sticky note written in a familiar handwriting Brim knew he'd seen many times before. It read simply: "Come on home. Contact me after you're settled in. As promised, I've got work for you." It was signed simply, "O." Brim held it out to Borodov with a raised eyebrow, "?"

The old Bear drew a monocle from his greatcoat and squinted at the note; presently he smiled. "Sent by man of great influence," he pronounced.

"Indeed." Brim seconded. "I assume you know nothing about this."

Borodov shrugged mysteriously, then turned and started back toward the base proper. "Come on, Wilfooshka," he called over his shoulder, "serious breakfasting is in order before travel…."

That Afternoon at the lakefront brow where he'd arrived, Brim bade farewell to both Borodov and Barbousse, then boarded the packet for Caer Landria, where he would catch a liner for the four-day trip to Avalon. In spite of his best efforts, he *still* had no clue whatsoever as to what kind of a job the Emperor had in mind for him—if any.

Chapter 6

. . .for better or for worse

Brim's voyage to Avalon/Asturius passed without incident, in spite of numerous bender alerts during the four-day passage. His ship, *S.S. City of Benoath,* had been converted into a fast transport shortly after the beginning of hostilities. Originally designed and constructed as a luxury liner, she could easily outrun any cloaked bender the League might field. Bender starships on either side of the war needed so much energy for their cloaking systems they were severely hampered in nearly every other attribute—especially speed.

Since before breakfast—ship's time—the Triad of Asturius had been bright in the liner's forward Hyperscreens. Brim found his excitement—and apprehension—growing in inverse proportion to the distance from Avalon City, capital city of Onrad's great Star Empire. By midday, the three stars of the famous Triad could be seen tumbling within their virtual globe, each trapped within the others' gravity bonds. By suppertime, all five planets orbiting the Triad were visible to the naked eye: Proteus, with its science colonies; Melia, the hub of commerce; Ariel, the galactic communications center; Helios, the shipping hub; and Avalon herself, containing the great city capital of the Empire.

Throughout nearly two years since Brim's court martial, life had grown more topsy-turvy by the day. For a man who been an active Star Sailor nearly 20 Standard Years, the transition to civilian life had been a challenge.

Clearly, being suddenly wealthy had eased the pain, if *pain* accurately described what had quickly settled into depression. However, that same wealth posed a formidable challenge to someone who had never possessed—nor needed—much personal money in the first place. What did a person *do* with all those assets? How did one handle them? At length, he'd taken care of the problem by hiring Porterfield Marston, an Assets Manager recommended by Emperor Onrad, himself. Afterward, with lack of anything to occupy a normally busy mind, he'd become more and more frustrated as each day passed. Now, with the utter impossibility of finding an official position in the war effort so sharply demonstrated at the Gantaclar Conference, he was more determined than ever to make some meaningful contribution—just as soon as he could determine the best way to do it. And at this juncture, the legality of any potential enterprise was far down on his list of important factors.

— o — 0 — o —

In what had once been a posh observation lounge during the ship's existence as a luxury liner, Brim passed the last Metacycles before landfall, standing before the huge Hyperscreens in thoughtful silence.

At the 200-c'lenyt limit, two flights of graceful, tri-hulled Starfuries came hurtling out of the darkness for a visual inspection. The astroplanes circled for a moment, then banked and were gone as if they never existed. Starfuries were graceful, 66-iral-long killer ships that could top 400 light years per metacycle, or LPM, and tangle with anything the Galaxy could throw at them. In their intended role as short-range interceptors, they were renowned—and feared—throughout the galaxy. Brim bit his lip. A long time had passed had passed since he'd commanded the helm of any starship; but he had special feelings for Starfuries; he'd been in on their development from the very first.

In a matter of clicks, *Benoath* began her fiery re-entry into the atmosphere. The Hullmetal glowed white hot, and even the slightest distortion in the air stream caused a wake of free ions that merged into a long comet's tail several thousand irals behind the ship. Below:

broken clouds, detritus of a storm passing off to Lightward still glowed fitfully with hidden lightning. Slowly, the big ship began to level out, then sank through shoals of pale, insubstantial shadows rushing at the forward Hyperscreens like colossal ghosts dissolving to nothing at the very moment of collision. Abruptly, they were in clear air over the streets and avenues of a colossal city extending past the horizon in all directions. Avalon City: A study in sparkling crystal towers and hoary monuments to antiquity—the very epicenter of galactic civilization. Ahead, Lake Mersin was a foreshortened expanse of darkness in the muted glow of wartime lights that surrounded it. As always, a chill of excitement raced along Brim's spine. How this great city had changed his life! But as the ship lost altitude, he could see how the city, in turn, had been changed by the ravages of war! *Devastated* was a better word.

The huge Starship banked slightly, turning to follow the park-lined Boulevard of the Cosmos, instantly recognizable by ancient, tower-like palaces it bisected every four c'lenyts as it split the austral environs of the city center. Once teeming with vehicles of every description, the great artery was choked here and there by tumbled masonry; craters obliterated many of the parks, and as they passed, a crew of large machines was struggling to remove the wreckage of what looked like a Leaguer Gorn-Hoff astroplane.

In moments, Locarno Square and the massive stone buildings of the Imperial Admiralty were slipping beneath the nose, nearly surrounded by piles of disruptor rubbish and partial walls with empty windows like yawning mouths. Then the ship was over the Grand Achtite canal that wound through the city to port and emptied into Lake Mersin. Nearly five years ago—during one of the worst Leaguer raids on the city—Brim had crash-landed a crippled Starfury in that very canal. His eyes followed the banks to a small turning basin where a great sooty blemish still blackened the retaining walls and loading plaza. The wreckage had long since been removed—and largely recycled, he supposed—but smudges left by the radiation fires would endure for centuries. It had been a *bad* night for him as well as the city—and it was clear the bad nights had continued.

With the Achtite in their wake, they coasted over dark squares of tree-filled parks in the ancient Beardsmore section; many of the parks now filled with defensive disruptor emplacements. In the center, Brim picked out graceful old Kimber castle. How many times he'd passed that landmark on his way to the Admiralty; so far it remained miraculously untouched by this and countless wars that preceded it. His eye traced Lightward from the castle along Kimber Boulevard to its intersection with the Allington Parkway. At its Boreal corner rose the apartment tower in which Brim had established a residence a month or so after his court martial: a *home*, such as it was. He grinned in spite of himself. Nice to see it was still standing.

Off to starboard, a moving forest of great loading cranes and goods houses slid by the suddenly rain-streaked Hyperscreens. Nearly half of the great warehouses showed some sort of damage, but the rubble-strewn streets were busy as the great city's commerce continued in spite of the war. Picking up speed, the ship thundered over the squat, glass-walled Estorial Library where more than two hundred years ago Hobina Kopp first presented her startling Korsten Manifesto on Rights and Responsibilities. Half of the east wing was a tumbled pile of charred rubble; he wondered how many priceless manuscripts had been lost in that one assault. The blind fury of war was a great equalizer, treating outhouses and palaces with equal fury.

Before long, they were over Courtland Plaza and the great Huntingdon Gate, both intact despite huge craters nearby that were clearly the result of a near miss for some disappointed Leaguer. From there, Brim's gaze followed Coregium Boulevard the short distance to the Imperial Palace. Even in the dark sky, he could see one wing of the huge building was still enclosed in builder's scaffolding after the Leaguer hit that had forever changed his life. That blow to the palace during the Battle of Avalon killed Raddisma—the woman who had given birth to Hope, *his child*. At least the little girl had survived to pass her mother's almond-eyed beauty on to future generations; she would be beautiful in spite of the rather plain Carescrian heritage of her father. Presently, she lived as ward of Emperor Onrad, himself, who had taken her in and was raising her as his own.

Many memories here—perhaps *too* many. Brim fought his way back to the present. Lake Mersin was just ahead, and the ship was filling with the thumps, bangs, and running feet he associated with imminent landing.

"All hands to stations for landfall," the blower buzzed. "All hands to stations for landfall. Passengers please find secure chairs immediately. Repeat, passengers please seat yourselves in secure chairs immediately."

Brim hurried to a seat at the forward Hyperscreens and activated his gravity restraints. Off to port, he spied the great hall where Cago JaHall composed *Solemn Universe* and other classics of the same idiom. Somehow, the hall had survived. But, nearby, the silver-and-gold-domed Tower of Marva with its fluted sides and curious winding concourse was completely gone, replaced by a blackened, irregular circle hundreds of irals in diameter. Then more reminders of war—huge craters, yawning foundations, and masses of rubble marked the Leaguers' continued attempts to punish a great city that had so far managed to withstand its worst onslaughts. Abruptly, Verecker Boulevard and the lake shore were racing at them. Off to the left, Grand Imperial Terminal dominated the end of Palidan Causeway. Then, moments later, the ship banked hard to port, dropped quickly, and was down in one of those silk-smooth landings only a Helmsman can appreciate. For better or worse, he'd returned once more to the great city where his present troubles had begun. This time, however, there was a distinct possibility things might change for the better.

Chapter 7

. . .Avalon

After retrieving his portmanteau, Brim caught a taxi for his apartment. With the tremendous destruction wreaked on the city by constant Leaguer attacks from space, traveling from one place to another took at least twice as much time as it should have—and for the most part, the view was downright depressing.

Yet as the cabbie picked his way through the often-fetid destruction, signs of the city's imperishability were everywhere. Where buildings had been overlooked so far, or even missed, nearly every storefront displayed an OPEN FOR BUSINESS sign. Elsewhere, storekeepers conducted their commerce from the ruins or in tents— often out in the open. Here and there, surviving children who hadn't been evacuated to safer locales played in parks or laughed among the wreckage—and occasional lovers still strolled the sidewalks. Brim pursed his lips. Life went on, all right. What choice did people have?

Almost centered in the fashionable Beardsmore Section of Avalon, Brim's residence tower had never seemed like much of a home, mostly because he'd spent so little time in it. Too, it was a little elaborate for his customary lifestyle, which leaned more to temporary rooms in Officers' Quarters than to richly paneled wood, high ceilings, magnificent portraiture, and fine furniture. He'd asked Porterfield Marston to furnish the place. Awed comments from the few visitors he'd entertained there attested to Marston's extravagant taste.

The only civilian home that had ever really registered with Brim was the ancient hillside residence of one-time lover Claudia Valemont in Haelic/Hador's Atalanta. He had long cherished that warm home, but never dreamed of living in such a dwelling himself. Nothing like it existed anywhere outside of the teeming Rocotzian Sector of that ancient city—nor would one like it sit well within the ultramodern, ever-changing Avalon. Besides, both Claudia and her home were practically a lifetime distant..., especially Claudia. He quickly pushed her memory from his mind.

Brim's elegant apartment suite did have a view, however. Unfortunately, Avalon had taken such a beating in the past few years of war that the sight of ruined buildings and piles of rubble outside depressed him in the daylight, and the blackout—which he suspected posed no hindrance whatsoever to crews of Leaguer attack craft—provided only a ghostly hint of what might have been a spectacular nighttime panorama.

He spent the next week at Marston's office managing various components of the vast holdings Onrad had deeded him. Most nights, he spent playing Cre'el at a number of gambling establishments, winning considerable sums—for which he had little need—as well as a number of interesting ladies whose charms often faded quickly in the harsh reality of morning. When he found himself lapsing into periods of boredom, he knew it was time to move on—and quickly. With his business dealing nearing an end, he thumbed a short text message to a confidential socket at the Imperial Palace:

"Mow your lawn, Your Majesty?"
Signed: "Brim."

Three days later, during an orchestral concert in Royal Basler Hall, his HoloPhone buzzed silently in his pocket, its rhythmic beat the one he'd associated for years with Royal Summonses. At intermission, while his lovely blonde escort—a Commander in the Imperial Fleet—adjusted her makeup, Brim glanced at the phone's deep blue display. It read:

"About time, Slacker. Lawn nearly
overgrown. See you at Grand Imperial
Terminal, central marquee, B:15
tomorrow. I shall bring mower."

~Signed: "O."

P.S. "Some Blonde!"

Brim chuckled to himself. Onrad might be bored at concerts, but he
always had an eye for a well-turned leg, especially if the other end was
blond. Grinning, he glanced around for Secret Service agents—as
usual they were blended perfectly with the crowd—then thumbed:

"B:15 tomorrow, Your Majesty."

~Signed: "Brim."

P.S. "You bet!"

He'd just sent his message when the Commander returned. "Wilf
Brim," she said with a faux pout, "were you on the phone?"

"I was," Brim admitted, "but with no one as gorgeous as you,
believe me."

"Well, I certainly hope not," she said, taking his arm with a low,
feminine laugh. "Just remember, tonight, you're all mine."

"Believe me," Brim said, starting back for their seats, "I should
have it no other way, Commander."

Chapter 8

. . .a long-time friend

AVALON/ASTURIUS, AVALON CITY, GRAND IMPERIAL
TERMINAL, 16 NONAD, 52016

No sooner had Brim stepped from his cab at the Grand Imperial Terminal than he was met by a Royal herald, dressed in a gold uniform with red piping. "Lord Brim?" the man asked, glancing at a hand-held display.

Brim nodded warily. "That's me."

"Message for your Lordship," the herald said, presenting a signature recorder. "Please sign here."

Brim pressed his thumb to the recorder, then stepped back until the authentication chimed.

The herald nodded. "A special astroplane waits your convenience in the Boreal Concourse, your Lordship. Please follow me."

Brim looked at the herald and raised an eyebrow. "An astroplane in the Grand Terminal?"

"Er, yes lord Brim. An astroplane. Please to follow me."

Must be some *lawnmower Onrad's got*, Brim thought. "All right," he said, "let's have a look."

Without a word, the herald set off at a rapid pace through the maze of moving walkways toward the Boreal concourse, where private and general-space-travel starships moored away from the rush of scheduled liners and interstellar ferry craft. They passed a section of ceiling covered by sheets of temporary roofing. Many of the boutiques lining its periphery were closed—blackened holes in the fabric of the terminal—but here and there, a few doughty merchants had set up shop on temporary tables. Brim shook his head sadly: even the magnificent Grand Imperial Terminal had lost a lot of its magic in recent years. "Here we are, M'Lord," the herald announced, stepping from the walkway at a berth on a close-in watercourse where a polished, ebony Wakefield Type-327 Tormentor gleamed in the sunlight as it bobbed gently at the end of a slim boarding tube.

Brim raised an eyebrow. Something about *this* Wakefield appeared *special* to him, though he couldn't put his finger on just what it might be. Special or not, Wakefield Tormentors were *serious* starships built by Wakefield Starship Ltd. in the small city of Hall on the planet Hatfield orbiting the star Salisbury—only a few Metacycles' flight from Avalon. Slim and elegantly shaped for atmospheric maneuvering, they even looked fast—and, unlike most starships, needed no gravity pool to support them when not in use. The broad-shouldered, teardrop shape that made them famous was unbroken except for a slight bulge to accommodate a small flight bridge placed well forward, just ahead of stubby, wing-like sponsons to port and starboard housing 3,420-SU Krasni-Peych Wizard 76/77 Drive units in large, radically streamlined nacelles. Little more than 82 irals from stem to stern, the tiny ships were considered delightful to fly under most circumstances, however, with high loading on their twin gravity repulsors, resultant landing speeds and steep approach paths were downright terrifying to some. If this was Onrad's "Lawnmower,"—and by now, Brim had little question about *that*—something big indeed was up.

Every WF Type-327 he'd seen had been coated in a light-gray tint and carried normal Fleet identification with Imperial Comets amidships. This one with its brilliantly polished ebony hull was without embellishment, save for a tiny Imperial flag and an Intergalactic registration number, "I.F.S. 9999," on either side of the tail cone—clearly a civilian vessel. Curious. Ordinary circumstances reserved these powerful little ships for military use, exclusively.

"Please to board immediately, M'Lord" the herald urged, breaking into Brim's speculations.

Smiling now, Brim nodded and started along the boarding tube; moments later, he was peering into a tiny, but generously appointed wardroom where a familiar figure was seated in obvious comfort. "Your Majesty," Brim exclaimed, feeling his face break into a grin.

"Hello, Brim," boomed Onrad V—Grand Galactic Emperor, Prince of the Reggio Star Cluster, and Rightful Protector of the Heavens—"come on aboard." Handsome and heavy-set, Onrad rose from a svelte leather sofa. He was dressed as a full Admiral of the Fleet: his privilege as supreme Chief of all Imperial forces. His thoughtful, humorous eyes were those of a man in the bloom of youth, but the gray in his small goatee and mustache revealed the first marks of advancing age—and the terrible pressures of his lonely profession.

Brim hurried forward to take the Emperor's proffered hand, taking in the exciting smells of a brand-new astroplane: heated logics, fresh paint, leather, plastics, solvents, and hot oil. "It's been a long time, Your Majesty," he said.

"A damned long time, Brim," the Emperor agreed. "You still speaking to me?"

"Why not, Your Majesty?"

"Well," Onrad said, "...there is the little matter of my letting your career go down the drain when Confisse Trafford needed someone to take the hit for his idiot daughter's botched attack on Eppeid."

Brim took a deep breath. "I understand a little about politics, Your Majesty," he said. "You wouldn't have let that happen if you could have avoided it. Besides," he added, "you did make me Lord Brim."

"Thanks for the nice words," Onrad said quietly, his gaze uncharacteristically cast toward the deck. "But I know how you feel about your beloved Fleet—and I also understand all the wealth in the Empire can't make up for taking away that Fleet Cloak, Star Sailor."

Brim smiled. "Perhaps someday I shall yet win it back, Your Majesty."

"Count on it," Onrad promised, now looking directly into Brim's eyes, "You will." Then he settled back into the couch and indicated a chair facing it. "Sit with me for a few clicks," he commanded. "Couple of things I want to get clear, then I'll go back to the palace and this ship becomes yours."

"*Mine?*" Brim gasped. "*This* ship?"

"I'll get to that," Onrad said. "Right now, I want to talk about an assignment for you, Brim."

"An *assignment*, Your Majesty?" Brim asked in surprise.

"Something's made you hard of hearing, Brim?"

"Er, n-no, your majesty," Brim stammered. "In fact, I'm all ears."

"Thought you might be," Onrad said breaking out in his own grin, "—especially after the debacle at Gantaclar." He placed a hand on Brim's shoulder. "Sorry I had to put you through it, but, well, it was the best way of demonstrating what I'm up against politically. That Zukeeds Trafford has Xaxtdamned near as many credits as m' treasury. And he uses them to buy everybody he can get his hands on."

"I pretty well got that idea watching Lord Cranwell," Brim seconded.

"Dan Cranwell," Onrad growled with obvious distaste, "I'd call him a snake if I didn't think I'd turn so many snakes against me. And yes, he's one of Trafford's toadies, all right." He shook his head for a moment, then shrugged. "Sooner or later, Brim, one of those zukeeds is going to make a mistake—just one thraggling mistake—and I'll use it to shut them all down. Believe me, the time's coming." He ground his teeth for a moment before breaking out in wry smile. "Right now, however," he continued, "those Zukeeds did me quite a favor in their own way by freeing you up for a very special job I need done right away—and even though it won't put you in a Fleet Cloak, you'll be in the thick of everything that transpired at Gantaclar. How does that sound?"

"Sounds good to me, Your Majesty," Brim replied. "Nothing wrong with *my* hearing."

Onrad grinned. "Guess I had *that* coming, didn't I?" he growled with a chuckle. "Do keep in mind, Brim, the office of Emperor encompasses broad powers—including exiling smart Alecks to a number of really pernicious locations."

"I'll certainly keep that in mind, Your Majesty," Brim said hastily. "Ah, what was it we were discussing?"

"Assignments," Onrad said, growing solemn once more. "Specifically, I need someone to run a little project for me, one that's so important the whole war might someday hinge on its success."

Brim grimaced. "Sounds serious, Your Majesty," he said.

"A lot more than just serious," Onrad said. "A better word is *crucial*. And it calls for the special skills you're famous for—

specifically flying fast starships: astroplanes like Starfuries, or *this* little beauty. And, of course," he added, "the gift of gab."

"Thanks, I think, Your Majesty," Brim replied noncommittally. "But the Gantaclar Conference I attended was mostly about starliners, escorts, and benders—big starships with enough range to fly half way across the galaxy if necessary."

"Precisely," Onrad said.

"Unless I'm missing something, Your Majesty, astroplanes like WF Type 327s and Starfuries don't have the kind of range those operations call for. Why, just a couple of years back I had to practically strip a Starfury squadron of all its weapons just to fly 'em from here to Haelic/Hador."

"You're right on both counts, Brim," Onrad replied with a deep chuckle. "Starfuries don't have much in the way of range, but you're still missing something."

"Once more, Your Majesty," Brim said, "I'm all ears."

Chapter 9

. . .Onrad's "loaner"

AVALON/ASTURIUS, AVALON CITY, GRAND IMPERIAL
TERMINAL, 16 NONAD, 52016

"**M**uch of what I need done has to do with *this very* Wakefield in which we're sitting," explained Onrad. "I've named her *Four Nines* and she's *by no means* a WF Type-327—she only *looks* like one. Actually, she's one of only two WF-400s Wakefield has built so far." He frowned momentarily. "What would you say if I told you she can fly from here all the way to the Bright Triad of Ely?"

Glancing around at the rich furnishings and accouterments, Brim needed moments to digest this piece of information. "Great Voot," he exclaimed, "from the Bright Triad, it's an easy flight to any of the nearby Carescrian stars... like Linfarne/Navron, for example. Your Majesty—that *is* big news."

"Unfortunately, it isn't the only big news," Onrad said. "And, the rest isn't anywhere as nice—at least for our side of the war. What couldn't be announced at Gantaclar—but will soon become quite apparent—is that Nergol Triannic's bender fleet is about to become a lot more troublesome than it is right now."

Brim raised an eyebrow.

"Let me bring you up to date about this bender problem," Onrad said. "By way of background, remember that benders were first developed during the First Great War by the League. Leaguers called 'em *Onsichtbarschiffe*, or *O-shiffe*, in their Vertrucht. And although the tricky little starships worked their effect—eventually on our side, too—they had little affect on *that* war's outcome." He frowned. "As

45

you *also* know, they've played a much more important role in *this* war. What you don't know is that things are going to get worse." He offered a mu'occo cigarette from a silver case—Brim turned it down—lighted one with a squared-off silver lighter, then drew a great draught. "Soon, the space lanes between Carescria and Avalon will become as important as the combat zones, themselves. From here on to war's end, our fate will ride in the bellies of transport ships carrying the endless supplies demanded by campaigns to recapture League-dominated territory. And Nergol Triannic's first line of defense will be to *stop* those transport ships—at any cost. Obviously, he'll attempt to do that with his benders."

"From what I see in the media," Brim observed, recalling the disappearance of numerous ships in the space lanes, "he's off to quite a start."

"He is indeed," Onrad continued. "Unfortunately for us, between the wars, The Congress of Intragalactic Accord—you remember those Zukeeds, I'm sure—dominated Fleet opinion and largely discounted the Leaguers' O-ships as solely an instrument of war on trade. At the time, this was essentially correct, of course, but the real aim of the secretly League-backed CIGAs was keeping our eyes off what the future held in store. The League's aim has always been to capture planets—and Triannic knew we'd need to do a lot of shipping if we wanted to capture them back. We began to see the results of that when he returned from exile to his capital Tarrott in 51008; he immediately directed his Chief of O-ships, L'rak Z'tinod, to produce 300 new benders, then assigned the necessary priority in resource allocation to implement his decision. Thereafter, the strength of Z'tinod's bender fleet has been increasing with each passing day. And it's quite apparent his gamble is about to pay off—handsomely." He stopped and looked Brim in the eye. "I'm sure you've already made the connection between what I'm saying and why this WF-400 is so important."

"I can guess," Brim said. "It doesn't take all that much theorizing to suppose our escort fleet will soon have a lot more work than it does now—and new long-range astroplanes can spot O-ships long before they get to the convoys. O-ships travel in cloaked mode only when they're attacking, don't they?"

"They do," Onrad said. "Imagine how much more space an astroplane can patrol at say—conservatively—two twenty to two fifty LPM than one of our Starship escorts that can't get past eighteen." He grinned evilly. "But they'll really come into their own when we develop them to a point where they can carry enough armament to do some good on their own."

Brim nodded. "And you want me to do *what* with them, Your Majesty?"

"That, friend Brim, is pretty much up to you," Onrad said thoughtfully. "Right now, they tell me this ship has a range of about 3500 light years—one way at an average speed of say, 220 LPM. It's not quite enough to make it all 3500 light years from here to Linfarne/Navron with any kind of useful load, and it makes no allowance for gravity storms or any of the million and one things that can go wrong on a long trip like that. But the fact is she can *easily* make it to The Bright Triad, and that's a start. I need somebody like you to take this little beauty to Hatfield/Salisbury and help the people at the Wakefield factory make the capability useful."

Brim took a deep breath. This was nothing even remotely like what he'd planned for getting himself back into the war. No combat here, no action, no challenges—only drawn-out, boring Metacycles wringing the last iota of performance from little starships.

"You've never taken so long to consider an assignment since we met, Wilf," the Emperor interjected softly.

"Sorry, Your majesty," Brim said, suddenly aware of his silence. "Of course, I'm honored to tackle the assignment."

"The Xaxt you are," Onrad said with a pained look. "I *know*. And I also know you've been going through your own version of Hell for nearly two years now. What's worse, I put you there by failing to back you up when the chips were down."

"Your Majesty," Brim protested, "as I said, you certainly did your best to…."

"Granting you a title was the least I could do," Onrad said with an imperious wave of his hand. "Emperors don't —apologize."

"No, Your Majesty," Brim protested, "that wasn't what I meant about doing your best for me. Even an Emperor's hands can be tied; I certainly understand that."

"So I still have your trust, Brim?"

"Voot's Beard, Your Majesty," Brim exclaimed, "of course. My trust in you was never in question."

"Good," Onrad said, glancing at his timepiece. "Guess that's all the time I have." He laughed wryly for a moment, then added, "If someone ever offers you the job of Emperor, turn it down flat. The perks are pretty attractive, but it takes a Xaxt of a lot of your time."

"I'll be sure to remember, Your Majesty," Brim said with a grin.

Rising majestically from the couch, Onrad fumbled for a moment in a pocket of his Fleet Cloak, then fished out a set of keys on a small chain with an Imperial fob. "Here, then," he said, tossing the keys to Brim and nodding toward the cockpit door, "consider this little beauty a 'loaner.'"

"Wow," Brim whispered, "you really meant that, didn't you?"

"Well, she *is* signed out to me, but since my Helmsmanship is a bit rusty these days, I'm loaning her to you. When you want to loan stuff like this to a friend, it's always good to be an Emperor."

"Sure seems like it," Brim observed. "And pretty nice 'stuff,' too."

"Oh, this is one hot *lawnmower*," Onrad said with a grin. "Little *Four Nines* here is powered by two K-P 77/77 drives. At max power consumption, she's faster than any WF Type-327 the Wakefield folks have built so far—and they tell me you're going to love what she'll do."

Brim frowned. "No question, Your Majesty," he said, "but I haven't flown anything at all for nearly two years. "I'm a bit rusty for this kind of ship."

"Figured you might feel that way, Brim," Onrad said. "At my request, the Wakefield people added a simulation mode to the controls and the Hyperscreens. You can make all the mistakes you like while she's nice and safe on the surface."

"But...."

"You've got this parking space as long as you need it," Onrad said. "When you're ready, just fire up and take off. I'm picking up the tab personally for everything. Of course, you *could* leave it to Chief Barbousse to fly you out to Hatfield. He's checked out in her, after all."

"?" Brim asked.

"Barbousse, himself," Onrad said with a grin. "While you were out of action, I had him sent him to flight school—turns out he's a damned good Helmsman."

"Yes, I discovered that at Gantaclar, Your Majesty. He had to be a *natural* Helmsman."

"Couldn't talk him into taking a commission, though." Onrad mumbled. "You know how stubborn the Chief is, even to his Emperor. He always argues he carries all the rank of whomever's orders he's carrying out—and I guess that does make some sense. The important thing is it makes sense to *him*, and I didn't want to break up the potential damage you two as a team can do to the League."

"I'll be glad to ride shotgun for him until I get some time at the helm," Brim said. "Probably be *a lot* safer that way, too."

"You might want to give that a little thought," Onrad replied, looking Brim directly in the eye again. "I happen to know the Chief is pretty well expecting *you* to be at the controls. Frankly, I think he'll be seriously disappointed if you aren't—as well as the other members of your crew. Barbousse has hand picked each of 'em."

Brim thought for a moment, then felt his cheeks burn. "I think I understand, Your Majesty," he said, taking a deep breath. "Please consider I'm back in command mode—after a *Long* time."

"You're on the right wavelength now, Brim. Shall I call the Chief?"

"He's here?"

"Chief!" Onrad thundered. "Chief Barbousse—front and center!"

Chapter 10

. . .'Skipper'

"**M**aster Chief Boson Barbousse reporting as ordered, Yer Majesty," the Chief said, exploding into the wardroom with a grin. "Lookin' forward to workin' with you again, too, Yer Lordship."

"Looking forward to working with *you*, Chief," Brim said, head whirling at the speed things were taking place.

"Brim," Onrad said, "I've got to get out of here in next to no time, so here're the rules: All but one of your crew is military, so they report to the Chief. And since the Chief's aboard to keep an eye on *you*, Brim," Onrad continued, "they'll all pretty much follow you around. Right, Chief?"

"Right, Yer Majesty."

"It's the only way I could set this up without a military man reporting to a civilian—which was your demand back when all this mess started right after your court martial. We'll keep it that way until I can finesse those Admiral's rings back on your cuffs."

"V-Voot's beard, Your Majesty," Brim stammered, "I don't know what to say.

"Don't say anything," Onrad interrupted. "Just get the kinks worked out of this little astroplane. I need a high-speed patrol ship with some useful range, and I need it fast. Once you have that in hand, I'll make sure you have a job that's a little more to your liking. Got that?"

"Got it, Your Majesty."

"Good," he said, peering through the hatch. "My honor guard's here. I'm supposed to dedicate some sort of memorial here at the terminal this afternoon. Enjoy the little bus, Brim, and drop me a line once in a while—the Chief will know what channels to use." With that, he handed a photo crystal to Brim and grinned. "Thought maybe you'd want a few pictures of Hope," he said, "especially since I'm not giving her 'Uncle Wilf' time to stop in and see her this trip. Cute kid, Brim," he added thoughtfully as he started into the boarding tube. "One of these days, it'll be time to tell her who her parents are; her real dad is someone she can really be proud of." Then, he turned and was gone before Brim could respond.

Brim absently watched the Emperor striding along the brow for a moment. All his thoughts were momentarily focused on his tiny daughter who lived the life of a true princess as ward of the doting Onrad. From the moment her mother, the Princess Raddisma of Fluvanna, was killed in a space raid on Avalon's Imperial Palace— where she and her nominal spouse, the Nabob of Fluvanna, were sheltering as war refugees—Onrad had treated the little girl as if she were his own daughter. The Nabob still believed she was his— confronting him with the truth would no doubt someday cause an international incident. Both Brim and Onrad had agreed to put that off until Fluvanna was liberated and the Nabob—who had very little real interest in the little girl—returned home. But one thing was clear, when the time came, Hope would remain a citizen of the Onrad's Grand Galactic Empire—and the "Uncle Wilf" who visited her now and then to shower her with gifts would be revealed as her true father. Forcing himself back to the job at hand, Brim pocketed the crystal, then turned to Barbousse. "Well, Chief," he said with a shrug, "think you might trust me at the controls again?"

"How long you plan to use that simulator, M'Lord?"

"Not very long," Brim said.

"In that case," Barbousse said, "I'll assemble the crew and start getting' her buttoned up right away."

"Hang on, Chief," Brim protested. "I haven't even had a chance to go back to my flat for clean clothes. All I've got is what's in my traveling case."

"Well, um, I took the liberty of packing a few things for you myself, M'Lord."

"How'd you...?" Brim started, then laughed—Utrillo Barbousse was one of the most talented lock picks in the Known Universe. "Chief," he said, clapping the big man on his shoulder, "I certainly hope the town house was in presentable condition."

"Your maid service maintains it impeccably."

"Thank you, Chief."

"All part of keepin' my eye on you for the Emperor, M'Lord...."

"Chief?"

"Yes, M'Lord?"

"Drop the 'M'Lord,' old friend, will you please?"

"You are Captain of this ship, M'Lord. We can't go around calling you by your first name. Doesn't really matter what markings she wears, this little starship is still military, pure and simple."

"All right, Chief, I understand—and appreciate—how you feel. But this *M'Lord* stuff has simply got to stop."

"Well," Barbousse said hesitantly, "how about 'Skipper,' again—like we agreed to at Gantaclar? That's a pretty neutral title, but it still puts you in command."

"Does it work for *you*, Chief?"

"It works fine, Skipper."

"Thank Voot," Brim said, rolling his eyes heavenward. "Give me about a metacycle, then get the crew up here to the bridge for introductions. If the Emperor is in a hurry, then we'd better get a move on."

—o — 0 — o—

Elsewhere, in Avalon, Count Tal Confisse Trafford steepled his fingers as he peered intently across an ornate table at Lord Daniel Cranwell, wondering what the man had unearthed in the last week about the upstart Brim. The two had just finished a gargantuan lunch in a private dining room of Trafford's club, and servants dressed in formal attire were silently clearing the table before serving cvc'eese.

"So, what have you learned about this parvenu?" Trafford asked. "How dangerous is he to.... *our enterprises*, shall we say?"

Cranwell carefully picked his teeth with a fingernail. "The man is more dangerous than I had imagined," he replied slowly. "When you destroyed his career nearly two years ago, I thought we'd seen the last of him—especially since Onrad's attempt to pay off his own guilt by making Brim a wealthy Lord. Most lower-class beggars would have taken that and disappeared forever."

"Well, it appears he certainly *didn't* disappear," Trafford commented drily. Cranwell's table habits simply made him sick.

"Now you mention it," Cranwell said with a nod, "he *did* disappear—for a couple of months. The man was seriously hurt."

"Well, I certainly hope so," Trafford grumbled. "He nearly ruined daughter Megan's career in the Army."

"What you *will* find interesting," Cranwell continued—avoiding *that* subject—"is *why* he came back out of his hole."

"Oh? Why then?"

"Because he was *called* to the Gantaclar Conference, not just invited."

"By whom?" Trafford asked in surprise. "He had no place there. He's nothing but an ignorant Helmsman."

"He may be an ill-bred Helmsman, Cousin, but he is *anything* but ignorant. In fact, this Brim is a rather brilliant character who has quietly developed strong connections all through the High Command and the civil Government. Had I not been there to stand up for our interests, he could have easily become DTOU—potentially an extremely powerful position."

"Really? Then who called him to Gantaclar?"

"His travel orders came from the Imperial Palace itself."

Trafford set down his cvc'eese. "I had no idea," he said. "*That* influential, eh?"

"Precisely, Cousin."

"Well, what about this Commander Hunt?" Trafford demanded.

"No problem with her," Cranwell replied. "She is an extraordinarily competent woman, and quite attractive as well. But she would never use the position as a springboard upward, as would have Brim's supporters had he been appointed."

Trafford peered idly at an ancient portrait on the dark wood paneling. "Nor will she be overworked if certain of our plans come to fruition," he said quietly. "But back to Brim. What do you recommend we do about him, Cousin?"

"At the present, Cousin," Cranwell replied. "We do nothing except watch his every step. Perhaps nothing will come of his recent presence—so far as our projects are concerned. But if he again appears within our sphere of influence again, then we shall probably be forced to take appropriate action quickly."

"Hmm," Trafford rumbled, feeling as if he'd overeaten again. He'd rather hoped his meeting with Cranwell would be useless and unimportant. Apparently it was not....

Chapter 11

. . .the crew

"Skpper, this is Nero Lu, our Navigator," Barbousse announced.

"Pleased to meet you, Lu," Brim said, climbing from the left-hand Helmsman's console. "The name sounds familiar. Where else have you served?"

"Many places, Captain," Lu said, almond-shaped eyes smiling behind thick glasses that clearly made him ineligible for Imperial military duty. "Probably we ran across each other when I was navigator for Captain Delacroix on his ship *Yellow Bird*. We operated out of Atalanta supplying Gontor."

Brim nodded. "Of course," he said, his mind spinning off half way across the galaxy to the sprawling Imperial outpost of Atalanta, where he'd hired the elegant rogue Cameron Delacroix to fly supplies to the great space citadel of Gontor during a final buildup before the Fluvanna invasion. The lovely face of a long-ago lover, Princess Margot Effer'wyck also briefly passed his mind's eye; in a wild turn of fate, she had become Delacroix's bride. "What made you leave the *Bird*?" he asked.

"A HyperTorp," Lu replied quietly. "Two of them, in truth. We managed to salvage her wreckage, but we scrapped what was left soon after we towed it home."

Brim grimaced. "I hadn't heard," he said, embarrassed. "What happened to Delacroix?"

"Vaporized," Lu said. "Only two of us survived the attack."

"I see," Brim said, fighting back a whole crowd of conflicting emotions, including more unexpected musings about Margot Effer'wyck. "W-we'll try to make that a one-time-only experience for you," he said, recovering himself.

"Ah! Excellent idea, Captain" Lu agreed with a grin. "I shall take you up on your kind offer."

"Warrant Officer Harmony Kermis and Leading Spaceman Josephine Treble, our Systems People, Skipper," Barbousse interjected, clearly in a hurry.

"Ladies, I'm pleased to meet you," Brim said, turning to shake their hands one at a time. "I'm sure you know this will be a very special assignment in the systems area."

The women couldn't have been more unlike; Kermis was tall with a pale, narrow face and black hair that resembled an experimental battle helmet; Treble was short, fat, red-faced, with hair looking as if she had just come inside from a hurricane. "Special assignments are why we volunteered, Skipper," Kermis declared with a proud look.

"Two of the most highly rated technicians in the Fleet," Barbousse added. "Dr. Borodov personally interviewed both after the Gantaclar conference."

Brim chuckled in spite of himself. Somehow, he never did seem to have much input into really big decisions affecting his life——he was always the last to know. But then, except for his court martial, he wouldn't have traded that life for anyone else's, either. "Ladies," he said, "we've got a an awful lot of work to do; I hope you won't end up wishing you'd signed on some normal ship."

"You just find stuff for us to do, Captain," Kermis declared, "We'll get it done, won't we Jo?"

"Best to stand back and not get in our way, Skipper," Treble quipped with a wink.

"I'll keep that in mind that," Brim said with a sham look of dread, then glanced around the cabin for a moment. "There's one more isn't there, Chief?"

"Aye, Skipper," Barbousse said. "Right here at his console checkin' out his new toys. Front an' center, Mister Steele."

"Chief Warrant Officer Greg Steele reporting, Captain," a huge, red-haired figure rumbled from aft. "Had to replace the master BKAEW just before we brought the Emperor over," he explained untangling himself from the COMM console. "Thought I'd better get it tuned while I have the chance."

To Brim, the man resembled a freckled version of a Sodeskayan Bear. "Glad to have you on board, Mister Steele," he said, wincing as his hand was crushed in an iron grip.

"I replaced Steele on I.F.S. *Truculent* just before you reported in, back in '94, Cap'm," Barbousse interjected. "He's a particular specialist in extra-long-range communicatin'."

"You'll have your work cut out for you on this ship," Brim observed.

"Couldn't ask for better," Steel declared. "Lots of challenges operating KA'PPAS over long distances in deep space——specially aboard a fast-movin' ship like this astroplane."

Brim smiled. Perhaps this wasn't the assignment he had dreamed of, but it promised to be an interesting one, if nothing else. "All right, people," he said, "let's secure for space and get rolling. As an old friend of mine once said, 'We're burning daylight here....'"

$$— o — 0 — o —$$

In less than a Metacycle, Brim was again seated at the left Helmsman's console with both SpinGravs rumbling smoothly at idle. Outside, the brow had retracted and two burly ground handlers wearing great metallic mittens had stationed themselves at the fore and aft optical bollards, ready to cast off. After one last sweep of the instruments, Brim glanced across the control console to Barbousse, who was relaxed in the right seat as if the two of them had flown the ship in earlier that morning. In the back of his mind, Brim still found himself concerned about taking the ship up so soon after spending so much time on the beach. Logically, he knew he could fly it; there was no ship in the Known Universe he couldn't master. Yet the ghost of a doubt nagged him: He wouldn't be the first cocksure Helmsman who had died trying to fly a ship he wasn't ready for—and there were other lives to consider as well. Certainly Barbousse could do it, even though he was fresh out of flight school. Whenever Barbousse put his mind to doing something, he did it well.

"All set, Skipper?" Barbousse asked expectantly.

Brim ground his teeth. He couldn't—*wouldn't*—let his old friend down. "All set here," he conceded, sliding the side Hyperscreen open beside him. "Single up those mooring beams!" he called to the waiting ground crew. Now, there would be no more time to worry.

"Singling the beams," one of the handlers shouted with a quick salute. He nodded to his partner at the stern, and a moment later, only a single, thin beam at each end of the ship held her in place.

Brim checked area around the ship: All clear. "Chief," he said, "let's raise ship."

"Raising ship, Skipper," Barbousse seconded.

As Brim moved his hands deftly over the ground controls, the ship lifted smoothly to the five-iral taxiing height above its thrashing footprint in the water.

Brim switched his globular link to ground control. "Four Nines Wakefield requesting clearance to, ah...." he checked the Terminal map hologram on his lap; it *had* been a while..., "exterior taxiway 86G."

A head in the display consulted something off screen, then turned and nodded. "Four Nines cleared to taxiway 86G."

"Thanks, GC. We're on our way." He turned to the dockworkers outside. "At my signal, cast off all mooring beams!" he shouted, giving a quick salute.

"Casting off at your signal," the dock worker shouted.

Brim slid the panel shut, watching an indicator change to green. "Ready, Chief?"

"Ready, Skipper."

"We'll go to internal gravity, then, if you please."

"Internal gravity comin' up, Skipper."

While Brim ground his teeth, Barbousse clicked on the blower. "All hands, prepare for internal gravity... all hands, internal gravity in five clicks." He paused a moment, then touched two icons in sequence on a control panel… and Brim nearly lost what little lunch he'd been able to snag while running the simulations.

As always, the queasiness passed rapidly, then he was ready to move.

Brim scanned his instruments: All normal except the core temperature in the port SpinGrav, which was running moderately cooler than its starboard twin: Not a problem. With a last check forward and aft, he signaled the dock workers outside; the last mooring beams winked out just before he released the gravity brakes and nudged the thrust dampers forward. Moments later, he'd pulled into the canal as if he'd been practicing the difficult maneuver for weeks—something about occasionally riding Gravcycles, he thought with a smile.

He taxied carefully: *Four Nines* was obviously a quick surface ship, a lot quicker than the WF Type-327s he'd flown in the past. Ahead, intersection lights shone green as far as the eye could see. One way or another, they were on their way to Hatfield.

Chapter 12

. . .in the left seat again

AVALON/ASTURIUS, AVALON CITY, GRAND IMPERIAL
TERMINAL, 16 NONAD, 52016

For the next 15 cycles, they taxied and detoured through a maze of canals—many blocked by debris and bomb damage—while Barbousse traced their path on a small HoloMap. Brim found it passing curious he seemed to have constant green lights as he passed each controlled intersection. Also at many of them, knots of people—mostly military—were standing and *waving*.

The first red light they encountered was at the entrance to Lake Mersin itself, and Brim brought the little ship to a halt just short of the breakwaters—almost relieved to have been stopped at least once in this ultra-busy terminal. He peered around the breakwater and smiled. Good reason for the stop, he observed to himself: A majestic old Queen Elidean-class battleship was thundering majestically past on her way to the military terminal—at least ten times the length of his Wakefield and an order of magnitude more in raw mass of Hullmetal. "We shall require a salute, Mister Steele," Brim prompted, noting her name, *I.F.S. Indomitable*.

"Aye, Skipper," Steele replied. Immediately, the KA'PPA beacon rose from the Wakefield's back, and ghostly KA'PPA rings spread through the sky like ripples in a pond. "MAY STARS LIGHT ALL THY PATHS."

Brim had to crane his head back to see the battleship's beacon when she made her traditional reply: "AND THY PATHS, STAR TRAVELERS." He glimpsed crowds of tiny figures peering down from the vast panoply of Hyperscreens atop her towering bridge as she passed; they were all waving. For a moment, he peered around the ship, puzzled. *What was so interesting about the Wakefield?* Was something wrong? Certainly nothing *seemed* to be amiss; the instruments all displayed normal readings—at least according to the simulator settings he could recall. Outside, all the hatches he could see from the bridge appeared to be closed and the fouled water around the ship looked as clean as Lake Mersin ever got. Then the battleship was past, the lake churning furiously in the wake of her massive gravity generators..

Brim shook his head for a moment as the WF-400 bounced in the big ship's gravity wake. How things had changed during his few years in the Fleet! When he'd reported to his first duty station on old I.F.S. *Truculent*, massive starships like the aging *Indomitable* ruled the galaxy, and speedy little astroplanes like the Wakefield were considered mere adjuncts to the fleets they served: Fast but with so little endurance and killing power they were used mostly for scouting beyond the limited range of BKAEW equipment available in those days. Now, only a few years later, vastly increased firepower and rapidly increasing range had turned the tables. In the past few years, astroplanes had become the point of the sword and the great, massive starships of old found themselves relegated to support roles as heavy cargo carriers or orbiting artillery. Brim himself had destroyed the huge Imperial battleship *Queen Elidean* from a Starfury in combat when he had been a part of Onrad's Imperial Volunteer Group. Now, it looked as if even long-range patrolling duty might about to be taken over by ships like his little WF-400.

Suddenly, the signal ahead was green and a voice from his display announced, *"Four Nines* Wakefield: you are cleared to marker nineteen; departure vector will be three forty-seven degrees."

"Four Nines Wakefield taxiing to liftoff marker nineteen departure vector three forty-seven degrees," Brim acknowledged. "Thanks, Terminal."

"Good bye and good sailing Admiral Brim," the controller replied.

Brim felt his face flush. Everybody military in the terminal seemed to know he was making a takeoff today. What was all the excitement about? Shrugging, he headed out onto the lake and made for marker

19, which was little more than a distant buoy on the windswept water. He needed the Hyperscreen wipers almost immediately.

"Taxi checks, Chief," he ordered, momentarily surprised at how easily the command came after so long on the beach.

"Lift modifiers, twenty one, twenty one, green."

Brim checked the control panel: 21 and 21; both indicators were back-lighted green. "Check" he acknowledged. "Yaw dampers and instruments?"

"Checked, Skipper."

"Weight and balance finals?" he asked, steering clear of a scorched, corroding freighter that protruded from the lake at an odd angle like some stranded whale. The wreck towered over the tiny Wakefield, ringed by green nun buoys warning STAY CLEAR. It must have been hit by tremendous energy beams, for the blackened, gaping hull had been blasted open like a ripe Ca'omba fruit, revealing smashed bulkheads and galleries of compartments littered with melted debris. Hatches hung open everywhere, and a thick band of oil from Mersin's filthy water had formed ring of sludge around her new waterline. Brim ground his teeth. No matter how you looked at it, war was a terrible thing.

"Two fifty three; eighteen at no-load," Barbousse announced, breaking into Brim's reverie

The check list! Brim admonished himself. *Weight and balance*. He quickly calculated... *253 at 18 and no load*.... "Okay, Chief. Put twenty-nine point three on the stabilizer."

"Twenty-nine point three it is, Skipper."

Back in synch with the takeoff, Brim clicked a display into life. "Engineers' taxi check, ladies."

"Complete, Captain," Kermis replied. "Everything's *go* here."

Brim glanced at Barbousse, still not entirely convinced he was ready to handle a hot ship like this '400. "Looks good to you, Chief?"

"Aye Skipper," Barbousse replied with a wink. "*Very* good... except I think the three-forty-seven departure vector they gave you from marker nineteen takes us directly over the palace. We'll want to watch our altitude and noise profile a bit over the Grounds. I understand the Palace Guards can get pretty ugly about noise."

Brim nodded. "I'll keep it in mind, Chief," he said, then smiled to himself. Seemed as if Onrad might be checking him out till the last click…. By now, the wipers were going top speed and spray was washing clear over the ship. The buoy was less than a half c'lenyt distant…, and for some reason, a number of watercraft had put out onto the lake; most seemed to be heading for marker 19. Frowning, Brim focused again on the task at hand. "Liftoff checklist, Chief." He glanced at the list he'd taped to the corner of his instrument panel. "Transponders and home indicator?"

"Both on, Skipper."

"FullStop cell?"

"Powered."

"See any warning lights?"

"Everything's green."

"Looks good to me, too. Configuration check, then. Antiskid first."

"Antiskid is….on."

"Speed brakes?"

"Forward, Skipper."

"Stabilizer trail?"

"Neutral."

"Give me a point zero five starboard on that, Chief."

"Stabilizer trail reset to point zero five Skipper."

"Lift gradient?"

"Twenty-three one… set."

"Course indicators, Mr. Lu?"

"Set… and checked, Captain."

For a moment, Brim's eyes swept out around the harbor: wrecks everywhere, the shoreline littered by tumbled wharves, smashed warehouses with crumbling walls and gaping windows, toppled gantry cranes. The Leaguers and their attacks had been greatly slowed, but not before they'd caused grievous damage to the Empire's great capital city. Nothing gallant about *this* war—or any other, for that matter. Suddenly, Ground Control interrupted his musing again. "*Four Nines* Wakefield, when you reach the marker, you are cleared for liftoff. Wind is out of sixty-five degrees at twenty-four."

Brim smiled to himself. The ship was just abreast Marker 19. "Acknowledge that, Control, and thanks," he replied, swinging the ship around the tossing marker. As the landscape skidded to starboard, he made a last check of the flight instruments: Looked okay. "Everything secure back there?" he asked over the intercom.

A chorus of "*Secures*" issued from another globular display at his right. Only moments later, in the distance along the takeoff vector, a violet beacon began to pulse, rapidly at first, then slowing as Brim swing the bow swung further to port. Any moment now....

Chapter 13

. . .straight on until morning

LAKE MERSIN, AVALON/ASTURIUS, 33 OCTAD, 52016

Abruptly, the beacon changed to green, then gradually shifted to pulsing red. Brim was ready; he nudged the steering engine to the left, stood on the gravity brakes, then eased both thrust dampers all the way forward to the stops as the beacon changed again to green.

"Lights on…, full military, Skipper!" Barbousse shouted over the swelling thunder of the Gravs.

In the aft display, receding waves had suddenly flattened along two backward flowing troughs. *Time to roll….* Taking a deep breath, Brim released the gravity brakes, and the ship surged forward, accelerating rapidly as it knifed through the waves sending great cascades of spray hundreds of irals to either side. For the briefest moment, he experienced one final vestige of doubt—*What in the name of Xaxt am I doing here?*—then a lifetime of reflexes took over and suddenly: *Elation!* Back in his own element at last! Confidence surged like a mantle of crackling energy. Lake Mersin rushed by in a suddenly reassuring blur, the big Krasni-Peych Gravs thundering their anthem of extravagant power.

"Alpha velocity, Skipper!"

"Alpha velocity, Chief." Grinning now in spite of himself, Brim rotated the bow a few degrees skyward: The amazing speed increased even more. Nothing, absolutely nothing he remembered took off like this. Of course, he managed to remind himself, it *had* been a while….

"Beta velocity, Skipper!"

"Beta velocity, Chief!" As Brim raised the bow a few degrees more, the faint drumming of the waves died away and ship lifted smoothly off the surface; at once, the Hyperscreens dried, and Barbousse parked the wipers. Brim leveled out as the speed built, thundering along only 500 irals off the surface. *Voot's beard, how he'd missed this!* It was as if he'd suddenly come alive again!

"Imperial Palace comin' up, Skipper!" Barbousse warned as Brim banked steeply to port and headed inland. "Ya' think 500 irals might be a *wee* bit low?"

Brim glanced out the Hyperscreens and grinned as the city rushed under the starship's bow like some wild travelogue. "I'm guessin' we're fine, Chief," he said with a grin, then—on an absolute whim—he yelled, *"Hang on, everybody...."* and executed a perfect slow roll. As they passed over the sprawling Imperial Palace up-side down, he glanced through the overhead Hyperscreens at a heavy-set man below in the gardens holding a small child: Both were looking up at the ship and waving wildly—as if they'd been waiting. Then he rolled level and continued his climb out, rocking the ship from side to side and hoping no one would notice the tears streaming along his cheek.

"Ground Control to *Four Nines* Wakefield...."

"*Four Nines* Wakefield... *SNIFF* ...."

"Are you experiencing problems, Lord Brim?"

"Everything's under control, GC," Brim replied with a great, broad smile: slow rolls at 500 irals altitude *were* downright illegal—especially over the Imperial Palace. Somehow, he felt certain he'd never hear of this particular transgression "Thanks for checking," he said.

"*Four Nines* Wakefield: you are cleared to Level-thirty-six buoy Cantrell and LightSpeed."

"*Four Nines* Wakefield. Thanks."

"May stars light all your paths, Lord Brim"

"And yours, GC...."

Abruptly, Brim's court martial seemed a thousand years in the past. At last, he was back where he belonged....

BOOK II

Campaigning

Chapter 14

. . .back to work

The ugly panorama of worn, patched streets and age-stained structures composing the city of Hall on Hatfield/Salisbury was little different from all the other terraformed industrial sites that had sprung up on marginal planets within a few Metacycles travel of Avalon. Salisbury, was a weak star giving off a minimum of light and heat, which left its only satellite—a watery little planet named Salisbury—damp, dark, and chillsome, but perfect for a noisy, dangerous industry like building starships.

No one really cared how much the planet was polluted, nor how chiselly it was to reside there because industry was of prime importance, not people. The key requirement for terraforming was that the average temperature in the temperate band be higher than the freezing point of water—which Salisbury's was—and grubby little Hall with its natural harbor, had naturally become the major industrial center. Unfortunately, for the same reasons, Hall had also become a frequent target of Leaguer raids, with obvious damage nearly anywhere one looked. War had turned a naturally ugly locale into a disaster. Yet somehow, work continued unabated. Something was indomitable about the human spirit, or so professed the Gradgroat-Norchelite communicants....

Four Nines' reception at the Wakefield plant had been mixed, to say the least. Because Brim and his crew were sponsored by a mysterious—but obviously powerful—government office in Avalon, the managers and officers of the corporation treated them with kid gloves, demonstrating respect as well as deference. Even the engineering divisions gave the impression of wanting to cooperate, at minimum. But there was always a quiet undertone of displeasure. Brim and his crew were interlopers—there by some mysterious outside decree—who were to improve a product many of them has spent many years to deliver. In spite of the smiles and cooperation, it was plain no one in Wakefield, Ltd. really wanted to see them succeed, for their every success meant something had been overlooked in the ship's design or testing. It was an uncomfortable milieu in which to work, but the crew of *Four Nines* dove in with purpose, and little by little, their collective skills began to pay off in many aspects of the new astroplane's performance.

For the remainder of Nonad and most of Decad, Brim and his crew explored ways to extend the already phenomenal range of their WF-400—while insuring the ship would still have sufficient loiter time over possible targets to make the extra range worth while. Much of their time had been spent actually flying the ship at Hyperspeed, testing combinations of reduced GCOMs (billion crystal oscillations per milliclick), damping the thrust-energy flow, and ever so slightly increasing the phase delay.

Tests like these lent themselves very little to simulation on logic machines. Rather, they required actual performance and called for long, arduous days of flying. No one complained, however, especially Brim, who was happy enough to spend all the time he could back in the left seat. And just as surely as the days passed, their experiments began to pay off. By early Decad, they were able to fly *Four Nines* over distances equivalent to flights reaching the Bright Triad of Ely—some 2300 light years—in a little under ten and a half Metacycles *with nearly* three-quarters of a Metacycle left over for operational work, like bender killing. Admittedly, Brim had slowed the little ship to little more than 220 light years per Metacycle: Less than half her normal cruising speed. But even that was more than ten times the velocity of a normal escort—and the number of cubic light years Steele would be able to search with his high-powered BKAEW on such a brief mission was no less than astonishing.

Soon, it was time to put that research into practice. At the Year's-End Holidays, Brim took the crew back to Avalon for a few days' leave before their real push began.

As *Four Nines* cleared the Salisbury traffic pattern, a slim, ghost-like man in a black cloak was HoloPhoning the news of their takeoff and destination back to Avalon City. A man with mysterious access to nearly everything in Hall, Covall the Wraith had already sent back a great deal of daily information to the same address about the ship's performance...

Chapter 15

. . .Grand Admiral Baxter Calhoun

AVALON/ASTURIUS, AVALON CITY, 34 DECAD, 52016

On Brim's first morning back in Avalon, his foremost priority was a call to Calhoun's office in the Admiralty to accept an luncheon invitation that had been waiting with the Concierge at the lobby desk when he arrived at his condominium tower. Subsequently, he spent a few Metacycles shopping for Year-End Holiday gifts and spending much agreeable time visiting shops specializing in children's wares. War clouds may have threatened the very warp and woof of civilization, but merchants nevertheless managed to fill their showrooms with so many items sure to gladden the heart of a four-year-old girl that Brim wound up so laden he could hardly walk.

After a wild taxi ride through downtown Avalon's rubble-burdened streets—nothing, not even the devastation of war, managed to slow the feral motorists of central Avalon—he reached Calhoun's ancient Chambers Society, housed only a block from the Admiralty. Since time immemorial, the Society had occupied a location on the top floor of the ancient, gray Imperial Bank and Savings Building which—with the exception of many boarded-up windows—had so far miraculously escaped Avalon's extensive destruction at the hands of the Leaguers.

Handing his packages to a dour doorman, Brim presented his card to am imposing Maître d', remembering full well that not too many years ago, his inexpensive clothing would have earned him a rebuff at the door. Now, outfitted in the costly garments that had become his habit since becoming Lord Brim, he lingered in the muted opulence of leather and dark wood with a confidence that would have astounded him only a few years ago. If clothes didn't necessarily make the man, he considered with no little irony, they certainly made for a big boost in the ego! Moments later, the Maître d' returned with an unctuous smile. "Please to follow, M'Lord," he said, bowing obsequiously, "the Admiral awaits at his table...."

"Ah, Brim!" Calhoun said, standing and offering his hand, "Welcome to Chambers. I'm glad ye could accept m' invitation on such short notice."

"I'm honored, Admiral," Brim replied, returning the Admiral's firm, masculine grip. "Besides, it's been a long time since my last visit to the Society."

"Ye'll soon be a member if I ha' onythin' to do wi' things." Calhoun said with a little grin. "We need mair Carescrians here to give the place a little class it's lackin'. Then he nodded as the Maître d' held an opposite chair. "Have a seat, auld friend," he said. "'Tis time for a wee bite to eat, an' then onless I miss m' guess you hae' much to tell me...."

They drank an excellent vintage of Logish Meem and dined leisurely on tomato Leopold, braised lamb chops boulangère with escalloped potatoes, and pears en cremè.

At the conclusion of the pears, Brim turned down a camarge cigarette from the Admiral's silver case, then relaxed and prepared his thoughts while the waiter cleared away the remaining plates. At last, the Admiral steepled his fingers, leaned back, and fixed Brim with an intense gaze. "All right, Wilf, let's have it. The Bears hae electronically swept this dinin' room so many times neither CIGAs nor Leaguers are willin' t' waste any mair expensive bugs on it. Ye can speak your mind."

For the next half metacycle, Brim presented a condensed summary of notes he'd prepared during his long trial flights across the stars: The power settings he and the crew had tried, the flying techniques they'd developed, the operational capabilities that were now possible with prudent use of the new WF-400's Drives. He focused especially on a list of modifications that might obtain even more utility from the powerful astroplanes in terms of augmented sensing capabilities and increased combat potential, i.e., bender-killing.

When Brim finished, Calhoun pursed his lips and frowned for long cycles, clearly deep in reflection. When he spoke, his eyes blazed with the kind of intensity that indicated to Brim that his words had found their mark. "'Tis a marvelous job ye've done, young Brim," he said in a quiet voice. "Nae' mair than Onrad an' I expected of ye, but deservin' o' much praise nonetheless." He glanced about the room for a moment as if in thought, then again fixed Brim with his gaze. "However, I sense there's mare to come, isn't there?"

"Aye," Brim said. "You know me well, because I'm about to suggest we do something about those studies I've made."

"Calhoun rolled his eyes and sat upright. "Why am I nae surprised?" he said with a chuckle. "All right, on what is it ye wad talk me into spendin' the Admiralty's credits now?"

This time, it was Brim who sat back in his chair and steepled his fingers. "What I want to do, Cal," he said, "is put my theories into actual operation."

"You're talking aboot...?"

"I'm talking about killing benders," Brim said. "Theories are wonderful in peacetime when all you do is debate 'em. But..., well, you've seen what's going on outside. This is all-out *war*, and unless we find a way to counter the Leaguers' head start in cloaked warfare, we stand a good chance of being on the losing side."

"So?" Calhoun asked warily.

"So here's what I need to prove out what I've been working on," Brim said, reaching into his suit coat for a sheaf of documents, which he handed across the table. "All the details are here," he explained, but basically, this is what I'm after."

Calhoun scanned the papers in silence. "Tall order, Brim," he said after a number of cycles. "You've got civilians aboard your WF-400. Armin' it wuld be against every treaty...."

"So. is what the Leaguers are doing to the Sodeskayans," Brim countered. "If we're going to win, we'll have to break a few rules ourselves. Like, for example, your actions a few years ago as a privateer."

74

"Wha'?" Calhoun demanded, pushing away from the table with a frown. "Wha' makes you think.... " then he sat back and shrugged. "I don't guess I hae many secrets anymair, Wilf Brim," he said, "do I?"

"Not from the people who most admire you, Cal," Brim said. "Without that privateering experience, we'd never have had our IVG in Fluvanna. Besides, there's only one astroplane involved with this operation. We'll be lost in the shuffle."

"Weell...."

"Second," Brim continued before Calhoun could voice more objections, "those documents in your hand also contain a list of supplies I'll want dropped off at the Bright Triad of Ely."

"The wha...?"

"The Bright Triad of Ely," Brim repeated. "A small, intensely bright star within a few hundred light years of Carescria. It's captured two large asteroids that reflect the star's brilliance so well the whole thing seems like a triad. The Space Transportation Safety Establishment mans a small MET station on the larger asteroid to monitor gravity storms passing toward Greater Avalon from the galactic center. I want to quietly start a small operation there, too. It's an easy flight to any of the nearby Carescrian stars—like Linfarne/Navron. And though everybody seems to know about the MET Station, neither side in this war pays it much attention, other than using its grav-storm reports."

Frowning, Calhoun leafed through the thin sheets of plastic again, stopped to read for a moment, then looked up. "In-flight sustainables, HyperTorps, BKAEW spares, military-spec, and at least one energy generator for refueling the WF-400, personal arms," he recited. "All contraband for a civilian as ye know. Looks as if ye're goin' to war, Wilf Brim—wi'out a Fleet Cloak."

"I am, Cal," Brim said, looking his old commander directly in the eye. "I'm going to set up a one-ship patrol between here and The Triad and see if I can't bag me enough benders to make a full-scale operation worth implementing."

Calhoun laughed. "Ye think all ye' are goin' to need grows on trees, do ye?" he demanded.

Brim laughed wryly. "No, I don't think any sort of thing—I was at the Gantaclar conference, too, remember? I also know everything you supply me with is coming out of somebody else's budget—somebody who's going to be mad as Xaxt he isn't getting what he thinks is his fair share."

"Ye've got *that* right, Laddie, Calhoun agreed with a wink. "But I can handle it. "After all, it's not as if you're askin' me to outfit a whole squadron of those new WF-400s." He frowned. "The tough part wull be makin' the stuff disappear."

"Oh, I'll make it disappear," Brim assured him.

"Not wha' I meant," Calhoun amended with a frown. "Wha' I mean is makin' it disappear so tha' it looks like it's merely bein' stolen—people expect tha' in wartime. But if it gets out tha' it's goin' to *you*, tha' zukeed Confisse Trafford wull surely raise the Admiralty roof. You're all tha' stands in the way of his daughter takin' her rightful blame for the failure of tha' attack on Emithrnéy/Bax, an' your ev'ry success puts more doubt on the charges she's brought against ye. Trafford's got his spies ev'rywhere."

"Yeah," Brim agreed, "I've noticed that."

"So where are ye going to work out of on the Avalon side?" Calhoun asked.

"Thought I'd lease a warehouse in one of the industrial sections off Lake Mersin. Seems to me I ought to pick up that share of the expenses myself, considering what the Emperor did for me."

"Guid thought, young Brim," Calhoun said. "It a' comes out in the wash, as they say. But this ground crew ye mention, they hae no need to be civilians, do they?"

"I'd rather have Blue Capes; they'll report to Chief Barbousse and have to be cleared for black operations."

"I'll tak' care of everything."

"I'm counting on that, Cal."

Calhoun tossed back the last of his Logish aperitif, then glanced at his timepiece. "'Tis time I'm back at the Admiralty," he said. "I'll have my personnel people get to work on locatin' your ground crew. An', can I assume our friend Barbousse still retains his, er, *contacts*?" Calhoun asked.

"Oh, I think so," Brim replied.

"Gud," Calhoun said. "Then we'll work the supplyin' business through him; it'll give one more level of indirection to the proceedin's." He drew a business card from a silver case and spoke a few words into it, then handed it to Brim. "Have him contact this lady at her office tomorrow," he said. "The twa o' them can set things up an' get 'em goin' afore you and I cauld ev'n list the details."

Brim chuckled. "A successful officer knows that people luik Barbousse run the Fleet," he quoted.

Calhoun nodded solemnly. "From Grand Admirals to the lowliest SubLieutenants. E'en Onrad himself is in awe of Barbousse—which reminds me: Ye'll be at the Imperial Calendar Ball?"

"I don't think so," Brim said. "I haven't been invited."

"Yes ye hae'," Calhoun said. "The invitation's at your apartment. His Majesty war surprised when you blew into town unannounced."

"I hadn't planned to bother him," Brim said in surprise.

"And how were you going to visit that *niece* of yours without him knowing?"

"My, er, *niece*? How did you know about...."

"Little Hope?" Calhoun guffawed. "That young lady's lineage is probably the worst-kept secret in the Imperial Court. She hae her mother's eyes, but the look in them—weel, Gallsworthy predicts she'll be a better Helmsman then either o' ye' ev'n hoped to be."

Chapter 16

. . .plotting

ABOARD THE S. S. *PRINCESS MEGAN*, IN PRIVATE MOORING ON LAKE MERSIN, 34 DECAD, 52016

Despite his considerable success in life, Cranwell had never owned a yacht. However, during his stay on Trafford's *Princess Megan* during the Gantaclar conference, he'd been impressed by everything he saw. The moment he'd stepped on the brow to Trafford's floating palace, he'd realized he would have to possess something just like it—or better. Private starships were a true measure of a man's success—and would thus beautifully set him off from the lower classes who could only dream of owning something like this sleek beauty.

Today, a uniformed civilian Captain welcomed him aboard and lead him to the grand-looking "Salon" where his host waited, ensconced at one end of a magnificent, ophet-leather settee.

"Welcome again to *Princess Megan*" a jovial Trafford exclaimed, as always, *conspicuously* keeping his seat and raising a goblet of what promised to be a fine Logish Meem. "Come sit, cousin and enjoy a goblet with me."

"Thank you, Cousin," Cranwell purred through a practiced smile, determined not to mention his growing envy Trafford's imposing yacht—one of the largest on Lake Mersin, he understood. As soon as he'd taken a seat on the settee beside his host, a Steward placed a large goblet in his hand.

"Try it," Trafford demanded expectantly.

Slowly, Cranwell swirled the violet liquid in its delicate goblet, inhaled the fragrance, and closed his eyes in ecstasy. At long last, he took a sip, savoring the complex flavors and sighed. As he'd expected, the Meem was truly Logish, of a classic vintage. He smiled at his host. "Magnificent, Cousin," he declared. "Magnificent!"

"Like my *Princess Megan*, right, Cousin?"

"Indeed," Cranwell admitted. "She is a *very* nice yacht."

"'Very nice'—that's all?" Trafford returned in faux anger.

"Well, Cousin," Cranwell allowed, stifling another surge of jealousy, I've never had much of an interest in owning a starship. But, yes, your yacht quite impressive."

"Well, that's better, Cousin," Trafford said, apparently mollified. "And before we savor more refreshments, shall we discuss our, say, *project?*"

"Well," Cranwell hesitated, glancing pointedly at the steward hovering near the bar, "perhaps...."

"Clear the room!" Trafford ordered, and the steward disappeared with the bartender. "I'd trust them all with my life," the Count declared, "but I respect your caution."

"Thank you, Cousin," Cranwell said with a scowl. "And I trust the room—er cabin—is completely secure?"

"Believe me," Trafford assured him, "this cabin is one of the most secure in the Known Universe."

Cranwell glanced around the cabin once more as if he could *see* everything was secure, then sat back and nodded. "All right, Cousin," be began, "in short: this Wilf Brim is more dangerous to us than I could have imagined."

"Indeed? He's nothing but a simple Helmsman. How can he be dangerous? What has he done?"

"In the short time he and his crew have been at the Wakefield plant on Hatfield/Salisbury with the new WF-400, they have stretched the little ship's range to some 2300 light years—and travel that distance in a little under ten and a half Metacycles."

"So?" Trafford demanded. "Those figures mean little to me."

"It's a matter of how much area the little ships can now patrol in a very short time," Cranwell explained. "They can cover in those ten Metacycles as much as an escort ship can cover in a week."

"Impossible," Trafford exclaimed.

"Not impossible to Lord Brim," Cranwell declared. "And that's not all."

"There's more?" Trafford asked in a concerned voice, peering over his goblet.

"Oh yes," Cranwell said with a deep frown. "Brim can make these flights with nearly three-quarters of a Metacycle left over for operational work—like bender killing—at more than ten times the velocity of a normal escort. The number of cubic light years he should be able to search with their new, high-powered BKAEW on such a brief mission is seriously difficult to believe. In other words, Dear Cousin, the very future of the Escort Service is at risk." *Not to mention my secret projects as well as yours, dear Cousin,* he thought.

Trafford held his goblet in both hands as if he was suddenly afraid to set it down. "I assume this information is quite current?" he demanded.

"Quite," Cranwell said. "It was delivered to me from data compiled on site at the Wakefield plant."

"So these developments are still new enough that, without Brim, they probably couldn't be duplicated?"

Cranwell pursed his lips. "No," he replied after considerable thought. "Once a genie like that is out of its lamp, it never goes back."

"Then what shall we do?" Trafford demanded. "We certainly don't want anything to happen to our *dear* Escort Service."

"Not to worry, Cousin," Cranwell assured him. "Even though the genie is out, it still must be *sold,* so to speak. New ideas seldom catch on until someone well-known champions their ultimate utility."

"And that someone is Brim?" Trafford demanded.

"Oh, it is," Cranwell replied. "Brim has become so well respected in the highest ranks of the Fleet, probably he *alone* can make people believe in the techniques he's developed."

"I see," Trafford mused. "Then disposing of him seems like an obvious necessity. Much as I hate to admit it, his existence also threatens Daughter Megan's military career." He paused a moment studying his fingernails, then nodded as if he had made a decision. "I shall take on the job myself," he said, staring down at the richly polished deck.

"*You?*" Cranwell gasped. "And how do you plan to accomplish such a thing?"

"In a way that will cast no blame on either of us, Cousin," Trafford assured him.

"And that is…?"

"No need for you to know at this point—perhaps ever," Trafford replied with a confident smile.

Cranford smiled, too. He'd rather hoped his wealthy cousin would decide to do the job for him. It had long been rumored more than one would-be adversary had simply disappeared when running afoul of Trafford. "In that case," he declared, "I am ready for more of that delicious Logish Meem."

"What a grand idea, Cousin," Trafford said, pressing a concealed button to summon his servants…

Chapter 17

. . .Hope

AVALON/ASTURIUS, AVALON CITY, IMPERIAL PALACE,
OCTAD, 34 DECADE, 52016

S hortly after lunch, Calhoun and Brim parted, the latter catching a taxi to Barbousse's quarters, where he dropped off Calhoun's business card and continued on to the Imperial Palace. Entering by a special rear gate, he was met by Nurse Tutti and the tall, elderly Imperial page, Joseph, who for the past few years seemed to be permanently assigned to "Hope Duty," as it was known among the Palace staffers. "Is she busy?" Brim asked.

"Never too busy for her Uncle Wilf," Tutti said, nodding toward a sunny courtyard where a little girl with long, black tresses was playing with a small orange cat. "In fact, she's waiting for you."

"C-could she even remember me?" Brim wondered aloud.

"No, I don't think so," Tutti said. "She was barely two when last she saw you."

"So I guess I'm starting all over again."

"That you are, Lord Brim," Joseph said with an encouraging smile. "But I don't think it will matter. She's quite the young lady; my guess is you two will be instant friends."

Brim bit his lip for a moment. "I picked up a few things here in Avalon, but I never know what will please," he said, shuffling his packages.

"Probably yourself is plenty," Tutti said with a chuckle. "You've already sent her enough gifts to spoil her rotten. But it is the Holidays, so I'm certain a few more won't go to her head."

Brim smiled uneasily, then opened the door and stepped into the courtyard. "Hello," he said, wishing he could think of something a lot more engaging to a four-year-old.

"Hello," the little girl replied soberly. "You must be my Uncle Wilf. The one who sends me things from all over."

"That's me," Brim said, once more totally unable to think of anything else appropriate. She was easily the most gorgeous child he had ever looked upon: Her jet-black hair and tawny complexion were the very picture of her mother, but it was her eyes that set her off from all others: almond-shaped and radiant, they had a unique *look*. Brim recognized it in other Helmsman. Gallsworthy had seen it too. Instantly, he realized that this little girl could very probably grow up to be one of the Galaxy's truly great Helmsman, if she wished.

"Do you like cats?" she demanded as a shaggy little orange cat bounded across to Brim and proceeded to rub herself on his boots.

"Oh, I love cats," he said, setting down his packages to lift the cat into his arms.

"That's good," Hope observed when the cat delicately licked his nose, "because she certainly likes you."

Brim laughed and set the cat gently on the floor beside the little girl. "What could be better than that?" he observed, "…and I have a clean nose, too."

Hope laughed happily. "I have a clean nose, too," she said with a secretive glance to the window where Tutti and Joseph stood smiling. "But *they* don't much approve."

"Well," Brim said, "probably they're right—but once in a while, it *is* nice to have a cat-clean nose."

"Yes," hope giggled, "a cat-clean nose. I shall remember, Uncle Wilf. It will be our secret." Suddenly, she peered up at him. "You're the man who flew over the palace up-side down in the noisy astroplane, aren't you?"

Brim grimaced. "Er, yes, that was me, too."

"What fun," she said with a giggle. "That made Uncle Onrad so happy. He laughed and laughed." Then, suddenly she became serious and frowned, looking Brim directly in the eye. "I'm so glad you're fun," she said thoughtfully. "That very day, Uncle Onrad said you would someday be the second most important man in my life."

"Your Uncle Onrad is too kind," Brim replied, nearly choked with emotion. "But it would make me very proud if it came true."

Abruptly, Hope glanced past Brim and grinned. "Oh, here comes Uncle Onrad now."

Brim spun 'round. "Your majesty," He exclaimed, "I didn't hear you coming."

Onrad grinned and extended his hand. "I'm usually not good at sneaking up on people, Brim—good to see you. And how are *you*, little Princess?"

"I'm fine Uncle Onrad," Hope said, holding her arms to be picked up. "This is the man who flew up-side down over your palace."

"Yes, I know he is," Onrad said, taking the little girl in his arms with a huge smile.

"You also told me he would be the second most important man in my life. Remember?"

Onrad looked embarrassed and rolled his eyes at Brim. "Yes I did. I can't deny it," he said.

"Well, since then," Hope said with the poise of a girl twice her age, "I have wondered who the *first* most important man will be. Do you know?"

"Hmm," Onrad grumbled, clearly taken aback by the direction of their discourse, "...I guess I don't. Perhaps. . ."

"Uncle Brim?"

"Um, well...."

"Will *that* man be the man I marry?" Hope interjected. "I suppose I shall have to do that some day. Nurse Tutti says so."

"P-probably a good assumption, Brim stammered, completely out of his depth with this outlandishly mature four-year old.

"W-whatever Nurse Tutti says," Onrad stumbled.

"If that's so," Hope continued, turning to Brim as though she had known him for years, "it very probably makes *you* my real father."

"W-what?" Brim stammered.

"Oh, it's all right," Hope said with a little smile. "We can make that our secret, too. He *is* my father, isn't he?," she asked Onrad. "Who else could be that important?"

Flummoxed, Brim glanced at Onrad. How could he deny this magnificent child? On the other hand, how could he entrust a four-year-old with such a perilous secret? "W-what about Nabob Eyren?" he parried.

"Oh, lots of people tell me Nabob Eyren is my father" Hope said, "but I don't believe them." She looked at Onrad. "You never talk about Mustafa Eyren the way you talk about Uncle Brim. Besides, Nabob Eyren never comes to see me."

"He never visits you?" Brim asked before he could stop himself.

Hope shook her head. "Nurse Tutti takes me to see him once in a while, but he soon acts as if I bore him."

"Well, I don't come to see you much either," Brim pointed out.

"That's true," Hope said, "but you send me things from all over *everywhere*. And I love it. It's almost like hearing from you. It shows you care."

"You like what I've sent?" Brim asked. "I'm never sure...."

"I like *everything* you send," Hope replied, "but what I like most is that you *send* stuff. I know you're thinking about me."

"Well, that's certainly true," Brim assured her. "I do think about you often."

"Then you *are* my real father, aren't you?"

Brim took a deep breath, considered for a moment, then decided the next words would probably be the most important of his life. But before he could say *yes*, Onrad spoke for him.

"Yes, Hope," he said, looking her directly in the eye, "It's time you know the truth. Uncle Brim is your real father."

"That makes me happy," she said, reaching across to take Brim's hands. "All the other little girls I play with have real fathers. It's nice to have one, too."

"But you won't be able to tell anyone," Brim cautioned. "You'll still have to pretend Mustafa Eyren is your father."

"Oh, I can do that," Hope assured him happily.

Onrad frowned and stroked his beard. "You really shouldn't have to," he said. "It's time the truth is told."

"But why, Uncle Onrad?" Hope asked. "As long as I *know* who my father is, why should we make Mustafa Eyren sad?"

Onrad glanced at Brim, then at the little girl. "Yes I suppose it would make him sad," he said. "Even though he doesn't come to visit, you do mean a great deal to him."

"Then it will be our secret," Hope pronounced, turning to Brim. "And I shall call you 'Daddy' only when the three of us are together. Won't that be fun?"

Brim met Onrad's gaze and nodded. "It's your call, Your Highness," he said quietly.

Onrad turned his gaze to Hope, his nose nearly touching the little girl's. "This is a *big* secret if we decide to keep it, Little Princess," he said. "Some day, the secret will be—must be—broken. But the longer we keep it, the less trouble the truth will eventually cause. Do you understand? It's *very* important you do."

Hope considered a moment, then nodded. "There's a lot I *don't* understand," she said in a very serious mien. "But I do understand it is important only you and daddy know, so I shall keep it that way."

Onrad nodded thoughtfully, then gently handed the little girl to Brim—who held her at first as if he had a fused HyperTorp in his arms. "So be it, folks," the Emperor said, his smile returning. Then he shook his head and chuckled. "I'd only dropped by to ask if you two would dine with me this evening."

"I'm so glad you did," Hope said. "All of a sudden, I've got a real Daddy, and I think that's a good excuse for a party—just between ourselves."

"Now *that's* a really good idea, Princess," Onrad said, slapping Brim on the back. "Sometimes," he said, leading the way into the palace proper, "the most important things in the Universe manage to happen quite by accident. Let's have us a party!"

Chapter 18

. . .completely out of place

TRIAD OF AVALON/ASTURIUS, AVALON CITY, 39 DECAD, 52016

O n the eve of the New Year celebration—and the 52017 Imperial Calendar Ball—Brim found himself completely alone in the city. Everyone he knew was immersed in family celebrations, urgent war work, or business matters. Even Barbousse had disappeared for a few days' leave with Nurse Tutti, and Brim was tired of the shallow wealthy who frequented the gambling casinos— besides, he was tired of parting them from their money, especially when he didn't need the winnings. Dreading yet another lonesome supper—the best catered repasts tasted bland when eaten alone—he took an elevator to the lobby and nighttime Avalon.

Waving away a resolute doorman who seemed determined he should take a taxi, Brim set off on foot along the dark, rubble-strewn streets toward the Admiralty, which he knew was surrounded by many public houses offering both good food and the solid company of spacemen. As he made his way along the ancient streets, debris crackled beneath his boots. The very air reeked of damp plaster, charred wood, death, and destruction. He wrinkled his nose. The wounded city seemed to shiver with the fevered blight of war. Wherever he looked, windowless silhouettes of shattered buildings slumped in among others that appeared to have gone unscathed. Along the street, bustling shops behind blackout curtains operated alongside others that by chance were little more than blackened, eyeless shells. Living or dying in wartime Avalon: it was *all* luck. He ground his teeth and pulled the cloak tighter around his neck as he trudged on.

Much better to be in it, fighting, rather than trying to exist as a bystander. Either way, luck pretty much determined who would live or die, but at least as a combatant, you could feel you were doing *something* in the way of defense:

In the near-darkness, he stumbled over a heap of bricks and nearly fell when a blacked-out lorry forced him close to the shapeless mountains of putrid rubble. Afterward, he gave in and hailed the next available hack

He halted the cab beneath a familiar sign topped by an ancient galleon—THE SAIL AND CANNON—relieved to find the hoary tavern beneath still intact. Providing a large tip for the cabby, whom he guessed must live an incredibly difficult life navigating the dark, cratered, streets, he moved a heavy blackout curtain aside and stepped into a dim, noisy Universe of life filled rich aromas of meem, Hogge'poa, mu'occo cigarettes, perfume, and spices, surrounded by an almost implausible ambience of cheer and vitality in the midst of ruin.

Pushing his way to the bar, he scanned the chalked menu board and was just about to order when a hand touched his shoulder. At the same time, a somehow familiar perfume wafted by his nose and a feminine voice inquired, "I say, you're Lord Brim, aren't you?"

Brim turned to face a woman seated at the bar with a sensible, intelligent mien, a lovely nose, sensuous lips, and full cheeks—all charmingly framed by straight blond hair, curled under at her shoulders. She was dressed in a stylish, obviously expensive civilian cloak, royal blue and trimmed in gold braid, beneath which she wore a dark red business ensemble and a white blouse. Clearly, he knew this stunning woman, but from *where*?

"The last time we met," she hinted with a puckish smile, "I was wearing a Fleet Cloak."

Suddenly, Brim recalled the conference at Gantaclar, the lovely Commander by whose side he'd sat, and the cosmopolitan warmth she'd radiated. Struggling desperately, for a name he came up with, "Hunt!" he exclaimed, "...Commander Ann Hunt! You got the job of DTOU, didn't you?"

"I did," she said, offering her hand, "how nice of you to remember."

"How nice of you to remember *me*," Brim returned. "What brings you to Avalon for the Holidays?"

"Admiral Calhoun," she replied. "A progress report."

"In the middle of the Holidays?" Brim asked.

"Well," she replied, peering over her eyeglasses, "as you may have noticed, there *is* a war going on outside."

"Even we civilians notice things like that," Brim grumbled mordantly, "And how are things progressing with the job?"

"Sorry," Hunt said with an embarrassed look. "I'd forgotten you were...."

"S'okay," Brim said quickly. "And I'm sorry too. How *are* things going as DTOU?"

"So far, so good," she replied thoughtfully. "It's just a routine progress report I'm here for; nothing more."

"Then my congratulations," Brim replied. "You drew a tough billet."

"Yes," she said. "I got the impression you understood that more than most others at the conference."

"A zillion years ago, "Brim said with a chuckle. "No more...."

"Nice of you," Hunt remarked as a bartender interrupted their discourse.

"Good to see you in the City again, Lord Brim," the beefy man said with a big grin. "What'll you have?"

Brim glanced at Hunt's plate; she was nearly finished. "Well...," he began, when a tall Vice Admiral stepped between him and Hunt.

"Ready, Ann?" the man demanded, as if Brim didn't exist.

"Stephen," she admonished, "I *was* in conversation with this gentleman."

The Admiral turned part way toward Brim. "Oh, sorry," he said, nodding absently over his shoulder. Then, "Ready to go, Ann? We don't have all that long, you know."

"*Stephen*," Hunt continued emphatically, her cheeks reddening, "I should like you to meet Lord Wilf Brim; Lord Brim, my Fiancée, Admiral Hendrix."

Helplessly, Brim watched the bartender shuffle off to service other, more adroit customers, then offered his hand as Hendrix turned.

"Pleased," the man said taking Brim's hand apathetically. Then he frowned. "I say," he mumbled, "You're the one who caught it for the cock-up at the battle of Emithrnéy/Bax, aren't you?"

"That's me," Brim admitted in a flash of discomfiture, while behind Hendrix, Hunt suddenly closed her eyes and bit her lip.

"Pity," Hendrix mumbled with a hurried shrug, then turned his back and took Hunt's arm. "We really *must* be on our way, Ann," he said, this time with clear annoyance in his voice.

"N-nice seeing you Lord Brim," she said.

"Yes, a pleasure," Hendrix muttered over his shoulder, as he pushed her toward the blackout curtain.

The next moment, a brawny Commando, wearing fatigues and a scarlet beret from Special Services had pushed his way onto Hunt's just-vacated bar stool, and was noisily signaling the bartender as if Brim didn't exist.

Peering around at the remainder of the clientele Brim understood immediately—he hadn't even noticed when he came in from the cold. Except for a few *Ornwald* "girls" dressed in the abbreviated green dresses of their singular profession, very few of the patrons wore civilian clothing! He felt his face reddened as he realized he was completely out of place here.

At that point, he decided perhaps a catered supper wasn't so much of a bad idea as he'd earlier imagined. Within the metacycle, he'd returned to his lonely apartment, where he ordered a light supper, watched media broadcasts about historic starships while he ate, and finished the evening at a gambling casino playing Cre'el and winning even more money he didn't need. All-in-all, he thought—as he climbed into bed with another gorgeous woman who had little appreciation for the sacrifices going on in the besieged city—the evening served as ample justification for the many absences from this grand city he'd enforced upon himself since his court marshal.

Chapter 19

. . .a shockingly familiar voice

AVALON/ASTURIUS, AVALON CITY 40 DECAD (CALENDAR EVE), 52016

Late in the afternoon of Calendar Eve, Brim answered an authoritative knock on his door to discover a smiling Barbousse, who strode through the front door and into Brim's bedroom, where he capably laid out an entire formal ensemble—including dancing slippers shined to an impossible luster. "Lucky you ordered these when you did, Skipper," he said without meeting Brim's eyes.

Brim had to smile; had it not been for Barbousse, he wouldn't have had them tonight—or probably any night. Somehow, formal clothing never gained much priority in Brim's view. During one of their overnight visits to the Carescrian port of Caer Landria on Burtis/Celeron, however, the Chief had quietly arranged for a tailor to visit the hotel where the crew was staying, giving Brim no choice but to take time out to be measured for civilian formal wear: a black, waist-length dinner jacket based on the standard Imperial Fleet Mess jacket—minus military ornamentation—black bow time, black trousers, pleated shirt with archaic wing collar, and a black cummerbund.

Barbousse himself tied the bow tie: "No pre-tied refuse for Lord Brim," he muttered, then stood back for an inspection. Pursing his lips, he minutely checked each item of clothing—buffed one of the six gold buttons against the cuff of his Fleet tunic—then, at long last, nodded. "You look terrific, Skipper," he declared.

Brim found himself grinning. "Now I know why you are so feared on the parade ground, Chief," he said. "It felt as if you could see through to my underwear."

"I can," Barbousse replied without missing a beat, "There's a wrinkle in your briefs, but aside from that, we've done a credible job, Skipper."

Brim shook his head. "Drat," he grumbled histrionically, "I thought you'd never notice the wrinkle."

"Can't keep secrets from yer old friends," Barbousse replied, then checked his watch. "I took the liberty of securing transportation," he said. "Unless you have plans I don't know about, I'll be your driver tonight."

"My *driver*?" Brim asked. "Don't you and nurse Tutti have plans for tonight?"

"You bet, Skipper," Barbousse said. "Don't forget, she's at the Palace, too; we'll just be celebratin' in a different part."

"How'll I get home afterward?"

"Well," Barbousse said, "If it turns out I don't drive you home, I'll have someone reliable t' take my place. Count on it."

"You think of everything, Chief," Brim said in genuine gratitude.

"I have to," Barbousse said with a sly grin. "Otherwise you might try walkin' like you did the other night. An' if anything happens to you, I'm in trouble with the Emperor himself."

$$— o — 0 — o —$$

Barbousse's "transportation" turned out to be a late-model Phantom-III skimmer with a De Ville body: Phantom's idea of a combination owner-chauffeur sedan, usually referred to as a *Touring Limousine Skimmer* in Avalon. It featured a divider and a slightly higher roofline than other Phantom-IIIs, but was generally more sporting in appearance than other vehicles made for the ultra-wealthy. "Voot's beard, Chief," Brim muttered when Barbousse opened the door for him, "this is the kind of skimmer people like Calhoun go around in. Not me."

"Nothin' like that at all, Skipper," Barbousse assured him, slipping into the front seat. "Calhoun's isn't as nice."

Brim was about to protest, but Barbousse raised a hand and winked through the rear-view mirror. "In the life we lead, Skipper, you never know when you aren't comin' home any more. Emperor Onrad made sure you have plenty of credits in the bank; perhaps it's time you spend some of 'em while you can—just in case."

"Did I *buy* this?" Brim demanded.

"Not *exactly*, Skipper, it's on loan from Phantom Skimmers," Barbousse admitted. "But I think you ought to consider it."

"Wha-a-at?"

"I checked with your assets manager friend, Porterfield Marston; he says it would be a great investment."

"He did, eh?"

"Aye, Skipper."

"And *you*, Chief?"

"Well, I don't know much about investments, Skipper, but it's a whale of a lot of fun to drive. You'll love it. Handles a little like a Starfury."

"It does, eh?"

"Oh, it *does*...."

At the Imperial Palace, the graceful Phantom-II/De Ville turned a few heads, but didn't seem all that out-of-place among the arrivals under the marquee that night. Even in wartime, Avalon remained the epicenter of galactic wealth and elegance—blamed by many as one of the root causes of the war in the first place. As Brim strode through the opulent doors of the palace ballroom lobby, he glanced over his shoulder while Barbousse slid back into the front seat of the new skimmer. It really was beautiful, he thought, then laughed at himself. *Tomorrow...*, he promised. *It wouldn't hurt to at least take a little drive in such a magnificent machine....*

$$— o — 0 — o —$$

At the ornate portal to the ballroom, Brim handed his invitation to a page dressed in Royal Scarlet, who inconspicuously scanned it in the palm of his hand, then tapped his AnGrail on a sounding block and announced just slightly louder than the hubbub of the elegant throng, "Oyez, Oyez, Lord Brim, First Duke of Grayson!"

A few heads turned in the glittering assemblage; one or two hands waved, then Brim descended the grand stairway, the AnGrail tapped again, and another name was announced. Immediately awash in a sea of unfamiliar faces, Brim accepted a goblet of Logish Meem from one of the attendants moving constantly through the crowd, then headed for a group of Fleet Officers he knew, but before he had gone more than a few steps, he felt a hand on his arm. "Hello Wilf," a shockingly familiar voice said, "Cousin Onrad said you were in town."

Chapter 20

. . .sleepy blue eyes

AVALON/ASTURIUS, AVALON CITY 40 DECAD (CALENDAR EVE), 52016

Momentarily closing his eyes in disbelief, Brim stopped in his tracks, then slowly turned as he felt his heart begin to race. "M-margot!" he stammered, nearly spilling his drink. "I h-had no idea you were…."

"I arrived only this morning," she explained quietly, more stunning and beautiful in maturity than Brim could have imagined—unchanged, but somehow transformed. Her sleepy, blue eyes flashed the same nimble intelligence, as always, yet behind it was a new depth of insight only heartbreak and torment could produce—no strangers to Brim, himself. The lovely oval face was still framed by loose golden curls she'd always favored, but the fair skin on her left cheek was now misshapen by a deep scar that slashed from near her eye to the corner of her mouth. Brim could hardly imagine a wound so terrible a healing machine would finish by leaving such a disfigurement. It was her slight smile, however—if one could even call it a smile—that caught him off guard. She still frowned as it formed on those full lips, but gone was the old confidence that once forged the very hallmark of her being. Something horrible had ripped at the very soul of Margo Effer'wyck… and had nearly destroyed it.

Impulsively, he tenderly kissed her ample hand, glanced for a moment at the long, tapering fingers, and remembered the magic of their caresses. Closing his eyes for a brief moment, he took a deep breath, then looking into her eyes, he whispered, "You are still the most beautiful woman in the Known Universe, Margot Effer'wyck. If I say nothing else that makes any sense tonight, that is the ultimate truth."

"Thank you, Wilf Brim," she said, her hand impulsively straying to the scar on her cheek. "Those are perhaps the best words I have heard in many long months."

Always a sturdy woman, she was dressed tonight in a simple, full-length gown of silken apricot, cut low across her small breasts and slit daringly to a point above her right knee. The waistline was high, just below her bosom, and for a moment, the recollection of those tiny breasts with their knobby pink aureoles, swollen nipples, and a half-sensed network of delicate veins in the creamy skin beyond swept his memory back to another night in this very castle when.... Somehow he snapped himself back to the present.

The almost smile was back on her lips and her eyes softened. "You were *looking*, Wilf Brim," she chided with a little laugh.

"I was," Brim said, again mesmerized by the woman who had captured his heart so many years ago in a different war, then shattered it in a completely different world. "How could I possibly stand here *without* looking?"

"Memories," she said, gently withdrawing her hand from his, "so *many* of them. I see them when I look at you, too." She closed her eyes for a moment. "If I am not blushing, I should be, Wilf Brim," she murmured.

Afterward, they stood for long moments while the whole of Onrad's court revolved around them nearly unseen, certainly unperceived. At last, Brim broke the silence. "C-can I get you a meem?" he asked, realizing he hadn't even thought of sipping his own.

"No thank you," she said. "Perhaps some time later. Only lately am I transported into a part of my healing that permits substances like meem, and I must be careful."

"Your *healing*?"

She nodded. "With help and time, I have nearly mastered the TimeWeed addiction that once owned my life and destroyed me."

"Margot!" Brim took her hand again, but this time, she pulled it away, gently but firmly. "Not yet, Wilf Brim," she said softly. "I am not prepared for what I know you can do to me—nor are *you* prepared for what I have become."

"I don't understand," Brim started, but she only smiled and held up a lace-gloved hand..

"Wilf," she said looking so deeply into his eyes he knew she could see within his soul, "I may look like the woman you once loved. I know I am still beautiful in your eyes, even with this mark on my face to remind me what I once allowed myself to become. And *yes*, Wilf, I would gladly share a bed with you tonight, for I know as well as you our bodies are still made for one another; but this is not the time."

Brim tried to speak again, but she pressed his arm with her fingers.

"The truth is, Wilf Brim, my once and *perhaps* future lover, I am *not* the Princess Margot Effer'wyck you met in I.F.S. *Truculent's* wardroom one night some twenty-one years ago. Since then, I have married *two* husbands: the second of whom I truly loved. I have born a child to the first, who is lost to me. I have seen my body—no, my entire being—stolen and ravaged, along with my pride and integrity." For a moment, she bit her lip, then grimaced as she gazed at him with horror in her eyes. "You of all people must remember my part in an attempt on your life, or," she shuddered, "one night in Tarrott allowing the Leaguers to offer my numbed body for your pleasure." For a moment—only a moment—her eyes regained their old intensity. "Margot Effer'wyck died during those years, Wilf," she said in a quiet voice. "For a long time, only Cameron Delacroix believed in me." She shut her eyes. "He was *so* beautiful, Wilf. Beautiful and *strong*. He truly loved me in spite of what I had become. He searched much of the galaxy before he found a healer for me—gave up all thought of fortune while we traveled among the stars in *Golden Bird*. He left me in the care of a family from the Lampson Provinces—near the home of your prescient First Officer when you were in command of your first Starfury squadron. Remember her?"

"Of course," Brim said. "Nadia Tissuard."

"And remember how she hated me?"

"Well…."

"Oh, she hated me," Margot said, "and it turned out she had ample justification. But her well-deserved hate is not my reason for mentioning her—except to relate that many people from the Lampson provinces have similar powers, and the family in whose care Cameron left me was a great spiritual teacher who agreed to see if she could save me."

"Looks as if she did quite a job," Brim commented.

"Neither she nor I are finished yet," Margot said. "The original cure emptied me. Now, I must try to become human once more—a woman. So far, the process of healing has been long and painful—I am warned the remainder may be even more so."

"It *must* have been," Brim agreed. "TimeWeed addiction was once considered unbreakable."

"For all I know, it may yet be," Margot said. "Only time, and what strength I still possess, will tell." For a brief moment, her eyes flashed with something of their old power. "But I shall not give up nor give in. I already know what living death is all about; the next time I die, it will be truly be the *Long Sleep*."

At that moment, The AnGrail sounded with a resounding note and Brim—with everyone else in the ballroom—turned his attention to the top of the Grand Staircase as the page announced, "Oyez, oyez, Onrad the Fifth, Grand Galactic Emperor, Prince of the Reggio Star Cluster, and Rightful Protector of the Heavens!" As a shout of acclaim went up from the gathered upper echelon of Avalonian society, Brim turned to Margot and..., *she was gone*! As if she'd been only a figment of his imagination. He whirled around in a wild attempt to follow, but as he searched, her blonde hair blended into the mass of revelers and she disappeared.

Chapter 21

. . .one *tough* Lady

AVALON/ASTURIUS, AVALON CITY 1 UNAD (CALENDAR
DAY), 52017

T hough genuinely disturbed, Brim felt obligated to remain at the
ball, dancing cheerfully with his share of great and not-so-great
ladies, recalling with a smile the days when he'd feared dancing
more than League disruptors. All evening and long into the morning,
he kept an eye out for Margot's blonde hair and apricot gown, but she
appeared to have truly departed, and he had no desire to initiate his
own search of the Palace.

A few cycles after the Change of the Calendar, Onrad dashed out of
the crowd between dances and took Brim's arm. "The Secret Service
people tell me she got to you before I did," he said with a grimace.

"I assume you mean Margot, Your Majesty?"

"The same—and I am truly sorry."

"Thanks, Your Majesty," Brim said. "But I think she'd have had the
same effect on me even had I known in advance." He shook his head
and shrugged. "Somehow, I didn't think I'd react the way I have."

"You do look like you've seen a ghost," Onrad observed quietly.

"I *did*...," Brim started.

"...And she is," Onrad finished for him. "From what I understand,
she literally materialized at the Effer'wyckean Embassy this morning
in an ordinary cab—from where, they still don't know, but they say
they're working on it. Evidentially, if one of the old-time
Effer'wyckean guards hadn't recognized her at the gate, they'd have
locked her up for a psychotic—and until their Secret Service manages
to noodle out where she came from, they *still* want her locked up.

She's here at my personal invitation—phoned me on a *very* private line—I've got her under guard while she's here, subtly, of course. I'm certainly not going to throw her out. But let me tell you, Brim, I was no more prepared to see her face than I imagine you were."

"Too true, Your Majesty," Brim agreed. "She pretty much disappeared after she married that Delacroix fellow—but I can't in truth state I *ever* forgot about her."

"No," Onrad said thoughtfully, "not the way you two were. I take it you still have feelings?"

This time, it was Brim's turn to grimace. "If you'd asked me this afternoon, Your Majesty," he said, "I'm not sure what I might have replied. But now…, well, it's clear *something's* still there—on my part, at any rate."

"I figured," Onrad muttered, frowning to inspect his fingernails. "And I can't just ignore her, either. She was one Xaxt of a fighter in the last war. Damn near got herself killed a couple of times."

"It was she who risked her life in the battle for the Zonga'ar space citadel. I think that's where she got the scar on her cheek."

"When your Starfury blew it up?"

"Aye, Your Majesty." Brim said. "Her LifeGlobe was much too close to the explosion. To this day, no one knows how or why she survived—or any of the others with her, for that matter."

Onrad grimaced. "She must have been a mess for a healing machine to leave her in that shape." He pursed his lips. "She may well be an Effer'wyckean, but she's also a bona fide Imperial hero, too." He stared at the carpet for a moment, then shook his head. "If it hadn't been for my Father insisting she marry Rogan LaKarn, none of this would have happened to her—and yes, you and she would be celebrating quite a few years of marriage by now."

"Water long over the dam and gone," Brim reflected. "Nobody's fault, really, Your Majesty. People with royal blood don't always get to live their own lives—as you must certainly understand. Poor Margot just had a run of bad luck."

"Bad luck for both of you," Onrad said, squeezing Brim's shoulder. "Why the Xaxt is it people like you two—people who understand why things happen and accept them for the greater good—always end up being kicked the hardest?"

"My life has turned out a lot better than hers, Your Majesty" Brim observed. "Nothing like TimeWeed ever got to me. I can't think of anything worse. I'm not so sure I'd have *wanted* to survive what she's gone through."

"Tough lady."

"Yeah," Brim said. "One *tough* lady, Your Majesty."

The two stood in silence for a moment, then Onrad nodded to himself and seemed to come to some decision. "Can't leave her to those 'Wyckeans," he said. "I'll put some Secret Service people on her full time and make sure she's got everything she needs. It's about all I can do until she sorts out the mess in her own mind."

"Thank you, Your Majesty," Brim said; he meant it.

"And I'll keep you posted," the Emperor added. "Count on it." Then he stopped and smiled. "Ya' know, Brim," he said, scratching his head for a moment, "if you keep moving in your kids and old girlfriends, I'll have enough family here I won't have to find myself a bride at all!"

Chapter 22

. . .TopLine SPC&R

AVALON/ASTURIUS, TOPLINE SPACECRAFT
PERFORMANCE, CUSTOMIZATION & RESEARCH, LTD., 14
DIAD, 52017

Admiral Calhoun was good as his word. He supplied everything Brim had requested to begin his "One-ship Operation"—and more. Following a brief search for suitable location, Brim and Barbousse established TopLine SPC&R in a leased brick warehouse on a backwater canal no more than a c'lenyt from the Imperial Fleet Base on Lake Mersin.

Within a month, the two had equipped it with a complete Hullmetal machine shop, a shielded Drive maintenance room, overhead lifts, and a ship lift suitable for the WF-400. Soon, the ancient brick warehouse had become a factory of sorts, filled with the fascinating odors of star travel: oils, solvents, ozone, hot machines, open logics, and all the arcania necessary to prepare astroplanes for star travel. With his usual aplomb, Barbousse supplied a sign for the building's facade that appeared as if it had weathered for at least a decade. A CLOSED sign hung perpetually inside the front door, and inside the tiny reception office, a blank-screen HoloPhone answered all incoming calls with:

> "Thank you for calling TopLine
> SPC&R. Our schedule is completely
> filled for the remainder of the Standard
> Year. We apologize for the
> inconvenience."

Inside the main hangar area, Brim and Barbousse watched a team of civilian-clad Blue Capes working on the WF-400's rotary launcher, inserting a sixth HyperTorp, then locking it in place. "What do you think, Chief," Brim asked, "…we good to go in the morning?"

Barbousse nodded thoughtfully. "I think so, Skipper," he said. "Steele says he's got the new long-range BKAEWs operating on the new DISTANT SEARCH setting; Lu's loaded all zillion charts in the database yesterday, and everything else about the ship is as ready as we can make it. I've got the rest of the crew reporting in tomorrow, Morning and Two. That ought to put us on the Lake for liftoff about Brightness on the nose."

Brim glanced at his timepiece: Twilight and Thirty—time for a brief visit to Hope. "Good work, as always, Chief," he said. "After the Palace, I'm going home and turn in. Anything else you need me for?"

"Everything's handled, Skipper."

Brim stepped through the tiny office and boarded one of the diminutive Zortech skimmers he and Barbousse had leased for work at TopLine; the Phantom-III would have drawn too much attention in the seedy neighborhood. Besides, it took him nearly a metacycle to pick his way through Avalon's rubble to the Palace, so he couldn't have made better time in the more expensive skimmer.

After a quick visit to Hope, he sent a text message to the Emperor's confidential socket:

> Your Majesty: Departing tomorrow
> morning for first hunting trip; thought
> you'd want to know.
>
> ~Brim.

At the palace gate, a Secret Service agent directed the Zortech to a detention lane. "Lord Brim?" the man asked.

"I am," Brim responded, though he knew the man had already made a quiet identification.

"The Emperor appreciates your notification, M'Lord," the agent said, attempting to stifle a little smile. "He suggests a 'chunk of bender,' in his own words, would be an appropriate gift for his upcoming birthday celebration."

"Please tell His Majesty I'll see what I can do," Brim said.

"Hmm," the agent said with a serious mien. "His Majesty thought you might just take that seriously, M'Lord. He adds that should you risk yourself, your crew, and especially his personal WF-400 on such an idiotic stunt, he will personally exile you to someplace extremely unpleasant."

Brim grinned. "Please inform His Majesty that I shall indeed keep that in mind." Soon afterward, he returned to his suite and was asleep within a few cycles.

— o — 0 — o —

Early next morningSeyess Inhardt, a tall, gray-bearded Tower controller at Lake Mersin watched Brim's WF-400 thunder skyward—carefully follow standard procedures for avoiding the Royal Palace—then disappear into the fading starscape. Within moments, he signed out to the lavatory where he placed a call from his HoloPhone to a receiver returning a blank display. "The Wakefield has lifted for deep space," he reported.

"Its destination?"

"The manifest reads, 'Bright Triad of Ely,'" Inhardt reported, "but I was not aware Wakefield astroplanes have that sort of ra...."

"You are not required to think, Inhardt," the voice from the HoloPhone interrupted. "You will be paid promptly—both for the information *and* your silence." The controller's HoloPhone disconnected.

— o — 0 — o —

For the past nine Metacycles, the WF-400 had been pounding through space at a steady, energy-saving 220 LPM. It had passed the point of no return nearly four Metacycles ago and was committed to reaching the MET station or running out of Drive energy, with all the complications—and danger—that would bring. So far, Steele had detected no uncloaked Benders, but no one had expected success on this first mission. As everyone knew, war mostly consists of long stretches of boredom punctuated by moments of intense action. The Bright Triad was now blazing in the forward Hyperscreens and it looked as if the first leg was going to be a dry run when suddenly a global display on Brim's console came alive with Steel's face. "Skipper, something strange."

"What's that, Chief?"

"The MET station up ahead: it hasn't made it's quarter-Metacycle report."

Brim frowned. "Strange. Could they be simply late?"

"Could be," Steele said, "but I've never known 'em to be half a Metacycle late before."

"Maybe you just missed it?"

"I don't miss things I'm watchin' for, beggin' the Skipper's pardon."

"Sorry, Chief; I believe you. So what do you make of it?"

"Don't know, Skipper. But there's somethin' else."

"Go on."

"About a metacycle ago usin' the new, long-range BKAEW, I got a faint hit on something like a standard starship in close proximity to the MET station asteroid. The ship wasn't moving—like it was makin' a stop. Now it's gone."

"Just, *gone*?"

"Just noticed it's gone, Skipper: must have taken off away from us because there's no trace of it on the screen."

"A bender, perhaps?"

"Too big for a bender."

"Very well, Chief, Thanks," Brim replied and glanced at Barbousse. "Any thoughts?"

"Does seem strange the Met-station folks haven't made their signal," Barbousse replied. "Specially since they had a recent visitor."

"Well, we've only got a little over a Metacycle and a half of energy left. I don't know of any alternate landing sites within our range, do you?"

Barbousse shook his head. "None where we can refuel, anyway."

"So I guess we're going to the MET station, no matter what."

"Looks that way, Skipper. But if somethin's seriously wrong, we're at least forewarned."

Brim grinned. "Wouldn't be the first time we've blundered into trouble together."

"Probably won't be the last, either, Skipper...."

Chapter 23
. . .suspicions

BRIGHT TRIAD OF ELY, ASTEROID 2, 16 DIAD, 52017

B rim took the long way around the triad, keeping the star off the left cockpit Hyperscreens while Steele tested a whole spectrum of radiations emanating from the MET station. "Anything new, Steele?" Brim demanded, coming through Hyperspeed just as the asteroid became visible in the forward Hyperscreens.

"Nothing," Steele reported, "...but it doesn't mean I think things are all hunky dory over there, either. Actually, things seem *too* quiet."

"We're committed to a landing, now," Brim said.

"I understand, Skipper," Steele said. "But I think we'd all best keep our eyes open."

"Will do," Brim said, pursing his lips as the little MET station hove into view over the craggy horizon of the asteroid. The Station was no more than a series of eight cylindrical Standard Habitats connected by a central communications tube. Nearby was a gravity pad. Brim had seen thousands of similar Habitats throughout the Galaxy—wherever temporary housing was needed in hostile environments. However, normal as this one appeared, he now viewed it with a certain feeling of apprehension. Grinding his teeth, he decided he'd been away from action for too long; he was letting Barbousse and Steele get to him. He needed to concentrate on putting the ship onto the gravity pad ahead.

"Lonely place," Barbousse commented absently, staring through the Hyperscreens.

"It is," Brim allowed. "Too lonely. I kind of expected some sort of welcome—a light signal or something."

"Well, the Karlsson lights are on around their gravity pad," Barbousse remarked, "so they must be expectin' someone. And look out back: there's the mobile energy collector for recharging our power cells."

"I noticed," Brim said, "…those stacks of space crates are probably the rest of the supplies the Admiral landed here for us."

At that moment, Barbousse magnified a section of his Hyperscreens and narrowed his eyes. "Skipper," he said, "there's something strange about the gravity pad."

Brim brought the astroplane to a hover and magnified his own section of the Hyperscreens. "What's that, Chief?"

"Maybe it's me, Skipper, but I don't remember that model gravity pad having six sets of repulsors. Do you?"

"*Six* sets…? Why, there *are* six, aren't there?"

"That's what I count, Skipper," Barbousse replied. "And If I'm not mistaken, except for those two center-mounted repulsors, that's a standard Model 800-B, just like what we used at the Helmsman's Academy."

Brim increased his magnification again. "Those repulsors don't seem to be connected to anything, do they?"

"Not like the ones at the corners.," Barbousse said. "And if I was going to booby trap a gravity pad, that's just where I'd put a couple of Doppler bombs, set do go off when they sense a ship approaching vertically. If it was up to me, I'd have 'em go off at about 30 irals— blow a ship like this right in half. What d' *you* think, Skipper?"

Brim took a deep breath. "You're the demolitions expert, Chief," he said. "I'll take your word for it. Chief Steele," he called into a globular display. "Anything like a sign of life down there?"

Steele appeared in the display. "Nothin', Skipper," he said. "It's like everybody's dead."

Brim thought about *that* possibility for a moment, dismissed it, then changed his mind and turned to Barbousse. "I'm not going to take any chances." He pressed the red STATIONS sensor. "Hands to action stations," he intoned, "Hands to action stations. Don battle suits and report when geared up." Setting the ship on auto-hover, he struggled into his own battle suit while Barbousse did the same. Shortly after both had returned to their seats, all indicators were green. "Folks," Brim announced, "it's possible there is be some trouble at the MET station below. I'm going to land using our pods instead of the gravity pad. We'll keep you posted." Then he turned to Barbousse. "I think we need somebody on the ground, down there."

"I think so, too, Skipper," Barbousse said, his voice hollow in Brim's battle suit headphones. "I'll go."

"And why *you*?" Brim demanded.

"Because I'm the demolitions expert aboard, Skipper. You said so yourself."

Brim hesitated a moment and frowned. "Looks like you've got me there, Chief," he admitted dourly. "How do *you* want to handle this, then?"

"If you'll land the ship about 100 irals from the pad, I'll simply walk over and have a look-see. Then we'll have a better idea about what we're facein'. All right?"

"Guess I don't have any choice," Brim said, "But you be careful."

"Oh, I'll be careful, Skipper," Barbousse promised. "I'm under Onrad's personal orders to look after you; I could be deported if…."

Brim rolled his eyes.

"I'll have this settled before you know it, Skipper," Barbousse said as he disappeared into the companionway.

Brim shook his head, lowered the four landing pods at the bottom of the hull, and brought *Four Nines* to the surface some hundred irals from the pad, then switched to local gravity. "How's that, Chief?"

"Perfect, Skipper," Barbousse said. "I've got the hatch open and…, here goes. I'll keep you posted."

Brim waited helplessly until Barbousse half-walked, half floated from under the ship and waived. "Spooky down here," he commented. "You'd think someone would have noticed us by now."

"You'd think," Brim commented with growing concern. "We'll keep an eye out for anything suspicious from up here."

"Thanks, Skipper; I'll appreciate that…."

Heart in his mouth, Brim watched Barbousse skip-glide to the gravity pad, then circle it, stopping every few steps to peer into the structure. At last, the big man looked up at the ship. "Don't see any anti-personnel devices anywhere, but those two extra repulsors sure look suspicious. I'm going up and have a closer look at them."

"Don't be in *too* big of a hurry, Chief," Brim warned.

"No booby trap before its time, Skipper," Barbousse quipped as he pulled himself onto one of the gravity pad's many ladders "I'll be careful." Within a cycle, he had climbed to the repulsor platform and was standing beside the suspicious device centered on the far side of the pad; it was nearly as tall as the Chief himself. After a few moments, he glanced up at the ship again. "This is no repulsor," he reported. "It's a plastic tube shaped to look like one, but...." abruptly, he took a knife from his tool kit and cut a large hole in the side of the tube. "Looks to me like there's... something like a HyperTorp inside," he said, peering through the hole with a flashlight. "And...," he sliced most of the way to the top, ripped it open like a ripe comboa fruit, then threw the empty tube to the ground, "...that's what it is!"

Brim gasped in spite of himself. In its place was the all-too-familiar shape of an Imperial MK-41 HyperTorp: sleek and narrow, with typical striations for launching from a standard Imperial torpedo tube—same as the ones in the belly of the WF-400.

"Uh huh...," Barbousse mused, pointing to the upper end of the torpedo. "There's a Doppler fuse at the top of this one, just like I thought." He shook his head. "Voot's greasy beard—if we'd tried to land, this one alone would have blown us to particles, even if the other one isn't a HyperTorp. " He glanced up at the ship again. "Someone's taken a real dislike to us, Skipper."

"Seems so," Brim agreed. "...and someone on *our* side, too—unless the Leaguers just decided on a whim to take out the MET station with one of our own HyperTorps." He took a deep breath. "Can you defuse that thing?"

"Easy, Skipper. This one's got only a simple Doppler fuse. Looks to me like a real rush job by somebody who was so sure we'd be taken by surprise he just threw the thing together." Drawing a tool from his battle suit, he made a few adjustments, then bounded up to the tip of the HyperTorp. "There," he added with a grunt as a puff of gray debris appeared above the HyperTorp. "It's as simple as burning off the Doppler fuse. That puts paid to this one."

While Brim continued to hold his breath, Barbousse strode around to the second faux repulsor, sliced it open, and turned to look over at the ship again. "Another HyperTorp, if you hadn't noticed, Skipper. Whomever those zukeeds were, they weren't taking any chances of havin' too little explosives." He quickly burned the fuse off the second HyperTorp, then glanced over again. "Hang on a moment, Skipper," he said, "while I check out the other four to make sure they're what I think they are. Then you can put the ship on the pad."

Brim was only too happy to delay permanently berthing the WF-400 until Barbousse had thoroughly finished the job.

Chapter 24

. . . ugly!

BRIGHT TRIAD OF ELY, ASTEROID 2, 17 DIAD, 52017

Within half a metacycle, Brim had the WF-400 secure on the gravity pad and was half-floating his way toward the air lock when someone grabbed the arm of his battle suit. It was Steele. "Skipper," he said, "are you planning to search the MET Habitats with Chief Barbousse?"

"I am," Brim replied, "What's up?"

"Begging the Skipper's pardon," Steele said, "but only you and the Chief know how to fly this crate home. What if somethin' bad happens over there? We're a long way from home."

Brim grimaced. "Well...," he began.

"Let me go instead, Skipper," the big man interrupted. "The Chief and I worked side-by-side for a lot of years. Together we can do almost any job—and if something bad *does* happen to us, you can at least get the rest of the crew back home. Alright?"

Brim thought for a moment, then nodded. "All right, Chief," he conceded. "I guess that makes sense."

With a quick salute, Steele pushed past Brim and disappeared along the companionway. "We'll keep you posted, Skipper," he promised over his shoulder.

Grimly, Brim started back toward the flight bridge, beginning to feel like a second-class bus driver. Strapping in at the helm, he watched Barbousse and Steele hurry to the first Standard Habitat. Barbousse was first at the door.

"It wasn't even closed," the big man reported, nudging the door open with the toe of his boot "I'm going in."

Brim watched the two battle-suited men disappear inside. Moments later, someone gasped. "Great Voot," Barbousse exclaimed, "I was afraid of that."

"What?" Brim demanded.

"All six of the MET crew, Skipper—murdered at the inside entrance to the vestibule cylinder," Barbousse reported. "It's pretty ugly; looks like each was shot in the head execution-style."

"None of 'em were even wearing atmospheric suits," Steele added. "Pretty clear they *thought* they knew whomever attacked them and let them into the airlock without a fight."

"Poor zukeeds didn't have a chance," Steele added, "They weren't even wearing their side arms."

"Anybody else in there?" Brim demanded.

"That's what we're going to find out now," Barbousse replied.

"Don't take any unnecessary chances," Brim cautioned.

"Count on it," Barbousse promised. "If those butchers are still around here, they've got nothing to lose by knocking us off as well."

— o — 0 — o —

At nearly the same moment, in a dark, richly paneled dining room at Avalon City's fashionably exclusive Oxford Men's Union, Count Tal Confisse Trafford was dining with third-cousin Lord Daniel Cranwell, Imperial Minister of Commerce. As the two made polite conversation over lemon sorbet following the *Entrée*, they were interrupted by the entrance of a svelte, gray-uniformed messenger carrying an envelope on a small silver plate. The woman came to attention beside Cranwell, bowed, then presented the envelope.

Dabbing his lips with a napkin, Cranwell examined the envelope, tore off one end, blew to open it, then extracted the message and read. In a moment, he raised his eyebrows, smiled coldly, then replaced both the envelope and the message on the messenger's plate, where they disintegrated in tiny flames. "No answer," he said in dismissal.

Count Trafford raised an eyebrow. "Good news, Cousin?"

"Indeed, Cousin," Cranwell replied. "It seems the upstart Wilf Brim has run into unexpected trouble that may well have cost him his life."

"How unfortunate. Did the message indicate how it happened?"

"An accident in space, one assumes Cranwell purred. No doubt details will be forthcoming, all in good time." He smiled. "An excellent sorbet, wouldn't you say, Cousin?"

"An *excellent* sorbet, Cousin. Just the proper nip of zest...."

— o — 0 — o —

It took Barbousse and Steele less than a half metacycle to check the remainder of the Habitat cylinders. Aside from the six bodies and themselves, they reported the MET station contained only standard gravitological equipment. Whomever had attacked the station—and booby-trapped the gravity pad—had done their work and cleared out with no delay. In Barbousse's estimation, the MET occupants had been dead no more than three Metacycles.

Lu, Kermis, and Treble joined the other three on the surface to help record the disaster, snapping Holophotos of anything that might provide a clue to what had transpired before their arrival. At last, they carried the bodies outside and buried them in the icy gravel. Subsequently, with nothing else to be done for the poor wretches, they stood in a circle around the six lonely graves and—led by Nero Lu— recited a few simple Gradgroat-Norchelite nostrums of respect, ending with the traditional Spaceman's Hymn:

> Oh Universal Force of Truth,
> > Which guards the homeland of our youth,
> That bidd'st the mighty cosmos deep,
> > Thine own appointed limits keep:
> Oh hear us when we cry for Grace
> > For those in Peril far in space....

As the others returned to the ship in respectful silence, Brim and Barbousse wearily started up the mobile energy generator's traction engine, drove it to the gravity pad, and aligned the collection head with the Triad. Brim climbed to the generator controls while Barbousse dragged its three output cables to the WF-400 and opened the hatch to

114

the ship's power cistern. When he'd plugged each cable into its proper socket, he signaled. Clicks later, Brim saw three white lights wink on above the cistern plugs, indicating the WF-400 was receiving energy.

In the two Metacycles before the ship was ready to fly, Brim and Barbousse carefully inspected the stores Calhoun had delivered to the asteroid. Like the mobile energy generator, everything appeared to be in perfect condition—another indication the attack on the MET station had been organized at the last moment and hastily carried out. It was a shoddy job from beginning to end. But, Brim reminded himself as he and Barbousse made their way back to the Generator, the deadly rouse almost certainly would have succeeded, had he and his crew approached the asteroid without previous suspicions raised by the Met Station's unsent report. It had been a Xaxtdamned close thing.

More important, now that he and his crew had survived: who was responsible for the shoddy attempt on their lives? The most obvious suspects were Imperials—even though the Empire was at war with the League. But *why* Imperials? Their one-ship experiment was such a small operation, it would hardly interest the League, at whom it was directed, much less someone on his own side. No matter which side had ordered the operation, whoever had given those orders was going to be mighty displeased when the WF-400 showed up on final for Lake Mersin—and would be a great deal unhappier when he, or she, eventually discovered the shoddy job they'd bought.

Of course, the shoddiness might simply be a ruse in itself.... Brim grimaced as he monitored the generator, idly balancing a million-odd possibilities as *why* the MET station had been raided—and *by whom*. He shrugged: until he reached Avalon, his job was to hunt benders, not to play detective....

And speaking of detective work, it was high time to report what he'd found; civilian lives were involved. Trouble was, there were so many implications to the incident, it was difficult to determine just who ought to receive the report. His mission in the WF-400 was so sensitive—and the report on the MET station so significant—that reporting the attack to customary authorities would effectively reveal their so-far black operations. And, of course, since the station wasn't sending its expected reports; every few Metacycles, more and more recipients would be noticing…. He'd have to do something soon.

At last, Barbousse reported three green lights at the cistern plugs, and Brim shut off the generator. Together, he and the Chief parked the machine where they'd found it, then hurried to the ship and prepared to take off.

— o — 0 — o —

As the Bright Triad shrank in his rear-view display, Brim made up his mind. He pressed the STATIONS button. "Attention all hands: Skipper speaking." Five STATION-READY indicators lighted immediately. Clearly, they'd been waiting.

"People," Brim began, "you've all seen what's happened at the MET station. And I'm certain you're asking yourselves who's responsible—as am I. I'm also certain each of you already knows from the grapevine that—within powerful circles on the Imperial side—ours is not a very popular project. So this attack could have just as well come from home as the League—especially since everyone knows the League depends on reports from this MET station as we do. I'm telling you this because right now, I'm officially putting a 'TOP SECRET' imprimatur on this whole episode and reporting it directly to our sponsors instead of through ordinary channels. They'll let us know how they want things handled. I'll keep you posted as things progress. Steele, send this message…."

Chapter 25

. . . surprise!

Grand Admiral Baxter Calhoun, Supreme Commander of the Imperial Fleet, had just arrived at his inner office and was sitting down to review his communiqués when his personal secretary, Captain Evan Barlow, opened the door and handed him a printed message under a Top Secret cover sheet. "This just in, Admiral," the Captain said. "I suspect you'll want to read it right away."

As Barlow waited, Calhoun scanned the message, then read it carefully before placing it in a large bowl beside his desk, where it caught fire and burned to a fine ash. "Ye've read it, Banta?"

"Of course, Admiral."

"What d' ye mak' o' it?"

"Doubt if the League's in on it, Admiral."

"M' thoughts exactly," the Admiral said, pursing his lips. "A'right, we'll start by keeping it quiet as possible. I'll want tha' MET station back in action soon as possible—ev'n sooner. We ha' a SpecOps detachment somewhere around there, don't we?"

"In Carescria, Admiral. The port of Chambre on Dorches/Orlena."

Calhoun nodded. "Right," he said. "Send a detachment o'er to the Bright Triad with the purpose of securin' that MET station, then gettin' it back in operation immediately. Highest priority. Their first MET message should begin wi' something about a malfunction—nothing specific. An', yes, everything about this hairball is Top Secret-Plus."

"Aye Sir, Top Secret-Plus. And what should the SpecOps people do while they're there, Admiral?"

"I nae kenna, yet, Barlow. Tell them to sit tight and pretend they're MET people until further orders. Surely those Ops guys can figure out how t' operate a MET station."

"Aye, Sir."

"Then hae' Brim report to me the moment he returns to Avalon...."

— o — 0 — o —

With the WF-400 on AutoHelm, Barbousse had set up a globular display ion the flight bridge between himself and Brim as a repeater to Steele's long-range BKAEW; both were almost wholly focused on the view with only an occasional glance at the flight instruments. A little more than 1,700 light years and nearly eight Metacycles into what had become a boring return to Avalon, they'd only picked up a few small convoys and a number of large starliners, traveling too fast for attacks by benders. "D' you suppose we've finally had enough excitement for today?" Barbousse quipped.

"You never know," Brim said grimly. "Old Voot seems to have his eye on this mission." Unconsciously, he scanned the flight instruments—which had switched the main display to a systems screen and was flashing the portion dedicated to the starboard Drive. He frowned, clicked his microphone on. "Starboard 77's starting to run a little hot, isn't it?" he asked Treble.

"It is, Skipper," Treble replied, "...Crystal's been a little out of balance since takeoff. It's just now picking up a bit of temperature, Kermis and I are keeping an eye on it."

"And?"

"At this speed, we don't think it'll give us much problem—at least not until we get back to Avalon. Then we'll see what's up."

At that moment, Steele's voice boomed in Brim's globular display. "Skipper, take a look at the blip in area J-34. I've set it on blink."

Brim swiveled to peer into the display. "Where in Xaxt did *that* come from?" he demanded.

"Just popped up," Barbousse growled, "as in something *coming out of cloaked mode*."

"Interesting shape," Steel commented. "I'm thinking we've got ourselves a bender."

Brim glanced at Barbousse. "What'd I say about Voot?"

"Hasn't failed us yet, Skipper."

"Treble," Brim asked. "Will that left seventy-seven hold up under a little maneuvering?"

"Depends on what you mean by, 'a little,' Skipper."

"I understand" Brim grumbled. He considered a moment. "Well, I guess we're going to find out, then." He clicked the blower. "Action stations, all hands," he said slowly. "I repeat: Action Stations. Battle suits sealed." With this, he donned his helmet, attached it to his battle suit collar, then sealed all couplings. When he glanced at Barbousse, the big man was already signaling "okay" with his thumb and forefinger. Behind his visor, he'd broken into a big grin.

"Let's get him, Skipper," he said, his voice muffled in Brim's helmet.

During the next moments, everyone else checked in with affirmatives. The "blip" was only light years distant; if it was indeed a bender, Brim guessed its commander would be getting his bearings, taking a look around, and preparing to broadcast a daily report back to his base. Here in deep space, many light years from habitable planets, he definitely wouldn't be on the lookout for astroplanes. "What sort of speed is he making?" Brim asked.

"Cruising about fifteen LPM," Steele answered. "Range is now five point three light years—and we're closing fast."

"What does she look like?"

"From the blip, I think she's one of the usual suspects: a Type Seven. It's what I'd expect out here in a void like this."

"I'll want two HyperTorps ready, Chief," Brim said.

Barbousse bent over his controls for a moment. "Two 'torps rotated to the rails, Skipper."

"Very well," Brim said, then slowed the WF-400 and set a course directly away from the bender. "Let me know when he's sent his report, Steele—if we can get him right after that, it'll be at least a Standard day before they know he's gone."

"I'm on it, Skipper."

Clicks dragged by like Metacycles while Brim flew a random pattern just outside the known BKAEW range of a Type-Seven S-boat. In spite of himself, he grinned—it had been a long time since he'd been action against the League. It felt good.

"He's sending Skipper."

"Very well." Almost in relief, Brim kicked the steering engine around, eased the thrust dampers forward, and took off toward the bender—it was now or never. "Ready 'torp one, Chief." he said.

"Ready, Skipper."

With the WF-400 traveling at nearly 300 LPM, the ugly little bender became visible almost immediately, growing larger in the forward Hyperscreens as the targeting system locked, beeped, and fired a HyperTorp. Then, without any warning, the left K-P 77/77 lost thrust and the WF-400 skidded wildly to the left, breaking target lock just as the 'torp blasted off the launching rail. Blind and without a designated target, the torpedo streamed away from the WF-400, obeying its self-destruct logic and detonating harmlessly a safe distance away as Brim fought to bring the ship under control. "'Torp number two-now!" he ordered as he used the ship's now asymmetrical thrust to make a tight left turn, then skidded the steering engine full right. For only a moment, the targeting system saw the bender as it momentarily skidded past, locked on, and-with Brim's finger mashing on the firing button, it fired the second HyperTorp,

"Voot's thraggling beard!" someone gasped from the rear of the cockpit, "...He's cloaking."

Peering into the forward Hyperscreens, Brim held his breath as the HyperTorp streaked for the bender—which was quickly winking into nothingness, panel-by-panel. Just before it went fully cloaked, he squelched the missile's self-destruct circuits, causing the confused HyperTorp to continue on its way—even though it no longer "saw" its assigned target. Clicks later, the forward Hyperscreens dimmed as space where the bender *ought* to be erupted in a terrific explosion, which instantly filled with what remained of the bender—bow and stern spinning separately—within an expanding cloud of un-collapsing Hullmetal debris and radiation fire.

Grinding his teeth, Brim did what he could to dodge the swirling debris, but with only one Drive unit and speed far in excess of any help from the SpinGravs, the WF-400 hurtled directly into the very core of the explosion. In the corner of his eye, he barely discerned the aft portion of the bender as he whizzed past to port, giving only a moment's view of the opened hull and its complex machinery before some unfortunate Leaguer smashed against the forward Hyperscreens in a blur of red that bubbled into nothingness. Someone screamed in horror just as—with a deafening BANG—the port Drive unit smashed into something solid, blipping the internal gravity and jerking the ship left—*away* from the bender's forward section, which had just spun directly into what would have been their trajectory less than a click ago.

Then quickly as they had entered the fireball, they were past it and the forward Hyperscreens filled with stars streaking right as the ship continued its curving path to the left. At that moment, Brim noticed he'd neglected to breathe for quite a long time. Gulping a quickly, he looked aft:, the great radiation fire that had once been a bender was beginning to fade and, the two halves of the ugly little ship had spun away into the starry void.

Chapter 26

. . .return to Gimmas/Haefdon

INTRAGALACTIC SPACE, 19 DIAD, 52017

"Crew check," Brim ordered, trimming the astroplane so she could fly a straight line with only the starboard Drive operating. "Everybody all right? Report!" As the reports came in, he glanced out to port, where a jagged piece of Hullmetal had embedded itself in the forward end of port Drive nacelle-clearly part of the late bender. No use trying to restart that one!

Aside from a few bumps and bruises from the moment their gravity had blipped, the WF-400's crew seemed to be intact. So did the WF-400 itself—at least there were no pressure leaks in the hull. "Very well," he said. "Treble, Kermis, let's have a systems report."

"All systems report normal operation," Kermis replied.

"Except the port Drive system," Treble added. "We'll have to take the Drive controls apart to find out what went wrong with the system during our attack on the bender, but it's pretty clear that right now, the piece of Hullmetal sticking out of the Drive nacelle shattered the crystal itself, so we're going home on starboard Drive alone."

"What about the SpinGrav on that side?"

"It's far enough back in the nacelle it *might* just be all right, but I'm not exactly trusting it, either."

"What kind of system readings are you getting?"

"Readings look good, but I'd sure like to do a 'hands-on' before we have to bet our lives on trouble-free operation. That was a big shock it took."

Brim nodded. "Got you, Treble," he said with a wry grin. "I'll be watching for a visit from Voot and his friends when we're coming in on final." He looked up from the display, considered a moment, then turned to Barbousse, "Think I'm going to take us to Gimmas instead of Avalon," he said. "The way the ship looks right now, we'll attract a lot of attention back on Lake Mersin."

Barbousse nodded. "Sounds right, Skipper," he said. "Especially with a piece of bender sticking out of the port nacelle—but," he added, "this civilian ship is going to need special clearance to land on a military planet."

Brim grinned grimly. "Somehow," he said, "I doubt if we'll have any trouble with that, once I send our latest report. Steele...."

"Aye Skipper."

"Take a Top Secret-Plus message to Admiral Calhoun in Avalon. Ask him to clear us into Gimmas' Complex 19."

— o — 0 — o —

Approaching Complex 19, one of the few *totally* restricted landing areas on Gimmas/Haefdon, Brim watched a landing vector begin to melt in Gimmas' perpetual ice. This one was at least three times as wide as normal for the WF-400's size. Brim laughed. "Not taking any chances, aren't they?" he said wryly.

"Doesn't look like it skipper," Barbousse replied with a chuckle. "Guess they don't trust that port SpinGrav any more than you do."

"Oh, I'm good," Brim quipped with a shrug, "it's Treble and Kermis who don't trust it."

"*Four Nines* Wakefield," a tower controller's voice crackled in Brim's ear. "You are cleared for final on the 08:31:22 landing vector in your path." Simultaneously, a ruby beacon began to flash from the far end of the vector.

"Thanks, Tower Nineteen," Brim replied. He checked his instruments. No mistake, he was on a 08:31:22 heading. "*Four Nines* sees vector at zero-eight, thirty-one, twenty-two."

"Can we be of any assistance?"

"Negative for now, Tower Nineteen. *Four Nines* sees crash vehicles pulling alongside the vector—we appreciate them."

"Tower Nineteen...."

"Okay, folks," Brim said. "Everybody strapped in? Can't count on the restraint systems. Let's see those lights."

Six diodes winked.

Brim forced himself to relax. Everything that could be checked had been checked—and cross-checked: vertical Gravs, lift enhancers, altimeters, flight instruments. Now, it was all up to him. He laughed to himself. Except for the crumpled port nacelle, everything seemed to be normal—actually *could* be for all anybody knew. In the corner of his eye, he checked the port SpinGrav's readings—everything on the money. He walked the steering engines; *Four Nines* was a little slippery at low speeds, but she was pretty well right on with the ruby beacon, despite a slight crosswind. Off to the left, an odd-looking structure with a great helical spiral in its center slid past, reminding him of an absurd opener for Meem bottles. Closer in, windows below the Tower glowed warmly. Nice touch on this life-forsaken planet. Scanning the instruments one more time, he eased in a little more thrust—better to be just a little fast just before touchdown. Now…. He eased off on the steering engines; the bow wandered slightly to starboard, and he banked to counter the drift. Nose up ever so slightly. Hold her off…. *Voot, if you ever turned your back, this is the time!* An instant before touchdown, he leveled the deck, then… cascades of black water and slush shot skyward in the side Hyperscreens, diminishing gradually as he pulsed the gravity brakes and slowed the ship until it came to a stop, about a thousand irals from the edge of the ice. Down in one piece.

Taking his first breath in what seemed to be a long time, Brim checked the area for clearance, then eased the thrust dampers forward to taxi through a side canal melting away from them toward a group of hangar-like buildings near a slight rise in the snow that appeared to be what passed for "shore." Suddenly—amid surprised outcries from every part of the ship—the WF-400 pivoted sharply to port, then spun completely around before Brim could bring her to a halt.

"What happened?" Barbousse asked in a dazed voice.

Brim could only shake his head in wonder. "The port Grav—It just quit cold."

"What'd I tell ya, Skipper?" Treble quipped in a weak voice from a globular display.

"I'll never doubt your word again," Brim swore. Rolling his eyes and trimming the steering engines to compensate for the dead port Grav, he began taxiing toward the canal once more. It had been a close thing, he thought with a shiver. If the Grav had gone out just off the surface, things might have been disastrously different. But, he had recovered from worse circumstances in the past, and, as he'd learned back at the Helmsman's Academy, any landing you can walk away from is a good one. By Voot, they all were going to walk away from this one—including, figuratively, the Emperor's personal WF-400, although the latter *was* a bit worse for wear. As he neared a portable brow hastily erected beside the heated waterway, he noticed everyone was wearing the distinctive blue of the Imperial Intelligence Services. "Talk about 'restricted areas,'" he muttered.

Barbousse chuckled. "I doubt if they get any more restricted than this," he quipped.

Chapter 27

. . .complex 19

GIMMAS/HAEFDON, COMPLEX 19, 19 DIAD, 52017

With *Four Nines* rapidly covered with a huge tarpaulin by warmly bundled handlers—all dressed in IS blue—Brim and his crew were directed toward a bright red omnibus skimmer As he climbed aboard, the driver smiled. "G' Mornin,' Admiral," he said, raising a freckled hand. "It's been a while."

Brim peered at the man, whose crested, reddish hair and chalk-white complexion did seem familiar. Then, with a shock, he recalled a narrow face, long, thin nose, and a name that didn't fit at all. "Blue!" he exclaimed. "By Voot, it's been years since...."

"Red Rock 9, Admiral", Blue said with an appreciative grin. "It was there we showed you how to fly your first astroplanes."

"Yes," Brim said, a long-past adventure bursting into his memory. "You worked for Colonel Dark, I believe."

"Well, I still do, and she's *Major General* Dark now," Blue corrected. "She's sure anxious to lay eyes on you again, too."

"By the way," Brim said as Blue put the omnibus into motion, "it's just Wilf Brim anymore. I, ah ran into some...."

"Gorksroar, Admiral," Blue said. "Every true Blue Cape knows what that court martial was all about."

"Well...."

"'Well,' yourself, Admiral. In a few ticks, you'll be at General Dark's complex, and *there*, you're Admiral Brim, make no mistake."

Brim took a seat beside Barbousse and shrugged.

"Your past has a way of catchin' up with you, Skipper," the Chief said with a grin.

"Did *you* recognize Blue?" Brim asked.

"Didn't have to, Skipper," Barbousse replied. "I was first off the ship, an' he had his hand out, ready like. Seems like General Dark is the only one on the planet who runs an area with the proper security arrangements to take care of us."

Brim rolled his eyes. "Probably has something to do with the MET station."

"Or perhaps the bender we put paid to," Barbousse added.

"Guess we'll find out soon enough," Brim said with a chuckle.

"If we're lucky," Barbousse quipped

"Yeah," Brim agreed. "I hear *that*, too."

— o — 0 — o —

Blue dropped them off at the building that looked like a meem bottle opener. Inside, Barbousse and the others were ushered into a comfortable lounge where orderlies were serving hot cvc'eese and yeasty breakfast fixings. Before Brim could sit, however, a very senior Sergeant let Brim down a long corridor, trough a ciphered gate, and past two guards wearing side arms to a door marked A. M. DARK, MAJOR GENERAL. The Sergeant knocked lightly.

"Show the Admiral in, Sergeant," a feminine voice replied from inside.

"Admiral," the Sergeant said with a little bow, then opened the door.

Brim's mind raced as he stepped into a sparse office whose only adornment to relieve its bare walls was a portrait of Emperor Onrad. Dark was standing, hand outstretched, with a little smile. Sixteen, perhaps seventeen, years had passed since he had last seen the legendary woman. Granted, he'd not spent much time with her then, but from what he could see, she had aged hardly at all. Dressed in the sleek blue coveralls of the Imperial Intelligence Service—which Brim understood she ruled with an iron hand—the close-fitting uniform still revealed a great deal more than it concealed. Her complexion remained the chalky white he recalled, but now she wore salt-and-pepper hair in a bob reaching only to her shoulders. The large, almond-shaped eyes had clearly not softened with age, but she no longer nervously fingered the fragment of Hullmetal Brim remembered had been the constant, companion of her long fingers. Major General Dark was clearly nearing sixty, but she had lost none of the energy that always seemed to crackle around her. Brim grasped her outstretched hand and kissed it. "General Dark," he said. "I am honored."

"As am I, Admiral," she replied with an appreciative smile.

"It's not 'Admiral,'" Brim protested.

"Never forget this is *my* bailiwick," she warned, her eyes suddenly hard as Hullmetal as she took a seat at her desk, "and *here*, you are 'Admiral' Brim, with all the particular appellation implies."

Brim gulped. "As you wish, General Dark."

The smile returned to her lips. "Much better, Admiral," she said, touching a sensor on her desk and motioning for Brim to sit in the room's only other chair. "Now that little matter is settled, in private, I hope you will call me Abby if I may address you as Wilf."

Sinking into the chair, Brim took a deep breath. "Abby," he said with a sigh, "I should be proud if you called me Wilf." On the moment, the door opened as a Sergeant wheeled a serving table into the room. The smell of cvc'eese and hot rolls made his mouth water. He'd been living on flight rations since takeoff.

"Excellent," Dark pronounced, then waited in silence as the Sergeant poured two cups of the sweet thick liquid and placed a basket of rolls in the center of the desk. When she'd left the room, Dark seemed to relax and took a long sip of cvc'eese. "I'm certain you'd like to be brought up to date about what has transpired since you reported the destruction of that bender."

"You've got that right Gen..., er, Abby," Brim replied tearing into a sweet roll. "It's a pretty good guess this first mission of ours has stirred up a nest of trouble."

"Some guess," she said with a dark laugh. "But then, you've been in one kind of trouble or another since I first laid eyes on you at Red Rock 9." She daintily broke a roll in half and took a bite.

Brim made a faux grimace. "Mostly for the League, I hope."

"Oh, *really*? From what I recall, you've been magnificently equal-opportunity about causing troubles: Leaguers and Imperials alike."

"I try to be fair."

Dark rolled her eyes. "But I did promise to tell you what I can, didn't I?"

"When you're ready, Madame," Brim said, refilling both cups from a carafe. "Right now, I'm more interested in fresh cvc'eese than anything else I can think of."

Dark smiled. "First: about that hot astroplane of yours. Soon after you KA'PPAed your report to Admiral Calhoun, I received orders directly from his office to put that little ship back into operation *post haste*—which I should be able to do before the next local Gimmas day is through. That should get you back to Avalon approximately four Standard Days following your departure. The Admiral wants you to be seen landing on Lake Mersin as soon as possible."

Brim frowned. "That '400' is a pretty special ship," he warned, buttering a second roll large.

"We're well aware of your '400,'" Dark said with a nod. "I've got a new Krasni-Peych 77/77 Drive on the way from Sodeskaya already. It's my long-lead time item."

"How are you going to get it here from Sodeskaya so fast?"

"Aboard another WF-400," Dark said. "With Admiral Calhoun, all sorts of things become possible."

"Wait a cycle," Brim exclaimed, setting down his cvc'eese. "Another WF-400? I thought the one I'm flying was the only one outside Hatfield/Salisbury."

"I worried about the same thing," Dark agreed with a chuckle, "but you never know when you're dealing with Calhoun. If I were to take a wild guess, I'd say he had so much faith in the performance you and that crazy crew would wring out of those little ships that he put them into production before the results were in." She shrugged. "And looks like he was right...."

Brim felt his cheeks burn. "How about the wrecked nacelle?" he asked?

Dark laughed. "My people can hammer out that damage so only close inspection will show it was repaired." She shut her eyes and laughed. "'TopLine Spacecraft Performance, Customization & Research, Ltd.,' indeed! Almost as good as that 'Payless' outfit you set up at Atalanta a few years back. Where *do* you get the names?"

"Mostly from Barbousse," Brim admitted with a chuckle. "But what about the Grav that went out on me?"

"A Grav's a Grav," she said with a shrug. "If we had to, we could completely rebuild it before you turn in for the night."

"Seems like you've got quite a place here on old Gimmas, Abby."

"Wilf, you don't know the half of what we've got in this complex— and probably never will."

"Somehow, I don't have any trouble believing that," Brim admitted, refreshing their cve'eese cups again. "What do you know about the MET station?"

Dark checked a display beside her desk. "So far, nobody has a clue about that," she said. "Doesn't make any sense; the Leaguers depend on that station as much as we do."

"That's what I understand," Brim agreed. "Looked like a rush job: poorly planned and badly carried out."

"The Admiral's got some ideas about who might be responsible, but he wouldn't even share them with me, Wilf," she said. "He forwarded us the Holophotos you sent ahead; I've got people studying them as we speak."

Brim grinned. "Kind of figured they'd end up here."

"You'd be surprised what ends up here."

"Not any more." Brim quipped.

Dark nodded, checked her timepiece, and stood. "I'm due at a meeting, Wilf" she said. "I've got it set up so you and your crew have access anywhere in this building, but I'll have to keep you out of anywhere else. How about if we dine together here at the Officer's Club, say Twilight and one?"

"T-that would be wonderful, Abby," Brim said in surprise. "But I'm hardly dressed for supper at an Officer's Club. I only packed spare flight gear."

Dark laughed. "You've been spending too much time in Avalon. Out here on Gimmas, we're a lot more casual."

Smiling awkwardly, Brim stood and took her hand. "Meet you at the Officer's Club, Twilight and one on the dot."

"Be there, Admiral…."

Chapter 28

. . .can't keep your nose out of trouble

GIMMAS/HAEFDON, COMPLEX 19, 19 DIAD, 52017

No more than a Metacycle later in the casino of the Officer's Club, Brim was passing time in a game of Cre'el with Barbousse, a most talented player. Brim—himself no slouch at the game—had just won a difficult play of linked Tomers when a Sergeant stopped by their table. "Urgent message for Admiral Brim in the secure section," he announced.

Brim shook his head. He was still down by six Tomers; leaving would give the game—and the pot—to Barbousse. He scowled. "Chief," he grumbled, "If you cooked this up...."

"Not me, Skipper," Barbousse said with a great smile. "Besides, face it, you were going to lose anyway; I feel lucky this afternoon."

Brim rolled his eyes. Beating Barbousse was nearly impossible. Grudgingly, he pushed the pot across the table. "One of these days, Chief...."

"Not if I can help it, Skipper...."

Chuckling wryly, Brim stood and slapped his old comrade on the shoulder, then: to the Sergeant, "I'm all yours." During the next few cycles, he followed the man through a number of corridors to a secure gateway where a retinal scan of both the Sergeant's eyes was required before the door swung open to a small, bare room containing only a table, a chair, and a KA'PPA set, facing the door

"When you're finished, Admiral," the Sergeant said motioning Brim inside, "please knock and I'll escort you back to the Officer's Club."

"Thanks, Sergeant," Brim replied, watching the door close and lock. He tried the lever—it didn't move—then walked around the KA'PPA set and took a seat. The display read:

MOST SECRET, EYES ONLY
PLEASE TOUCH CONTROL TO BEGIN

Brim touched CONTROL. Immediately, the display changed to:

ADMIRALTY: PLEASE SIGNAL WHEN READY FOR
ADMIRAL CALHOUN.

"Ready," Brim said, then waited at least four cycles until:

CALHOUN: HELLO, WILF. YOU ALL RIGHT??

"We're all fine, Admiral," Brim said.

CALHOUN: GLAD TO HEAR IT. CONGRATULATIONS
ON BAGGING THE BENDER. FROM OUR
INTERCEPTS, WE THINK THE LEAGUERS
DON'T HAVE A CLUE AS TO WHAT'S
HAPPENED.

"Piece of good luck on my part, Admiral. We just happened on it at the right time: when it was coming out of cloaked mode. I think we got it right after the crew made their regular report."

CALHOUN: SPLENDID. NEVER KNEW WHAT HIT
THEM ONE SUPPOSES. WHAT HAPPENED TO
YOU?

"Trouble with one of the drives—I lost control in the middle of my attack." He grimaced in spite of himself. "Must be out of practice—should have had better control."

CALHOUN: NOT ACCORDING TO STEELE'S
REPORT—SAYS YOUR FLYING IS THE ONLY
REASON THEY'RE STILL ALIVE. FROM PAST
EXPERIENCE, I LIKE HIS STORY BETTER.

"Can't believe everything you read, Admiral."

CALHOUN: WE'LL TAKE THAT UP OVER SOME
GOOD MEEM SOMEDAY, BRIM. RIGHT NOW, I
WANT TO TALK ABOUT THE MET STATION.
ANY IDEAS?

"Not a lot, Admiral"

CALHOUN: I CHECKED YOUR MANIFEST. JUST AS I
ORDERED: YOU SIGNED OUT FOR THE BRIGHT
TRIAD.

"That's right, Admiral, it was there for anybody with the proper clearances to see, including any Leaguers who cared to look. SECRET isn't all that high, although there is always a need-to-know requirement."

CALHOUN: NEED-TO-KNOW IS PURE GORKSROAR
AND YOU KNOW IT. WHAT'S IMPORTANT IS
THAT THIS PUTS PEOPLE ON OUR SIDE UNDER
SUSPICION.

"Well, people with secret clearances and above."

CALHOUN: CORRECT. AND I'VE GOT SUSPECTS
WHO HAVE MORE THAN ENOUGH CLEARANCE
TO READ THOSE MANIFESTS.

There's always an access trail to classified documents; I assume you've checked those. Do any names look suspicious

CALHOUN: YES, I'VE CHECKED THEM AND NO, I
HAVEN'T FOUND ANYBODY'S NAME THAT
SHOULDN'T BE THERE. BUT THAT DOESN'T
PROVE MUCH. DATA CAN ALWAYS BE PASSED
BY WORD OF MOUTH FROM SOMEONE WHO
HAS CLEARANCE.

"I understand, Admiral, but, who would want to kill someone aboard our ship? We're not threats to anybody I can think of—at least not Imperials."

CALHOUN: YOU HAVEN'T BEEN DOING MUCH IN
THE WAY OF THINKING ABOUT THAT, HAVE
YOU BRIM? I KNOW A NUMBER OF PEOPLE
WHO MIGHT LIKE TO SEE YOU DEAD. BUT IF
IT'S NOT PERSONS YOU THREATEN, HOW
ABOUT YOUR MISSION?

Brim thought about that a moment. "Even though we were signed out for the Triad, very few people knew we were armed," he said, "I can't think of anybody outside your circle, the crew at TopLine, and the Emperor who knows anything about that part of the mission. And the WF-400 carries its HyperTorps internally, so they weren't visible when we took off."

This time, a number of clicks passed before Calhoun replied:

CALHOUN: SO I CAN'T SEE WHY THE LEAGUERS WOULD
CARE ENOUGH ABOUT AN EXTRA-LONG-RANGE
MISSION IN A SINGLE, UNARMED ASTROPLANE THAT
WOULD CAUSE THEM TO DESTROY A WHOLE MET
STATION—ESPECIALLY ONE THEY DEPEND ON
THEMSELVES.

"I guess I can't think of any reasons, either," Brim replied. "Besides, if the Leaguers had been in on it, they'd have done a much better job."

CALHOUN: BY VOOT, THAT'S A FACT, ISN'T IT?
ALL RIGHT, LET'S GO ON THE ASSUMPTION IT
WAS AN IMPERIAL JOB. HANG ON A MOMENT
OVER THERE WHILE I TALK TO SOME OF
YOUR OLD FRIENDS, HARRY DRUMMOND
AND BOS GALLSWORTHY, WHO, BY THE
WAY, SEND THEIR GREETINGS.
GALLSWORTHY, ESPECIALLY WANTS TO
KNOW WHY YOU CAN'T SEEM TO KEEP YOUR
NOSE OUT OF TROUBLE.

"Tell him I blame it all on Barbousse, Admiral."

> CALHOUN: THOUGHT THAT MIGHT BE THE CASE.
> HOLD ON WHILE WE TALK THIS OVER.

After a few cycles:

> CALHOUN: WE'RE ALL AGREED YOUR BEST
> COURSE OF ACTION IS TO COME BACK TO
> AVALON AS SOON AS POSSIBLE, ACTING AS IF
> NOTHING OUT OF THE ORDINARY HAS
> HAPPENED SINCE YOU DEPARTED. DARK
> REPORTS SHE CAN HAVE YOU ON YOUR WAY
> SOMETIME TOMORROW, OUR TIME.

"That's what she says, Admiral."

> CALHOUN: OF COURSE, YOU'LL IMMEDIATELY
> TAKE THE SHIP BACK TO TOPLINE BEFORE
> ANYONE HAS MUCH OF A CLOSE LOOK AT
> HER.

"Immediately, Admiral."

> CALHOUN: AFTER THAT, GO ABOUT YOUR LIFE AS
> IF NOTHING HAPPENED. I'M ASKING YOU AND
> BARBOUSSE TO TRAIN THE FIRST BATCH OF
> WF-400 HELMSMEN, SO YOU CAN PUBLICLY
> MAKE YOURSELF BUSY GETTING READY FOR
> THAT.

"*Batch* of Helmsmen? Until I talked to General Dark, I thought I had the only WF-400 in captivity."

> CALHOUN: WELL, I DID A BIT OF CHEATING WITH
> THE FLEET FUNDS, SO WE HAVE A FEW NEW
> ONES IN STORAGE WITH ALL THE
> MODIFICATIONS YOU ASKED. AS SOON AS WE
> CAN TRAIN THOSE HELMSMEN, WE'LL PUT
> THEM ON PATROL.

Brim shook his head and smiled. "Somehow, I'm not surprised Admiral."

CALHOUN: OF COURSE YOU AREN'T. YOU KNEW
I'D DO SOMETHING LIKE THAT— SOON AS
YOU PROVED THE SHIPS COULD DO THE JOB.
NICE WORK,

"I'll train them, Admiral," Brim replied, wondering what was coming next.

CALHOUN: AFTER THAT, I'VE GOT AN
INTERESTING ASSIGNMENT FOR YOU, TOO, IF
YOU'LL TAKE IT. WE'LL TALK AFTER YOU
RETURN.

"I'm all ears, Admiral."

CALHOUN: ANYTHING ELSE ON YOUR END BEFORE
I BREAK THE CONNECTION?

"Nothing, Admiral. See you when I see you."

CALHOUN: OUT, THEN.

Brim's display went dark

Chapter 29

. . .Abby Dark

W hen Brim returned to the Officer's Club, another Sergeant delivered a note from Dark:

> Admiral:
> With regret, I must cancel our plans for
> dining this evening. I'd looked forward
> to the chance of knowing you better, but
> if anybody understands the service life,
> you do. With luck, I shall have a chance
> to see you before you leave tomorrow.
> ~Dark

"Will there be an answer, Admiral?" the Sergeant asked.

Brim thought a moment. "Yes," he said with a smile. "Please tell General Dark I am deeply disappointed, but hardly surprised,".

"I'll convey your message," the Sergeant replied, then saluted— though the gesture was unnecessary indoors—and disappeared at a brisk clip.

Brim shrugged, looked around the Club Lounge—lonely at this time of the Gimmas' day—then started off for his room in the Visiting Officers' Quarters. A few Metacycles remained before the dining room would open, and he might as well catch up on his mail. He was halfway there when he met Barbousse in a corridor. "Skipper," the big man said. "I understand you no longer have supper plans."

"News travels fast around here," Brim said with a grin.

"No finer Logus vine than in the Imperial Intelligence organizations, Skipper." Barbousse explained. "And will you be joining the rest of the crew and me now you're free? We're dining at the NCO club."

"The NCO Club, eh? Had I known you had *that* set up, I'd probably have turned down Dark's invitation."

"In a gratzl's eye, you would, Skipper. Dark may be on the far side of sixty, but she's a true hottie."

"Yeah, well, no denying that, but good food's a great recompense."

"So you'll join us?"

"Of course. When?"

"Twilight plus one—same time you were to meet Dark."

"By Voot, it's good to have so much privacy," Brim said with a grimace.

"Glad to know you feel that way, Skipper," Barbousse replied with a chuckle. Then, winking, he turned and continued along the corridor toward his quarters. "Pick you up at Twilight plus three quarters" he called over his shoulder.

"I'll be ready, Chief," Brim shouted after him, then continued on to his own door. Later, using the room's communicator, he answered a number of posts from long-time friends, including a steamy missive from Claudia Valemont-Nesterio in far-off Atalanta. Somehow, despite her ostensibly indissoluble marriage to a Atalantan barkeep, their quiet, passionate affair had managed to survive and continued to smolder. Metacycles passed quickly as he composed; he liked to correspond with friends and had all too little time for it.

Supper at the NCO Club was more a banquet than a simple meal—as Brim expected: everywhere the Imperial Fleet Noncoms established a permanent headquarters, the NCO Club quickly became famous for its faire. Moreover, once the sommelier opened his reserve meem cellars, Barbousse chose some of the finest Logish Meem Brim had tasted for years. It helped stem some of his angst left over from the mission and its surprises. For victuals, the waiters served no dominating main course; instead, they brought what seemed like endless small, sophisticated dishes until everyone at the table was perfectly stuffed with victuals and excellent Logish Meem. Long after the last plates had been cleared, good camaraderie continued with countless salutes to Emperor Onrad and anyone—or anything—the revelers could summon to mind. At last, Brim noticed very few diners were in the room—and the waiters were giving their table sidelong glances. "I think," he said ruefully, "it's time to let these people clean up and go home."

This was met with groans and grumbles, but eventually, everyone managed to stand and make their way from the dining room. Barbousse quickly palmed the bill and slipped it into Brim's pocket before they were in the lobby. Shortly thereafter, cold Gimmas air restored everyone quickly to some semblance of sobriety, and the little party split up for their own temporary domiciles.

"Good night, Skipper," Barbousse said. "Sorry to say I'm glad your supper with Dark didn't materialize. Our night out together meant a lot to the crew."

"I've gotta' agree," Brim said as they approached the Officer's Quarters. "That was an opportunity we shouldn't have passed up, even though Dark is one magnificent woman. It would have nice getting to know her a little better, though—even she is a bit odd." Inside, they stomped snow from their boots, checked for messages, then headed for their rooms.

"Any idea what time we'll get out of here tomorrow?" Barbousse asked.

Brim shrugged. "Another of the secrets this place likes to wallow in," he chuckled. "I for one am going to sleep in and let them tell us what's what when they've figured that out themselves."

"Sounds like a good idea, Skipper," Barbousse agreed, stopping at his door. "I'll see you when I see you."

"See you then," Brim said, continuing on down the hall to his own door. After a long day—if the mission could even be called a *day*—he was in need of some sleep, which he got the moment his head hit the pillow.

— o — 0 — o —

In the middle of the night, Brim was awakened by someone opening the door to his room although he remembered he'd carefully locked it as soon as he'd entered. Instantly awake, he sprang to his feet, ready to defend himself—then quickly changed his mind when he recognized a small female figure in a great white bathrobe silhouetted in light from the hallway. "Abby?" he whispered in surprise.

"Well, shall I come in?"

"I surely hope so, Abby" Brim replied, reaching for the lights. "Be a terrible shame if you'd come to the wrong room."

"No mistake, Wilf," Dark said, stepping inside and shutting the door. She smiled, staring at him quite obviously as she opened her bathrobe. "Seems as if you've forgotten to pack your jimmies."

"I *have*," Brim assured her.

"Pity," she said, "you seem to be growing a nice place to hang them now."

"Like to try that bathrobe of yours?"

Dark let the bathrobe drop to the floor. "Something tells me if we concentrate, we can find better uses for that hanger," she whispered. She was wearing some sort of blue negligee that was all lace in front. It left nothing to the imagination—including a million freckles.

Brim walked slowly to her, taking in everything. She was more beautiful than he'd imagined! He pulled her to him; she wrapped her arms around his neck and drew him to her face, then whole Universe simplified itself into a wild confusion of lips, tongues, and teeth until—mysteriously—he found himself on the bed beneath her, panting as if he'd run a c'lenyt or more. With an expert wiggle, she managed to fling the negligee over her head, then, raising her haunches, she bent forward so their lips touched. Time stopped in its tracks....

$$— o — 0 — o —$$

At last they lay side by side, sweaty and exhausted, she on her back, he resting on his elbows. Peering into his eyes, she chuckled. "Wilf Brim, if I'd had any idea back at Red Rock One you were so talented, I'd never have let you go on that mission."

"Abby," Brim replied, "...had I known anything about you, I probably wouldn't have gone." He chuckled. "Except I doubt if you spend much time in bed with SubLieutenants, do you?"

Dark laughed out loud. "Yeah," she admitted, "there *is* that."

Brim leaned over and kissed her lips gently. "You know I am terribly honored, Abby," he whispered. "I've always thought of you as a great lady."

"You're pretty great, yourself, Wilf," she said. "Someday, you'll get that Fleet Cloak back and you'll realize you've only just gotten started with your life" With that, she sat on the edge of the bed, then retrieved her negligee from the floor. "It's time I get back to my day job. Your ship will be ready by the time you've gathered your crew and had a decent breakfast. Is there anything else I can get for you before I become General Dark again?"

Brim thought for a moment, then an idea that had been forming since his run-in with the bender came complete. "Ya, know, " he said, "...aside from an invitation for a special visit to you some day in the future, there is one other thing."

Dark grinned. "You've got your invitation, Wilf Brim—an open one at that. Now what else?"

"That chunk the bender your people have by now removed from our Drive nacelle. I need a piece of it—not big. Maybe just enough to fill in a shoe box."

"A piece of *Bender*," she exclaimed, slipping on her robe and fastening it. "What in the name of Voot do you want with something like that?"

"I'd like to have it gift wrapped for Emperor Onrad," Brim explained. "His birthday's coming up shortly, and he once jokingly asked me to bring back a piece of bender. Then he threatened to have me exiled if I tried a trick like that in his personal WF-400."

"So, you *want* to be exiled?"

"Well, if it was exile to *here*—with you—I might consider, but...."

"I'll give you exile," she said with a laugh. "What a great birthday gift! Soon as I get back to my suite, I'll make sure a proper piece is waiting for you at breakfast. Now, is there anything else I can do for you?"

"Absolutely," Brim said with a grin "but I'm too worn out to do anything about it."

Dark laughed. "So am I," she said, then opened her arms, "….but I'd love one more *long* hug before this lovely evening is over."

Brim complied, and a long time afterward, the two held each other before Brim gently let her go. "I'll never forget you Abby."

"Nor I you, Wilf," she said, taking his hand, then walking to the door and turning out the light.

"How'd you get here with nobody seeing you?" Brim demanded.

"Simple," Dark said, opening the door and stepping into the hall. "Until I'm back in my suite, every door on this floor is locked except yours. It'll be chocked up to a malfunction, of course." Then, after a peck on Brim's cheek, she disappeared along the corridor and around a corner.

BOOK III

Uh oh!

Chapter 30

. . .a lot easier dealing with Leaguers

AVALON/ASTURIUS, LAKE MERSIN, CONTROL TOWER,
AVALON CITY, 21 DIAD, 52017

Tall, gray-bearded Tower Controller Seyess Inhardt was engaged at his terminal catching up on administrative duties when, by chance, he overheard a neighboring Controller handling a ship with a familiar call sign:

"*Four Nines* Wakefield: turn new heading of five zero two five zero to join the Covington-32 radial inbound. Descend and maintain ten thousand at velocity of two fifty; the altimeter two nine nine one."

Inhardt looked up from his work, listening intently. Something familiar about....

"*Four Nines* Wakefield: Fly new heading two thirty five and descend to seven thousand."

Yes: *the ebony civilian Wakefield with 'four nines' as a call number*. The one whose departure he'd been asked to report on. Inhardt wondered why his mysterious contact hadn't asked for information on the ship's *return*. Perhaps the man *had wanted to*—and simply neglected to call. Or, possibly, the ship's return was a surprise, and he'd appreciate knowing about it. Either way, Inhardt decided it was worth a call. One could always use a few more credits in one's pocket—*if* the information was deemed valuable. While the neighboring controller continued working the incoming ship, Inhardt put his terminal on HOLD, then hurried to a nearby observation balcony, where he entered an address in his HoloPhone.

After a few moments the ONLINE indicator lighted, but the display remained dark, as he expected: "Inhardt? How dare you contact this address on your own?"

"I h-have information y-you might find useful, sir," Inhardt whispered hesitantly.

"What information?"

"The *F-four Nines* Wakefield you w-wanted me to report on the Fifteenth."

"What about it?"

"It's in the landing pattern here on Lake Mersin, s-sir."

"Why would I want to know about that?"

"Perhaps because you wanted me to notify you when it lifted off"

"I did?"

"Yessir."

"Wait… yes, I see here I did. You say it's in the landing pattern?"

"It is."

"Tail number ISS nine-nine-nine-nine?"

"I can't see; it's at the wrong angle."

"You will see the astroplane when it lands?"

"I shall, sir—in moments."

"Record it with your HoloPhone, then call me back."

Inhardt's HoloPhone went dark. Frantically, he pointed it toward the landing vector and began taking photos as the Astroplane smoothly touched down and skimmed the surface, trailing a long wake of spray. The landing was at some distance out on the lake, but Inhardt's HoloPhone was an expensive model; it could record details like the tail number. As the little ship slowed, it turned abruptly and disappeared into a side canal—almost as if its crew was in a hurry to be out of sight.

"Inhardt for Voot's sake—what on Avalon are you doing out here on the observation deck taking pictures? On *my* time!"

Taken by surprise, Inhardt nearly dropped the HoloPhone. His supervisor! "I, ah, wanted some pictures, Supervisor Clarke."

"And for *what*?"

"T-testing my new HoloPhone, S-supervisor."

"Hmm," Clarke sniffed. "Looks like an expensive one. Perhaps I am overpaying you?"

"I don't know what to say, Supervisor."

"No, I should think not," Clark sniffed. "Well, consider your pay docked for the afternoon. I shall look for you tomorrow *on time* ready to work a full shift. Understand?"

"I u-understand, Supervisor Clark."

"See you do, Inhardt," Clark growled, as he turned on his heel and walked away. "Oh, and enjoy your afternoon," he added over his shoulder.

Inhardt ground his teeth as he entered the address in his HoloPhone again and pressed TRANSMIT. When the ONLINE indicator lighted again, he said, "I have recorded the landing as you requested."

"You took long enough, didn't you?"

"There was trouble."

"Trouble? What kind of trouble?"

"My supervisor; he docked me the afternoon's pay. I'll expect...."

"Send the recording immediately. If it is of any worth, I shall notify you."

"But...."

"Send it *now*."

Impotently biting his lip, Inhardt shifted the HoloPhone to INTERNAL, then pressed TRANSMIT; moments later the 'phone went dark. He took a deep breath and walked toward a down-moving stairway. A nice little tavern was close by; a few drinks wouldn't hurt right now... going home early to the wife would produce questions leading to still another spat he was bound to lose....

— o — 0 — o —

At TopLine, Brim was last to exit the ship, carrying his package in an innocuous-looking shopping bag adorned by the emblem of a tony Avalon boutique. Inside, Dark had set Onrad's birthday present in an exquisite wooden chest, then placed the chest in the bag beneath a spray of red tissue paper. Brim glanced around the hangar as soon as he was on the brow and chuckled; he had a good crew. Even before the canal door closed, they'd swarmed the 400, inspecting every thumb as if its intimacy with "foreigners" might have adversely affected something.

Somehow, he'd expected the plain-clothed stranger with Imperial Secret Service credentials waiting for him in the office—or the perfectly ordinary black skimmer idling at the curb outside. "Special Agent Callay," the man said by way of introduction. "May I give you a lift to Admiral Calhoun's office, Lord Brim?"

With a grin of capitulation, Brim clapped the man on the shoulder and nodded. "Agent Callay, I can't think of anyplace I'd rather go." Turning back into the shop, he shouted, "Barbousse! You're in change."

"Aye Skipper!"

While Callay picked their way through Avalon's smoking, rubble-clogged streets—clearly, there had been a raid early that morning—Brim prepared himself for the questioning that lay ahead, trying to summon every detail to mind. Calhoun would have had time to study all the pictures he and the crew of the WF-400 had taken. But this questioning would be a lot more personal. Nobody had mentioned Brim's personal enemies, but even at this early stage of the investigation that was sure to come, he knew it would be one of the main vectors.

Flocks of pidwings swooped past the little skimmer as Callay skillfully eased through swirling traffic and dodged into the cavern-like approach to a parking area below the grand old Admiralty building. Clearly, the skimmer was broadcasting special arrival signals, for they passed through the blast-proof tunnel with no interference from the force fields that would have stopped them short, had they been riding in an unprepared vehicle. Callay pulled to a stop at a bank of transporters.. "You know the way from here, don't you Lord Brim?" he asked.

Brim smiled wistfully. "I've been here a few times," he said as an armed guard opened the door for him. "Appreciate the lift, Special Agent," he said.

"Tell Calhoun's girl when you and the Admiral are done," Callay advised with a salute, "...one of us will get you back to TopLine."

Brim saluted his thanks, then strode into one of the old-fashioned lift capsules—it smelled of oil and ozone—then touched a warm Identity Sensor glowing red. In a moment, it turned green. "Your destination, Lord Brim?" the capsule asked as the door rolled closed on silent rollers.

"Admiral Calhoun," Brim announced. Cycles later, after having been lifted along what felt like a complex path through the ancient building, the door opened and he stepped into a richly paneled anteroom, where a comely young Blue Cape stood and smiled. "Welcome, Lord Brim. The Admiral asks you go right in," she said, indicating a door embellished with the Great Seal of The Fleet.

As she spoke, the door swung open ponderously. Inside, behind a huge desk, Calhoun rose and stood, a serious mien on his leonine face. Clearly the war was having its affect: new lines seemed to appear on his forehead each time Brim saw him, but his icy gray eyes showed none of his powers were affected. "Damme guid seein' you here, Brim," the Admiral said, extending his hand.

"Good to seen, Admiral," Brim replied, returning the Admiral's warm handshake. "As always, it was Barbousse who saved us. He spotted the hidden HyperTorps on the Gravity pool before I set the ship down and killed us all."

Calhoun chuckled. "Weel," he said, indicating a facing pair of ophet leather arm chairs, "tha' probably maks ye twa a wee mair e'en then. Ye've saved his life at least as many times."

Brim waited until Calhoun had settled into one of the chairs, then took the other. "I don't think we're keeping track any more," he said. "We've shared a lot of close calls."

"I'll wager this was ane o' your closest," Calhoun declared.

"Don't think I'll take that wager, Admiral," Brim replied.

"How about tellin' me aboot it first hand?" Calhoun said. "I wad hear all details ye couldn't remember on the KA'PPA COM."

Brim nodded., bracing himself for questions that had made Calhoun the most feared debriefer in the Fleet. "Well, Admiral," he said, "let's take it from a couple moments before Barbousse spotted the HyperTorps.... "

— o — 0 — o —

By the time Calhoun had finished—nearly a Metacycle and a half later—Brim and the Admiral had gone through a generous snack tray and two pots of cvc'eese. Brim knew for a fact he'd been interrogated by the Empire's best.

Opposite, Calhoun sprawled in the chair, steepling his fingers and frowning. "So ye still nae think it war Leaguers, do ye?" he asked.

"Haven't changed my mind yet," Brim replied firmly. "Leaguers are too professional for that hack job. And another thing: our little WF-400 isn't important enough to the Zukeeds that they'd take out a whole Met station to get it." He chuckled momentarily. "Of course, that's only until they figure out what happened to the bender we blasted."

"Yon Leaguers wadn't like tha' at all," Calhoun agreed with a dark laugh. "But sae far as ye Met station's concerned, ev'eryone kenn those zukeeds use information from there themselves." He frowned. "So there's still another reason why it isn't them."

"Perhaps someone else has declared war on us?" Brim suggested.

"Nae' I recall as of this morning," Calhoun said with a guffaw "But then ye never know, either." He frowned. "It's almost *got* to be some of our own people who tried to kill ye."

"Imperials?"

"Aye, Imperials. And pretty highly placed anes, at tha'. Only the very highest-placed people are in on the secret o' tha' daft Astroplane of yours."

"But that's crazy," Brim said. "Why interfere with WF-400 research? It's one of the biggest threats against the Leaguer bender fleet since the discovery of N-rays."

"Your discovery, by the way, Brim."

"Thanks, Admiral," Brim said. "That was just a lucky accident a long time ago and deserves to be forgotten."

"You and Barbousse *do* make a habit of bein' in the right places at the right times," the Admiral said with a chuckle. "But back to our mystery. I'm also thinkin' tha' a job like the ane on the Met station— even a hack job—wad cost an arm an' a leg, so whoever set it up has got be someone wi a whole lot of credits behind him."

152

"Oh? But, again, *why*...? Who would benefit? I mean, we're all in this war together... aren't we?"

"Some less than others," Calhoun rumbled. "I don't suppose it ev'r occurred to you, Brim, tha' some people count on this war for their positions o' power, ev'n their wealth—and tha' you and your WF-400 might be a threat to *them*?"

"I don't understand."

"Bein' Wilf Brim, you wouldn't," Calhoun said. "Listen: wha' wad happen, say, t' Escort Command, if a fleet o' relatively inexpensive astroplanes could do a better job o' guardin' convoys than they do with their slow, expensive starships?"

Brim felt his eyebrows rise. "I think I understand *that*." He said. "You feel maybe someone in Escort Command wants to shut us off?"

"Weel, tha' gang certainly hae' nae' love for ye, as you may hae' noticed."

"Oh, I've noticed *that*, Admiral." Brim said, "but...."

"They re not the only ones, Brim," Calhoun interrupted. "How aboot Count Tal Confisse Trafford? He sure as Xaxt doesn't want you lookin' good at onythin'—especially since there's plenty o' suspicion about who caused the disaster at Eppeid. Daughter-General Megan maun have won the Court Martial tha' put ye out of business in the Fleet, but ev'eryone knows it's not a completely done deal, an' onythin' that looks good for you reflects badly on daughter Megan. Right?"

"Somehow, I hate to think either of them would sabotage the war effort for any reason. What would happen to them if the League won? Everybody knows Leaguers shoot collaborators first—they're not considered trustworthy."

"Easy, Brim," Calhoun said with a gentle smile. "I'm nae' accusin' anyone right now. I'm just sayin' tha' if it's not Leaguers who destroyed that Met station—in an attempt to put and your WF-400 crew out o' business—then 'tis wise to look elsewhere. An' that gang o' self-servin' Zukeeds stick out luik the proverbial sore thumb."

Brim shrugged. "I guess they do," he said. "But I'm not going to let anyone come between me and finishing this WF-400 project—certainly not our own people." He pursed his lips a moment. "Tough

when the enemy is on your own side," he said staring into nowhere.
"It's a Xaxt of a lot easier dealing with Leaguers..."

Chapter 31

. . . deserved rewards

THE GREEN STAR BAR AND GRILLE, A WATERFRONT
TAVERN IN A SEEDY NEIGHBORHOOD AT THE AUSTRAL
END OF LAKE MERSIN, 24 DIAD, 52017

Archibald Greller, gaunt, bearded Captain of the ancient, Banta-class star freighter *Argonaut*, looked expansively around the small banquet room he'd rented for the occasion, smiled proudly, then counted noses again—everyone was present, from the engineers to the bridge crew. Carefully, he entered an address in his HoloPhone. Immediately, the ONLINE indicator lighted, but the display remained dark as always.

"Are all present?" a harsh voice demanded.

"They are all here, M'Lord."

"You are certain? Count them again."

Patiently, Greller counted again. "They are all here, M'Lord," he said.

"Keep them where they are," the voice ordered. "I shall present your awards only once. Anyone who is not present will lose all remuneration. Do you understand?"

"I understand, M'Lord," Greller said, only moments before the HoloPhone disconnected.

Presently, he rapped a fork against his goblet of meem, bringing his unkempt crewmen to a surly attention. "Keep yer seats, boys," he ordered. "You probably wonder why I've called you here for this great feed, don't you?"

A chorus of affirmative grunts came from the four other tables in the room.

155

"Well," Greller explained proudly, "tonight's the payoff for the job we did on the Met station. We must have pulled it off damn well. The stiffs that hired us have set up this big feast and drinks to show their appreciation—while they deliver our payoff in *cash*. They wanted to make sure everybody was here."

"Who the Xaxt are they, anyway?" one of the diners demanded. "Ain't often we get hired ta' do a gov'ment place like that."

"*And* rig the gravity pool ta' boot," another piped in. "Those guys were really sore about something!"

"Since when did we start askin' questions about our, er, *clients?*" Greller demanded. "Specially when they pay off like this." He glanced at his timepiece. "Listen, they're due ta' show up any click, now, so try ta' look a little more professional than usual. We want as many jobs from those stiffs as we...."

Greller never finished his sentence. Instead, he whirled around in bewilderment to confront a muffled commotion at the only doorway to the banquet room—which had suddenly burst open to admit four masked figures firing silenced blast pikes almost at random. Greller was about to shout something in protest when his whole universe burst inward in an icy burst of raw energy. His last thought was a perplexed, "*Why?*"

— o — 0 — o —

Some days later, as Brim exited a small auditorium in the Admiralty where he'd addressed a class of Helmsmen qualifying on the new WF-400, a man in dark business dress met him in the hallway. "Lord Brim?" he asked.

"That's me," Brim replied. "What can I do for you, Agent?"

"Burns," the man replied with a little grin. "Admiralty Special Security. Admiral Calhoun asks you contact him at this HoloPhone address," he said, slipping a strip of plastic into Brim's hand.

"Thanks," Brim said. "Anything else?"

"That's it," the man said, touching his forehead. Then, without looking back, he continued along the hall toward an exit.

Brim took a seat on a leather couch in an alcove, entered the address in his HoloPhone and pressed CONNECT. Moments after the plastic strip disintegrated, Calhoun's visage appeared in the tiny instrument's display.

"Hullo, Brim; luiks as if Burns had nae trouble finding ye."

"Your guys are good, Admiral—at finding me, anyway."

"Actually, a couple o' them came up with summat quite interestin' tha' maun have to do wi' thee, Brim."

"With me?"

"Wi' thy wee adventure at yon Met Station."

"I'm all ears, Admiral."

"You a-keepin up wi' the local news?"

"Not much…. Um, why?"

"Hear about tha' little massacre at the Green Star aboot a week ago?"

"What's the Green Star?"

"A local hang-out nigh the waterfront—where someone gae a bloody massacre."

"Begging the Admiral's pardon, but what does a massacre at a waterfront bar have to do with me?"

"Thought ye'd never ask," Calhoun said with a grin. "As a hint: wha' kind o' Starship did your BKAEW operator think he detected at the Met Station 'afore ye got there?"

"Starship at the Met station? Brim asked in confusion, then snapped his fingers. He'd almost forgotten. "I think Steele said it looked like an old Banta-class freighter. But what does that have to do with anything—especially a massacre?"

"The massacre war a bunch o' professional assassins shootin' up the whole crew of an auld Banta-class freighter named *Argonaut*. An' tha' particular ship were in space, 'NO DESTINATION LISTED,' almost a Standard Week *afore* the Met station got worked over—then returned here nearly a week *afterward*."

"Long time for an old ship to be 'NO DESTINATION LISTED,'" Brim considered. "She almost had to stop somewhere—otherwise, she'd be losing money every moment."

"Not at a'," Calhoun objected, "My guess is the whole trip were contracted to *ane* client."

"Still kind of a stretch connecting the two, isn't it, Admiral?" Brim asked.

"Not when ye consider tha' whomever worked over the Met station failed to get *ye*. And since we're nearly certain ye and your WF-400 war the real targets o' the raid, we're pretty much chalking tha' whole operation as a failure—which earned wha' maun be normal mob-style punishment."

Brim shook his head. "...Just hard to imagine people sabotaging their own side in wartime merely for credits."

"Or for *power*," Calhoun added. "The people who *hired* tha' ship: power was their motive, mak nae mistake about tha'."

After a few moments thought, Brim asked, "So what am I supposed to do about all this, Cal?"

Calhoun smiled wearily. "Aside from bein' *very* careful from here on in, there's nae much ye can do—least not for now. But I felt it war important ye know what ye're really up against. Whoever set this up made quite an investment in getting' rid of you."

"Guess I'll simply go about business as usual, then," Brim said a little helplessly. "Can't just stop what I'm doing because someone wants me out of the way. Xaxtdamned Leaguers have been trying to do that for years, and look what it's got 'em!"

"Kind o' thought tha' would be your reaction, Brim!" Calhoun said. "Sae ye'll finish helping train those new crews?"

"Of course, Cal. We ought to be complete about the middle of Triad—just after Onrad's Birthday Ball on the 15th."

"Guid," Calhoun said, "because soon after tha', I should hae' another assignment tha' maun interest ye."

Brim laughed. "I'm interested in nearly anything at this point."

"We'll get together on the details by and bye," Calhoun promised "but what it amounts to is puttin' ye back with thy old friends in Sodeskaya. What do ye think o' that?"

Brim felt himself smile. "You know I've always had a soft spot for the old G.F.S.S."

"I ken it well, Brim," Calhoun said. "An' ye're probably the only ane in The Empire who we maun send on such a mission."

"You know I'll give it my best, whatever you have in mind, Cal."

"It's all I'll ever expect of ye, Wilf."

"I'm available whenever you're ready to talk."

"I wull be soon—after Onrad's Birthday Ball. First things first, as we say. In any case, see you at the Ball."

"See you there, Cal...."

Thoughtfully, Brim slipped his HoloPhone in a pocket. Baxter Calhoun wasn't in the habit of giving out easy assignments....

Chapter 32

. . .there will be other times

AVALON/ASTURIUS, AVALON CITY, A DRAWING ROOM IN
COUNT TAL CONFISSE TRAFFORD'S RAMBLING MANSION,
15 TRIAD, 52017

Porcine in spire of his finest formal outfit, Count Tal Confisse
Trafford eased his bulk into a comfortable armchair near his
daughter, Major General Megan Trafford—also replete in her
finest dress uniform. "What seems to be troubling you, my dear?" he
asked solicitously.

"You know very well what's bothering me, Daddy," the General
pouted.

"That awful Brim fellow?" Trafford asked, sagging cheeks
reddening in spite of the makeup.

"*Of course* I mean that Brim fellow!" Trafford replied. "What else
would be worrying me? Since his court martial, I've been stuck at
Headquarters as if it were *my* fault the operation at Eppeid failed."

"Now, now, Megan...."

"Don't, 'Now, now,' me, Daddy. General Hagbutt won't let me
near anything that has to do with front-line operations. Nearly two
months ago, you said Brim would be out of the picture—and he's still
on the guest list tonight. *See!*" she raged, holding a guest list before
her father's nose. "And I'll probably have to *meet* him tonight!"

Frowning, the Count pushed the list aside, grinding his teeth with
irritation. "You know," he said, "you didn't exactly *have* to attend the
ball tonight. You could have remained home for any number of
reasons."

"Hmpf," the General sniffed, "If I don't show and *he does*, everyonc will know why."

At that moment, a butler stepped into the room., "My Lord, Madame Major General: your limousine awaits."

"Well, Megan?"

After a long pause, the General wrinkled her face, then shrugged. "I suppose I have no choice, do I?"

"No, Megan," her father replied pointedly, "you do not—unless, of course, you want people to suspect those rumors about Operation Eppeid might be true...."

— o — 0 — o —

Later, at the Palace, when Barbousse drew up under the Palace marquee, Brim handed his gift for the Emperor to a Royal Valet, who saluted stiffly, then placed Dark's colorful bag in a satin-lined hand truck, in which dozens of other, handsomely wrapped gifts for the Emperor waited to be thoroughly inspected before Onrad got within a c'lenyt of them. Glancing around the gold-encrusted vestibule, Brim nodded to a few friends preparing themselves to be announced, then, handed his cloak to a waiting footman, and strode into the announcement foyer, where he was engulfed from below in a refined babble of voices along with odors of spirits, perfume, and rich comestibles. He passed his calling card to the scarlet-clad page, then peered over the glittering assemblage below as an AnGrail sounded and his name boomed out: "Oyez, Oyez, Admiral..., er, *L-lord* Wilf Ansor Brim, First Duke of Grayson!"

"Sorry, My Lord," the man whispered as Brim started down the long staircase. "I'm a retired Blue Cape, and...."

Brim, stopped, turned, and gripped the man's arm—noticing for the first time the man's empty sleeve was pinned to his tunic. "Believe me, I'm *honored*, Star Sailor," he whispered with a wink. Then, starting down the grand staircase again, he noticed two pair of eyes glaring up from the crowd: Count Tal Confisse and Major General Megan Trafford; it looked as if they had just cleared the reception line. The Count fat, and daughter Megan in Imperial Army uniform with a skirt slit nearly to her waist. Brim emotionlessly returned their stares until both the Trafford and his daughter averted their eyes and moved off toward a Page offering goblets of meem from a golden tray. Chuckling to himself, Brim noted Megan Trafford still had a magnificently turned ankle, whatever else he thought about her.

At the foot of the stairs, a second, grandly uniformed page ushered him to the foot of the reception line with a loftily-whispered, "Madame Colifels, may I present Lord Wilf Ansor Brim, First Lord of Grayson?" Brim kissed the gloved hand proffered by the pudgy, middle-aged wife of Vice Admiral Colifels, then felt himself swallowed up in the latest of which, he estimated, were at least a billion-odd reception lines since his first a long time ago at a place he could no longer recall.

As he shook the last hand at the far side of the line, he saw a gloved hand take his arm. "I've been waiting for you, Admiral," a mellow feminine voice whispered in his ear.

Startled, Brim turned and felt his heart leap. "Margot," he said, pressing his hand over hers, "I've been waiting for *you* all my life." She was exquisite in another long, strapless gown in a pale yellowish orange cut low across her bust to show off what he remembered as smallish, but perfect, breasts. With her perfect skin, she always came off as the most beautiful creature he had ever encountered. "How are you," he asked, looking deep into her blue eyes.

She squeezed his arm and smiled, her red lips forming a perfect bow. "Better than yesterday, not quite as well as I shall be tomorrow." For a moment, she closed her eyes, then looked at him with that half-sleepy look he remembered so well. "Buy a lady a drink?" she asked.

"I, ah, I thought you weren't drinking," Brim stumbled.

"That was then; now is now," she said in a half whisper. "It's time I tried, and if it doesn't work, I'm not too far from home."

Brim nodded to a page carrying goblets of what where sure to be excellent Logish Meem—Onrad's cellars were legendary. He took a goblet from the tray and handed it to Margot; the second goblet he raised and gently touched its rim to hers. To you, Margot," he said, "both beautiful and strong."

She raised the goblet to her lips, closed her eyes momentarily as if gathering herself, then sipped as Brim sipped his. For a moment, her eyes became distant as she savored the taste, then gave a sad little smile. "I still love the 'beautiful,'" she said, "the 'strong is wearing a bit thin these days."

"Sorry," Brim backpedaled.

"Oh, it's all right," Margot whispered. "But I've been recuperating for so awfully long. Perhaps it's time to declare I'm cured and take up living again." Then she smiled. "Right now, though, I'm quite happy to simply hang on to your arm as if I should fall without it." She looked directly into his eyes. "You don't mind, do you?"

Brim chuckled. "How could I mind having the most gorgeous woman in the Known Universe on my arm?"

Again, Margot unconsciously touched the scar on her cheek. "Thanks, Wilf," she whispered, "even if you are the only one in the Known Universe who would say that."

Brim gently led her to a sideboard at one end of the room and set his drink on it. The noisy ball around them seemed to have disappeared: only he and Margot existed in this special universe.

Margot slowly set her Meem beside his with both hands. "It's enough," she said in a small voice, still peering at the goblet as if it were alive. "I've proved I can set it down. It's a huge step for now."

Brim put his arm around her shoulders and pressed her to his side. "I can only imagine what you have been through," he whispered in her ear, "but I truly believe what you have just shared with me." As he spoke, he felt her arm glide around his waist.

"It's been a long time and many lives since we touched so, Wilf Brim," she whispered.

"Too long—and too many lives," Brim agreed, more shakily than he wanted to admit. "W-where do we go from here?"

"I don't know," she replied, taking her arm from his waist, "but your closeness is having effects I don't think I am prepared for just yet."

Reluctantly, Brim released her, but instead of stepping away, she took his arm again. "Is this all right?" she asked.

"Anything and everything you do is all right," Brim assured her. "What would you like to do?"

She got a faraway look for a moment. "With the meem, I got past some of my addiction fears tonight," she said softly. "If I had my way—and you were willing—I'd smuggle you back to my suite and try to make up for all the years we've been apart. But I'm not quite ready for emotions strong as, well, making love. Especially with you, my wonderful lover. From what I have been told, I am still capable of falling completely apart again—I don't want that."

Brim his breath for a moment, terrified he might not be able to speak. Then, desperately grabbing his own emotions, he looked into her eyes. "Margot...," he began.

"Don't say anything, Wilf," she breathed, placing a finger to his lips. "Not now.... Not yet...."

"Bu...."

"Wilf, dearest," she interrupted again, "Never mistake me for the Margot you once knew. I am not that woman—she died a number of years ago— *Standard* Years. I exist in the husk of what she was, trying to fill it with life again, a little at a time, as I find strength to do so."

"What can I do to help?" Brim asked.

Margot drew a deep breath, then gently took his hand. "I don't know, Wilf," she said softly. "Since the hazy beginnings of my cure, I have avoided as much sentient contact as I could, except the family of healers from the Lampson Provinces—the 'Speakers to All.' But, especially tonight, I sense the time approaches when I must attempt more contact with my own kind—like you, Wilf Brim."

"I shall be at your service whenever I am able," Brim swore with more emotion than he'd felt for a long time. "Margot," he whispered, "you only have to ask."

"And I *shall* ask, Wilf," she promised. Then, squeezing his hand, she dropped her eyes. "I must go now," she said in a small voice.

"No, Margot we've only...."

"Please, Wilf," she said. "There will be other times. Be patient with me, please...." Then, before Brim could react, she turned and disappeared into the crowd.

Helplessly, Brim knew better than to pursue, gradually surfacing back into the noisy, glittering ball. Dumbly, he glanced at the little sideboard where their two goblets of Meem sat side by side, nearly untouched. He lifted hers to his lips and drank deeply. Then, replacing it on the table, he took his own and made his way across the room to where a grandly outfitted Porterfield Marston—sporting a gold, paisley brocade vest—appeared to be in deep discussion with a short man dressed in a severe business suit....

Chapter 33

. . .a modicum of mystery

AVALON/ASTURIUS, AVALON CITY, A BALLROOM AT THE
IMPERIAL PALACE: ONRAD'S NAME-DAY BALL, 15 TRIAD,
52017

Frowning, Count Trafford, watched Brim stride across the room. "That *was* Princess Margot Effer'wyck with Brim wasn't it?" he asked.

"Certainly looked like her," his daughter replied. "Wasn't she involved with him a number of years ago?"

"Well, there *were* rumors about something like that—*while* she was married to that Rogan LaKarn, as I remember. She always had a reputation for, shall we say, *adventurous living.*"

"Yes, there were always rumors of one sort or another," the General replied. "I heard she'd been killed a while back—something like that."

Trafford narrowed his eyes. "Clearly, *that* rumor was false," he said grumpily. "You know, Megan, it's said she has the ear of her cousin Onrad."

"*She's* Onrad's cousin?"

"Megan," Trafford said angrily, "you *must* keep better track of potential dangers in the Court."

"Who said she is a danger—and to whom?"

"To *you*," Trafford growled.

"But why?"

"Because if Effer'wyck is indeed a close relative of Onrad—and if Brim and Effer'wyck again become lovers—then that Carescrian will gain even more traction with Onrad. Surely you know what that means."

166

Suddenly, Megan Trafford closed her eyes and clenched her fists. "Why does everything think that I'm to blame for the disaster Operation Eppeid turned out to be? It certainly wasn't my fault."

Trafford rolled his eyes. "Of course, my dear," he reassured her. "But Brim is the typical wily product of the space slums—he should never have been permitted into the Helmsman's Academy. We of the privileged class must forever be on our guard against such people who want to deprive us of what is rightly ours."

"Yes. Imagine his sort of trash here at the Palace on a night like this. Disgraceful. Daddy. You must not fail to take care of him the next time."

"Unfortunately," Trafford said, "because the idiots I hired to do that job failed so spectacularly, it will be at least twice as difficult the next time. Perhaps impossible."

"But you will try Daddy—won't you?"

"Oh you may be sure I shall, Megan, dear. You may be sure!"

— o — 0 — o —

Brim felt himself break out in a grin as he pushed his way through the crowd toward Porterfield Marston.

"Mmmm, yes," Marston called out, "...it's M' Lord Brim, if I'm not mistaken!" Outfitted in a rich, blue-velvet coatee with expensively embroidered collar, cuffs, and pocket flaps, he also wore black-velvet trousers festooned by a gold oak-lace stripe and shiny, patent-leather buckled shoes.

"Guilty as charged, Porterfield," Brim said, taking Marston's proffered hand.

"Yes, yes," Marston mumbled, "..and you must meet this handsome gentleman beside me: Doctor Factovar Zinnkin, an old friend from the mysterious World of Forensic Finance."

"Honored to meet you, M'Lord," the slim, elegantly dressed man said, extending his hand with a piercing look. "I've certainly heard a bit about you."

Brim made a faux grimace. "Anything good?" he asked, returning the man's firm handshake.

"Well," Zinnkin said, indicating Marston with an airy gesture, "this gentleman certainly speaks well of you."

"I fool people a lot," Brim quipped. "But thanks friend," he said, with a wink.

"How about if you gentlemen allow me buy you two an excellent Logish Meem," Marston offered expansively, "Hmm—with Onrad's money, or course?"

Brim felt himself break out in a grin. "The price is certainly right," he said.

All three lifted a Logish Meem from a convenient tray proffered by one of the ever-present servants, then raised their goblets. "To Voot," Marston toasted, "...may his beard be ever clean and starchy."

"To clean and starchy beards," Brim and Zinnkin returned in unison, touching their goblets to Marston's.

When all three had toasted, Marston turned to Zinnkin and nodded. "Yes, Hmm. Rather hoped to put you two together tonight," he said. "Especially with Count Trafford and Madame General in such close proximity. Hmm."

"Oh?" Brim asked, raising an eyebrow.

"Provides a chance to judge body language," Zinnkin explained. "People reveal so much about what they're thinking that way."

"And what *are* they revealing tonight?" Marston asked, indicating the Traffords with a nod.

"Most upset," Zinnkin said, stroking his elegantly trimmed beard, "Especially when you, M'Lord, were with Ms. Effer'wyck."

"Margot?" Brim asked, surprised. "You've been watching *me*, too?"

"Of course," Zinnkin said with his mysterious little smile.

"Marston," Brim demanded, "what's going on here?"

"Hmm, yes...," Marston mumbled. "...all part of a quiet plot...."

"A quiet, *what*?"

"Hmm... a plot to avoid seeing you killed, my wealthy client."

"Huh?"

"Well, yes.... Mmm." Marston explained, "Admiral Calhoun seems to want you alive as much as I do."

"Admiral Calhoun?"

"Of course. He suspects very wealthy people are attempting to off you, so he suggested I find someone who is skilled at following money trails."

"I don't get it," Brim protested.

"Hmm. Yes.... You explain it, Factovar," Marston rumbled.

Brim turned to Zinnkin with a raised eyebrow.

"Simple, M'Lord," the elegant little man said, "—extremely wealthy people like your suspected enemies hire others to do their dirty work. That costs credits—often *lots* of credits. I follow the trails their money leaves behind. Simple as that."

"Hmm, yes.... As *complicated* as that," Marston interjected. "Factovar's the best in a hazardous and secretive business."

Zinnkin made a little smile. "Porterfield," he said with a frown, "I hardly know hazards, compared to the dangers Lord Brim here has faced."

Brim held up a hand; in the corner of his eye, he'd spied a flash of blond hair. He glanced in that direction—in time to momentarily lock eyes with Ann Hunt, as she was swept by into the swirl of dancers. "Er," he stuttered off guard, "...e-each of us faces his own unique risks".

"You look as if you've seen a ghost," Zinnkin said with a smile.

"An old friend," Brim said, recovering.

"Yes. Hmm," Marston remarked. "That blonde didn't look *old* to me."

"An acquaintance, then" Brim explained with a shrug. "Met her at a conference some time ago."

"Hmm, yes... a fine looking acquaintance, nonetheless," Marston said. "I'll wish you luck with that one."

"But...," Brim began, but he never had a chance to continue....

"Uh oh," Zinnkin interrupted, sliding a tiny HoloPhone from his coat pocket and glancing intently at the display. "Interestingly enough, I believe we've begun to make a little progress on this very project." He nodded to Marston. "Porter," he said, "it's time for both of us to leave this elegant party. We have work to do...."

Moments later, The two men had made their adieus, and were working their way toward the grand staircase, leaving Brim to finish his second goblet of Meem and reflect that he might well no longer wear a Fleet Cloak, but even so, his life never lacked at least a modicum of mystery.

Chapter 34

. . .a top-secret *request*

AVALON/ASTURIUS, AVALON CITY, A BALLROOM AT THE
IMPERIAL PALACE: ONRAD'S NAME-DAY BALL, 16 TRIAD,
52017

As the evening wore on, Brim traded glances a number of times with the elegant Hunt woman, but each time, she seemed almost wholly consumed by the tall, handsome young Admiral she'd introduced that night at the bar.

Wryly, Brim chuckled to himself. Somehow, the man's name eluded him—but not his rank. Oh, he was a very junior, bottom-of-the-ladder Rear Admiral, but if nothing else, he was a genuine Blue Cape. And like himself, when he'd been privileged to wear *The Cape*, he'd often had no use for civilians. He was just about to signal Barbousse to bring the car, when once again he locked glances with Ann Hunt—and this time, she was seated at one of the many tiny bars scattered throughout the huge ballroom—*alone*. She was absolutely stunning in a red cocktail dress that revealed a great deal of lovely flesh, long, shapely legs, and diminutive feet in high-heeled, golden sandals.

She smiled and gave a shy wave.

With a strangely familiar sensation in his gut, Brim made his way to her side, expecting any moment to be shooed away by her apparent captor. "Commander Hunt," he said, bowing to kiss her hand.

"Lord Brim," she replied apparently surprised by the gesture from another age.

"I'd much prefer, 'Wilf,'" Brim said.

"And I, 'Ann,'" she returned with a friendly smile.

"Always nice to break the ice," Brim said, much encouraged. "What brings you to Avalon this trip?"

"Took some leave this time," she said. "Coriander was invited to Onrad's Name Day Ball, and he wanted me here with him, so here I am."

"Coriander?"

"Rear Admiral Coriander Hendrix, my fiancée," she explained. "I introduced you the last time we met here in Avalon."

Brim smiled in spite of himself. "Ah, yes," he said blandly. "I should have recalled."

"He *was* very unpleasant at the time," she admitted.

"Why, I recall nothing of the sort," Brim equivocated.

"*Of course*, you don't," she said with a sad little smile. "But I do, and I've felt rather bad about it ever since. He has no regard for... civilians," I suppose. "No even a *retired* Admiral," she added pointedly.

Brim felt his cheeks burn. "Unfortunately," he said, "I wasn't given the option of retirement."

"Oh, I know, M'Lord..., er Wilf," she said shaking her head for a moment, then looking directly into his eye. "But like most of my military colleagues, I saw your trial for the travesty it was." She shrugged. "By the way, I noticed General Trafford is here tonight with her Father. Don't suppose you two have had any long conversations."

Brim chuckled with a mock frown. "For some *imponderable* reason, we've kept missing each other all evening."

"Imponderable," Hunt repeated with an impish smile.

"Hey," Brim interjected, "It's not as if I'm no longer in the fight."

"I'm quite sure you're in it right up to your ears," she replied. "Rumor has it you're on another super-secret assignment. It's just that if something like that can happen to you, then all us Blue Capes are at risk when we run afoul of politics."

"No comment," Brim said. "Sometimes, it's just a matter of being in the right place at the wrong time."

"Or the other way 'round," she said with an ironic smile.

"So how long will you be in town?" Brim asked, changing the subject.

"Not long," she replied. "I'll brief Admiral Calhoun tomorrow afternoon, then leave by the end of the week. Soon as I can cadge myself a ride back to Gantaclar."

"When did you get here?" Brim asked.

"Yesterday."

"Not much of a visit," Brim observed. "Especially with nearly four days' travel on each end."

"Lucky to get that, I suppose," she said. "These days, it's difficult to take the leave one earns."

"A big job you've got on your hands, Ann," Brim observed.

"Yes," she said, "but in this case, I really had no choice but to take the time. Coriander made it clear my being at the Ball tonight was extremely important to his career."

"How about *yours*?" Brim asked, but never got an answer…

"Well come *on*, Ann," a clearly overwrought Rear Admiral Hendrix interrupted, stepping in front of Brim as if Brim never existed. "There are so many important people I want to meet before this is over."

"Coriander!" Hunt complained. "I *was* talking to Admiral Brim."

Hendrix turned around. "Admiral?" he asked. "Oh, Brim. Hello. Surprised to see you here, old man. How did you find your way into such an occasion?"

Brim shrugged. "Like everyone except Onrad," he said with a smile, "I had an invitation."

"Clearly taken aback, Hendrix frowned. "Surprising," he said. "After the mix-up with General Trafford, I wouldn't have thought to see you at events like this."

"Coriander!" Hunt interrupted.

"Coriander, *what*?" Hendrix demanded, clearly irritated.

Brim stepped in quickly. "Ann," he said placatingly, "I'm certain Admiral Hendrix meant nothing…"

"Certainly, not, Old man," Hendrix said. "Just wondered what would get you invited to something like Onrad's Name Day Ball."

Brim paused to take a deep breath. "Oh, I still have a few friends in the right places, Admiral," he said patiently.

"I guess you do," Hendrix allowed, then turned to Hunt. "Well, come on, Ann," he urged, taking her hand, "There are ever so many more people I have to meet tonight. I'm sure Mister Brim knows how important contacts are to one's career."

"*Lord* Brim," Hunt corrected.

"Oh, well that explains everything," Hendrix said, practically pulling Hunt from her bar stool. "No wonder you've stayed here in Avalon, Brim."

"One lives where one must," Brim said, once again mastering his temper. Then, reaching into his vest pocket, he withdrew a business card: TopLine Spacecraft Performance, he handed it to Hunt. "Commander," he said, "If you'll contact the third link on this card tomorrow—and ask for Chief Barbousse—I believe he'll be able find you an extra-fast ride back to Gantaclar."

"Seriously?" she asked. "Can you just… .*do* that?"

"I can," Brim assured her. "It'll give you and the Admiral a week of extra time here before you head home."

"W-well, …thank you, M'Lord," she said with a little curtsy.

"Yes, thanks, Brim," Hendrix said pulling Hunt off into the crowd. "Damn good of you," he called over his shoulder. Then, they were gone.

Brim shook his head, then shrugged—it took all kinds of people to make a Fleet—some climbed the ladder with actions; others with "contacts." He smiled to himself. Whatever else Hendrix had going for himself, he had one Xaxt of a sweet, good-looking Fiancée.

After private drinks with Emperor Onrad, Admiral Calhoun, and a few old friends, Brim, said his Good Evenings, then summoned Barbousse and the Phantom III to the Palace marquee. On the way home, he suggested to the Chief that a special WF-400 training flight might be in order during the next few days—perhaps to set a record from Avalon to Gantaclar.

"To Gantaclar, Skipper?" Barbousse asked picking his way through late night traffic.. "That would be some run! We could do a quick refresh at the Met station, then make it to Gantaclar in a couple of Metacycles. When d' you suppose we ought do it?"

"Don't know, Chief. Probably in the next couple of days," Brim said with a grin from the back seat. "I think you'll get a HoloPhone call tomorrow from that nice Commander Ann Hunt we met at the Gantaclar Conference

"*Ah!* She's in town?"

"Yeah. Saw her and her fiancée at the Ball tonight."

"Nice looking lady."

"Oh, she *is*."

"And I'll bet she'd really be pleased to get a quick ride back home," Barbousse suggested.

"I'm sure she would," Brim assured him. "It would give her an extra week with the boyfriend, too."

"Why don't I schedule the test run to coincide with her trip home?" Barbousse suggested.

"What a great idea!" Brim exclaimed.

"I'll set it up, Skipper," Barbousse said. "In fact, since you're shippin' out soon, I'll put some newbie from the training pool in the right seat, then fly the mission myself—in our own *Four Nines.* How about that?"

"What?" Brim demanded. "*I'm* shipping out?"

"That you are, Skipper," Barbousse said. "Surprised me too. Day after tomorrow. The orders are waitin' on yer mail server."

"Voot's greasy beard!" Brim exclaimed with a chuckle. "Don't I have *any* privacy."

"Only when you want it," the Chief replied.

"Okay, I understand *that*, Chief. Who are the orders from?"

"That Case guy over at the Interspace Transport Bureau."

"Barny Case? How can he issue orders to me?"

"Kind of a top-secret *request*, Skipper."

"For what?"

"They want you to ride a freighter in a convoy from here to that big harbor Caer Landria on Carescria's Burtis/Celeron—then write a paper an how to improve the convoy system from a merchantmen's viewpoint."

"Makes sense," Brim observed thoughtfully. "Probably I can do some good there—and we're practically finished with our WF-400 training assignment tomorrow. Still," he said scratching his head absently, "Wonder why Calhoun didn't mention this."

"Have no idea, Skipper"

"Doesn't matter, I suppose," Brim said. "Calhoun hasn't come up with the job in Sodeskaya he was talking about anyway, so I ought to be back in plenty of time before he makes up his mind."

"Sounds good to me," Barbousse replied. "Now about this Commander Hunt: I assume you want the VIP treatment for her?"

"Everything first class; wouldn't have it any other way."

"Skipper," Barbousse said, "Commander Hunt will think she's died and gone to heaven. How about that?"

"Chief," Brim said rolling his eyes, "you always did have a way of reading my alleged mind…"

Chapter 35

. . .the S.S. Purple Abigail

ORBITING AVALON/ASTURIUS, APPROACHING *S.S. PURPLE ABAGAIL*, A MERCHANTMAN, 18 TRIAD, 52017.

O rbital dockyards above Avalon were anything but orderly, with ungainly, non-landing-capable starship freighters in orbit at a dozen levels in seemingly random patterns. Whole fleets of lighters careened among the freighters in every dimension at breakneck speeds, reminding Brim of the awful traffic below in Avalon City—only worse. He grinned as the Helmsman of the little orbital buss picked her way through the confusion, steering as surely as if her many destinations had been at their locations for ages, instead of days, at the most.

His companions in the passenger compartment were a mixed lot at best, from neatly uniformed civilian officers to grizzled Star Sailors whose eyes had seen a thousand different worlds throughout the galaxy—none of which could be called *home*. S.S. *Purple Abigail*, Brim's destination, was the buss' sixth drop-off of the morning, according to his unofficial orders, she was nearly loaded and ready to join a Convoy 33A-98G bound for Carescria.

As the bus approached, Brim contemplated the elderly freighter that would be his home for the next weeks, wondering how she'd managed to survive all the years of hard use—as well as the exigencies of warfare in space. She was older than he was! If nothing else, this *Abagail* was clearly a survivor.

Peering through the windshield of the bus, Brim compared what he could see of the hull against ancient plans Barny Case had included with his "orders" from the Interspace Transport Bureau the previous day. The little freighter appeared to be all of her promised 350 irals in length, but not an iral more—a good point because many of these aging ships had been expanded to hold more cargo, and often such expansions disastrously failed after only a few years in service.

Built for easy loading and unloading rather than beauty, she was little more than a large pressure vessel, dented and pockmarked by thousands of collisions with space debris and Voot knew what else. She mounted ancient RG-199A Drive Units, located at the end of skeletal pylons on either side of what, by default, *had* to be her aft end. Eight large—also antiquated—spin-gravs open to space ringed the hull just aft of the Drive pylons to provide what limited maneuvering a ship like this would possess. An awkward, circular "bridge"—looking more like a can of fish than anything else—perched perilously at the "top" of the forward end of the ship, ringed by a thin line of Hyperscreens. Eight small LifeGlobes were set into a half deck beneath the aft end of the bridge. Brim sincerely hoped his experience aboard the old freighter would not provide a ride in any of *those* antiques.

Built for commerce rather than comfort, Brim knew she would offer a minimum of habitation to her hard-working crew. This was how the majority of spacemen made their meager livings—spending most of their lives, shuttling back and forth in the nothingness of the void. He shivered. By the grace of Voot, he *could* have spent his life that way, too.

When the Helmsman had secured the bus to the old freighter and clamped her hatch to the boarding tube, Brim summoned his valise, paid his fare, and glided through the air curtain into a tiny airlock. As the hatch clanged shut behind him and locked, the atmosphere reeked with dozens of odors left over from countless uncrated cargoes of Voot knew what—all overlaid with the rank stench of a bilge that hadn't been cleaned for generations and a galley located somewhere nearby in which someone was cooking garn cabbage. Brim chuckled to himself. This voyage did not promise to be one of gastronomic delight.

"Lord Brim?" crackled from a wall speaker.

"That's me."

"Welcome aboard *Purple Abagail*. Come on up to the bridge and I shall show you where to stow your gear."

"Which way's the bridge?"

"See the red line painted on the deck?"

"I do."

"Follow it; you'll be on bridge in a couple cycles—depending on how fast you move in zero gravity."

"On my way." Brim said, frowning. *Could the Captain be a Sodeskayan?* He thought to himself. *Sure sounded like one.* Summoning his valise, he skipped off into the ship itself. Six cycles' worth of making his way through narrow passageways, and high galleries overlooking the vast cauldron of a hull—which was nearly filled by countless containers of Voot knew what—he arrived at an open hatch with a faded sign overhead reading, "WIPE YOUR FEET," in Avalonian script.

Brim wiped his feet, then knocked on the bulkhead beside the hatch.

"Lord Brim?" came from inside.

"*Wilf* Brim, Captain," Brim corrected.

"Well, come on in, then, Wilf Brim."

Stepping over the coaming, Brim entered and found himself in a surprisingly modern-looking starship bridge within a completely circular planform. At the forward end, a heavy-set man rose slowly from the left-hand Helmsman's console and made his way to where Brim was standing. "Name's Verger," the man said, offering his hand, "Verger Antillies. I'm Captain of this old wreck."

"Wilf Brim," the Carescrian said, grasping the Captain's warm, dry hand. "Guess we're going to be seeing each other for the next couple of weeks."

Antillies laughed. "Well, we'll hope so," he said, "but these days, ya' never know. Guess that's why you're here, *Admiral Brim.*"

Brim Grimaced. "Not 'Admiral' lately, Captain."

"The once and future Admiral," Antilles said with a guffaw. "Seems I've heard that somewhere.

"Not from me, Captain," Brim said. "I'm here to work—and to learn everything I can about what it's like in a convoy."

"Ya' must really want learnin' pretty bad, then," Antilles said mordantly. "Benders are picking off more and more of us every convoy."

"That's why I'm here."

"Damned if I'd be out here if I didn't have to be—and you *don't*, as I understand."

"But you're not me, Captain."

"Aye, that's for certain, Carescrian," the old Captain said, "but doesn't say I don't admire you for doin' it—'specially if you manage to bring about some results while you're along."

"I'll try," Brim promised.

"That's all any of us freighter jockeys ask," Antilles replied, pushing past Brim and gliding for the hatch at the aft-most portion of the bridge. "Now, let me show you to your stateroom. Whoever picked this old tub for you to ride in did you one favor—we've got a couple of decent staterooms. Used to rent them out before Triannic decided he wanted a couple of wars."

"Guess that ruined the tourist trade," Brim observed as he followed Antilles through the aft hatch and down a long companionway.

"*Ruin* ain't the word for it, Brim," Antilles said, opening a hatch at the lower end of the companionway, then signaling Brim to follow. "Can't remember when I've had a taker in years." He stopped at the first entryway he came to. "Give you the bridal suite," he said with a laugh, and opened the hatch to a roomy compartment with a large, round Hyperscreen, two ample bunks, and two large dressers with mirrors. "Ya' got your private head through that hatch," Antilles explained. "And the mess is open all day. Just serve yourself. If you want anything special, let me know. I make it a point of eating well on these trips, so I doubt if you'll starve to death."

"Couldn't ask for more," Brim replied, considerably impressed. He signaled his valise onto the bunk, then checked his timepiece. "When do we shove off, Captain?"

Antilles drew his own, huge timepiece from a vest pocket, squinted at it, and frowned. "Lessee," he mumbled. "It's Morning plus two and fifteen. I figure we'll get underway in another metacycle, so say Morning: plus three: fifteen—local gravity five cycles before. We'll

180

form up the convoy while we're moving and ought to be pretty well into deep space no later than Brightness plus three."

Brim checked his own timepiece, glanced at Antilles' mechanical antique, and decided *close enough.*

"See you on the bridge in half a metacycle," Antillies said. "Long enough to settle in?"

"Be with you in a lot less than that," Brim promised with a serious mien. As always, he found himself eager to get on with the new mission.

— o — 0 — o —

From information accompanying his "orders", Brim knew *Purple Abigail's* crew was made up mostly from refugees of the Fluvannian Fleet; none spoke Imperial Avalonian—or at least would admit to it. Since he could barely make his way in Fluvannian, he planned to communicate—when he had to—by means of smiles and gesticulations. Because he was merely an observer, responsible for nothing, he was free to concentrate on his surroundings.

As soon as he reached the Bridge, Antilles assigned him a comfortable console with a good view of the forward Hyperscreens. From that point on, the Carescrian stayed out of the way as much as possible while the ship got underway.

— o — 0 — o —

While Brim concentrated on learning everything he could about the complex process of forming up a convoy, he failed to notice an elderly mess-hand who entered the bridge to place a tray of cvc'eese mugs on a bulkhead table. At changeover to local gravity, the tiny woman was back, taking a careful look at Brim while he was desperately attempting to swallow his gorge. At this, nodded to herself with a secret smile, and scuttled back to the galley where she quickly made a call on her *darkened* HoloPhone before the ship could travel beyond range in the harbor.

Chapter 36

. . .Convoy 33A-98G

IN SPACE ABOARD *S.S. PURPLE ABAGAIL* 19 TRIAD, 52017

During the next Metacycles, *Purple Abagail* and 23 other merchantmen became Convoy 33A-98G bound for the sprawling Carescrian port of Caer Landria on Burtis/Celeron. Struggling into a ragged, three-dimensional formation, the lumbering starships slowly, painfully increasing their speed through HyperLight. Only after nearly a half-day's acceleration did the convoy reach an agreed-upon cruse velocity of 12 LPM and begin the complex maneuvers of zigzagging in formation.

From years' experience, Brim knew the convoy would roughly approximate a matrix of three layers, each consisting of eight merchantmen, each separated from its nearest neighbors by half a c'lenyt. Surrounding *this* convoy, he understood, two destroyers and five picket ships would maintain a steady patrol, constantly on the lookout for Leaguer activity—especially benders. He wished them good hunting, but knew at best they could provide only reactive protection to their charges. Long before benders got within detection distance of their victims, they dodged into cloaked mode and stayed that way until they were ready to attack.

Occasionally, squadrons of conventional League warships ventured into the space to attack important convoys too—usually a pair of capital ships plus escorts. The result was almost sure destruction for the thin-skinned merchantmen as well as their escorts, the latter obliged to sacrifice themselves in hopes some merchantmen might escape in the confusion. Luckily, these disastrous attacks occurred rarely, as Leaguer Grand Admiral Kabul Ana was clearly adverse to risking his capital ships on unimportant targets—especially since benders were small, relatively inexpensive, as well as much easier to replace.

But cloaking had its disadvantages: uncloaked, Benders were relatively speedy for conventional starships and normally traveled in this mode except when making an attack. When cloaked, however, speed was cut by two thirds at a minimum—more often, three fourths. Moreover, cloaking worked *both* ways. To see "outside" its own cloaking, a bender was forced to open "windows" in the cloak itself— and these were "visible," even at Hyperspeed. Windows were also necessary to aim and fire HyperTorps—but even at that, cloaked benders were difficult to spot under most circumstances. Occasionally, when they encountered lone merchantmen, benders attacked uncloaked, using small-diameter disruptors mounted on their decks to save HyperTorps for cloaked attacks. Nevertheless, from the standpoint of the average merchantman, benders existed as terrifying wraiths because they attacked, seemingly out of nowhere—and *anywhere*.

At relatively short ranges, escort vessels could defeat a bender's cloaking by smothering the little starships with the same N-rays that are universally used to combat radiation fires. But, without long-range, high-speed patrolling by astroplanes—with the speed to catch uncloaked benders when they are cruising—these little starships were a severe problem for the Empire and her allies.

— o — 0 — o —

During the next eight days, Brim carefully noted the complex rhythms of life aboard a slow merchantman half-lost in the middle of a Convoy. The more he studied, the more the convoy began to resemble a living creature, with its individual starships—merchantman and escort alike—acting as organs and the senior destroyer its brain. Its one purpose during a short life was to arrive at some set destination with as much of itself intact as possible: not an easy trick in wartime.

This was a far different war than the one to which he had become accustomed over the years. Since his first tour on IFS *Truculent* back in 51994, his war had been one of attack: destroying, killing, capturing—all aggressive actions. To sit and wait—helplessly—for an attack to occur was disconcerting at best. He quickly built a deep respect for these Star Sailors who plied space in slow, ungainly starships that served as easy prey for any sort of enemy that happened to cross its route.

Convoy 33A-98G's first attack came ten days into the mission. Brim was snoozing in his stateroom toward the end of the second, eight-metacycle Watch when the ship's siren announced "Action Stations." Attuned to a lifetime of such alerts, he was instantly awake and aware of his surroundings. Swiftly—but carefully—donning his battle suit, he sealed the helmet and gloves, then pushed his way to the bridge through a tide of crewmen in the narrow corridor.

On the bridge, he felt the freighter rock slightly from gravity anomalies caused by a huge asteroid shoal the convoy was paralleling for cover. The rocky formation extended for light years into the distance forward.

"Looks to me like the real thing, Brim," Verger warned, turning in his seat to make his point. "You'll want to be solid on your recliner."

"Thanks, Captain," Brim said, setting the old-fashioned seat controls to a point where his restraints were quite tight.

Glancing out the starboard Hyperscreens again, he guessed the initial attack would probably come from the port side, high or low. He forced himself to relax even while his muscles keyed to the stress he knew was coming.

Off to port—as he predicted—a few suspicious lights winked on and off.

Abruptly one of the escorts—a Corvette—sped past on the starboard side at full speed—disruptors indexing and Drive plumes blazing as it curved to the left leaving a glowing green wake as its Drive crystals were throttled up to maximum power.

Ahead and to port of the speeding escort, a muzzy image began to materialize. The corvette's N-ray projectors were defeating a bender's cloaking mechanisms. Like most of its sisters, the deadly little bender resembled a sort of hooded asp, with the control room immediately above the hood and six torpedo tubes spread across what would have been the creature's mouth

"Look," someone shouted, "he's uncovered the bender!"

"Get the Zukeed!" another exclaimed.

Before the bender was fully visible, the corvette fired and missed, its disruptor beams drilling into space to disperse harmlessly in the distance.

"Come on. How could you miss at that range?" someone exclaimed angrily.

"Yeah, don't let 'im get away...."

As if the Corvette's gun crew had heard, the little ship fired again, this time her gunners didn't miss. A bright ball of roiling radiation fire engulfed the bender's port side. Immediately, the viperish little ship became fully visible and a HyperTorp shot spasmodically from one of its tubes.

"Got 'im good!"

"Yeah! That one won't give us much more...."

The corvette—now nearly on top of the stricken bender—fired again. This time, the Leaguer disappeared in a huge, red and orange blossom of radiation fire, with the corvette pulling up sharply to pass over the roiling fireball.

As the *Purple Abagail's* bridge crew cheered wildly, Brim ground his teeth. After such an explosion, there would be no operable LifeGlobes in the bender—so the crew was cheering while men died slow painful deaths from radiation burns or suffocation.

Only an instant later, a HyperTorp's long fiery tail appeared to come from nowhere, homing in on the corvette with tremendous speed. On the bridge, the cheering turned to shouts of horror when the corvette, itself, disappeared in pulsing, red-and yellow paroxysm of radiation fire, trailing only a sparse few LifeGlobes before guttering out like a spent candle.

No sooner than the corvette's glowing remains had passed astern, out ahead another merchantman blew up, trailing no LifeGlobes Brim could see.

Too late one of the destroyers rushed in from high port, but evidentially found nothing as it curved away toward the front of the convoy.

Moments later, two more merchantmen were hit simultaneously off to port. At once, the remaining escorts blasted away at the area where the two stricken merchantmen were attempting to continue on, but appeared to hit nothing. Brim found himself straining helplessly against his restraints, wanting—*needing*—to fight back, yet all he could do was watch helplessly as the benders wreaked their slaughter.

Then, as suddenly as the attack had begun, it was apparently over. After nearly a metacycle of enormous stress, the ship's siren sounded all clear, and—almost as if the attack had never happened—the diminished convoy continued plowing through space toward Burtis/Celeron and Caer Landria.

— o — 0 — o —

On the 12th Standard Day out from Avalon, *Purple Abagail's* siren sounded again, sending the crew members scuttling to retrieve battle suits then racing for their action stations, there to wait for another attack to begin. From long experience, Brim kept his battle suit rolled into a tight cylinder at the foot of his console, along with his helmet. Heart in his mouth, he donned them quickly and rushed to the forward Hyperscreens, but nothing outside had manifested itself when— unexpectedly— "ALL CLEAR" sounded at the same moment a familiar shape sped between the convoy and a bright gas giant nearby, silhouetting itself for an instant against the light. Brim recognized the shape immediately—a Wakefield, obviously throttled 'way back, circling the convoy in lazy orbits.

For a moment, Brim wondered who it could be, then smiled. *Of course*! It was Barbousse out there, taking Ann Hunt back to Gantaclar on Linfarne/Navron via the Met Station. For a moment, he wished he could somehow send a greeting—a message of some sort—but here in the convoy lanes, everyone kept strict KA'PPA silence. As the little ship sped into the distance and disappeared, he shrugged. Long as he could remember, space and the vehicles plying its endless light years had been his chosen element. But astroplanes had changed everything. Guiltily, he glanced around the bridge of the little merchantman. He'd left this part of his age-old trade and stepped into a whole new dimension of speed. Only Voot knew how these swift little machines would affect the peace that, eventually, would follow the war—no matter what side managed to come out on top when the fighting stopped.

Chapter 37

. . .HyperTorped!

IN SPACE ABOARD *S.S. PURPLE ABAGAIL*, 32 TRIAD, 52017

Less than a day later, Brim had only just taken his place on the bridge and was scanning ahead through a haze of flickering radiation from a nearby gravity storm when the deck leaped under his recliner with tremendous concussion; the ship's local gravity pulsed violently, then failed—along with the bridge's unprotected crew-restraint system.

Suddenly. Brim found himself floating above the deck in the midst of total confusion. Feeling his breath pulled from him, he jammed on his helmet and sealed it, taking long gasps of air while he donned and sealed his gloves. Throughout the bridge, those who refused to wear battle suits until an actual attack were spinning helplessly, writhing in agony as boiling blood foamed out of every orifice. Others, already dead, floated like rag dolls. Summoning all his energy, Brim pushed off from a seat back toward a crewman who couldn't seem to lock his helmet, but in the cycles it took to reach the man, he suddenly stiffened, eyes popping out of their sockets.

Death everywhere! Nobody likes wearing battle suits, but in the Fleet, when under threat, you wore them all the time. In this civilian fleet, they didn't. Something he would make sure he changed—when—and *if*—he made it back to Avalon.

Suddenly, "Abandon ship!" thundered over the COMM circuits. "Abandon Ship." Gently pushing the corpse's eyes back into their sockets, Brim closed the helmet, then pushed himself away and floated aft—along with pitifully few survivors, none of whom seemed to know anything about LifeGlobes.

Quickly taking charge on the LifeGlobe deck, Brim filled 'Globes One and Two with ten survivors each—including Captain Antillies — put an Engineer each at their controls, then pushed them out into space, where they bobbed off into the gravity storm toward the nearest habitable planet, their emergency KA'PPA beacons broadcasting distress signals. *At least they'd have a chance*, Brim thought grimly as the powerless wreck of *S.S. Purple Abagail* began its inexorable slowdown through the great constant of LightSpeed, where it would continue to coast forever through the cosmos. Grimacing, he watched the other merchantmen and escorts rapidly disappearing into the starry darkness ahead. Then he waited for other survivors, watching radiation fires creep aft toward his solitary position on the LifeGlobe deck.

At last, when it was reasonably clear no one else would make his or her way to the LifeGlobes—and the radiation fires were no more than a few irals distant—Brim slid open the hatch of the LifeGlobe Three and clambered aboard. Activating the ancient controls—half surprised they worked!—he was just about to shove off, when a tiny figure in a battle suit many sizes too large floated helplessly out of the companionway and pushed off clumsily toward the hatch. Brim reached out to grab an arm and dragged whomever it was into a seat, then shoved against the 'Globe's attachment arm with all his might as the tiny Spin-Grav unit chattered under his feet. "Belt in," he shouted over his communicator, but the tiny, crumpled figure inside the battle suit clearly had no idea how to activate the suit's own communication system, so—expertly swimming in the zero gravity—Brim set the slumping figure's belt, closed and sealed the hatch, then settled into the helm and secured. Only moments later, *Purple Abagail*, blazing over nearly the whole if her hull, collapsed inward, nearly dragging LifeGlobe Three into a roiling maw of radiation fire before shock waves sent the little craft darting off into the starry emptiness of space.

— o — 0 — o —

At the Imperial Commerce Building in downtown Avalon's Financial District, Lord Daniel Cranwell rocked back in a chair and peered around the office of Denny Case, Director of the Interspace

Transport Bureau. He pursed his lips and frowned as he looked across Case's desk, regarding Count Tal Confisse Trafford. *You cheap bumbler* he thought, *with all your credits, how you could foul up something this important is beyond belief.* Then he gave an inward shrug "Well," he said aloud, "I suppose the ball is in my court, so to speak, Cousin."

"Seems that is so," replied Trafford, uncomfortably inhaling a giant mu'occo cigar in a plush divan. He released a great draught of smoke and grimaced. "My attempt certainly came to nothing. The Carescrian zukeed continues to breathe, and my foolish daughter's commission is still on the line. Not to mention the family reputation." He rolled his eyes helplessly. "And *our* shared problem worsens each moment those WF-400s continue to prove themselves on bender patrol."

"A combination of bad luck and...." Cranwell let his voice trail off while he battled to control an inner rage. "Let's chalk it up to luck only."

The Count frowned. "Kind of you Daniel," he muttered, "...but much of it was my attempt to do an important job on the cheap. The city is filled with potential pirates. I simply didn't offer enough credits to attract a top crew."

"Bygones be bygones, Cousin," Cranwell said placatingly. "One eternally needs to find the correct price in everything, doesn't one?"

Trafford bit his lip. "That fiasco also cost me the price of hiring a death squad. And even locals are expensive in the midst of this war—speaking of which, you mentioned you have launched your own attack on the lowlife Brim. Pray tell?"

Cranwell smiled, slyly. "I have already taken certain steps to make *sure* this Brim will never bother us again."

"And those steps are..?"

"First, I have placed Brim aboard a slow merchantman in a convoy to the Carescrian port of Caer Landria on Burtis/Celeron."

"So?"

"Dear Cousin, you certainly know the toll Benders take on those convoys."

"I do," Trafford said, "...but I also know significant numbers of merchantmen reach their destinations."

"Ah, but Cousin," I have certain, *connections*, shall we say, who practically guarantee, Brim's ship will be one of the ones that do not "

"B-but in the in the rare case he *does*?" Trafford demanded.

"Believe me, Cousin," Cranwell promised soothingly, "I have taken additional insurance against such a possibility." I have hired an assassin to accompany him on his last journey."

"An assassin?" Trafford demanded with raised eyebrows. "I thought we had agreed eliminating Brim should not raise attention to itself. Single murders are *ever so* traceable these days."

"But not *this* murder, my good Count," Cranwell said. "I have employed a professional woman from the Lampson Provinces: tiny but deadly. There is no way he can escape her."

"All right, Cousin," Trafford relented after considerable delay. "As you have trusted me, I shall trust you in this endeavor. But how did you manage something like getting Brim aboard a cargo ship in the first place?"

Cranwell laughed proudly. "I issued 'orders' from *this* office."

"*Orders* from *here*? This office can't issue official orders to anybody, can they?"

"Well, I *did.*" Cranwell said with a crude smile. "I had official-looking orders drawn up, got Barny Case to sign them, then I backed them up with a statement of Calhoun's urgent need for such action. It was *so* easy: nobody asked any questions at all. I also had the documents hand-delivered to Chief Barbousse instead of to Brim himself—the way Brim normally gets his orders. After it was clear everything had been accepted, I simply finished the job by contacting my Lampsonite Assassin."

"Lampsonites," Trafford mused, still filled with uncertainty, "…'speakers to all.' By Voot's very name, Cousin, those people are dangerous—as much to the persons who hire them as to their victims. If this woman fails in her mission, she will be obliged to kill the individual who hired her. Have you put us both in danger?"

"Of course not, dear cousin. Of course not."

"Then…, how…?"

Cranwell smiled again. "Because I did nor hire her," he explained. "I had Barny Case do it?"

"By that, you have possibly written *his* death sentence, poor chap."

"She will not fail, Cousin There is nothing to worry about. She is perhaps the best professional in the business."

"All the same, Cousin, in case she doesn't complete her, er, 'original mission,' what will you say to Case's father, Brandon?"

"Simply nothing, Cousin," Cranwell said. "Young Barnabas has been on his own for years: totally worthless—in and out of trouble. It should come as no surprise to anyone—leastwise Brandon, who has been paying for Barnabas' 'indulgences,' shall we say, since the young fellow reached puberty."

"All well and good, Cousin," The Count demanded, "but with whom shall we replace him? After all, he *is* Director of the Interspace Transport Bureau and completely under your thumb—as well as our insurance the Escort Service will never reach its potential."

"There are always replacements among children of the wealthy," Cranwell said soothingly. "Never any shortage of spoiled, worthless young scions who need jobs with impressive titles and will keep clear of the *actual* work going on."

The Count wrinkled his upper lip and shut his eyes. "Yes," he agreed bitterly. "You needn't remind me of *that*."

A moment later, the door opened and Barny Case stumbled into the office with a great, drunken smile on his face. "Good to see you, Gents!" he slurred. "Sorry I'm a bit late, but have I got a superb place for us to enjoy tonight," he gushed, "...and completely untraceable. More beautiful—*young*—woman than you can shake your walking stick at, Count."

"Then let us be off, friend Barny," Cranwell said with a thrill of anticipation. Barny Case seldom failed in his promises for ribald evenings of nubile young women, wild gambling, and other pleasures available to the fortunate individuals who could afford them....

Chapter 38

. . .Serena Morgan

IN SPACE ABOARD P-A LIFEGLOBE 3, 33 TRIAD, 52017

After sleeping in what was clearly an uncomfortable position, Serena Morgan woke with a start, her dreams filled by flames, explosions, and presentments of imminent death. Opening her eyes slowly, she shivered uncontrollably in the dim light until she remembered where she was—in a LifeGlobe! She hadn't counted on anything like *this*.

Still dressed in the ill-fitting battle suit she'd grabbed in panic when the explosion came, she turned her head to the left as far as she could without moving the helmet—only to encounter a metal wall. Turning the other way, she found herself facing the man she knew as Wilf Brim, sitting in one of the LifeGlobe's recliners and peering intently at her. He had on coveralls instead of the battle suit he must have worn when he'd pulled her aboard just before *Purple Abagail* blew herself to kingdom come. "You breathing air?" she called, then bit her lip, feeling both stupid and very much afraid.

"I am," the Man named Brim replied. "I'll bet you'd be a lot more comfortable out here than in that oversized battle suit."

"I'd like that," Serena declared, "But I barely got it on, and I don't know how to get off."

"Mind if I help?"

"I'd love it," she said, as Brim walked over to her.

"Can you sit up?" he asked.

Serena struggled for a moment, then lay back. "I'm going to need a lot of help, I think."

Brim helped her into a sitting position, then moved her legs over the edge of the bunk. "Hang on," he said. "Here goes the helmet."

In a moment, he turned her helmet nearly a third of a turn, then lifted it off as cooler air replaced the closeness of the battle suit. "Hello," he said, taking a step back. "I'm Wilf Brim."

She smiled wryly. "Well," she said, "by way of introduction, I'm definitely not who I look like."

"Okay" Brim said raising an eyebrow, "Then... who are you?"

"Name's Serena Morgan," she said. "And, as you're about to discover, I am not the old woman you think I am."

Brim stepped back farther looking embarrassed. "I didn't say you were, er..., Serena."

"Help me out of this horrible outfit."

"You can do it easier yourself," Brim said.

"I can?"

"Turn the lever on the neckpiece yes, that one... a full turn, and...."

Well, that was easy enough. "Now what?"

"Just pull the slide all the way to your waist."

Good grief, I didn't have much on when all the excitement happened..... "All the way?"

"If you really want to get out of the battle suit...."

"Okay, here goes...." Stifling a giggle, she watched his eyebrows rise. *I'll bet that was a little shock, Mister—Lord—Brim. You've seldom saw a wizened old hag a body like* this!

"Um. . . Let me get you something to put on," Brim sputtered, turning his blushing face and opening an overhead locker. "Let's see, I suppose you'll need a size SMALL?"

"Good guess," she said, climbing all the way out of the suit and joyfully scratching a few itches she'd developed in the Battle Suit. "Throw it over here."

Brim tossed the coveralls with his back turned while she laughed to herself. *Typical man: completely flustered by a naked woman.*

Dressing quickly, she massaged her face back to its original features. "Okay, Mister Brim," she said, "you can turn around again," then watched his jaw drop. "Told you I wasn't whom an old woman."

Looking completely nonplussed, Brim shrugged. "Well, it's pretty obvious you aren't *now*."

"I wasn't *then*, either," she said. "It was a disguise."

"...A good one," Brim admitted, still blushing. "Sure had me fooled. I thought you were the little old lady in the Mess."

"You noticed me, then?" she said with a bit of disappointment.

"It was my job to notice everything," Brim said. "I was on board as an observer to see if I could improve operations in the merchant fleet."

Serena laughed. "Guess you observed a lot more than you'd expected."

"You've got that right," Brim admitted with a wry laugh. Then he frowned. "But how about you? What was with the disguise?"

"My little secret for the moment, Mister Brim," she said, "...if it won't interfere with our little *relationship*."

"That disguise is your business," Brim replied with a shrug. "So far as I understand, Space is still free."

Nice guy, Serena thought. Too bad he's the very person I've been hired to kill. As a Lampsonite, his saving her life had automatically canceled her mission—but only until she might save *his*, then her mission would be valid once more. As a businesswoman, she naturally hated to give up the fat commission she'd been paid, as well as kill Barnabas Case, the silly little man who hired her. She mentally shrugged; she would bide her time—things had a way of changing in the assassination business; one always needed to be patient. "So now we're here in this oversized balloon," she demanded, "what's going on?"

"I don't understand," Brim said. "What do you mean?"

"I mean, what happens next," Serena asked. Like most people on advanced planets, she rather took untroubled star flight for granted— something that got her from one place to another. "For all I know, we could just go on drifting for the next zillion years."

Brim smiled reassuringly. "Nothing like that is going to happen, trust me. This little LifeGlobe will take good care of us."

"Save the platitudes for your brainless girlfriends," Serena growled. "I want to know what's going to happen to us step-by-step until we get rescued."

Brim rubbed his chin, which had already grown considerable stubble. "You really want to know?"

"Xaxtdamned right."

"Okay. Well, first, we have to bleed off velocity before anything else happens. While we're still traveling greater then LightSpeed, there's not much anybody or anything can do to help us. When *Abagail's* Drive crystals failed—sometime after we were hit by the HyperTorp—we were traveling twelve light years every metacycle."

"So what's to slow us down?"

"The First Law of Travis Physics," Brim answered. "When a body with a velocity faster than LightSpeed looses its propelling force, that body decelerates until it slows to a velocity just *below* LightSpeed."

"Okay," Serena said. "I think I remember something from grade school. But what happens then?"

"Then" Brim said with another of those reassuring smiles she was already beginning to like more than she wanted to, "we have the use of the LifeGlobe's little SpinGrav—a powerful anti-gravity engine—that will do two very necessary things for us."

"Like what?"

"First," Brim explained, "it will slow our speed to something a lot more rational than one hundred, eighty-six thousand c'lenyts per click."

"That's LightSpeed, isn't it?"

"Correct," Brim said. "See—you know more about this stuff than you think."

"Thanks," Serena said, feeling herself calm slightly in spite of her fear. "And what good will that do?"

"That's when the logic engine built into this little craft will guide us to a planet on which we can land and wait to be rescued. Simple as that."

"Somehow, I'm highly skeptical about your use of the word, 'simple.'"

"Well," Brim said, his face reddening again, "of course it's more complicated. But it does mean our chances of rescue are a lot better than they might be."

196

Taking a deep breath, Serena felt a sudden rush of relief. "All right, Wilf," she said, turning to more immediate needs, "Is there anything to eat aboard this Hullmetal bubble…?"

Chapter 39

. . . the best friend I ever made

GANTACLAR HARBOR, IMPERIAL PROVINCE OF
CARESCRIA, LINFARNE/NAVRON, 33 TRIAD, 52017

Many light years distant, Utrillo Barbousse had completed final return arrangements following the record run from Avalon/Asturius in *Four Nines*. Presently, he was relaxing alone in a waterfront café, enjoying a fine Logish Meem while feeling the glow of setting a record, and ruminating on the trip itself— especially Commander Ann Hunt.

The lovely officer had proven to be a most gracious—and comely—passenger. He shook his head sadly. He'd known Wilf Brim for most of his active-duty life, and so far as he could see, Hunt would make the perfect mate for his long-time Skipper and friend. Oh, with Brim, there were *always* plenty of women—two the Carescrian had even loved: the Princess Margot Effer'wyck and dark-haired Claudia Valemont back in Haelic/Hador's Atalanta. But this Hunt, she was somehow *different*. Nothing he could put his finger on. Nevertheless, she was one *unique* woman—and, *of course*, she was paired with the absolute wrong man—a self-adoring idiot whose mind was so concentrated on himself, the only thing for sure he'd be capable of enjoying to the fullest was Hunt's long, beautiful legs wrapped around his neck. He shook his head again and finished his Meem. So terribly often, the best women in the Universe went to the absolutely wrong men.

On his way back to the ship, he checked the dispatches shack to be sure he had the most up-to-date information before departing for Met asteroid—and from there to Avalon. He was just leaving when the

KA'PPA Administrator called his name. "Chief Barbousse," he announced with a frown, "I think you'll want to see this."

Nodding, Barbousse opened a nearby display.

"Item five," the KA'PPA Administrator advised.

Barbousse scanned to the fifth item, then his heart stopped.

DKLD03127360 DNC# ADD318448411 SECRET

1. CONVOY 33A-98G UNDER ATTACK BY
BENDER PACK SECTOR K95:G1276:7694GR187.

2. LOSSES INCLUDE THE FOLLOWING: S.S.
FALSTRIA, S.S. ILSENSTEIN II, S.S. ORBITA, S.S.
PURPLE ABAGAIL, S.S. LEERDAM, S.S.
LISMORAIDA.

END DKLD03127360 DNC# ADD318448411 SECRET

Throwing a quick salute to the Administrator, Barbousse took off at a run for *Four Nines*. Climbing the boarding ladder two rungs at a time, he drew up the forward hatch, locked it, then slid into the left helm. "Baun," he barked to the young Helmsman he'd chosen to accompany him on the record run. "Is the preflight checkout done?"

"Aye," Sub Lieutenant Baun replied from the co-helm. "T-twice, actually, Chief Barbousse."

"Good man!" Barbousse said and activated the blower: "Attention all hands:" he puffed, slipping on his helmet. "Prepare for immediate liftoff. Repeat: prepare for immediate liftoff."

"Need five cycles for the Drives!" Kermis replied in a startled voice.

"Everybody else ready?"

A chorus of "Ayes" exploded in his helmet.

"Kermis: report when you're ready," Barbousse ordered, "We're taxiing!"

— o — 0 — o —

At nearly the same moment, back at the Admiralty in Avalon, Captain Bradley burst into Calhoun's office carrying a scrap of plastic flimsy: "Admiral, did you see this"

"See wha'?"

"This communiqué. Read the highlighted portions, sir."

"...Anither Convoy savaged?" Calhoun demanded, donning his eyeglasses. "Sae wha' else is new?"

"Check the 'Personnel Missing List' aboard *Purple Abagail*, Admiral."

"Wha'?"

"The *list*, Sir. The PML, Sir."

"...Voot's greasy beard! *Wilf Brim!* Wha' in Xaxt war he doin' aboard a freighter?"

"I thought *you'd* know, Admiral."

"Nobody told me onything aboot Brim bein' on a freighter. Wha' were he doing there?"

"Seems he was ordered there."

"Orders? From whom?"

"Wasn't anyone here at the Admiralty, Sir. I checked."

"Then...?"

"Appears to be the Interspace Transport Bureau over in the Commerce Building."

"Barny Case's outfit? Na' possible!"

"The order seems to have come *directly* from Mr. Case's office."

"Canna' be! Onybody workin' wi' tha' drunken idiot wud ha' checked wi' me first."

"Perhaps Case himself, Admiral?"

"Case ony' fills a chair in tha' office. Besides, who wad order Brim t'do *anything*? Officially, he's still a civilian."

"Well, Admiral, Brim would do anything for the Emperor."

"Aye, but I certainly can't see Onrad puttin' Brim on a freighter."

"You're right, Admiral. Nevertheless, Brim is so desperate to get back into the war, he'd probably follow anybody's orders. Even orders from Case."

"Summat's up, here, and I mean to find wha' it is."

"Meanwhile, Admiral, what about Brim?"

Calhoun grimaced and took a deep breath. "See if you can raise Barbousse while I notify the Palace. Onrad's nae' goin luik this a' all!"

— o — 0 — o —

In space aboard *Four Nines* on a general course for Avalon/Asturius, SubLieutenant Baun glanced across the cockpit at Chief Barbousse. Like everyone who'd lately graduated from flight school at the Helmsman's Academy, he'd heard of the legendary Chief, but never thought he might actually share a cockpit with him. He'd also heard of the big man's powers of concentration, which were quite evident since leaving the refueling stop at the Bright Triad of Ely. Ever since entering sector K95:G1276:7694GR187, Barbousse had flown a complex search pattern while Chief Steele monitored the emergency KA'PPA frequency in hopes of picking up transmissions from LifeGlobes in the area. So far, however, nothing had turned up, and now, the WF-400 was reaching critically low energy levels. "Chef Barbousse," he said. "Have you checked our energy levels?"

The big man nodded heavily. "Thanks, SubLieutenant," he said without turning his head, "I have. We'll have to head back home now." With a grimace, he took the controls and set course for Avalon/Asturius. "Going to be a lot of angry people at the Admiralty," he muttered. "Especially since it was me who passed the Skipper those orders to join the convoy...."

"But it wasn't your fault someone issued those orders," Baun said consolingly.

"I understand," Barbousse growled. "In this case, what the Admiralty thinks doesn't matter."

"C-Chief...," Baun started, But Barbousse held up his hand.

"The Skipper was so anxious to get back in the war, I didn't even question that the orders came from Denny Case's office—and I should have done that under any circumstances."

"But orders are orders," Baun protested. "Everybody in the Fleet follows orders."

"Only orders that make some sense," Barbousse said. "Somehow, those didn't, and now, I may have lost the best friend I ever made...."

— o — 0 — o —

Back in Avalon City, at Roberto's Ironstone Restaurant, Avalon's most exclusive club, Lord Daniel Cranwell, Imperial Minister of Commerce relaxed in a plush chair and gazed around at the magnificent artwork and furnishings that filled this private dining room. Cranwell hadn't always enjoyed such luxury, normally available only to the top strata of the Imperial capital. But he did *now*; it was all that mattered—except perhaps *keeping* himself in this elevated level of existence. Across the table, a single chair waited for Count Tal Confisse Trafford, whom he had invited for a "Special Celebration." Cranwell treated himself to a generous sip of the libation that had been rushed to the table the moment he arrived, smiling in anticipation. A *true* celebration it would be! Cranwell was not a man to embellish.

In a moment or so, a velvet curtain in the vestibule was drawn aside to admit his guest. "Cousin Tal, welcome!" Cranwell exclaimed, rising to extend a dry, skinny hand across the table.

"Cousin Daniel," Trafford said, doffing his evening cape and gloves into a pair of hands that appeared magically from the alcove. He gripped Trafford's hand with pudgy fingers as he glanced around at the elaborate surroundings.

"I take it the *atmosphere* is to your liking."

"You can, my good Lord," Trafford replied with a satisfied smile. "You can."

"Excellent," Cranwell purred. "Then let me assure you our supper will be of the same standards of excellence. I have ordered it specially for our celebration."

"Must I wait until we dine before I shall know what it is we are celebrating?" Trafford demanded with faux sadness.

"Not at all, my good friend," Cranwell said, reaching inside his severely tailored coat. "I have the necessary documentation with me."

"Documentation?"

"Documentation, *indeed*, dear Cousin."

"What sort of *document* could evoke such a grand celebration for two?" Trafford demanded, his voice suddenly edged with suspicion. "We are both inordinately wealthy, so what could be so important

202

Bill Baldwin

about a new business deal? *Unless....*" Suddenly his eyes opened wide above porcine cheeks. "By Voot's filthy beard!" he exclaimed, "does this have something to do with the dastard Brim?"

"But of course, dear Cousin!"

"Then, by Xarksoar's yellow toenails, *Tell me!*" Cranwell pleaded.

Cranwell merely handed the cheap sheet of plastic across the table. "I have here a dispatch reporting the Merchantman *SS Purple Abagail* was destroyed on its way to Caer Landria on Carescria's Burtis/Celeron."

Trafford studied the document for a few cycles, then looked up with a frown. "And the point of this *is*?" he demanded.

"The point of this is, my dear Cousin, is both Wilf Brim *and* my assassin were aboard that merchantman."

"By the Gods!" Trafford exclaimed. "Then...."

"Then," Cranwell said, failing to squelch a proud smile, we may assume both that Brim is at last out of the way, *and* we don't have to pay our assassin the other half of her blood money. Our hands are clean!"

"Oh *really*?" Trafford demanded with a frown. "And what is to prevent them from returning should they have successfully made their way to the ship's LifeGlobes?"

"No cause for concern, dear Cousin," Cranwell said soothingly. "After all, space is limitless. How many civilian Star Sailors actually return from these torpedoings? Very few, and you know the odds are nearly insurmountable. Why, most freighter crews don't have the faintest idea how to manage their LifeGlobes. Besides, that sinking is only one of literally dozens that occur each convoy. There aren't enough rescue craft to search out even a small fraction of them. I mean, what is there to worry about?"

"Well," Trafford admitted, brightening somewhat, "it certainly does seem as if we've seen the last of those two—at least in this war."

"Correct, my dear Trafford," Cranwell assured him. "...and after the war, who will even care about a long-lost Admiral? Who remembers Admiral Penda, or even the great battleship *Neume* that was lost with him?"

203

Trafford thought for a moment, then smiled. "Well, my dear Cranwell, that does make sense. Let us then celebrate!"

Cranwell nodded and clapped his hands twice. Instantly, the room began to fill with nubile serving girls bearing trays of appetizers. He had promised a celebration; *he* intended to celebrate during supper, *and* afterward....

Chapter 40

. . .Onrad

AVALON/ASTURIUS, AVALON CITY, 34 TRIAD

Back over Avalon City, Barbousse watchfully let Baun take the landing on Lake Mersin. As the WF-400 glided to a stop, the big man reached across the control console. "Nice go, young man," he said, clapping the young SubLieutenant on the back. "Take her back to the barn and get her ready for immediate takeoff."

"Aye, Chief."

No sooner had they taxied into the canal toward TopLine, than Barbousse spotted a huge, black limousine skimmer in the parking lot. Clearly, it was going to be a long day. While Baun secured the ship, he hopped onto the dock and made directly for the big skimmer, determined he wasn't going to waste valuable time making reports. The damn Admirals could wait.

Just as he reached the Limousine, a uniformed footman hopped out and opened the rear passenger door. "Please step inside, Chief Barbousse."

The Chief stopped in his tracks, heart in his mouth. Inside the spacious passenger cabin, both Admiral Calhoun and Emperor Onrad were waiting.

"Come in, Chief," Onrad said, motioning for Barbousse into the seat beside him. "I'm assuming you're ready to fly back out as soon as the ship's ready."

"Er, I am, Yer Majesty," Barbousse stumbled tiredly.

"Wha' do ye have to tell us aboot Admiral Brim?" Calhoun demanded.

"Not much, Admiral," Barbousse replied. "The Fleet Rescue Office reports only three planets capable of supporting life are within LifeGlobe range of the *Abigail's* last reported position. That alone should give us a lot better chance of finding the LifeGlobes before their supplies run out. But even with that, we can't spend too much time lookin'. We wring a lot of range out of that WF-400 of yours, Yer Majesty, but those little ships burn a load of energy flyin' low and slow close to the surface."

"I understand they do," Onrad agreed. "What can the two of us do by way of helping?"

Barbousse thought for a moment, then nodded. "I'd like maybe three additional WF-400s to fly with us. The more eyes in a situation like this, the better."

"Ye've got 'em," Calhoun swore.

Onrad snapped his fingers. "And I've got a way around your fuel problem. Don't know why I never thought of it before. The Fifth Battlecruiser Combat Group is in that area. I'll divert some heavy iron to the general vicinity; the four of you can refuel from those whenever you need. "

"Couldn't ask for more than that, Your Majesty," Barbousse said. "I'll be out of here within the metacycle."

"You'll need some sleep, Chief," Calhoun observed.

"I can sleep on the way out, Admiral."

"Kind of thought that might be your answer," Calhoun said.

"Anything else we can get for you," Onrad asked.

"Hang on," interrupted Calhoun, "...there *is* something. If he could be landing on a populated planet—which is probably is—it maun very well be a guid idea t' tak' along a language translator—like a Lampsonite—'speakers to al',' ya' know."

"Great idea," Onrad agreed, "...but where are we going to find ourselves a Lampsonite on such short notice? Those people stay home in droves."

"Turns out, Your Majesty, we hae' our own *domesticated* Lampsonite right here in Avalon City," Calhoun said. "Anyone remember Nadia Tissuard?"

"Nadia Tissuard?" Barbousse broke out in excitement. "Who could forget her, Admiral? Shc and thc skippcr commanded the original *I.F.S. Starfury* a number of years ago—but I hear she's driving benders these days, isn't she?"

"By Voot's collar buttons!" Onrad exclaimed. "I remember her, too! Quite a heroic little lady, joining our Fleet when most of her fellow Lampsonites trip all over themselves avoiding even hints of war. What *is* she doing these days?"

"Still blowin' up Leaguer ships fast as she can," Calhoun replied. "She's a senior Captain in charge of the 15th Bender Flotilla. An' best of all, she's wi' us in Avalon today givin' a briefing to the Chiefs of Staff."

"She *was* giving a briefing" Onrad said. "If you don't mind, Baxter, I'll have the Secret Service handle this. You'd have to issue orders and all that sort of garbage to cancel a briefing to The Chiefs; I'll simply have her arrested. She'll be on her way here before the Chief has his ship ready to go."

"She hae' better be," Calhoun said with a grin. "I rather doubt if Mister Barbousse wad' wait for anyone on this mission, would ye, Chief?"

Barbousse felt his cheeks burn. "I guess I am in a pretty big hurry, Sirs, but in this case, I promise to wait."

"Poor Nadia. Tha' briefing of hers is goin' t' be seriously delayed," Calhoun said with a chuckle.

"And I'm on the phone right now," Onrad added, grabbing a HoloPhone from his uniform. "Anything else, now?"

"Only your blessings, Your Majesty," Barbousse said with a little smile.

Onrad broke into a big grin. "You've been running with that Brim guy far too long, Chief. When you find him, tell him you've *both* got my blessings."

Barbousse opened the door and stepped into the street. Coming to attention, he pursed his lips for a moment, then nodded. "I'm deeply your debt Gentlemen. I won't be back until I find him." With that, he saluted, made an about face, then marched off toward TopLine Spacecraft Performance, Customization & Research, Ltd.

— o — 0 — o —

By 36 Triad, Brim's SpinGrav had been running steadily for almost a day, and details of the little planet with its single satellite was now quite visible in the cupola's windows. Like most habitable planets, it appeared properly sized to exhibit "normal" gravity and had the unique blue complexion swirled with white that promised an ample atmosphere with plenty of life-giving water. In the 200 Standard Years since the first robotic survey ship had marked the little planet as "habitable," it had come a long way. From his seat at the 'Globe's helm, Brim was studying the instrument cluster. "As you say, it's a pretty looking place," he said with a frown, "but now it seems to be emitting a tremendous volume of radiation in the radio spectrum."

"What does that say about the natives ahead?" Serena demanded

Brim shrugged. "It could mean literally *anything*. I'm picking up what could very well be dialogues between sentient beings in a tremendous number of frequencies. But, so far, there's no indications of KA'PPA radiation—and *that's* important information, too."

"Oh?"

"Well, for one thing, without KA'PPA communications, it's pretty doubtful they have any idea of HyperLight transportation. The amount of radio traffic indicates they're pretty advanced—at least some of them—but they're still a long way from joining the HyperLight Community. One thing for sure, though…."

"What?"

"There *is* some sentient kind of life down there, because radio traffic like what's coming from below requires *somebody* to modulate it."

"You think they'll be like us?"

"It's anybody's guess," Brim said with a smile, "but if *we* can survive on the surface the way they do, we might just have *a lot* in common."

Chapter 41

. . .whoa!

Aboard the new super Battlecruiser *I.F.S. Barfluer*, Rear Admiral Tobias Moulding relaxed, standing with hands clasped behind his back on a bridge wing, looking aft at the wide, green wake of his command ship as it rushed away into the cosmos and disappeared. He'd been part of this great warship since she was only a set of specifications—many he'd laid down personally. His job then had been to ensure those specifications were fulfilled with excellence; he knew he'd done it well.

Now, five Standard Years later, he commanded this magnificent starship: 5,200 irals long, just short of a full c'lenyt in length, and capable of nearly 44 LPM with a range of more than 51 thousand light years at economical cruise. Streamlined for fighting in atmospheres as well as outer space and armed with a battery of largest disruptors ever constructed, she was arguably the most powerful warship in the Known Universe. And unlike many other space-only fighting ships, she was *beautiful*.

Moulding, himself, was distinguished by blue eyes that sparkled with good-natured humor, a grand promontory for a nose, and the droll, confident sort of smile that fairly shouted wealth. He was tall, blond, and about the same age as Brim, with whom he'd shared a close friendship since the days of the Mitchell Trophy races back in 5100. He wore the distinctive blue cape of an Imperial Fleet officer with the device of Rear Admiral on its left collar just above his Helmsman's insignia. He also wore the discreet red-on-green insignia of the semi-official Imperial High Speed Starflight Team. Not always a large-ship man, he had also been an early believer on astroplanes, and late in 52009 became the first human to exceed the absolute velocity of 400 LPM.

As he turned to peer around the big ship's Spartan, no-nonsense bridge, his thoughts were interrupted by a young SubLieutenant who came to attention before handing over a folded sheet of message plastic. "V-very High Priority, Admiral." The Orderly announced in an awestruck voice.

"Thank you, SubLieutenant," Moulding said with a smile. "First time on the bridge?" he asked.

"Aye, Admiral Molding," the SubLieutenant said.

"She's a big ship," Moulding said, "Sometimes that happens. What's your name, Son?"

"S-SubLieutenant B-blair, Admiral."

"Well, SubLieutenant, let's see if we can't get you a tour while you're here. One of these days, I suspect you'll have seen quite enough of these places." He reached out and touched the arm of a Chief Warrant Officer who had just come on duty. "Chief Reilly," he said, "this is SubLieutenant Blair. Would you be so good as to take this young officer for his first tour of *Barfluer's* Bridge?"

Reilly smiled. "I shall be honored, Admiral," he said, taking the Blair by the sleeve. "Come on with me, SubLieutenant," he said. "Let me show you how we run things up here."

"Learn as much as you can, young man," Moulding called after them with a smile. "This is a good place to start." Then, with a quick nod to Reilly, he unfolded the communiqué. It was short and to the point, carrying Onrad's coded autograph.

> Toby. Our troublesome friend Wilf Brim
> has got himself missing. I've promised
> your battle group to help find him. Get
> in touch with Chief Barbousse for
> details—contact him through that crazy
> TopLine Ltd. he's set up in Avalon.
> Good luck. ~ Onrad

Moulding chuckled and shook his head for a moment, then strode across the bridge. "Captain," he said, handing the Emperor's message to Captain Voshell, the ship's commander. "Find out where we are supposed to go, then alter course immediately and proceed there at top cruising speed. Seems Onrad and I have an old friend who could use some assistance...."

— o — 0 — o —

The LifeGlobe began slowing noticeably soon after the planet and its large, cratered satellite had quite filled the Hyperscreen ports. Brim found himself considerably interested with what might lay below. He and Morgan were traveling in a Nightward direction, opposite to the planet's rotation, and the radiosphere surrounding the planet was filled with radiation at all frequencies, some of it containing what sounded as if it contained human speech. "Hey, 'Speaker to all,'" Brim asked, "can you understand any of this?"

"I might if you'd stop changing frequencies," Morgan complained. "You are driving me crazy!"

"Oops, sorry," Brim said, offering the radio controls to the tiny Lampsonite

"I can't work that fast," Morgan said with a little blush. "I'd really need a couple Metacycles listening to a single channel before I could begin to understand—*if* I'm even listening to what turns out to be language."

Brim smiled. "Okay, Serena, he said. I'll put you to work when, and *if*, we run across a frequency that holds some promise."

Morgan shook her head as the dark side of the globe rolled almost imperceptively beneath them. "Look at the concentrations of artificial light down there," she said in amazement as she peered through the binoculars they'd found in the 'Globe's survival kit. "Many are almost as bright as Avalon!"

"Clearly, this is no primitive society," Brim observed, "even if they don't have KA'PPA communications."

Suddenly, Morgan stiffened. "By Voot's greasy beard—*what in all get-out is* that?"

211

"What?" Brim asked, looking up from the controls.

"Here," Morgan said, handing Brim the binoculars. "See for yourself—strange-looking thing. Maybe these guys aren't so backward at all."

"Really?" Brim said, lifting the binoculars to his eyes. "Now where should I look—and what for?"

"See those three light concentrations in a row down there—almost straight ahead?"

"Okay, I see them," Brim said, then, "Whoa! Looks like something is slowly passing between us and the largest one—just a silhouette, but...."

"What do you think it is?"

"I have no idea," Brim said, but it looks like it's a lot closer to us than it is to the light concentration on the surface, so it's almost got to be in some sort of orbit. What say we go down and have a closer look?"

"A closer look? Why?"

"Well, since we're absolutely committed to landing *somewhere* on this planet, perhaps we oughtn't to start with a reputation for sneaking around. And who knows, it might simply be some sort of space debris."

"Somehow it didn't look like debris," Morgan countered. "It had kind of a regular shape. You know.... like maybe it comes to a... point?"

"We're never going to find out until we go for a closer look."

"Yeah, you're right," Morgan said with a sigh. "I'm game if you are—but be *careful*. We have no idea what might have developed down there in the last couple hundred years."

"Oh, I hear you," Brim replied, switching off the AutoHelm, "We Humanoids are certainly a bloody minded lot, wherever in the Universe we're found. But sooner or later, you and I have to make ourselves known here. Maybe we'll be lucky"

"Or maybe we *won't*," Morgan added under her breath rolling her eyes.

Chapter 42

...jingling bells

IN SPACE, ORBITING A BLUE PLANET, 37 TRIAD, 52017
15 DECEMBER, 1965

As Brim and Morgan carefully approached the mysterious orbiting body, it became clear the object was quite small, perhaps no more than 20 irals in length, but certainly no random space debris. It was clearly *constructed* in a roughly conical shape. "Looks like a big funnel," Serena suggested chuckling "—with the wide end perhaps ten irals in diameter at most."

Brim was approaching from the wide end because he reasoned the opposite, narrow end might be the front, and he wasn't terribly anxious to startle anyone inside, if indeed the orbiter was manned.

From what he'd seen at a distance, the closed-in front of the ship was surfaced in ribbed metal, colored matt black with indecipherable white lettering on its curved sides. The closer, larger "aft" end was painted a brilliant white, open at its widest circumference. This large opening was covered by what appeared to be a golden fabric stretched tightly across a circular framework from which a number of long, golden streamers floated lazily. Two interesting circular holes opened aft at the "top" and "bottom" of this fabric; they looked as if they could be small rocket engines to move the little ship forward. Other similar holes placed around the circumference might well be used for rotation.

As he moved even closer, concentrating fully on maneuvering the unwieldy LifeGlobe, he heard Morgan gasp. "Wilf, look at that!"

"What *now*, Serena?" he demanded stopping their ship's movement relative to it's neighbor, then looking up.

213

"There," Morgan said, pointing to the surface of the planet. "You don't even need the binoculars to...."

"Whoa!" Brim exclaimed. "Now *that* is something else!"

"What is it?"

"Don't know for certain, but I'd almost bet it's a large, chemical rocket being launched from down there. Look at those flames...!"

"...And the long smoke trail behind it. You suppose they're shooting at us?"

Brim shook his head and stroked the rough stubble covering his chin. "Of course it could be anything, but I'm betting it has nothing to do with us and everything to do with this little obiter in front of us."

"Ya' think?"

"Just to be on the safe side, I'm going to put some distance from us and this thing to wait and see what goes on. One way or another, I have a strong feeling we are going be involved with both of them."

"Okay," Morgan said. "I *hate* waiting for stuff like this."

"Well, you've got plenty to do until it arrives."

"Like what?"

"Well, there's a lot of the 'new' gibberish coming and going from the one up here now on 296.9 million cycles per click. Why don't you start 'studying' *that* language they're speaking? Clearly, that rocket you saw doesn't have enough power for a purely vertical ascent, so you've probably got a few Metacycles until it arrives."

"You sound like you're pretty sure it's coming here."

"Sure as any WAG can be."

"WAG?"

"Wild-assed Guess," Brim explained.

— o — 0 — o —

Back in Avalon at TopLine, Barbousse was catching a quick snooze while he waited in the left seat of *Four Nines'* tiny control bridge. The sliding side window was open beside him because, so far as he was concerned, there would to be considerable noise when Nadia Tissuard arrived under Secret Service arrest. He was correct.

"Help!" a female voice screamed out on the street, waking him instantly.

This was followed by a "Ow! F' Xaxt's sake, Lady, we're just following orders! Ow!"

"Orders my ass! Help! I'm being kidnapped!"

"Ow!"

"Somebody come get this woman. Ow! *Help!*" As Barbousse raced aft for the boarding hatch, he noted this last plea was definitely in a masculine tenor.

Sliding down the boarding ladder, he heard, "Barbousse! Thank Voot! Help! Somebody's trying to kidnap me!" coming from the broken window of a limousine parked in front of TopLine. Running along the top of the canal bulwark, he arrived at the big skimmer just as a back door opened violently and Tissuard backed out dragging a wide-eyed man in a black suit. "Com'on, Chief," she panted, "help me pin this Zukeed down, then we'll...."

Suddenly, the limousine raced away, back door still ajar.

"Hang on, Nadia!" Barbousse roared "This guy's okay—believe me!"

"Like Xaxt!" Tissuard growled, knocking the agent sprawling into the street with a roundhouse to the jaw. "Now pick him up, and we'll report him to the Authorities!"

"Um, Captain," Barbousse interrupted, hurrying to lift the unconscious man in his arms, "this guy *is* the Authorities."

"Whadda' you mean, '*Authorities*?'" Tissuard puffed, "This son of a Gorker and his buddy were trying to kidnap me!"

"Well, matter of fact, they *weren't*," Barbousse explained gently. They were special Secret Service agents attached to the Emperor's own detachment."

"Whaat?"

"Seriously, Nadia."

Tissuard frowned and thought a moment, nursing her bruised knuckles. "Hmm.... Well, they did say I was under arrest. But by who's orders?"

"Onrad's"

"Onrad's? F' Xaxt's sake, why *me*?"

"Because we need you right here right now—and arresting you was the quickest way to get you." He nodded toward *Four Nines*, noting Baun had already started the Gravs. "Hop in and take a jump seat on the flight deck. Young fella' there is named Baun. We'll be taking off soon as I get this poor Zukeed to someone inside who can give him treatment."

"*Taking off?* To freaking *where*, for Voot's sake? And what about my presentation to the Chiefs of Staff? Why all the hurry?"

"Because we're searching for a friend of yours who's somewhere out there in a LifeGlobe."

"Who?"

"Wilf Brim."

"Wilf? Well why didn't you say so before?"

"Didn't have a chance, Captain," Barbousse replied, but he wasn't sure she heard—she was off for the WF-400 at a dead run. Shifting the unconscious man to a more comfortable position over his shoulder, he started out for the TopLine office, shaking his head. *Women....*

The ebony astroplane thundered off into space less than ten cycles later....

— o — 0 — o —

Some five Metacycles after Brim and Morgan watched what appeared to be the launch of a large chemical rocket from the surface, another funnel-shaped spacecraft maneuvered into orbit nearby its twin, using the tiny rocket engines placed around the white aft section of its fuselage. "Wow!" Brim exclaimed, "Unless I miss my guess, there's a Human at those controls, and he's one *Xaxt* of a Helmsman! Look at that! He's got that slippery little ship under magnificent control—and all he's got to work with are little rocket engines!"

"*He* could very well be a *she*, you know," Morgan corrected sharply."

"Have you been listening the gobbledygook coming from over there?" Brim demanded.

"Of course I have," Morgan retorted, "...and I'm making progress at understanding the words."

"Good," Brim said with a grin. "You suppose that 'woman' over there has a hormone problem or something? Or perhaps a bad cold?"

"Well, I admit, both voices from over there seem pretty deep."

"*Deep* as in *masculine*?"

"*W-e-l-l....*"

"'S okay," Brim allowed with a chuckle. "Anyway, check this," he said, handing her the binoculars, "looks like the new guy is going to touch the two noses together. I'm pretty impressed."

"What's impressive about that?" Morgan asked.

"Well," Brim replied, peering at the distant spacecraft with a glimmering of understanding. "I'll bet they haven't done this very often. Yet the Helmsman of the recent arrival handles complex orbital mechanics as if he's done it all his life. Man, I'd love to see him helm of a Starfury or a WF-400."

"He probably wouldn't understand anything," Morgan replied, returning the binoculars.

Brim raised the glasses to his eyes. "I've got a feeling, Serena," he said, peering out into the distance, "we're looking at a pure natural—who might not completely understand what's going on, but wouldn't have much trouble learning to fly it."

After the newcomer had maneuvered all around its sister ship like a wary animal, it slowed when its nose was within some 20 irals of the other and stopped. In a few moments, all voice-like transmissions to and from the little ships ceased. Morgan raised an eyebrow.

Brim shrugged. "Something's still sending data back to the planet," he said, staring at the radio display. "But nobody's saying anything."

"A rest period, maybe?" Morgan suggested.

"Don't know...." Brim began, but he was interrupted by a strange noises from what they'd previously thought were voice channels. "What in all Xaxt is *that*?"

"I think it's... *music*, Wilf," Serena said with a confused look. "Played on a very simple instrument—and now there are sounds of little bells. Listen. It's got a little beat: dá *da da* ... dá *da da* ... dá dé da da *daaaaa*."

"Yeah, I get that," Brim said in consternation, but what's with the little bells?"

Suddenly, the simple tune and the jingling bells ceased, replaced by gales of what could only be human laughter mixed with quizzical transmissions coming from the surface.

"I have no idea what the bells were for," Morgan said. "I'm catching on to this pretty quickly. I'd even bet the last was some sort of joke. One of those *guys* has quite a sense of humor."

"Let's hope that's true," Brim replied, glancing out one of the side portholes while he started the SpinGrav, "because when we rotate into the bright hemisphere again, it'll be time we go over to meet our new neighbors."

At last, the hubbub dwindled and the two orbiters separated to about 10 c'lenyts. Soon, all voice transmissions were replaced by silence, which was, in time, replaced by gentle snoring.

"Bet you have no trouble translating *that*," Brim remarked.

"None at all," Morgan said. "Sounds like a pretty good idea. It's been a long day, when you get right down to it."

"Me too," Brim agreed, with a sudden yawn. "And my guess is tomorrow's going to be a lot busier."

"If we share a bunk again, we're not going to spend a lot of time sleeping," Morgan said with a little smile.

"But think how well we'll sleep afterward," Brim countered,

Morgan thought for a moment or two. Then, slipping out of her coveralls and slippers, she padded to the bunk. "You've got a point there, Mister Brim," she said, pulling down the sheets. "In fact, you've got a *magnificent* point there."

Grinning, Brim headed for the bunk, too....

BOOK IV

Voot's beard!

Chapter 43

. . .What in heck is that?

IN SPACE, ORBITING A BLUE PLANET,   38 TRIAD, 52017
                                           16 DECEMBER, 1965

Aboard NASA's Gemini-6A spacecraft, Astronaut Walter Schirra turned to Astronaut Tom Stafford and frowned. "Uh, Tom, do you see what I see out there?"

"Huh? What? Where, Wally?" Stafford asked, waking out of a deep sleep.

"Over there," Schirra replied pointing through Stafford's window. "See? Something shiny is out here—gold—and it seems to be moving closer."

"Yeah, I do… and… good grief! What in heck *is* it?"

"Don't know—doesn't show up on the radar."

"Hey: Gemini-Seven: Frank, Jim! Wake up! Do either of you see what we see?" Schirra demanded.

Frank Borman's voice from Gemini 7 crackled in Schirra's headset. "Uh oh! Roger that; we see it too—like a shiny, gold ball. Seems to be going your way."

"That's what it looks like to me," Stafford said, "…and it's got a little cupola on top with portholes. Whoa! Doggone thing's coming right at us, now!"

"Firing the OAMS thrusters!" Schirra barked. "We're getting out of the way!"

— o — 0 — o —

Aboard the LifeGlobe, Morgan shouted, "Voot's beard!" as she peered out of a cupola Hyperscreen. "Look at those flames! They must be 15 irals long. Looks like he's in a hurry?"

"Clearly we startled the guy," Brim said. His fingers few over the controls and the clumsy little spacecraft somehow responded as if it were a much more pliable machine. Lately, Serena had been experiencing feelings for her target that were anything but professional. "Don't get us too close, Wilf," whispered under her breath. "Those flames kind of scare me."

"Don't worry, little friend," Brim said, still peering out of the windshield. "This 'Globe may be old, but it would take a lot more than those flames to hurt it. Let's go and take a closer look. I've got a hunch those two slanted openings near the nose are windows."

— o — 0 — o —

"Hey, Guys!," Alan Shepherd radioed from Mission Control in Houston, "…what are you four babbling about?"

"Whatever it is, Schirra reported breathlessly, "it's turned around and is catching up to us, fast."

"Hang on, Al," Stafford radioed back. "I'm switching to our secret, encoded frequency—Frank and Jim in Gemini-Seven, you'd better do the same."

A chorus of "Rogers" filled the airways. Then silence….

Moments later, when the two NASA spacecraft—as well as Mission Control—had switched to the secret DOD encoded channel NASA never admitted to, Alan Shepherd radioed again. "Guys," he warned, "you've just busted NASA's dirty little secret about having encrypted DOD code frequencies—so you'd better get serious. Everybody from Houston is listening, including Doctor Gilruth. What the Hell's going on up there—and it better be good!"

Schirra took a deep breath, glanced across at Stafford, then shrugged and announced calmly, "Al, the fact is we've got visitors— and they're looking through those little oblong windows at us!"

"Tom," Shepherd radioed, "is this another of Wally's jokes like the mouth organ and Jingle Bells?"

"Nope, Al; they *do* seem to be looking at us."

Chuckling to himself, Schirra heard Shepherd radio to Gemini-7. "Frank! Jim! Do you see this thing too?"

"Absolutely, Al," Borman's voice crackled in Schirra's helmet. "Shiny gold ball, with a little... um...."

"It's a kind of a cupola with oblong windows—pushed up from the top of the ball," Lovell finished for him. "The whole ball is about thirty, thirty-five feet in diameter."

"And you can see *people* through those windows?" Shepherd asked.

"Sure can," Schirra radioed back. "At least the *look* like people. One's a guy—got a real five-O'clock shadow on him. The other is pretty clearly female: long hair, at least. Right, Tom?"

"He's not kidding, Al," Stafford seconded. "Two of 'em in there."

"How close is this, er, 'thing?'" Shepherd demanded.

"Well," Schirra radioed back, "it's about twenty feet away. I don't dare fire any of the OAMS thrusters. I might burn 'em."

"Don't suppose they're green and have lots of eyes, or anything," Shepherd radioed.

"They look pretty normal to me," Schirra replied. "Actually, the female has waved a couple of times," he reported. "And if she's anything like her face, she could be a real looker. What do you think Tom?"

"Oh yeah. Could be a real looker."

"You know we can't pick up that ball on the biggest radars at Cape Canaveral," Shepherd radioed.

"Doesn't show up on ours either," Stafford reported.

"...Or ours," Bormann radioed from Gemini 7.

A fifth voice joined the conversation from Houston: "Gentlemen," the unmistakably patrician voice of Dr. Robert Gilruth broke in, "we have quite a historic situation here. Any of you have suggestions as to what we do next...?"

— o — 0 — o —

"What do you think, Serena?" Brim said asked. "Do those guys look like star-shaped people to you?"

"You mean, like *us*?" the tiny woman asked, peering intently into the oval window of the little spacecraft. "From what little I can see, they appear to be pretty human."

Brim chuckled. "Just another proof that what the Gradgroat-Norchelites preach is probably true."

"The Gradygroats?" Serena asked. "Where did *you* run into those crazies, Wilf?"

"In Haelic/Hador," Brim answered. "Found they had admirable things to say—especially about how life got started in so many places."

"Like what?"

"Well, very basically, they believe a race of Ancients seeded planets all over the Universe at something they call 'the beginning of time.'"

"Wonder when that was supposed to be?"

"Don't have any idea," Brim admitted, "I'm just a simple Helmsman."

"Yeah, right," Serena said sarcastically, then frowned. "Wait! What's that? Hey, I can't understand them any more. Like they've changed their language—totally. What can *that* be?"

"Don't have any idea," Brim admitted. "Sounds the same to me."

"Believe me," Morgan said, "it isn't."

"I believe you," Brim said, "But if you can master *this* one too, we'll be a lot better off."

Morgan nodded. "I'll do what I can, Meanwhile, one of them over there looks to be smiling at us."

"You're sure he's a *he*?"

"Looks like one—and he appears to be friendly."

"He does," Brim said, waving and smiling to the figure in the other ship. "Let me get into my Battle Suit, Serena. I'd like to use the airlock and take a short trip over there."

"You're really going to do that?"

"Absolutely. As long as we're visiting, we might as well be friendly."

"Better be careful," Serena warned. "Those flames…."

Brim smiled. "I'll be okay," he said reassuringly. "Don't forget, I'm wearing the latest Battle Suit money can buy."

Chapter 44

. . .Now that's interesting

ON THE SURFACE OF PLANET AN-543298157531-A31, 38
TRIAD, 52017

A t the same time Brim prepared for his impromptu spacewalk,
some 300 light years distant, Barbousse and Tissuard stood on
the shore of a small, clear lake surrounded by blue, cactus-like
plants—some of which appeared to be at least 200 irals in height. The
air was heavy with the perfume of a thousand smaller plants with
riotous colors. In a clearing behind them, two LifeGlobes rested on
landing pods, cupolas retracted and locked, hatches welded
permanently shut, flashers and KA'PPA beacons dark.

"Always seems so wasteful to just leave perfectly good LifeGlobes
behind," Tissuard commented with a shrug.

Barbousse shrugged. "Never gave it a thought before," he said.
"Does seem pretty wasteful."

"What can be more wasteful than war?" she mused. "These little
machines would be worth a fortune in the right places—and since
they're built of Hullmetal, they'll literally last forever. Seems when
nations—including our ours—gear up for war, all ideas of economy go
out the window."

"From what I understand," Barbousse said philosophically,
"abandoned 'Globes have provided at least two civilizations their last
technological push into the HyperLight Community."

Tissuard smiled and took Barbousse's arm. "Utrillo," she said, "you
have the doggondest way of finding some good in everything."

"I always try, Nadia," the big man replied. "It's a lot less stressful
than lookin' at things from the other way 'round."

"Speaking of stress," Tissuard mused with a twinge of fear, "there is only one more planet for us to search, isn't there?"

"Only one," Barbousse repeated with a slight nod.

"And if Brim's not there?"

Barbousse looked down at the tiny Lampsonite and smiled. "Then I'll keep on looking, Ma'am," he replied quietly, "because he *is* somewhere, and I won't rest until I find him—alive or dead."

Close by, a single Fleet launch waited to take the last survivors up to the Light Cruiser I.F.S. *Darter*, a unit of the Fifth Battlecruiser Combat Group, standing a few hundred c'lenyts off the surface of the planet. A hundred irals farther along the shore, *Four Nines* and three other WF-400s were beached with their Spin-Gravs rumbling at idle. As the two Imperials stood quietly, Captain Antilles approached, bowed to Tissuard and offered his hand to Barbousse.

"Sorry you lost *Purple Abigail*," Barbousse said, shaking the old Captain's grizzled hand, "but at least we found your two 'Globes before your provisions ran out."

"Ten saved out of 41 people we had on board," Antilles said, wearily. "I don't know if anybody got off after me. That man Brim you asked about helped launch our 'Globes, but then he stayed behind for some reason. Probably waiting to see if anybody else got off. Xaxt! If he hadn't forced me aboard the 'Globe, I'd never have left the old *Purple Abagail*."

Sympathetically, Tissuard patted him on the arm. "I understand," she said. "Unfortunately, war is all about breaking things and killing people."

"Terrible shame about that man, Brim, too," Antilles said, as the three started off toward the waiting launch. "Didn't realize the fellow had so many friends."

"He did," Barbousse assured him. "And you didn't see him take to a 'Globe?"

"As I said, Chief, when our 'Globes drifted out of sight, he was still standing there on LifeGlobe deck like he was waitin' for more survivors."

"That's Wilf Brim," Tissuard declared, trying hard not to use the past tense.

"Makes sense," Barbousse said shaking his head. "Well, Captain, have a good trip home. I'm glad insurance will replace the *Abagail*."

"Yes," Antilles agreed, "but it can't replace the people who died in her—or your friend Brim."

"Just so you know, Captain, that man is Admiral, Lord Brim of Grayson."

"Voot's greasy beard!" Antilles gasped. "I thought he looked familiar. But he was so…, normal, I guess. I'd never have known. What in all Xaxt was such a man doing on a little tramp freighter in the first place?"

"Doing what he thought was his duty for the Emperor," Tissuard said.

"B-but…."

Barbousse smiled as he helped the old Captain into the launch. "Neither of us know, Captain, but there are a lot of people trying to find out how it happened." He clapped a SubLieutenant manning the hatch on his shoulder. Take good care of these people, SubLieutenant," he said. "They've been through a lot, lately."

"Aye, Chief Barbousse," the SubLieutenant said, coming to attention and saluting.

Dumbfounded, Barbousse returned the man's salute. "How did you know my name?"

"Voot's Beard, Chief," the young officer exclaimed, "everyone knows who you are, sir."

Barbousse shook his head—in the last years, his world had changed radically, and there was no turning back time. "Thanks, young man," he said gently. "Good luck on your way through the Fleet"

"Thanks, yourself," The SubLieutenant grinned. "And good luck to you, too, Chief," he replied.

Barbousse winked, then he and Tissuard started off at a trot for the ebony WF-400. Climbing the ladder and settling into the left seat, Barbousse checked that Tissuard was properly seated, then glanced over the controls. "Baun," he demanded , "this tub ready to fly?"

"She is, Chief," the SubLieutenant replied.

"Okay, young man, take her up. After this, there's only one possible planet within range of the *Abagail's* old R-103 LifeGlobes. And we *are* going to find The Skipper...."

— o — 0 — o —

Aboard Gemini-6A: Schirra listened to Astronaut Allan Shepherd from Houston: "Wally: what's going on up there now?"

"Not much, Al," Schirra replied. "The other ship—if that's what it is—hasn't moved for the last five minutes, and as I said, I don't want to fire any of the thrusters for fear I burn it."

"Um," Shepherd radioed back, "Dr. Gilruth wants to know if you think your ship is in danger. Apparently, the Visitor isn't interested in Gemini-Seven."

Schirra looked over at Stafford and shrugged. "What do you think, Tom?"

"Well," Stafford replied, "we've got plenty of supplies aboard. I'm not in any hurry to get out of here."

"Either am I," Schirra agreed. "Al, tell Dr. Gilruth and everybody else down there that we're cool with sitting tight for a while. Right now, we don't feel as if we're in any kind of danger."

"Kind of suspected that," Shepherd commented. "Your heart rates are pretty normal."

"If that gal shows up at the cupola windows again, everything might change," Schirra joked.

"You two taking lots of photos?" Shepherd asked.

"You bet," Stafford said. "I've taken a couple rolls of already."

"Uh oh," Schirra exclaimed. "Now *that's* interesting...."

"What?" Shepherd demanded.

"Well," Schirra explained, "somebody's just opened a hatch in the side of the Ball."

"A hatch?"

"That's what it looks like to me...." Schirra said. "How about you, Tom?"

"It better be a hatch," Stafford said, "because someone is standing in it... wearing what looks a lot like a *really* lightweight space suit...."

Chapter 45

. . .space walk

IN SPACE, ORBITING A BLUE PLANET,   38 TRIAD, 52017
16 DECEMBER, 1965

"Floating" in space outside the LifeGlobe, Brim radioed to Morgan as he latched the hatch open and peered out into the void, "What's been going on over there since I left the cupola?"

"Not much," Morgan reported, "except the two guys behind the windows look surprised—and there's a lot of radio talk going on between them and ground stations as we orbit the planet."

"Yeah," Brim said. "I can hear 'em in my phones. Any luck understanding what they're saying, yet?"

"I'm getting there," she announced, frowning. "Shouldn't be too long…."

"Soon as you do, let me know" Brim said, securing the end of a stout, fifty-Iral line he'd attached to his battle suit to a sturdy handhold just inside the hatch. Next, he leaned out of the hatch to wave at the two beings in the orbiter and carefully launched himself across to the little craft. Right away, he saw he was going to miss!

By now, radio traffic to and from the funnel was nearly nonstop. He smiled and waved at the two beings in the little spacecraft as he floated feet-first past the windows, then grabbed the line and pulled himself back to the 'Globe's hatch. On a whim, he bowed from the waist and clapped his gloves together as if he were applauding. This immediately resulted in a great deal of human-like laughter from the little spacecraft, applause, then even more radio traffic. By Voot, they were *communicating* more or less!

"Nice try, clumsy!" Morgan giggled in his earphones.

"Watch me this time," Brim grumped back. "You'll think I was raised in a circus."

"Good luck," she said. "I'll be watching."

This time, Brim took more care of his aim and —pushing off with less force—found himself moving directly toward the small end of the funnel.

"Looks like you've got it this time, Wilf," Morgan radioed from the cupola.

"Seems that way," Brim agreed, as he bumped gently into the nose of the little spacecraft, noting what he took to be small thrusting rocket engines spaced around its periphery. Mumbling a quick prayer to Voot they wouldn't need firing for the moment, he maneuvered himself until he was straddling the nose of the spacecraft as if he were riding a Sodeskayan Droshcat. Now for some more communicating.

He peered into the window on his left and was met by a puzzled but smiling face from inside. A similar face met him at the right window. He held up an index finger to make sure he had their attention, then switched to the little spacecraft's frequency, and pointed to his chest with his thumb. "Wilf Brim," he broadcast.

Both occupants looked surprised for a moment then began talking gibberish into microphones. For moments, the frequency filled with a dozen native voices, which stopped abruptly when the man behind the window on Brim's right held up his index finger, pointed to his chest, and broadcast, "Walter Schirra."

Next, the man behind Brim's left window pointed to himself and broadcast, "Thomas Stafford."

Grinning, Brim instinctively held up his thumb in triumph. "Walter Schirra," he broadcast to the right window; "Thomas Stafford," to the left. Pointing again to himself, he repeated, "Wilf Brim," then, simply "Wilf."

"Wally" and "Tom" rapidly came back as replies.

Brim waved his right hand at the two men and broadcast, "Hello."

The two waved back in unison, broadcasting something that sounded like a greeting: "Hullo."

"Hullo," Brim returned. He'd learned his first native word! Now, he was getting somewhere! He twisted sideways, pointed to the other funnel-like spacecraft, and held his hands palm up in what he hoped was some sort of interrogative.

"Frank Bormann and James Lovell," the man named Schirra replied.

"Bormann *and* Lovell," Brim broadcast with a nod—he'd another native word—*and*!

"I like the one in the right window," Serena remarked.

"You keep out of this," Brim warned, but was too late.

The man named Schirra spoke what was obviously a question, even though Brim couldn't comprehend what he said. Before he could formulate an answer in sign language, Morgan replied in gobbledygook.

At that, Schirra exclaimed something in surprise.

"What did you say to him?" Brim demanded

"I said, 'My name's Serena and I think you're cute!'"

"What'd he say to that?" Demanded Brim.

"He said he understood—and 'thanks.'"

"Understood *what*?" Brim demanded.

"…What I was saying, silly. I can talk to them now."

"You didn't tell me," Brim grumped.

"I simply forgot," Serena retorted.

"Find out what in Xaxt they're doing out here in orbit," Brim prompted.

Serena spoke a few words to the funnel ship, waited while a number of verbal exchanges took place—including some laughter—then replied, "The Man named Schirra claims he and his partner Stafford are on a scientific expedition in orbit."

"Scientific expedition?"

"That's what he says—and the people on the surface back him up."

"People on the surface?"

"Yes. Sounds as if there is quite crowd down there somewhere. I've been talking to an Alan Shepherd and a guy named Gilruth who has some sort of a title—like 'Doctor.' They're in a place called 'Houston.'"

"What about the other funnel-ship?"

"They were up here together to see if they could meet nose-to-nose. Schirra used the word *rendezvous.*"

"Wow, these guys *are* fairly advanced."

"They are," Serena said, "...and they claim this is all in preparation for an expedition to their satellite.... Um, hang on, Wilf...." With that, she began another spirited exchange in the native language. After considerable time, she said, "Wilf, they want to know who we are and where we come from—they've already figured out we're aliens. What d'you think I should tell them?"

"What do *you* think?" Brim countered. "*You've* been talking to these dudes."

"Well," Serena said after a pause. "They certainly seem friendly—both Schirra and the one on the ground they refer to as 'Al Shepherd' have wonderful senses of humor."

"Tell 'em the truth, I suppose," Brim said. "We're unarmed and riding in an ancient LifeGlobe, so we don't appear to have much of an upper hand, do we?" As he spoke, Schirra rapped noiselessly on his glass window and held up a finger.

"Okay, that makes sense to me," Serena started, then "...Hang on, Wilf, the guy Schirra is talking again...."

Brim held up a finger and nodded as Schirra talked with Serena.

At some length, Serena said, "Schirra and Stafford are going to open their hatches. They want to shake you hand."

"Shake my hand?"

"That's what they say. Both call this an 'historic occasion.'"

"Well, " Brim replied, "I guess if we are their first 'aliens,' then this definitely qualifies as historic." As he watched, the two individuals inside the little spaceship were donning helmets and gloves of what appeared to be primitive battle suits. For a moment he absently considered what he'd do if they attacked him sitting there, straddling the nose of their little spaceship, but, considering their clumsy battle suits, he'd likely come out on top in any fight—*whatever that meant,* he added with a silent chuckle. He and Serena were, after all, their guests—with all the rights, responsibilities, and privileges that went with the situation.... Then, without any more warning—a substantial puff of ice crystals from the side of the funnel revealed the two occupants were depressurizing the cabin of their spacecraft...

Chapter 46

. . .handshake

IN SPACE, ORBITING PLANET EARTH,   38 TRIAD, 52017
16 DECEMBER, 1965

"Schirra, Stafford," Dr. Gilruth spoke from Mission Control, "I really don't advise opening your spacecraft! Is that understood?"

"Um, ..understood, Doctor," Schirra replied, "but Tom and I, we've decided we'd like to shake Mr. Brim's hand up here where we met him. Pretty clear, he's come a long way to meet us."

"W-what if he attacks you?"

"Well, there *are* two of us here, Doctor—and Tom's a pretty tough character. I figure we can handle him if he's unfriendly…."

"You two are not equipped for EVAs," Gilruth argued, even though Gemini-Six *is*. What if you simply float away….?"

"Doctor," Schirra promised in an even voice, "We're only going to open the hatch and stand up. I promise we'll both hold onto something at all times. Besides, we are always attached to the ship by our ECS lines."

"One other matter," Gilruth warned. "I assume you've read about what European bacteria and viruses did to the natives of North and South America."

"Wow," Schirra replied. "Yes I have."

"Are you willing to take that risk yourself?"

Schirra considered that for a time then nodded. "I am, in fact," he answered, turning to Stafford. "How about you, Tom?" he asked.

"Count me in," Stafford answered firmly. "I'll take a chance, too."

"All right, but keep in mind the chance you two taking is real...." Gilruth warned, however he was interrupted by Shepherd.

"Pressurization is now at zero, Wally," the Navy Astronaut reported. "You guys can open your doors—and good luck!"

Taking a deep breath, Schirra turned to nod at Stafford, then turned the release lever for his hatch, pushing upward and outward until he felt the tabs lock. He took a moment to acclimate himself to the awesome grandeur of Space before he raised himself in his seat to confront a man-like figure dressed in a golden space suit straddling the nose of Gemini VI-A. Obviously grinning behind the visor of his helmet, the figure offered his hand. Surprised by this completely human gesture, Schirra flipped open his quick-release belt and carefully stood upright. "Hello, Wilf Brim," he radioed, gripping the proffered glove.

"Hello, Wally Schirra," the other returned as Tom Stafford stood in his own opened hatch photographing the little ceremony of Earth's first known contact with the Universal Community of the Stars....

The three men remained in place for considerable time until the voice of Alan Shepherd broke the spell from Mission Control. "Hey, up there! Everything Okay?"

"Yeah, Al," Schirra returned. "I'd say everything is *very* okay."

"Anybody recording all this?" Dr. Gilruth demanded?

"I've taken a whole roll of photos with the Hasselblad, Doctor," Stafford replied "Surely some of 'em ought to turn out well."

"Good," Gilruth said. "Then hello from Earth, Mister Brim."

"Thank you, Doctor Gilruth," Morgan said. "On behalf of my colleague, Lord Brim, may I say, 'Hello to the planet Earth from the stars.'"

"Wait a moment," Schirra interrupted, "did I hear '*Lord* Brim'?"

"That's his title presently," Morgan assured, "but he's really what you call an 'Admiral' in the Imperial Fleet."

"Why am I not surprised," Schirra said, coming to as much a position of attention as he could in his clumsy space suit and snapping a military salute. "Lieutenant Commander Walter M. Schirra, United States Navy," he said proudly. As he watched, amazed, the figure he knew as Wilf Brim silently raised the tips of his fingers to his helmet in a perfect military salute of his own—even before the Morgan woman translated his words into the gobbledygook of the alien language.

"Gentlemen," Dr. Gilruth interrupted. "I dislike breaking into this historic meeting, but I feel it is imperative to urge all three of you back into your respective spacecraft. We have much more to discuss and at least our two Astronauts will be much safer inside."

"Aye, Doctor Gilruth," Schirra replied. "I think you're correct. Miss Morgan, will you please inform Admiral Brim that Commander Stafford and I are going back inside?"

Morgan made the translation, and Brim nodded a moment later. As Schirra watched, the alien Admiral began pulling himself hand over hand back to the hatch in the golden ball. It took nearly fifteen Metacycles before the two NASA Astronauts had once again seated themselves and swung their hatches closed.

— o — 0 — o —

Later, when both spacecraft were secured, Gilruth asked, "How can you understand us?" Gilruth demanded. "Especially since we're talking in a supposedly secret code."

"I really cannot answer that, Doctor," Morgan replied. "Simplest explanation is I come from a planet system whose inhabitants have a natural ability to translate from listening to emotions, not words. We're called, 'Speakers to all,' and even I have no idea how it works. We're born with the power."

"Um, Serena," Schirra interrupted hesitantly, "with all due respect, what are you and Lord Brim doing there in orbit above this planet we call 'Earth?'"

"Oh, sorry, Commander" Serena replied. "I was about to explain when you decided to open your hatch...."

"Yes," a number of voices chimed in from Mission Control, "....please go on!"

"Well," Serena said, "Lord Brim and I are, what? ...*Survivors*, I suppose. Our Starship was hit by a HyperTorp, and...."

"Whoa! What's a *Starship*?" Stafford demanded

"...and what's a *HyperTorp*?" Alan Shepherd piped in from Houston.

"Um:, you'll have to ask Lord Brim about the 'Torps,'" Serena parried. "But *Starships* are, well, ships that travel through space—like from star systems to star systems...."

"Um..., all... right," Gilruth said hesitantly, "I *believe* I have that as a *concept* so far. Now what about these *HyperTorps*?"

"They're things launched from starships to blow up other starships, I guess.... Again, you'd have to ask Lord Brim."

"Sounds like you're in some sort of a *space war* out there?" Schirra burst out in surprise.

"Well, *yeah!*" Morgan said in disbelief. "I mean, why else would someone blow up our ship?"

"Ok, ok," Schirra said quickly. "Sorry, I didn't know...."

"It's all right," Morgan assured him.

"So that shining gold ball you're riding in is a *lifeboat* of sorts?" Schirra asked.

"That's right, Commander," Serena replied. "We call them *LifeGlobes*."

"Figures," Schirra mused, "Figures...."

"What about other life boa... er, Life *Globes*?" someone from Mission Control asked. "Were any others launched from your er, starship?"

"A moment," Morgan asked, before speaking briefly to Admiral Brim in the alien tongue. "Lord Brim says he managed to launch two LifeGlobes before this one," she replied.

"Where are *they*, then?" Schirra demanded. "Can we help them, in any way?"

"Another moment, please," Serena asked, speaking with Brim for considerably more time. "To answer your question, Commander: at present, we can do nothing to help them."

"Howcome?"

"It all has to do with the speed of light," Serena explained after considerable deliberation. "Let's say our ship was traveling at ten LightSpeed, and...."

"*Light speed?*" Gilruth demanded. "You're talking about the speed of light?"

"Well yes, Doctor, but the ship on which we were traveling was only making about ten light years' distance per metacycle—a time unit comparable to your 'hour.'"

"*Faster than* the speed of light? B-but that…. That's *impossible!*"

"I understand that sounds rather slow, Doctor, but our ship *was* an old merchantman and…."

"No! I mean it's impossible to…."

"…Um…, Doctor," Schirra interrupted gently, "why don't we let the lady finish her story?"

"…Er, yes. Sorry Miss Serena. Please go on about why we can't help the other two life globes."

"No problem, Doctor," Morgan continued. "It's just that after Lord Brim launched the first two LifeGlobes, he waited quite a long time for other survivors while the Starship was slowing from approximately ten LPM. As the last person to escape, I managed to reach the LifeGlobe deck only moments before the ship blew up, so when Lord Brim launched us, we had traveled a number of light years beyond the others—therefore their LifeGlobes would have sought out other planets."

"You said, 'Sought out?'" Alan Shepherd asked in an awed voice. "How did they do that?"

"I have no idea, Mr. Shepherd," Morgan replied. "It's simply what LifeGlobes do. They seek out the nearest planets that will support the life of their occupants—like this one did in bringing us here to your 'Earth.'"

"How in the Sam Hill do they *know?*"

"Again, you'd have to ask the Admiral," Serena deferred. "He'd have a much better description, but unfortunately he doesn't speak your language."

"Yes, *very* unfortunate," Gilruth echoed ruefully.

At this point, Schirra broke in. "For crying out loud, people—what's the matter with us? We need to find out what we can do for these folks instead of beating our gums. Madame Serena, please, what can we do for you? Are you in any kind of immediate danger?"

Chapter 47

. . .twelve Metacycles out

IN SPACE, 38 TRIAD, 52017

Barbousse peered through the Hyperscreens at his little formation of WF-400s racing at top speed through the starscape, heedless of energy burn. He glanced behind him to check on Tissuard slumped in the jump seat, sound asleep. Across the console, Baun was conning the ship. Everyone was on edge. The star whose planet was their destination now appeared as a faint pinpoint on the horizon. "How long now, Nero?" he whispered into the blower.

"Should be there in less than twelve Metacycles, Chief," Lu replied.

"Good," Barbousse growled. "Chief Kermis, how are the systems holding up?"

"Everything's cool down here, Chief," Kermis replied. "But the Drives are gobbling energy like there's no tomorrow."

In the corner of his eye, Barbousse saw Baun glance at him and nod agreement. He already knew the energy situation; Helmsmen on the other three ships were complaining, too.

"We'll worry about that when we get there," Barbousse returned grimly. "First, we're going to find The Skipper!"

"Aye, Chief," Baun said and returned to the controls.

"Gettin' any KA'PPA traffic from around that star?" Barbousse demanded."

"Not yet, Chief," Steele reported, "but it's still a long way off, too."

"Keep tryin'" Barbousse growled.

"Count on it, Chief," Steele replied. "That's what earns me the big credits."

— o — 0 — o —

Back in the LifeGlobe, Brim listened absently to Morgan reassuring Commander Schirra that neither they nor the LifeGlobe were indeed in any immediate danger. Afterward: "Serena, ask if the Commander would recommend a good place for us to land this 'Globe."

"Okay," Morgan replied, and immediately began another dialogue with Schirra. After a considerable time, she returned with, "The Commander asks us if we will follow him down to a safe landing as his guest. He says he's prepared to de-orbit almost immediately."

"Serena," Brim replied, "inform Commander Schirra I am prepared to follow him *anywhere!*"

As Serena translated, Brim could hear Schirra chuckling inside the little orbiter.

"He says he kind of figured," she translated.

"You're doing a great job, Serena," Brim said, taking her arm for a moment.

"Thanks, Wilf," she said. "Sometimes it's handy to have us Lampsonite 'Speakers to All' around, even if we do seem a little weird sometimes."

"Weird is good," Brim reassured her with a wink. "Now, all we've got to do is get ourselves to the surface in one piece."

"Well, Admiral," Morgan said with a chuckle, "count on me to do everything I can toward that important goal. Kind of looking forward to discovering what kind of situation we get ourselves into next."

— o — 0 — o —

During the next Metacycle, Morgan translated lengthy technical dialogues between Brim, the occupants of both native spacecraft, and their controllers on the ground. As Brim had surmised, the little craft used rocket engines, firing them in the reverse direction from which they were traveling until the little craft was slowed from orbital speed and descended in a great arc toward the surface.

"You look concerned, Wilf," she observed with her hand over the microphone.

"Well, I am," Brim admitted. "They'll be taking a ballistic path to the surface. And at some time, they'll passing through the atmosphere so rapidly they'll be enclosed by fiery plasma."

"Sounds terrifying."

"In a way, it is," Brim assured her. "Their little orbiter's friction with the atmosphere will generate tremendous heat—enough to burn them up as if..., well, you've seen meteors. Everybody has. That little spacecraft will become nothing more than a meteor."

"You mean it's going to burn up?"

"Serena. Do those guys seem suicidal?"

"Of course not."

"Then you can be sure they've got some way of shielding themselves.... Hey, ask them if they've got a 'heat shield.'"

Moments later, Serena replied, "Commander Schirra says, 'Absolutely,' and asks if we've got one, too."

"Tell him no, we don't," Brim instructed. "But that doesn't mean we can't follow him down—even at the speed he'll be traveling. Our SpinGrav can take us as fast as they can fall, and our Hullmetal will protect us from most of the heat we generate. Just in case we become separated, ask them if they'll broadcast a beacon from their landing place."

After much more discussion with native technicians on the ground, Morgan reported they could indeed set up a beacon if Brim could follow a radio beam. "Can you?" she asked.

Brim scratched his head and studied the LifeGlobe's radio set. "Uh-huh," he mumbled after a time. "Absolutely. Tell 'em if they'll supply a strong, directional signal, I can home in it by monitoring its strength."

After a short conversation, Serena nodded. "That's taken care of, then," she said, scribbling a radio frequency on a scrap of plastic, then handing it to Brim. A moment later, she held up a hand as the voice of Dr, Gilruth interrupted from the speaker. After more conversation, she smiled and nodded to Brim. "Dr. Gilruth wants us to land on a 'ship'—the kind that floats on water."

"Interesting," Brim said. "Tell him it's okay with me as long as it has enough flat surface for me to park the LifeGlobe."

Serena spoke a few words to Gilruth, whose reply brought a smile to her lips. "Dr Gilruth informs me this particular ship has enough flat surface to park a whole *squadron* of LifeGlobes."

Chapter 48

. . .the plot thickens

AVALON/ASTURIUS, IMPERIAL MINISTRY OF
INTELLIGENCE (IMI) CAMPUS NEAR AVALON CITY, 38
TRIAD, 52017

W hile Brim started preparations for landing on "Earth," back on Avalon/Asturius, Porterfield Marston and his associate Dr. Factovar Zinnkin arrived for their appointment at the sprawling IMI Campus exactly on schedule. In its wooded location some ten miles Lightward of Avalon City, the shadowy Ministry looked more like a college than an organization rumored to be one of the deadliest in the Galaxy. Marston's Chauffeur deposited his two passengers under the portico of the mirror-clad, domed office building marked IMI.

"I say, Doctor," Marston declared as a first set glass doors opened before them, then closed rapidly behind them, confining both for a few clicks in a glass chamber. "Not a comfortable place for claustrophobics," he observed.

"Hmm," Zinnkin observed with a frown. "Imagine it was designed that way." He chuckled darkly. "Doubt if they exactly welcome visitors."

"Yes, hmm. Should be interesting," Marston mused while a second set of glass panels opened before them, granting entry to a wide, circular lobby ringed by display cases containing odd mechanisms he guessed were historic devices for secretly gathering information. "You ever met this Tazmir Adam before?"

"Shook his hand at a party at a party last year," Zinnkin said, tightlipped as they walked quickly toward a reception desk. "But, that's it." Above them in the golden dome that overlaid the lobby hung an ancient spacecraft believed to be the prototype for all modern bender spacecraft.

"Gentlemen," an attractive, middle-aged blonde said by way of greeting. "Welcome to the IMI." Flanking her were two stone-faced, black-suited men who looked as if they could easily smack down an entire regiment of Leaguer Special-Forces Agnords.

"Hmm. Yes. Good morning, Madame." Marston announced with an old-fashioned bow. "I am Marston; my companion is Doctor Zinnkin. We are here to consult with Doctor Adam."

"You are expected," the Receptionist said, handing each visitor a metallic badge. "Keep these with you at all times, Gentlemen," she directed pleasantly. "They will unlock any door authorized by your clearances. Doctor Adam's office is on the second floor, Suite One. Elevators are to your left."

"Hmm That's all?" Marston asked in amazement.

"Oh yes," the receptionist replied cheerfully. "You were searched as you entered, and you cannot enter anywhere you are not authorized. Please, enjoy your visit with Doctor Adam."

Nodding, the two men made their way to an elevator bank, entering an empty car that closed its doors and lifted gently in what felt like a gyrating course with no further directions. When the doors opened again, Marston and Zinnkin entered a comfortably furnished lobby, where another attractive woman motioned to a door marked only by ADAM. "Please enter gentlemen," the woman said. "Doctor Adam is expecting you."

Opening the door, the two entered a room dominated by a large wooden desk—mostly empty except for a few folders—behind which a scholarly, white-haired man rose to his feet. Wearing a camel's-hair sport coat, open white shirt, red sweater, and denim trousers, he looked more like a fatherly college professor than someone who was known to kill from across the galaxy with the touch of a button. "Messers Marston and Zinnkin," he said softly, offering his hand to each. "Thank you for coming." Afterward, he indicated a round table with four leather-covered chairs, "please have a seat. I understand we have much to talk about."

"Hmm, yes, I believe we do, Doctor," Marston began. "And it was a convoluted road that brought us here."

"Admiral Calhoun forwarded your report," Adam mused. "Interesting reading. He also mentioned back-up documentation. Do you have it with you?"

"That depends, Doctor Adam," Zinnkin said with an uncomfortable smile.

"Depends on what, Doctor Zinnkin?"

"On how much you care about *how* and *where* we got much of our information, Doctor Adam."

Adam laughed. "I suppose one can assume Forensic Finance requires the same sort of techniques we use at the IMI?"

"Good assumption, Doctor Adam," Zinnkin replied, "…only one *also* assumes you are not so much in danger of breaking the law as are 'normal' civilians."

"We like to refer to the process as merely 'bending' laws," Adam replied with a smile. "Let us say all 'bending' in this room becomes legal under the Wartime Security Act. How's that?"

"Ah, yes, Doctor Adam, hmm" Marston replied, his face reddening, "the good Doctor Zinnkin and I have indeed committed some serious bending, so that sounds fine."

Adam laughed a deep laugh. "Wonderful!" he said with a good-natured chuckle, "then we shall exchange trade secrets and *both* profit. When do we start?"

Marston exchanged glances with Zinnkin, then shrugged and grinned. "Yes …Hmm. As you've read, Doctor Adam, it all began with the tragedy at Operation Eppeid more than a nearly two years ago when Count Tal Confisse's daughter General Megan Trafford lost control of the situation and managed to transfer her guilt to Wilf Brim—Admiral Brim at the time."

"In most government circles," Adam corrected with a steady glance, "Lord Brim is still referred to as *Admiral* Brim."

"Hmmm. Yes. Understood, Doctor Adam," Marston said quickly. "But as stated, I believe that's where Trafford—normally a careful, conservative man—began taking chances. To bring off the court martial of a national hero like Admiral Brim, he was forced to, shall we say, open doors that, for him, would better have remained closed."

"It's worth mentioning," Zinnkin interjected, "that we believe this period is when Trafford began operating in conjunction with his cousin Lord Daniel Cranwell. Significantly, we discovered Cranwell is often as adventurous as Trafford is conservative."

"Hmmm. Yes. The modifying influence each had on the other's extremes made then an effective team for a time," Marston pointed out, "...until ongoing success gave way to the carelessness that lead to our meeting today."

"And you say both these two were linked into the League?"

"Absolutely, Doctor Adam," Zinnkin assured him. "At first, only Cranwell was directly involved, heavily insuring certain ships, then informing League agents of the secret coordinates through which the convoys would pass in space—and when."

"That's must be how the Leaguers HyperTorped the *Purple Abagail* with Brim aboard," Adam exclaimed.

"Yes. Hmmm. Precisely, Doctor Adam," Marston said. "But as Cranwell previously learned to his fiscal discomfort, often as not, the League benders missed his specially insured freighters, and he took a bath paying off the insurers."

"And that, Doctor Adam," Zinnkin said, "is why he made his big mistake—he couldn't really trust the Leaguers to target the right ship in a convoy, so he needed a backup in case that occurred during this extremely critical operation."

"Please go on," Adam urged.

"First," the Forensic Economist declared, "a bit of history. And from here on, we—Marston and I—are treading on rather thin legal ice. You see, Cranwell had devised a system of blind cutouts that made tracing these money transfers impossible. Believe me, Doctor Adam, I am very good at what I do, yet each time I began a trace—legally or most often *illegally*—I came upon a totally dead end somewhere along the transfer's path that totally nullified both source and destination."

Adam frowned. "I had no idea this Cranwell was a financial genius."

"Either did I, Doctor," Zinnkin replied, "and in point of fact, he was only *clever*. His real expertise came from a mysterious figure who goes by the name of Covall the Wraith."

"Interesting name," Adam commented.

"Apparently, he named himself—hmm," Marston interjected. "An extreme autistic, he is really Count Trafford's illegitimate son who suffers from a rare development disorder that manifests itself with extreme ability in a single, narrow area of expertise at the expense of nearly all other forms of development."

"*Savantism*," Adam pronounced.

"That is what we believe, Doctor Adam," Zinnkin said. "He can not live on his own, but follows his father like a dog, doing menial tasks Trafford's servants often refuse. His sister, General Megan Trafford, has no idea the man exists. The poor wretch's single area of expertise is Finance—and it is *he* who invented the brilliant system of cutouts and offsets that kept both Cranwell and Trafford safe for so long. That's the history lesson."

"Nevertheless, you did manage to crack this system of Covall's, didn't you?" Adam said.

"I did, and I *did not*, Doctor Adam," Zinnkin said. "Marston and I are here only because *Cranwell* became so self-assured he committed the single mistake that opened his whole financial scheme to my view."

"Great Voot," Adam whispered. "What was *that*?"

"It had to do with the murder of Wilf Brim," Zinnkin said.

Adam shook his head for a moment, then smiled. "Why am I not at all surprised it had to do with Admiral Brim? Please go on."

"Well," Zinnkin continued, "remember I said Cranwell's scheme of insuring freighters, then giving Leaguers the convoy's position, wasn't always successful because at times the League Benders didn't nail the special ship Cranwell had insured?"

"I remember," Adam assured him.

"Trafford and Cranwell so desperately wanted the Admiral dead that Cranwell independently decided to provide a backup for his plan. He hired the famous Lampsonite assassin Serena Morgan to accompany Brim aboard the freighter, then bring about his death in case the Leaguers failed to destroy the *Purple Abagail*."

"And...?" prompted Adam.

"And Cranwell decided he had no need for Covall's services when he paid the enormous down payment Morgan demanded. He was dead wrong. His fumble-fingered delivery of that payment into the topsy-turvy milieu of Lampsonite finance momentarily opened a window into Covall's magnificently crafted system which—after considerable study—revealed the hierarchy of financial links which eventually produced a record of every illegal transaction that had occurred."

"Hmmm. Unfortunately for Zinnkin," Marston continued, "our breakthrough occurred too late to prevent Admiral Brim from taking his, shall we say, *fateful* voyage aboard the *Purple Abagail*. But here we are with the details you need to dismantle Covall's entire network—as well as bring both Cranwell and Trafford to justice before they can cause even further damage to the Imperial transport system." He took three, tiny DataVaults from his vest pocket and handed them to Adam. "Zinnkin and I have copies elsewhere—just in case—but please feel free to use all the proofs we have garnered to bring down these powerful traitors."

"Believe me," Adam promised, "if these proofs are even half as damaging as I suspect, we'll have those two shut down before they even realize what is happening to them."

After a few more brief remarks of appreciation, Adam escorted the two men to his lobby, leaving them with one final statement. "Before you give this briefing to Admiral Calhoun, gentlemen, don't count Admiral Brim out of the picture just yet. This is not the first tight situation from which he has walked away safely—nor likely to be the last...."

Chapter 49

. . .and down we go!

IN SPACE, ORBITING PLANET EARTH,   38 TRIAD, 52017
16 DECEMBER, 1965

Aboard the Gemini-VIA spacecraft: as the two NASA Astronauts were beginning their de-orbiting procedures, Schirra eyed the panel clock: "Thirty minutes to retrofire," he said. "Time to head downstairs. What d' you say we start the checklist?"

"Might as well," Stafford replied. "C-band beacon to 'continuous.'"

Deliberately, Schirra moved the C-band beacon switch to CONT. "Roger that. Let's get the gyros out of the way too." For the next minutes both Astronauts carefully aligned the gyro platform one last time.

"Okay, Tom," Schirra warned, "I'm going to turn the ship around."

"Roger that."

Using OAMS thrusters in the Adapter Module aft for the final time, Schirra maneuvered the spacecraft to the Blunt-End-Forward position, in effect, traveling backward. "We're in position, Mission Control," he reported.

"Telemetry looks good from here," Shepherd replied from Houston.

"Serena," Schirra radioed to the LifeGlobe, "are you and Wilf set to follow us down?"

"Check," Morgan replied. "Wilf says he has your radio beam loud and clear."

"Okay, you two," Schirra said, "be sure to keep clear of my ship; I'm about to fire the retrorockets—they're a lot bigger than our maneuvering thrusters."

249

"Thanks, Wally! Wilf says we're clear."

"Okay, then, Tom and I are going to have our hands full for the next half our or so. We'll talk again when we're down."

"Wilf says 'good luck.'"

"And to you, friends," Schirra replied fervently.

Moments later, an electronic timer energized a set of switches and relays to place the spacecraft on battery power instead of the fuel cells in the Adapter module. The BRTY PWR indicator turned amber along with a number of other indicators. "Go to internal power," Stafford read from the checklist.

"Roger that," Schirra replied, moving the four switches under MAIN BATTERYS to the ON position. "Battery Power is green. We're on internal."

"So long Fuel Cells," Stafford commented. From this point, the little spacecraft was on its own power, independent of electricity from the powerful fuel cells, aft in the Adapter Module.

"Electrical system to retro-mode, Wally," Stafford read.

Schirra pressed the amber IND RETRO ATT switch-indicator, setting the spacecraft's electrical system to retro-fire mode as well as placing the inertial-platform gyros into a special retro-firing mode. "Roger Electrical system to retro," he repeated.

"Okay, let's pressurize the forward Reaction Control System."

"Pressurizing the forward RCS," Schirra replied, pressing the RCS switch-indicator.

For the next clicks, both astronauts listened to squibs firing to pressurize fuel and oxidizer lines for use by the reaction-control thrusters in the nose that would later be used during re-entry to roll the spacecraft clockwise and counterclockwise. The Gemini spacecraft had a clever, off-center heat shield, so that when rolled, the spacecraft would steer left and right.

When the indicator turned to green—indicating successful operation—both astronauts busied themselves setting up special retro-mode communications that would keep the spacecraft in active communication with the ground as much as possible during the reentry.

At this point, things began to happen quickly. "Separation timer coming on," Schirra called out, "thirty seconds to retrograde."

"Roger the timer," Stafford replied. Moments passed like hours while the Astronauts watched the SEP OAMS LINE, SEP ELEC, SEP ADAP, and ARM AUTO RETRO indicators illuminated to amber, indicating when the spacecraft was ready to sever all ties to systems in the Adapter Module aft

"Got four lights," Schirra reported,

"Roger four lights," Stafford seconded. "Time to cut the aft OAMS."

"Roger the aft OAMS," Schirra replied, pressing and releasing the first switch.

Holding their breaths, the Astronauts listened to pyrotechnic guillotines fire to sever and seal the OAMS propellant lines in the Adapter Module. This was always a bit dicey because had the propellant lines not perfectly sealed, a disastrous explosion would result the moment the hypergolic fuels touched each other.

"Ya' think we can breath now?" Stafford quipped after a few moments.

"Once more we've cheated death," Schirra chuckled as the SEP OAMS indicator changed from amber to green.

"Roger—and checked off," Stafford replied. "Let's cut the electric lines."

"Roger the electric," Schirra said, pressing and releasing the SEP ELEC switch-indicator to guillotine the electrical busses. Another explosion aft in the Adapter module turned the SEP ELEC switch to green.

"Checked off," Stafford noted. "Adapter Module next, then down we go!"

"Jettisoning Adapter Module," Schirra said, depressing and releasing the SEP ADAPT switch-indicator. Instantly, two powerful shaped charges rattled the spacecraft, severing the Adapter Module and sending it out of the way. In a few moments, the SEP ADAPT switch-indicator changed from amber to green as module floated off into space.

"Checked that," Stafford said, penciling off another box on the checklist. "Let's arm the retros."

"Arming retros," Schirra repeated. Thoughtfully, he pressed and released the ARM AUTO RETRO switch-indicator, changing it from amber to green. "Got a green light," he reported. "Timer's running; I'm moving the four retro rocket squib switches to ARM."

"Roger Retro Squib arming," Stafford reported.

Both Astronauts watched the panel clock count off 45 seconds.

"Brace yourself," Schirra warned. "…And *away-y-y-y* we go!" Abruptly it seemed as if the little spacecraft—still traveling some 18,000 miles per hour—had smashed into a brick wall with a deafening roar. Instinctively, he pressed and released the MAN FIRE RETRO switch, firing the other three retrorockets redundantly—just in case. For the next 22 ear-splitting seconds, he and Stafford found themselves pressed—*smashed*—into their seats as the spacecraft decelerated, bleeding off speed at a tremendous rate.

"Wow!" Schirra exclaimed in the startling silence after the last retrorocket ceased firing. "…That's what I call *brakes*!"

"Amen!" Stafford quipped. "I'll have to be pried from this seat after that!"

"Okay," Schirra said, "let's get rid of the Retro Section, then." He moved the JETT RETRO SQUIB ARM switch from SAFE to ARM. "Arming the jettison retro section," he said.

"Check that," Stafford said. "'Jett Retro' switch armed."

For the next few seconds, Schirra intently watched for the switch to go amber. "Okay," he reported after a few moments, "…got us an amber."

"Roger 'Jett Retro' to amber," Stafford seconded.

"Got a green, now," Schirra reported. "Hang on!" Pressing the JETT RETRO button, he set off another set of explosions that rocked the ship while separating and jettisoning the retrograde section—and uncovering the all-important heat shield that would protect them as they entered the atmosphere like a meteor.

"Roger that green," Stafford exclaimed. "Now let's see how close to the recovery ship you can come."

Schirra laughed, as he took the control stick and rolled the little spacecraft upside down so he could see the horizon. "*Close?*" he teased. "Just you watch. We're about to set a record for *close*."

In point of fact, they did....

Chapter 50

. . . "X" marks the spot

IN SPACE, OVER PLANET EARTH,   38 TRIAD, 52017
                                            16 DECEMBER, 1965

Brim and Morgan shielded their eyes watching bright retrorockets fire aboard the much-shortened orbiter, slowing it abruptly from the velocity necessary for remaining in orbit. Little by little, it plummeted in a long curve toward the surface. Brim followed in the LifeGlobe, using the SpinGrav to match the orbiter's descent, which began trailing long, intermittent fiery tongues from the heat shield.

"What are they going to do now?" Morgan asked, completely spellbound by the tiny craft's descent. "Looks like they're going to burn up," she gasped.

"Don't think that's going to happen, either," Brim said, placing a calming hand on her shoulder. "Remember, they've got what Schirra called a 'heat shield' on the leading end—although I doubt if I'd volunteer to be in that little orbiter with them right now."

Sharing the binoculars, Brim and Morgan silently watched the orbiter become enveloped a in fiery plasma—like the actual meteor it had become—which lasted nearly ten Metacycles before tapering off. As he followed, Brim stared in near-disbelief watching the spacecraft rotate right and left, modifying its direction toward a large object just appearing on the horizon—some kind of ship. "Now *that's* what I call *clever,*" he exclaimed. "That little orbiter is *really* impressive. Whomever designed it certainly knew his business."

"Or *her* business," Morgan corrected.

"That too," Brim mumbled apologetically. "But what in Voot's name is *this?*"

"Something's broken off the small end!" Morgan said tight-lipped. "Now they're *really* going to die!"

"Don't think so," Brim said, handing over the binoculars, "Look: it's attached to the orbiter by a cable. And it's doubling its size."

"So it is. Wonder what it's supposed to do?"

"Well, it certainly has slowed their rate of descent, he agreed, reducing power to the SpinGrav. Maybe that's what it's supposed to do. Look: we're catching up quickly."

"Oh Voot!" Morgan shrieked. "*Now* they're in trouble! Look, the slow-up thing has come off now!"

"Don't think so," Brim said. "See, now it's pulling something from the nose section—and *that* is opening like a huge, orange-and-yellow-striped umbrella! It's a... a... a *parachute!*"

"A *para... chute*? What in Xaxt is a *parachute?*"

Brim found himself thinking back to a History class at The Helmsman's Academy. "I haven't seen one since I was kid, Serena," he said, "but it's a really primitive way of slowing something falling through a liquid or gaseous medium—and it looks like this one works. See, the orbiter is just drifting slowly toward the surface. Now if it just floats!"

"Looks like it's got a reception committee waiting," Morgan remarked. "Bunch of weird-looking flying machines. What in the name of Organ's big toe are they?"

"One's a *Rotorcraft,* I think they called them back in the day," Brim said. "The other one looks like a fairly normal winged flyer. And you were right—they are clearly a welcoming committee for the orbiter."

"Yeah," Morgan said, "including a huge, crazy-looking monster of a ship's heading our way."

"Whoa," Brim exclaimed. "Hard to miss!" Looking like nothing he had ever experienced, this giant had a vast, elongated expanse of level deck cluttered with a number of flying machines, both rotorcraft and winged. A tiny superstructure sat off to one side; on the other, an odd, angular planform jutted out over the water for more than half the

255

vessel's length. Where the hull met the water, however, it appeared nicely shaped for efficient passage through a liquid medium, and at present, it was moving quite well through the surface of this huge body of saline water—which, according to the LifeGlobe's brief information section, covered nearly three quarters of the planet's surface

"Wow!" Morgan exclaimed, "Doctor Gilruth wasn't fooling, was he? That ship really does have room for a whole squadron of LifeGlobes on its deck...."

As the orbiter splashed into the water, the rotorcraft dropped a number of orange-colored, boats that looked as if they might be inflatable, while figures slid to the water along cables until, within mere clicks, the little spacecraft was surrounded by rubber rafts and swimmers. The latter quickly applied a large, yellow, bladder-like device around the floating orbiter as Brim brought the LifeGlobe to a hover a short distance from the swarm of air vehicles circling the orbiter's landing site.

"Now what?" Morgan asked.

"Don't know," Brim replied. "I'm going to hover here until someone tells is what to do."

Morgan chuckled. "Doesn't sound like the take-charge Wilf Brim I know," she said.

"Believe me, Serena," Brim assured her, "Not only am I *not* in charge, I don't *want* to be in charge—of anything around here—at least not until we get a better idea of what's going on."

Abruptly, one of the rotorcraft broke from the hovering formation and flew directly toward the LifeGlobe. A native began to speak in a friendly sounding voice from the 'Globe's radio, which had been silent since the orbiter fired its retrorockets.

"What'd he say?" Brim demanded.

"He says 'Ahoy the LifeGlobe,'" Morgan translated.

"Tell him 'ahoy,' and ask if our friends the Astronauts made it down safely."

After a few moments of dialog, Morgan replied, "The Astronauts made it down safely and they're looking forward to meeting us on the *carrier*."

"What's a *carrier*?" Brim asked.

"Thought you might want to know," Morgan said. "The guy in the rotorcraft says it's that monster boat approaching—a special ship for launching and recovering aircraft."

"Sounds like a good place for us, then," Brim commented, watching the hatches of the floating orbiter open while two of the swimmers climbed aboard to assist. In a few clicks, both Astronauts, minus headgear, were standing and stretching—Brim assumed they must have been severely cramped in the tiny orbiter. Suddenly, both Schirra and Stafford turned toward the LifeGlobe and began waving. At the same time, the voice from the rotorcraft announced something.

"What was that?" Brim demanded.

"Astronauts Schirra and Stafford say, 'welcome to their planet,'" Morgan replied. "Seems we're to land our 'Globe on the carrier as soon as it comes to a stop. They've marked an "x" on the deck where we're supposed to land."

Brim looked over at the giant carrier which had slowed considerably and was now creeping ahead. Its deck was considerably higher than the altitude of the 'Globe. Quickly, he checked overhead—clear of aircraft for the moment—then climbed rapidly until he could see the deck again.

To his surprise, there was a considerable crowd of figures waiting for him, each waving and pointing to a large x on the deck. As Brim hovered, an obviously capable Helmsman brought the massive vessel to a gentle halt only a few irals from the orbiter. He felt himself smile in admiration. These natives might be primitive by Galactic standards, but they were certainly magnificent at driving the machines they'd built.

At that moment, a section of the crowded deck lowered itself almost to the water and a derrick swung away from the ship's side. Moments later a cable descended which the swimmers attached to the orbiter, and within a matter of cycles, the dripping spacecraft was safely stowed on a kind of wheeled cart while the Astronauts were shaking hands with a crowd of natives dressed in all kinds of clothing.

With his friends safely aboard, Brim gently landed the LifeGlobe exactly in the center of the X, scattering people right and left. Now it time for getting on with his own rescue—such as it might be.

Chapter 51

. . .Covall's moment

AVALON/ASTURIUS, AVALON CITY, 38 TRIAD, 52017

At the same time Brim was landing aboard the "carrier," back in Avalon, Lord Cranwell sat in his quiet office concentrating on a column of figures that, with some manipulation, might considerably increase his fortune—perhaps enough to purchase his own space yacht.

Suddenly he felt the hair stood up on the back of his neck—he was not alone in the room. He swung around from his desk to confront Covall the Wraith standing silently behind him. "Covall" he exclaimed angrily, "who let you into my private office?"

"It matters little, Cousin," the gaunt man said from within the hood of his cloak.

"You are not my cousin," Cranwell growled. "Not get out!"

"Ah, but I *am* your Cousin, Cousin, only *once removed*, as they say. And I suspect you *will* need the news I bring, even as it upsets you…, *Cousin*."

Cranwell felt himself shiver. Though he, like Count Trafford, Covall's father, always treated this chance product of random debauchery like a mongrel hound, the man's unholy aptitude for finance had always made him useful. "Very well, *Cousin*, Cranwell said as if he had a bad taste in his mouth, since you are here, say your say and leave—as quickly as possible."

"Oh, I shall, Cousin Cranwell," Covall said, shrinking even farther into the great hood that all but hid his face—but not his sardonic smile—"I enjoy your presence as little as enjoy mine. However, it is my belief you recently made a blunder affecting you, Father, and me. I

258

thought you ought to know, lest you make other blunders that put us further at risk."

Cranwell felt an icy finger of anxiety climb his spine. In fact, he *had* been attempting to send funds to a risky destination using the complex series of cut-outs and blind alleys he'd watched Covall use— and he'd made at least two *near*-mistakes from which he believed he'd retreated in time. *Had they been recorded?* "What are you talking about, wretch?" he demanded.

"I believe you know quite well," Covall said with an edge to his voice Cranwell had never before experienced. "When I discovered you had made a large credit transfer—to someone in the Lampson Provinces, no less—I quickly traced your clumsy path through financial territory in which you have no business and discovered you had set off *two* secret alarms."

Cranwell shivered as if the temperature had plummeted in his office. "B-but I retreated from those links before an alarm could have been generated, didn't I?"

"I said *secret* alarms," Covall hissed. "And you certainly did set them off. Now, all three of us must hope your retreats were timely, because at that level, I easily traced the destination of your large transfer to a well known assassin. And worse, someone—or *something*—tracing *forward* to the assassin in the Lampson Provinces can also track *backward* to some of our most illicit credits. If anyone—or any*thing*—notices those alarms and decides to investigate, we shall all find ourselves in a spotlight we cannot afford. Onrad deals harshly with treason, employing the same gusto with which he rewards heroes."

When Cranwell managed looked up from his desk again, Covall had departed, as mysteriously as he had arrived. But the chill he had created in Cranwell's gut: *that* was not departing any time soon.

— o — 0 — o —

"Chief," Steele reported breathlessly from the communications room, "I think our long-range KA'PPA is picking up KA'PPA signals from the LifeGlobe."

"You sure?" Barbousse demanded, waking instantly from light slumber in the Helmsman's seat.

"Pretty sure," Steele replied. "Signal's week, but it's emitting the right packet headers for *Purple Abagail*."

"Great," Barbousse exclaimed with a twinge of excitement. "We're on course then?"

"You may want to alter course by 17L, R21.55, HT4" Steele replied. "But you made a Xaxtdamn good guess when we started out, Chief. Near as I can tell at this distance, we're about eight Metacycles out if you maintain this velocity."

"What say, SubLieutenant Baun?" Barbousse demanded. "Can we make it eight more Metacycles at this velocity?"

"A bit of a squeeze," Baun replied, focused on the flight instruments, "but if you don't mind burning reserve energy, we'll make it."

"And after we get there?" Barbousse asked.

Baun chuckled. "With all due respect, Chief," he replied, "we'd better hope some of Admiral Moulding's units show up or we won't be much more than LifeGlobes ourselves."

"Sounds good to me," Barbousse said, entering "17L , R21.55, and HT4" into the AutoHelm. "We're wastin' daylight!"

— o — 0 — o —

Seated at his massive oak desk, Grand Admiral Baxter Calhoun, Supreme Commander of the Imperial Fleet, was pouring over a stack of TOP SECRET intelligence reports when a polite chime signaled his next visitors were ready to enter. Placing the documents in his middle drawer, he pressed a hidden button, then relaxed as the door opened. "Come in, Gentlemen," he said with a grim smile and indicated two armchairs before his desk. "Cvc'eese?"

"Mmmm. Thank you, Admiral," Porterfield Marston said, "I'll have mine extra sweet. How about you, Doctor?"

"Regular, please," Zinnkin said, settling comfortably into the other armchair.

"Well, ye twa money men," Calhoun said, leaning toward them. "Word from Doctor Adam at the IMI indicates uncovered some pretty smelly financial stuff."

"'Smelly' isn't quite the word for it," Marston growled. "More like 'putrid.' Believe me, Admiral. I've seen rotten financial dealings, but this takes the cake—and mixes all sorts of criminal activity together with a large dose of what I call 'Treason.'"

Calhoun nodded, hoping to appear as calm as he was upset. Admirals never showed emotion; that was for underlings—and mistresses. "A'right," he said deliberately, "suppose I'd better hear it."

Marston settled back in his chair and indicated Calhoun with a nod. "Hmmm, yes, Doctor, please tell the Admiral what you've dug up—and on whom."

The slim Zinnkin took a sheet of plastic from his coat pocket, adjusted his eyeglasses, and nodded thoughtfully. "Admiral," he said, "here's a summary of what we've reported to Doctor Adam." He walked to a huge situation panel and activated a crayon, then began to write.

For the next metacycle and a half, Calhoun found himself first shocked, then downright infuriated by the machinations of these two tycoons who owed everything they owned to the Imperial way of life. When Zinnkin was finished, the wall-sized display contained three key points against Trafford and Cranwell, each one serious enough to earn the worst sentences in the Imperial legal system.

1. Trafford, 4th-Generation shipbuilder, owns a number of important commercial shipyards. His crimes include delaying new ships to replace the ones lost in wartime. He doesn't want to see the Escort Service (Under Cranwell) get any better because every loss means big profit on new ships. He has become so wealthy and powerful he has hopes of unseating Onrad. To this end, he has made overtures to Zoguard Grobermann, the League's Minister of State and is supplying high-level information to establish himself when (and if) the League wins.

2. Cranwell keeps control of the escort service for inside information about when convoys sail. He profits from secretly insuring certain transport ships, then passing information about them to the League, marking them for special attack.

3. Lord Brim innocently run afoul of both, first by being a scapegoat for Trafford's prized daughter, General Megan, then by perfecting the WF-400, proving its worth, demonstrating its abilities, and lastly championing its use among people who respect him. Their attempt to murder a senior Fleet officer alone is enough to send both into exile.

"In summery, Gentlemen," Zinnkin said, "these are two clever men. They played for extremely high stakes and played *excellently*. Their financial networks were so carefully crafted—with brilliant cutouts—it would have taken years to break in to them, if we broke in at all." He stroked his bead for a moment as if preparing himself for one last point, then smiled. "We so-called Humans," he began, "have stretched ourselves out across the Galaxy, conquered time, space, and distance, yet we are no more than average, star-shaped beings—with all the frailties endemic to our species. In the end, it was simple greed and hubris that defeated these two, highly developed Humans. Each had built such a bitter hatred for Wilf Brim, the lowly born Carescrian, that they became careless in their desire to put him in his place, so to speak. The key to their inner workings was hiring the infamous Lampsonite assassin, Serena Morgan. The large funds transfer to her Lampsonite account opened a tiny window into the financial labyrinth they had created. From *that* moment, they were mine—and now, they are yours!"

As Zinnkin returned to his seat, obviously tired, Calhoun pursed his lips for a moment, then nodded thoughtfully. "I ony hope tha' Admiral Brim survived his banishment, because we all owe tha' man a deep debt of gratitude."

"Hmm. Yes. Is there any word?'

"None yet," Calhoun growled with a deep frown. "But the Emperor has a new Fleet Cloak for him, an' we are doin' ev'rythin' possible t' ensure he lives t' wear it...."

Chapter 52

. . .all at sea

As Brim shut down the 'Globe's SpinGrav and switched to local gravity, he grinned at Morgan and shrugged. "For better or for worse," he said, "here we are."

"Whatever 'here' is," she said, glancing through the Hyperscreens at the huge expanse of deck on which they'd landed. "We still have to make it to the actual surface."

Brim chuckled. "Yeah, there is *that*, Serena."

"Also, most everyone I can see seems to be wearing some sort of uniform," she added with a frown. "Suppose this is all military?"

Brim rubbed his stubbled chin. "Hard to tell," he said. "Back home, both civilians and government own big ships, but generally, civilian ships are more... what? ...Well..., 'civilian looking,' I guess."

"Your powers of description simply amaze me," Morgan said mordantly

"Thanks," Brim said with a slight bow. "My pleasure."

"So what *does* this one look like?" Morgan asked watching a large group of helmeted men surround the 'Globe and began to shoo away anyone who came close to their perimeter.

"For my money, we're aboard some kind of warship," Brim said.

"—and what the Xaxt is going on out there now?"

"Don't rightly know, but it looks as if we've been surrounded by a ring of guards."

"Why? Do we look dangerous?"

263

Brim pursed his lips and thought for a moment. "Maybe we do," he said with a nod. "Alien bacteria and viruses for example: These people can't know we've taken care of those problems ages ago."

"You mean they think we're 'dirty?'"

Brim nodded thoughtfully. "Not so much unclean," he said, "but early on, there were instances of aliens wiping out native cultures and visa versa, until space-faring races banded together to eradicate the threat. In fact, The Institute of Life Sciences on Avalon/Asturius was where the basic research went on."

"Never heard of it," Morgan admitted.

"Doubt if you would," Brim said. "Most everyone takes its work for granted because they've been around for so long. For example, your Lampson Provinces have been a part of the Intergalactic Federation for as long as anybody remembers, but I'm sure at one time, a complete generation of your ancestors was treated—as was some past generation of Imperials." He glanced through the Hyperscreens. "As soon as this lot is detected in Hyperspace, they'll be treated, too."

"Sounds good to me," Morgan said. "But I'm guessing these guys don't have a clue we're no threat to them right now."

"Probably true," Brim agreed.

"So what do we do now?"

"Until our friend Wally shows up," Brim replied, "I'm going to see if I can raise Doctor Gilruth at the place they call Houston. I never disconnected the channel—and everybody's still using it to talk to us."

"I'm ready," Morgan said, picking up the microphone. "Doctor Gilruth, are you still on this channel?"

"Serena?" the voice of Alan Shepherd asked.

"Yes, Al—is Doctor Gilruth there?"

"He is," Shepherd said. "Hang on, I'll get him."

After a moment, "...Serena, I hear that you and Lord Brim are safely aboard the carrier."

"Yes we are, Doctor, thank you."

"Any problems?"

"Well, yes and no, Doctor."

"Tell me, Serena."

"We're quite safely landed, thank you, Doctor Gilruth, but for some reason, our LifeGlobe has been surrounded by a ring of what appear to be guards with helmets. Have we done something wrong?"

"Nothing I'm aware of," Gilruth replied. "I have no idea why they're deployed."

"Perhaps there are worries about bacteria and viruses?"

Gilruth paused for a moment. "Hmm," he mused. "I suppose that could be it, but I've already spoken to the Life Sciences people here and elsewhere. They don't see you two as much of a threat. Besides, you are totally quarantined aboard the Carrier."

"According to Lord Brim, we were made quite safe generations ago, but there's no way we can prove it," Morgan admitted.

"Tell you what," Gilruth said, "I'll phone President Johnson—our 'Emperor'—and see what is going on. Be back to you as soon as I know something."

"Thank you, Doctor," Morgan replied. "We'll sit tight until hear from you."

Chapter 53

. . .receiving visitors

Confisse Trafford was not particularly surprised when a servant announced that Lord Cranwell had appeared, unannounced, at the door of his palace-like residence in downtown Avalon. "Show him to my office," he ordered, then paused to rehearse how he would handle their dialogue. At this point, it was critically important to insure all blame pointed to Cranwell alone, not himself. Hurrying through a secret passage, he arrived at his desk a number of cycles before his guest. Calming his anger, he waited for the man he was now determined to destroy. A few cycles later, a knock on the door signaled the time had come.

"Lord Cranwell," The butler announced.

"Send him in," Trafford replied.

Moments later, the door opened and Cranwell stepped into the office. "Good afternoon, Cousin," Trafford said, rising and feigning surprise. "What brings you to my home?"

"I think you know as well as I," Cranwell replied uneasily.

"Cousin," Trafford replied with a feigned frown, "I have no idea why you have honored me with a visit, but welcome. Please have a seat."

"Come on, Trafford," Cranwell growled. "This is serious business—and we need to talk it over or we're both in deep trouble."

"Talk *what* over, Cousin?"

"Voot's beard, Trafford. You Xaxtdamn well know. Your own son told me about what I might have done—and it affects you, too, don't forget."

"Cousin," Trafford replied with faux concern. "I have no conception of this imagined trouble you mention, but, *please*, leave my poor, benighted son out of it. He has only half a mind."

"By the Gods, Trafford. You *are* going to leave me swinging in the wind, aren't you?"

"*Cousin*! Dear Cousin! Please calm down. What is this about 'swinging in the wind'?"

"You know Xaxtdamn well what I'm talking about, Trafford! You're in this as deeply as I! Don't think your own dealings with the League have gone unnoticed. I know all about your liaisons with Zoguard Grobermann, the League's Minister of State."

"Stop this, Cousin," Trafford ordered, suddenly—chillingly—aware Cranwell had somehow unearthed information about his, Trafford's, own traitorous culpability and his recording of their conversation now contained information that would have to be expunged. "Guards!" he shouted. "Guards! Seize this man!"

Instantly, a crew of large men appeared from hidden openings in the wall and tackled the furious Cranwell, whose struggles were swiftly overcome when his arms were pinioned painfully behind his back.

Groaning, Cranwell bared his teeth. "Trafford," he growled, "no matter what you do, I'll take you with me. You must know that."

"And how will you do that?" Trafford spit back, feeling an unfamiliar terror crawl along his spine.

"Do you *really* want your guards to share this?"

"They are trusted servants," Trafford replied—then realized that with sufficient pressure from any of a myriad sources, *no one* could be fully trusted. After considerable moments of thought, "Release him and leave us," he ordered. "All right, Cranwell," he said when they were alone, "I suppose we had better discuss this...."

— o — 0 — o —

"Looks as if we're having company, Serena," Brim said as the two stood in the cupola of the 'Globe watching six figures dressed in white coveralls hurrying along the deck toward them.

"Hey," Serena whispered, "I think one of them might be Wally."

"Uh-huh," Brim agreed. "I've only seen his face..., although one of the others could be Tom Stafford."

Keeping a respectful distance behind the six was a motley crowd of civilians carrying boxes looking similar the photo recorder Stafford used in the orbiter, only these were mounted on what appeared to be collapsible tripods. This last group stopped a considerable distance from the six, forming a circle around the front of the 'Globe, with bright lights flashing here and there among them.

The one who looked like Schirra proved his identity by looking up at the cupola and waving. Then Stafford did the same.

"Well," Brim said, "guess it's time to go down and meet our benefactors. All set, Serena?"

Morgan adjusted her coveralls, looked in the 'Globe's mirror, then grimaced. "No matter what happens," she grumped, "I'm going to look awful for this historic occasion."

"You'll never convince me, Serena," Brim said as they descended the ladder. "I _know_ you're beautiful."

"Thanks," she wisecracked, "but none of these guys have enjoyed me naked so often."

Brim hugged her shoulder for a moment, then opened the hatch and the pair looked out onto a troubling sight: helmeted natives guarding the 'Globe were clearly preventing Schirra and Stafford from stepping closer—and neither of the latter seemed happy about the situation. Schirra was talking in an angry voice; Stafford stood beside him, leaning well forward with hands on hips.

After much heated conversation and hand waving, Schirra simply pushed his way past; but other guards moved to block his way before he could reach the 'Globe. Instantly, Stafford pushed two more guards aside to help his friend, and at this point, the four men in white coveralls reading MC DONALD joined the fray. More of the surrounding guards began to arrive— soon a brawl erupted. When Brim saw Schirra go down with two guards on his back, he jumped from the hatch and dragged one of them off—who quickly turned his attention to Brim. Schirra downed his first assailant, then pitched in to help Brim.

Just as Morgan scrambled onto a guard's shoulder, beating him over the head with only Voot knew what, Brim downed another native with a roundhouse to the chin, then spotted a group of uniformed men carrying what are clearly kinetic weapons and firing them into the air.

From her vantage point, Morgan clearly saw the same thing. "Back in the LifeGlobe!" she shouted, but Brim knew she was already too late—he and his native comrades were clearly cut off from the hatch.

Stafford, himself struggling with burly guards, shouted a warning Brim's way but, instantly, Brim found his arms pinned to his sides— then metal rings were clamped to his wrists.

In moments, all eight struggling comrades were immobilized, while Schirra continued yelling at a native wearing different headgear. None of his words seemed to any good, and at last, Brim and his companions were carried and dragged off below decks to what was clearly the ship's brig.

Chapter 54

. . .with a little luck

U.S.S. *WASP*, IN THE SARGASSO SEA,   39 TRIAD, 52017
16 DECEMBER, 1965

Morgan wrinkled her nose as she considered her new quarters. Even the 'Globe was better than *this*! The Carrier's brig was small, sterile-smelling, and brightly lit, being quite crowded by the eight beings incarcerated within its four metal walls—along with a what was obviously a metal sanitary toilet behind a curtain, a metal sink, and a single bunk. Only Voot could imagine who might be supposed to sleep on *that*—certainly not Serena Morgan.

At least she had a number of interesting companions, not including Brim, whom she had long-ago decided was definite long-term companionship material. The two American "Astronauts" were brilliant men with great senses of humor—especially "Wally," the roguish one who kept everyone in stitches with outrageous humor that bubbled to the surface at the most unpredictable moments. He was also handsome. Stafford, the serious one, was an affable, self-depreciating scholar who loved to use engineering terms, most of which passed over Morgan's head.

Inside the brig, the prisoners had gotten to know one another quickly, considering the sudden circumstances that brought them together. Everyone was still talking excitedly about the donnybrook when one of McDonnell Technicians declared, "Damn good fight we made!"

Another technician said, "Yeah! I'll drink to that," while another shouted, "Hey, Don," another called out, "We could all use a drink!"

"Okay, Okay I'll share," replied a grizzled old MC DONNELL Technician said, pulling a large, silver flask from his coveralls. "Pass this around. See if it'll relax ya'!"

As the flask circulated among the occupants, Morgan watched Brim take a tentative sip.

"...Wow, Great stuff!" Brim said with a cough, then took another, sip.

"What'd he say?" The others in the cell demanded

Morgan translated, to howls and cheers.

Another Technician added, "Hell, he's no alien—he's one of us!"

Suddenly, Brim handed the flask the flask to Morgan.

Hesitating only a moment, she took a delicate sip that burned all the way down her throat, in a wonderfully civilized manner—like a fine, Logish meem. "Whoa! GOOD!" she exclaimed. "What *was* that?"

"Bourbon," Schirra replied. "Smooth, eh?"

"*Smoooooth*," Morgan repeated in the native tongue, then carefully took another, larger sip.

After a delicious supper of native food—a dish called "spaghetti and meatballs," hot fresh bread, a kind of boring vegetable, and a surprisingly delicious cold dessert called "ice cream"— one by one, the prisoners began falling asleep. Triad 39—or December 16, depending on one's system of keeping time—had been a *long*, eventful day for everyone in the brig.

$$— o — 0 — o —$$

Back in Avalon/Asturius—following long, rancorous discussions with Cranwell—Trafford was fully aware of the damage his cousin had caused to them both. By now, it was late evening and The Count realized he might have only Metacycles to act before the ponderous Imperial justice system might begin turning its wheels. "I am prepared to flee, Cousin," he growled to Cranwell. "Since our situations are so tightly linked in this, er, *emergency*, I am also willing for you to accompany me to a neutral star system until I can work out something with contacts here in Avalon to permit my return."

"And *my* return?" Cranwell asked weakly.

"We shall discuss that once we have made good our escape, Idiot," Trafford spat back. "Keep your mouth shut before you change my mind about taking you in the first place."

With that, he palmed his HoloPhone and entered an address. Moments later, the phone came to life.

"Captain?" The Count demanded.

"Princess Megan," a voice reported.

"…This is Trafford. Prepare *Princess* for immediate liftoff. File a flight plan to the nearest independent star system. Got that?"

"I've got that, Count Trafford," the voice replied. "Your voice and phone are verified."

"Get busy, then, Captain. Tonight, you will earn your keep." With that, switched off his phone and started along a long hall toward the garage and his private skimmer—with Cranford stumbling along behind like a frightened child.

— o — 0 — o —

Coming out of Hyperspace at only the last moment, Barbousse led his little squadron in a tight circle around the Blue Planet, searching…. Space around the globe was absolutely alive with radiation throughout the entire electromagnetic spectrum. In no more than a few clicks, Steel reported KA'PPA signals whose packet headers contained identifiers for S.S. *Purple Abagail*. Moments later, the other ships reported the same. "Got a position, Steele?" Barbousse demanded. Instantly, a set of coordinates appeared in a display. "Okay, people," he announced. "We're going down to have a look."

As the four ships approached the surface, it became apparent the LifeGlobe had come down somewhere on an *ocean*—ignoring great masses of available land. *Wonder why he's out there on the water?* Barbousse asked himself, with a tinge of worry. He was about to voice his concern shortly after the four astroplanes sped over a longish, semi-tropical island when Tissuard, who was standing between the two helms, broke into his thoughts.

"What in all Xaxt is *that*?" she exclaimed, pointing ahead through the Hyperscreens.

272

Barbousse narrowed his eyes, straining to see details of an immense, flat-decked watercraft slowly moving through the sea and leaving a wide wake.

"Don't have any idea what it is, Captain Tissuard," Baun replied excitedly, "but, see, there's a LifeGlobe parked at the front of it, just beyond what appears to be a gathering of rotorcraft."

"Okay!" Barbousse exclaimed. "Let's go have a closer look." Executing a tight wingover, he led his little squadron in a low-level pass along the length of the vessel, only a hundred irals above its long, flat deck.

Chapter 55

. . .arrivals and departures

U.S.S. *WASP*, IN THE SARGASSO SEA,   39 TRIAD, 52017

17 DECEMBER, 1965

Below, in *Wasp's* brig, the ship's majestic silence was shattered by a tremendous roar overhead, then three more at close intervals. Brim woke with a start amid surprised shouts. "What was *that*?" Morgan demanded.

"It's all right, Serena, believe me." Brim whispered. "I think we've just heard from home."

"Huh?"

"Serena," Brim whispered, "nothing else in the Known Universe makes thunder like two Sodeskayan TBN-998 SpinGravs running at medium cruise."

"Just what is *that* engineering gibberish supposed to mean?"

"Um, sorry, Serena," Brim said, feeling his cheeks burn. "No astroplane makes that kind of noise except the ones I fly. Sounds as if someone from home has come to get us."

Suddenly Schirra hunkered on the deck beside them and said something in the native tongue. To Brim, It sounded like a question.

"What did he say?" Brim demanded.

"Wally asked if you might know what those noises are. I told him your answer."

Abruptly, sirens went off all over the ship and the natives jumped to their feet. "What in Xaxt was *that*!" Brim demanded!

Serena shrugged. "Don't know" she hollered over the din. "Everyone is shouting something like, 'Battle Stations.'"

"Voot's greasy beard!" Brim shouted. "Tell 'em not to fire their weapons. Those are our rides home!"

— o — 0 — o —

In the darkness of D:1:45, the low, graceful shape of Count Tal Confisse Trafford's magnificent yacht, S.S. *Princess Megan*, ghosted into Lake Mersin as it left the dew-covered anchorage and stole off onto the active liftoff area.

Inside the yacht's dim control room, Trafford and Lord Cranwell sat uncomfortably behind the ship's two Helmsmen waiting for takeoff clearance. Their destination: the Arelida Star System, a neutral Star Nation recognizing only its own sovereign laws. On three tiny planets, the Arelideans maintained independence from interstellar law by offering popular perversions to tourists of the Home Galaxy—for a price. Within its borders, Arelida's laws had more to do with money and power than actual legislation. A number of Trafford's close associates had previously escaped to it's borders due to violation of any number of laws.

"Where is our Xaxtdamn clearance?" Trafford demanded.

"Don't know, Count," the left-seat Helmsman quipped. "Tower control often moves in its own mysterious ways."

"Don't try to make smart with me," Trafford growled nervously. "Isn't this a long time to make is make us wait?"

"Indeed, this morning is a little longer than average, Count," the Helmsman replied, "but certainly nothing out of the ordinary...."

He was interrupted by the voice of a tower controller, "Tower to S.S. Megan...."

"S.S. Megan...."

"S.S. Megan: Clearance is delayed until your ship is inspected."

"S.S. Megan copies. Please clarify."

"Tower: Understand routine pre-Arelida check."

"S.S. Megan copies. Thanks."

"So?" Trafford blustered. "Am I to understand my *Princess Megan* is to be inspected? Does the tower know whose ship this is?"

"Aye, Count Trafford. The information is part of the ship's manifest."

"Then why would they want to inspect *Princess*?"

"Government regulations, no doubt, Count Trafford."

"I am not accustomed to regulations."

"I copy that, Count Trafford. But I suspect you will have to submit this time. See four those blue lights approaching?"

"Yes. What are they?"

"They have identified themselves as Police cruisers, Count."

"Coming here?"

"That is what they say."

"Then take off! I command you to take off! Now!"

"Um, Count Trafford. That's *completely* against the law. If I do that without clearance, I'll lose my papers."

"I'll make it worth your while!"

"Sorry, Count, but nothing you can pay will make up for my Helmsman's papers."

Suddenly, Trafford pulled a small blaster from his vest and placed its muzzle against the Helmsman's ear. "You will lift off or you will die," he growled. "Follow my orders! Lift off!"

In that moment, Trafford, himself, jumped at the sensation of chill metal on his *own* neck.

"Put the blaster down, Father," he heard Covall whisper from behind. "It is time to end this sham of a life you lead."

"Covall, you wretch! How dare you threaten me—your Father?"

"Ah, Father," Covall said, "I make no threat; instead I simply state a truth. I shall fire my blaster unless you drop yours before I count to three. One...."

"Covall, you idiot! You have no idea what you are...."

"Two...."

"Covall, I demand...."

"Three."

Trafford's startled eyes and ears reported the flash and snuffle of a blaster. Immediately, his severed brain registered intense pain, surprise, and bitter cold—then a dizzying drop and sharp blow as the cranium hit the yacht's deck and rolled to a stop. Before all faded to darkness, he cast his eyes up to see his headless body slump in its seat, pumping blood like a fountain.

Chapter 56

. . .attacked!

In the morning light, with his other three ships cruising overhead, Barbousse made a third pass over the gigantic ship's flat deck, frowning. No sign of Brim out on the deck or even a KA'PPA message received. By now, the great deck had filled with human figures staring up at him and pointing. As he pulled back to altitude, proximity alarms sounded in the cockpit.

"Check your tail!" Someone warned from above.

Barbousse glanced back to see a large, sleek-looking winged vehicle pulling into position behind him. It was shaped like an elongated teardrop with two large blisters running along each side that Barbousse thought might be thrust engines. At least 20 irals of its forward end was painted light blue; directly behind this rose an ugly blister with oddly placed windows, probably housing the vehicle's small crew. Swept-back wings protruding from amidships were matched by smaller wings near the tail and a high, raked fin aft. Warnings from the other WF-400s indicated they were being followed by similar air vehicles. "Where in Xaxt did these guys come from?" Barbousse demanded.

"Probably from the large island we overflew on the way here," Baun answered. "They were coming from that direction, at any rate."

Abruptly, Barbousse spied a bright flash from the wing of the vehicle trailing him. This was immediately followed by some sort of missile—a *HyperTorp?*—leaving a smoke trail and heading directly for him at high speed.

"Action stations, everyone!" Barbousse shouted into the COMM system, then easily accelerated away from the missile, made three successive square left turns, and shot it out of the sky.

"Everyone in battle suits?" he demanded, quickly donning his own.

A chorus of "Ayes" fills his own helmet.

"Okay," he said tightlipped, "let's see what this Zukeed is up to!"

"Before the attacking ship could recover, Barbousse quickly maneuvered onto *its* tail.

The native ship began skidding all over the sky like a hooked fish—but not doing it very *well*, Barbousse noted—no way it was going to escape a WF-400. Unwilling to harm its native occupants, he decided to disable it before having to shoot it down. Opening two Disruptor ports, he pulled close behind, then carefully fired two low-energy blasts close underneath the aircraft, sending it struggling wildly for control—*so much for any electronic devices* that *pilot might employ.*

Seemingly unfazed, the occupants of the aircraft continued trying to evade Barbousse, so he maneuvered beside its portside windows in the cockpit hump from which two helmeted natives stared him; they appeared to be wearing some sort of battle suits topped by dark bubble-like helmets. Each helmet displayed a red, five-pointed star painted near its top—matching the red stars applied to the aircraft's fuselage and wings, now that Barbousse noticed. While one of the natives shook a fist from a rear side window, the other abruptly dumped power as panels popped up at the edges of the aircraft's larger, forward wing. Instantly, the aircraft fell behind, turned abruptly, then fired another missile from only a few irals distance. Instantly, it hit and exploded near the WF-400's cockpit, sending a jagged piece of metal into one of Barbousse's Hyperscreens and showering both helms with shards of crystal.

"Everybody okay?" Barbousse asked.

Another jumble of "OKs" filled Barbousse's helmet. He considered the situation for only a click, then growled to himself, *You asked for it, Zukeed.* Abruptly pivoting the WF-400, he fired a quarter-power disruptor salvo at the aircraft—which, following a great flash of light, abruptly ceased to exist, except for a small puff of sparkling vapor, that dissipated in mere clicks to nothing...

Moments after another WF-400 destroyed a second attacking aircraft, the remaining natives turned tail and headed back in the way they had come, leaving heavy smoke trails in their wake.

"Don't chase 'em!" Barbousse, ordered the other WF-400s, watching the native aircraft disappear into the distance. "We're all too short on energy."

Rude catcalls filled his helmet from the other Helmsmen.

"Okay, let's take a click or two and figure out what we're going to do until some major reinforcements show up."

"Uh oh, Chief," Baun warned above the proximity alarm's buzz, "...here comes another aircraft."

"Just thraggling WUN-der-ful!" Barbousse growled. "Where?"

"There," Baun said, pointing out through the undamaged starboard Hyperscreens.

"Hmm," Barbousse mused, peering at this new aircraft through binoculars. "Certainly doesn't look anything like our late enemies—no red stars anywhere, either."

"Besides which, it appears to be powered by two big fans, one on each wing," Baun added. "Don't think it's any attack craft."

"Doesn't look particularly dangerous to me, either" Barbousse declared. "Let's see what it's going to do. Just don't feel right about blastin' these primitives into vapor."

As they watched, the stubby airplane—less and less appearing to be any kind of threat—smoothly banked left behind the flat-decked ship, lowered what looked like wheels, and proceeded to land along the large, angled section of the port deck.

"Didn't see anybody shooting at it," Barbousse commented. "Guess he's okay—with the natives down *there*, anyway."

"And now we know the proper approach for landing on that deck ourselves—just in case," Baun commented.

"*Just in case?*" Barbousse seconded, rolling his eyes. "We're going to do it *right now*, before these ships of ours simply fall out of the sky...."

"Okay, guys," he broadcast to the other WF-400s, "follow me onto that deck *and keep plenty of room from the ship you're following!*"

Chapter 57

. . .what in Xaxt was *that*?

U.S.S. *WASP*, IN THE SARGASSO SEA,   40 TRIAD, 52017
18 DECEMBER, 1965

In U.S.S. *Wasp's* brig, the prisoners stood tensely, listening to baffling sounds from outside. Through Morgan, Brim explained what he believed was a small furball involving WF-400s and what he took for native aircraft. Surprisingly, he'd heard only a few, medium-power disruptor blasts—*after* sharp explosions with little meaning to him.

He pursed his lips helplessly, wondering what the natives had loosed on his little squadron in the way of weaponry. In his brief time to look around the great upper deck, he'd seen nothing even approaching directed-energy weapons, only kinetic weaponry of the most primitive kind—dangerous, but easily dealt with. As he shared another swig from the flask, he heard a sharp, whirring growl punctuated by a light thud on the flight deck.

"Serena," he asked, "see if anybody knows what *that* was?"

Clearly, Stafford guessed what he had asked and whispered something to Morgan.

"Tom says it sounds like an *airplane* landing on the deck," she relayed.

"Ask him what an *airplane* is."

In a few moments, Morgan returned her gaze to Brim. "It's a sort of indigenous air vehicle." She shrugged. "I guess our analog would be an astroplane."

Brim took a deep breath. "Thanks, Serena," he said, grinding his teeth. How he *hated* blindly sitting around waiting for something to happen!

— o — 0 — o —

Landing Systems Officer, Lt. Commander DeFazio, wiped his forehead and finished covering the communications and data board that controlled the ship's "Lens" optical landing system. With everything secured, it was time to turn in after a long, bizarre day aboard ship. He'd begun climbing down from his little platform when he turned aft and his eye caught all four of the strange "aircraft" —led by the black one—entering the landing pattern like normal Grumman Stoofs. Hurriedly, he climbed back to the platform, grabbed the phone, and was dragging canvas off the Lens as fast as he could when the Combat Center answered. "Hey, Darrin," he yelled, "we've got four of those super fighters in the pattern. Anybody down there know what we're supposed to do about em'?"

"*Do?*" his friend replied from below. "What the Hell *could* we do? Our radar can't see 'em. Even if we didn't want 'em on board, every weapon on the ship is radar guided."

"Oh, *that*'s nice," DeFazio answered sardonically.

"Plus you might have noticed, they took out a couple of those new, long-range TU-128 *Fiddlers* from Cuba without even breakin' a sweat."

"Yeah, I noticed," DeFazio said, "then we'd better do what we can to help them in, 'cause they're coming aboard whether we want them or not." He activated the ship's "Lens" optical landing system, hoping the pilots of the fast approaching aircraft—they were *big*—could understand the lights. "Raise the arresting wires," he shouted to a nearby rating through a Loud-Hailer and then gasped. The first ship was *not* trailing a hook! "*Drop* those arresting wires *immediately!*" he shouted, "…and deploy the crash barrier *now!*"

— o — 0 — o —

With his lightest touch on the WF-400's controls, Barbousse carefully began approximating the path used only cycles ago by the stubby, little twin-fan air vehicle. As he gradually lost altitude over the ship's wake, he first noticed a display of colored lights on his left at the forward end of the canted section of the deck—then at the near end of the ship, a man pointedly faced his way with his arms out from his shoulders and each hand gripping a round, paddle-like device. Instantly, he recognized this man's purpose.

He rolled the ship slightly to his left, the man ahead slightly lowered his right paddle and raised his left. Smiling, Barbousse leveled the ship and the man leveled his arms. Afterward, Barbousse concentrated on his landing, making certain the man with the paddles kept his arms level. Then, just before the WF-400 flashed over the end of the deck, he noticed the signal man take the right paddle and run it past his throat as if it were a knife.

"Cut!" a smiling Barbousse whispered to himself as he sped along the center of the inclined deck blipping short blasts of gravitons forward until he had come to hover just before the forward end of the inclined deck. There, he turned his ship to face the large, complex structure jutting upward from the starboard side of the ship; lowered the landing pods; and gently dropped the WF-400 to the deck. Before he shut down the flight systems he glanced across the helm. "Baun," he ordered quietly, "...open all the disruptor slots and set the charges at MAX. No sense lettin' our guard down until we know we're safe...."

Chapter 58

. . .the aliens have arrived!

U.S.S. *WASP*, IN THE SARGASSO SEA, 40 TRIAD, 52017
18 DECEMBER, 1965

The Texas twang of U.S. President Lyndon B. Johnson was unmistakable, even from the tinny speaker on the bridge of the carrier. "Here's mah problem, Captain," Johnson drawled. "Gilruth yonder at Houston thinks these so-called alien ships are little danger to us. Yet, ya'll jest told me they shot down two of them Rooshan Tupolev 128s like they was Piper Cubs. Now *y'all* say four of them Aliens is comin' in to land? What do *y'all* think, Captain? Are they tryin' to steal our Gemini like MacNamara thinks?"

"Mister President," Captain Hartley replied carefully, "...with the technology these aircraft display—if they *are* aircraft—I somehow doubt they have much interest in our Gemini. ...Um, with all due respect to Secretary MacNamara."

"So?"

"I am not certain there is much we *can* do at the present moment, Mister President. Those things seem to be invisible to radar, so we couldn't even aim our Phalanx guns or launch Phoenix missiles at them if we didn't want them to land."

"That's what y'all would *like* to do? Get at 'em—like *shoot them down*?"

"*No*, Mister President, I didn't even *suggest* that. In fact, since they completely ignored one of our Stoofs when it was clear they could easily have destroyed it, I think...."

"What in Hell is a "Stoof?" the President interrupted.

"A Stoof is the nickname pilots give to the Grumman S2-F that landed a few minutes ago, Mister President."

"So they didn't bother our Stoof, eh?"

"They did not, Mister President."

"Then what d' ya'll recommend, we do about em', Captain?"

"I think we should take a chance and let them land on the ship, Mister President."

"That's ya'all's recommendation, then, Hartley?"

"It is, Mister President."

"Okay, I agree. But don't dare let them other aliens out of the brig yet. McNamara thinks they might really be valuable—so does McCone."

"Aye, Mister President," Hartley said, wiping his forehead with a handkerchief. As telephones and alarms began to ring all over the bridge, he took the phone out on the port wing to see for himself what was going on. In the distance aft, the jet-back alien aircraft was approaching in a perfect landing pattern, leading the other three aliens in line-astern formation, nicely spaced for uncomplicated landings.

As he watched—half deafened by what sounded like chords from huge pipe-organs—the first big aircraft swept in over the stern, firing what must be powerful reverse thrusters until it slowed and stopped near the forward end of the canted landing deck. There, it hovered for a moment as it slowly turned its nose toward the carrier's island, then gently set down on four stubby pods that suddenly popped down from the fuselage.

There was clear damage to what Hartley guessed was the vehicle's cockpit area—a shattered window-like opening surrounded by a large, sooty area. It must have been hit by one of the Russian's infrared-homing R-4TM missiles, he mused, because the Soviet R-4TR radar-guided missiles would have been useless. Clearly didn't do much damage, at ant rate.

He shook his head, doubting the alien crew out there on the flight deck could be very happy with Earthlings—they could know nothing of the Cold War. Then, one by one, the other three landed and taxied to positions in echelon with the first. Immediately, six narrow doors slid open around the circumference of each nose. Hartley shook his head grimly; it was obvious these openings were weapons of some sort, and each looked like it was pointed directly at where he stood. "For better or for worse, Mister President," he said soberly, "the Aliens have arrived."

BOOK V

Tying Up Loose Ends

Chapter 59

. . .initial conversations

U.S.S. *WASP*, IN THE SARGASSO SEA, 40 TRIAD, 52017
18 DECEMBER, 1965

"**O**kay, what now, Chief?" Tissuard demanded, rising from her jump seat and peering over Barbousse's shoulder at the expanse of steel decking stretching out from the Hyperscreens to a curious structure rising from the opposite side of the ship.

"Well," Barbousse replied, "first of all, Mister Baun here is going to keep the ship ready to take off at a moment's notice"—Baun nodded—"then you, Nadia, and I are going to step outside and take a little walk. We're going to find someone who is in charge here."

"Wearing battle suits, I presume," Tissuard said, nodding toward the forward Hyperscreens. "Just look out there: people are running our way with all sorts of things that ought to be weapons."

Barbousse chuckled. "Of course they are," he said chuckling. "Who can blame them? I'd do the same if the situation were reversed."

"Ironic the poor natives don't have a clue that just one of us could cut this ship in half if we wanted to," Tissuard added.

"Okay, guys," Barbousse broadcast to the other ships. "I'm the one who led us into the mess; I'll take responsibility for getting us out."

— o — 0 — o —

As a cordon of white-clad men ringed their ship, the two Imperials—fully dressed in Battle Suits—descended the boarding ladder and begin walking toward the first cordon of guards, who were pointing what looked like powerful kinetic weapons.

Tissuard chuckled. "Looks like they intend to make negotiations difficult."

"Yeah, it does," Barbousse, agreed, stopping a few irals short of the first rank. "Ya' know, maybe we're going at this all wrong."

"What do you mean, Chief?"

"Well, over the years, I've observed you can't negotiate very well if you aren't taking some sort of a risk, yourself."

"And?"

"And, I'm going to even the negotiations a little," he said. With that, he removed his Battle Suit helmet and set it on the deck.

"What in Voot's name did you just do?" a shocked Tissuard demanded. "Any one of those guys with kinetic weapons can blow your head off."

"Because right now, we're here on a peaceful mission. Can't imagine we look all that friendly in battle suits."

"Okay; I'll do the same," Tissuard said, but Barbousse put a hand on her arm.

"Don't Nadia," Barbousse warned. "If something happens to me, I'll expect you to take over and get The Skipper out of here. Okay?"

Stunned, Tissuard only nodded. *Voot's beard,* she thought, *How Brave! No wonder Brim trusts him with his life.*

"You understand?" Barbousse repeated.

"Okay, I understand, Chief," Tissuard said, "but you're taking an awful risk,"

"Perhaps," Barbousse said with a little smile, "and perhaps not. Let's see how things go." With that, he continued walking toward the marines as if he were holiday. "Tell them we come in peace," Barbousse ordered.

Tissuard nodded and said something in the indigenous language that must have struck a chord. The men look thunderstruck, but continued to point their weapons.

Barbousse peered at Tissuard and shrugged.

"You've got me, Chief" Tissuard replied.

"Okay, next step," Barbousse said, approaching one guard and stopping just before the midsection of his battle suit touched the end of the man's weapon. Smiling, he gently pushed it aside—but went no farther. The man looked stricken, but immediately leveled the weapon again.

"Ask them why they keep pointing weapons at us," he ordered, absently peering up at a red, white, and blue flag streaming from a stubby mast atop the strange structure.

Tissuard queried them and turned to Barbousse. "They say they have orders to keep us from going farther onto the ship," she explained.

"Ask them *whose* orders."

After a few more words, Tissuard reported, "The Ship's commander's orders. They say his title is 'Captain.'"

Barbousse nodded. "All right, then," he said, "tell them we demand to speak to this *Captain.*"

Tissuard was about to speak, when, instead, she pointed to a slim man of about 50 who was approaching them at a fast stride, taking salutes from all whom he passed. "From all the junk on his uniform," she mused, "I'd say *that's* him on his way right now."

Moments later, the man barked an order and the armed men immediately lowered their weapons, one guard rolling his eyes heavenward as if in prayer.

At this, Tissuard stepped forward, offering a military salute with, "Captain Nadia Tissuard, Imperial Fleet."

Clearly surprised, the man came to attention and returned the salute. "I am Captain Gordon Hartley, United States Navy and commander of this ship" he said. "Are you a machine or a human, like your companion?"

"I am a human," Tissuard replied, taking her own helmet off and laying it on the deck. "Now your guards are no longer pointing their weapons, I feel safe to take my helmet off, too, as my brave companion did in the face of their implied threat."

"An unfortunate situation," Hartley said. "I hope you will forgive my suspicions."

"As I hope you will forgive ours," Tissuard answered with a little bow. Then, with a quiet, "One moment, please, Captain," she turned toward the parked WF-400s. As she had hoped, Baun had his side window open. "Close the disruptor ports, please," she called out.

"Closing disruptor ports," Baun shouted back, and the ring of six disruptor ports slid closed noiselessly. In moments, the other ships had closed theirs, too

Hartley, took a deep breath, and nodded. Tissuard knew immediately he had guessed that powerful weapons were staring him in the face. *Quite a combination we have here,* she thought. *Two extremely brave men.* She took her own deep breath. *Such a combination could produce the best outcome possible—or result in disaster.*

Chapter 60

polite gorksroar

"So you are another woman who speaks our language?" Hartley demanded, interrupting Tissuard's reverie.

"*Another*, Captain?" Tissuard replied, completely taken off guard.

"Er, yes, Captain," Hartley, replied. "A young woman accompanied the man we know as Wilf Brim in, er... their... *globe* there on the forward flight deck."

Has to be another Lampsonite, Tissuard thought. *Interesting.* Then, remembering the question, replied, "Like myself, Captain, some from the community of planets I call home indeed have the ability to understand spoken conversations by interpreting the emotions of the speaker and answering in his or her native language."

"Amazing," Hartley mused. "...a *community* of planets. Then, you are truly..., aliens to this planet."

"Oh, we *are*, Captain," Tissuard assured him. "Our homes are spread throughout this galaxy." Then, suddenly remembering her companion, she turned to Barbousse. "Captain Hartley, may I present Master Chief Warrant Office Barbousse, I.F., commander of the astroplane on which we arrived?"

Taking as a queue, Barbousse stepped forward and saluted.

Hartley returned the salute gravely, repeated his name and rank, and continued with a few more words.

"The Captain says he is pleased to meet you, Chief," Tissuard whispered with a smile.

"Please return the compliment," Barbousse replied, then pursed his lips. "Enough of this polite gorksroar," he growled. "I want to know where the Skipper is. *Now.*"

"Ya' think it might be a little early to get tough, Chief?"

"Nadia," Barbousse said quietly, "you yourself said we could cut this steel tub in half if we wanted to."

"Yes, and likely fry our friend Brim while we're at it."

"Okay. Okay; you're right. Ask the man *nicely* if we can see the Skipper, then. How about that?"

"Better." Tissuard replied, then smiled and spoke to the native Captain, who frowned and—after considerable delay—made a suspiciously long reply.

"What'd he say?" Barbousse demanded immediately.

"He said we can see The Skipper, but he can't release him," Tissuard replied.

"Why?"

"Looks like the Skipper is a prisoner in the brig."

"Wha-at?"

"That's what The Captain said."

"What did Brim do?"

"The Captain said the Skipper and his friends got in a fistfight with guards he posted around the LifeGlobe."

"Wait. Stop. Did he say who these *friends* of Brim's are?"

"Natives: Astronauts and spacecraft technicians."

"What in the name of Voot's greasy beard are *astronauts*?" Barbousse demanded. "There's a lot more to this than meets the eye, and I want to know what it is."

"I'll see if I can't get some background, Chief," Tissuard promised. "Hang on." With that, she entered into a conversation with the captain while Barbousse stood by helplessly watching their expressions for telltale signs of stress.

At last, the two appeared to finish their talk and Tissuard turned to Barbousse. "Some story, Chief," she said, then chuckled. "But a story worthy of Wilf Brim, I assure you. Even their Emperor—called a *President*—is involved. *He's* the one who wants the Skipper locked up."

"Why am I not at all surprised?" Barbousse quipped. "Okay, let's have it."

"How about we follow Captain Hartley to where we can talk directly to the Skipper."

"You mean to the *brig?*"

"Well, if that's were they've got him, then yes, to the brig."

"You think that's wise?"

"Possibly not," Tissuard replied. "But right now, I think it's time you call in the big-time help you were promised. The closer to the Skipper we are physically, the better we can help him during the end game. What do you say?"

Barbousse smiled and shrugged. "Admiral Moulding and the Fifth Combat Group," he mused. "Wait till these natives catch sight of the new *Barfluer!*" With that, he took a HoloPhone from his pocket and contacted Steele in the WF-400. "Greg," he asked, "How about calling Admiral Moulding and asking him to come down for a *close* look?"

"Right on it, Chief," Steele replied. "Gonna' impress the natives?"

Barbousse chuckled. "If that *doesn't* impress them, then we're probably in for quite a furball."

"We'll give 'em Hell, then Chief," Steele said, and Barbousse slipped the HoloPhone back in his pocket.

"Ready to go?" Tissuard asked.

"Ready as I'm ever going to be," Barbousse said with a little smile.

After a few more words in the native language with Tissuard, the man named Hartley smiled and lead them across the ship's great expanse of deck to the structure Barbousse now understood was the *Island.*

Chapter 61

. . .words from home

Abored Wilf Brim was snoozing lightly with his back to a bulkhead and Morgan's head cushioned in his lap, when a familiar voice broke into his drowsy musings.

"Hey, Skipper!"

Brim jumped, waking Morgan with a start as he scrambled around to see where the familiar voice came from. "Who's that?" he demanded.

"Up here," the voice said through a spy panel in the metal hatch to his prison.

Jumping to his feet, Brim ran to the door and peered through the opening. "Hey, Chief," he shouted. "I thought I heard *Four Nines* flying around outside. Who's with you?" By now, all eight prisoners were crowded at the door.

"Well, outside of *three other* WF-400s on the deck upstairs, I'm here with Captain Gordon Hartley, commander of this ship, and Captain Tissuard"

"Nadia?"

"You bet, Skipper. Best Lampsonite in the Fleet."

"Whoa," Brim exclaimed, "*She's* your 'Speaker to All'?"

"None finer, M'Lord Brim," Tissuard teased, replacing Barbousse at the spy panel. "And I'm curious, who's yours?"

"Um..., Serena Morgan, here," Brim said, stepping aside so Tissuard could see. "We were the last two off *Purple Abigail* before she blew up. Captain Tissuard, meet Serena Morgan."

"Good day, Captain," Morgan said with a suddenly apprehensive look. "H-have you come to take us home?"

"Yes, Dear," Tissuard assured her. Then: "Skipper, before I meet your other partners in crime, let me have a few words with my fellow Lampsonite, please."

"Sure, Nadia," Brim said and stepped aside, ushering Morgan to the spy panel.

For one lengthy moment, the two stared silently at each other, then Tissuard whispered, "Come here and listen to me carefully." As Morgan obediently stood on her tiptoes with ear to the spy panel, Tissuard whispered three short, forceful-sounding phrases before Morgan stumbled back from the spy panel with a stricken look."

"Hey Nadia," Brim demanded, "what in Xaxt did you say to Serena?"

"N-nadia said n-nothing, Wilf," Morgan interrupted. "Trouble in our homeland I was not prepared for, that's all."

"Looked pretty personal to me," Brim said, glancing outside at Tissuard, whose whole demeanor had suddenly returned to normal.

"Nothing to worry about, Skipper," the pert Lampsonite said airily. "You know how we women are."

"That's what I'm afraid of," Brim returned with a frown.

"Same to you, Brim," Tissuard replied with a wink and a faux-rueful glance. "Now, how about introducing the Chief and me to your friends here?"

"All in good time," Brim said. "First, I want to know when Captain Hartley is going to let us out of this Xaxtdamned brig."

A wisp of concern passed Tissuard's face, and she pursed her lips for a moment. "He tells me he is under orders to keep you and Morgan locked up."

Frowning, Brim stroked his chin for a moment. "I kind of suspected," he said. "What about my friends here?" he demanded.

"Better talk to the man himself," Tissuard said.

"Oh great," Brim growled, watching Tissuard step to a slim man with badges of rank on his uniform and lead him gently to the spy panel.

"Lord Brim," she said in Avalonian, "this is Captain Hartley, commander of this warship, the U.S.S. *Wasp*. Then she switched to what sounded like the native language and said something that ended in, "...Imperial Lord Brim of Grayson."

Hartley replied with a look of obvious embarrassment.

"What's he say?" Brim demanded.

"He said, 'Welcome aboard the U.S.S. *Wasp*.' He added that he's personally honored to make your acquaintance."

"Some thraggling welcome, Nadia."

"I know, Skipper," Tissuard said. "But right now he's got all the cards."

"Voot's beard," Brim exclaimed. 'Our little *Four Nines* alone could sink this rusty tub in clicks. What do you mean he has all the cards?"

"Hey, " Tissuard reminded him, "better respond to the Captain first, Skipper."

"Hmmf. Tell Hartley I am honored to make his acquaintance, also."

Tissuard made a little speech in the native tongue, then turned to Brim. "What about saying something nice about his ship?"

"Make something up, Nadia," Brim grumbled. "When I can roam his decks a free Imperial, I'll say something nice."

"Well, you *did* get in a fight, you know."

"*They* started it."

"You sound like a little naughty little boy, Skipper."

"The fact is, I've *always* been one of those." Brim replied, rolling his eyes. "Go make the Captain happy, then find out who says he can't let any of us out of the brig."

"Serena," he said, glancing at the six battered natives with him in the brig, "please tell our friends...."

He never got a chance to finish., interrupted by the Astronaut, Schirra, who rushed the door, bellowing something that included, "Captain Hartley," and didn't sound very friendly at all. Stafford joined his fellow Astronaut at the door and the two began yelling and pounding on it. Whoever these Astronauts are, they don't seem particularly afraid of their superiors. "Serena," he yelled over the hubbub, "What are they shouting?"

"Something about how terrible it is to treat the first visitors from space this way," she explained. "Schirra is threatening some sort of legal action. Evidently, the Captain's power doesn't extend to either him *or* Stafford."

Suddenly, the two Astronauts stepped away from the spy panel, revealing Hartley's face, strained and clearly under pressure. "Lord, Brim," he began, following these words by more of the native gibberish.

Brim gave the man his best military salute while continuing eye contact. "What'd he say?" he demanded from Tissuard.

"The Captain says he wants to explain the situation," She replied,

"Sounds like one Xaxt of an idea to me," Brim replied. "Tell him, 'Please do.'" Then he saluted again.

Chapter 62

. . .here comes the cavalry!

U.S.S. *WASP*, IN THE SARGASSO SEA,   40 TRIAD, 52017
                                             18 DECEMBER, 1965

Hartley returned Brim's salute, nodded, then turned to begin a conversation with Tissuard .

At the same time, Brim clapped Schirra on the shoulder. "Morgan," he directed, "tell these guys I'm with them one hundred percent."

Morgan translated, resulting in great grins from the Astronauts.

After considerable dialogue with Hartley, Tissuard returned to the spy hole. "At last I think I understand what's going on," she explained with a frown. "And like you, Skipper, the Captain finds himself between a rock and a hard place. Actually, you're both prisoners against your wills."

"*He's* a prisoner?"

"You bet, Wilf," Tissuard said. "He's under orders from his 'Emperor' to keep you locked up—and he can no more break those orders than you could break orders from Onrad. Now do you understand?"

Brim stepped back rubbing his chin and frowning. "Well, now that *is* a problem, isn't it?"

"It is," Tissuard agreed.

"That apply to our six native friends, too?"

Tissuard raised an eyebrow. "I forgot to ask," she admitted, "but I'll find out right now." After only a few more words with Hartley, she turned back to Brim with a little smile. "The Captain says he's willing to release them immediately and call the whole thing a misunderstanding."

"Great," Brim pronounced. "How about letting our friends in on the situation?"

"Will do," Tissuard said, and motioned the natives toward the spy panel. After a few moments conversation, they shook their heads angrily and turned their backs to the door.

"What are they saying now?" Brim asked Morgan.

"The natives—including our two Astronaut friends—refuse to leave until everyone is released," she said. After this, all six natives in the brig began cheering while they lined up to shake Brim's hand.

"Serena, tell these guys we *deeply* appreciate their gesture, but question if it's wise on their part."

Morgan nodded, then spoke said, "Mister Schirra says they've taken an oath to remain with us," Morgan explained.

Brim bowed deeply to his friends, but held up a finger as he had when they first met in orbit.

The natives immediately silenced, clearly waiting for his thoughts.

"Serena," he began, "please ask these good men to consider that they might do us a lot more good if they weren't penned up in this cell with us."

"Good idea," Serena said. "I'll see what they have to say," then translated his question.

This had considerable effect on the natives, who immediately began talking among themselves with serious mien. After considerable discussion, the man named Schirra turned from the group, pointed a finger at Brim, and spoke a long string of words.

"What did he say," Brim demanded.

"He said he and the Astronaut Stafford believe you are correct in your assumption."

"Good," Brim said with a wave of relief.

"But that's not all," Morgan warned.

"What else?" Brim demanded.

"The four technicians have renewed their pledge to stay in the brig for as long as it takes to free you."

"Voot's Beard," Brim Said, clearly impressed. "Tell everyone we certainly appreciate the help—especially the support."

When Morgan had translated these words, Schirra and Stafford stood at attention—Schirra's black eye was quite noticeable by now—saluted, then marched to the hatch, and called out to the captain. Only clicks later, the hatch opened and the two men exited. Through the momentarily open door, Brim studied the armed guards, holding weapons ready at their chests. He turned to Morgan and shrugged. "Serena," he said with a chuckle. "It must be you, because I know I don't look quite *that* threatening...."

— o — 0 — o —

In the anteroom, Schirra and Stafford immediately made for the two Blue Capes, stopped, and saluted military style—which the Imperials returned. Then, all shared handshakes.

"Commander Schirra," Tissuard said, "how nice to meet you. I am Nadia Tissuard, Captain, Imperial Fleet." With a nod, she indicated Barbousse beside her, "Gentlemen, may I present Master Chief Warrant Officer Barbousse?"

"Captain," Schirra replied, greatly impressed, "H-how do you and Ms Morgan know our language so well?"

"Difficult to explain, Commander," Tissuard said with a little blush, "Serena and I come from a group of stars and planets where such abilities are not uncommon, but little understood in spite of the best technology." Then she smiled again. "I understand you are called, 'Wally.'" I would be greatly pleased if you and Commander Stafford would call me Nadia."

"Copy *that*, Nadia!"

"And I'm John," the tall Astronaut said.

"I am called 'Chief,'" Barbousse said in heavily accented English, offering his hand. "Happy to be meeting both you." Moments later, they were joined by Captain Hartley.

Wasting no time, Schirra saluted Hartley, then, "With greatest respect, Captain," he said, keeping tight reign on his temper, "but what is the *real* reason you are keeping Lord Brim and Serena Morgan in

302

the brig and under guard? This is perhaps the most significant event in Human history, and you are making a disaster of it, Sir."

Hartley pursed his lips and nodded. "You are correct, Commander Schirra," he said gravely. "And I completely aware of the pending disaster I am causing—but it is not by my command this is happening."

"Then whose, Captain?" Schirra demanded.

"As I have informed Captain Tissuard and Chief Barbousse, it is President Lyndon B. Johnson who personally issued the orders," Hartley replied with a troubled mien.

"*President Johnson,* f' gosh sake," Stafford blurted out. "What's *his* problem with our visitors?"

"I doubt anything," Hartley replied. "I think perhaps our President's advisors, have caused him to issue these orders."

"Uh oh," Schirra whispered, looking to Stafford with a chill running along his spine. "Ya' think maybe it's like that 'flying saucer' stuff that was going around a few years ago—like *Area fifty-one?*"

"Been on my mind," Stafford seconded.

"More to the point of learning as much as possible from them—and *about* them," Hartley added.

"Not good," Schirra muttered. "With even the slightest possibility that's true, then we've got to get them out of here." He turned to Hartley. "Captain," he said, "again with all due respect to your orders and rank, the situation may require a small mutiny—and I'm ready to cause it."

Hartley nodded his head and his shoulders slumped. "I understand and respect your concerns. We must insure our visitors are kept safe from all, shall we say, *inquiries.* However, if you two provide this *necessary* mutiny, it will save my career and destroy yours. Therefore, as your Commander I shall make that important decision. The U.S. Navy has plenty of Captains, but very few astronauts. No options exist; I and I alone must release our guests. And that, I issue as an order from my position as commander of this ship."

"What is this about 'destroying careers'?" Tissuard broke in.

"Well, Nadia," Schirra explained, "we understand we must release your countrymen before even more diplomatic damage is caused—or worse."

"Thank you, Wally," Tissuard replied.

"Unfortunately," Schirra continued, "there are only two options by which this can happen—both requiring sacrifices."

"How so?" Tissuard demanded.

"Well," Schirra explained, "either option will require Captain Hartley or Stafford and me breaking orders from our superiors—and the punishments that will surely follow."

"Hmm," Tissuard mused, thoughtfully rubbing her chin, "...and your decision?"

"Captain Hartley has decided to carry the burden on his own shoulders. He will order Ms. Morgan and Lord Brim be released immediately, which will end his career in the U.S. Navy." Schirra explained. "He is a brave man."

"Wow," Tissuard exclaimed with an admiring smile. "You guys from Earth here seem to be pretty good people. But while I certainly appreciate Captain Hartley's decision, we are about to have a visit from some of our own people who will do their best to avoid making trouble for *any* of you."

"Oh?" Schirra demanded. "Who else is coming?"

"Well," Tissuard said, tipping her head slightly, "if my ears don't deceive me, we are about to be visited by one of the newest and largest warships in the Known Universe."

Chapter 63

. . . Only Wilf Brim

U.S.S. *WASP*, IN THE SARGASSO SEA,   40 TRIAD, 52017
18 DECEMBER, 1965

As Tissuard spoke, Hartley noticed a Warrant Officer rushing into the anteroom with a radio telephone. "Captain," he puffed, passing over the handset, "the President demands to speak with you immediately." Even as he spoke, a low-pitched, pipe-organ chord—more felt than actually heard—seemed to surrounded the ship

Taking a deep breath, Hartley keyed the phone and spoke. "Captain Hartley, here, Mister President."

"Hartley," Johnson shouted from the phone, "Y'all got Big trouble comin' y'all's way. One of our SR-71's is up there over y'all. He's sendin' back pictures of the biggest damn thing ya' ever seen. Looks like a skinny ol' Zeppelin—only the pilot of the SR-71 says the damned thing is almost a mile long!"

"We do hear something approaching, Mister President," Hartley replied.

"Well, Keep an eye out, Cap'm, *'cause it's sure a-comin' your way.*"

Hartley raised his eyebrows and glanced at Tissuard. "Captain," he said above the rumble—now more like a powerful chord from a thousand pipe organs—"is *that* the unit of your Imperial Fleet you mentioned?"

"I do believe so, Captain," Tissuard replied calmly.

"Mr. President," Hartley yelled into the phone. "Our visiting aliens here believe it's is a unit of their fleet. Shall I order a defense of *Wasp*?"

"Hartley, are y'all out of yer bleepin' mind? Don't do nothin' 'till we see what it is they' wants."

"Ah, Mister President, "Hartley replied, now practically hollering over the phone. "I already *know* what it's here for."

"Wull, then, whut?"

"To pick up the aliens we've got in the brig."

"Y'all mean...?"

"That's it," Hartley interrupted.

"Shee-e-*it*," Johnson roared, "...then release 'em. I think they'all have us outnumbered."

"Right away, Mister President," Hartley, shouted into the phone, then turned to the guards. "Release the prisoners," he shouted. *"Now!"*

Hartley watched the guards stumble over one another to unlock the hatch as the huge Barbousse, Fleet Cloak flying, flung it open, accidently bumping a number of sailors to the floor. In the next moment, he grabbed the man named Brim and exploded from the brig like a cannonball—followed by the cheering NASA technicians.—with Serena Morgan riding the leader's shoulder.

"Hey, everybody!" Schirra whooped, "let's hustle up on the flight deck and see what's goin' on up there! I think we're about to see something we'll remember!"

Smiling, Hartley followed the cheering procession to the flight deck. Great leaders, he remembered, often find themselves followers in certain situations. Clearly, this was one of them....

— o — 0 — o —

Hands clasped behind his back, Admiral Tobias Moulding stood on the bridge of *I.F.S. Barfluer*, watching through clear Hyperscreens at an extremely advanced air vehicle circling his ship at a most respectable speed. "Hmm," he mused, "Beautiful ship out there. These people have come along way since our robot explorer checked them out years ago."

"Indeed, Admiral," Captain Voshell agreed. "With that kind of technology, it shouldn't be much more than a hundred Standard Years or so until they join us in the Hyperspace community."

Moulding smiled as their big ship descended rapidly through gauzy banks of clouds, following the KA'PPA signal broadcast from the LifeGlobe. "Perhaps," he said, "...but with all the radioactive hotspots below, my guess is they have only recently discovered atomic power—and believe they have mastered it—which they'll eventually find they haven't."

"Maybe these will be lucky" Voshell said, then glanced at the Helmsman. "Er..., how close will you want to approach the target, Admiral?"

"Rather closely, Captain," Moulding said with a little smile. "My latest reports indicate our friends are being held prisoner inside some sort of a ship, so about all we can do is frighten them a bit, at least for now."

"Probably won't have much trouble doing that," Voshell mused. "Tell you what: I'll have the Helmsman descend until our displacement cavity in the water just begins to affect the target, then back off and see what happens."

"Sounds like a plan," Moulding said, peering through the forward Hyperscreens. "I say, d'you suppose *that*'s our target down there?"

Voshell checked his conning board, then nodded. "Might well be," he acknowledged.

"Strange-looking vessel," Moulding commented, "...although there do seem to be a number of winged vehicles parked on it. Might explain the long, flat decks."

Voshell rubbed his chin as *Barfluer* quickly erased the C'lenyts ahead. "If I'm not mistaken, there seem to be four WF-400s parked at the far end of the canted port deck...."

"...And a LifeGlobe all the way at the bow," Moulding added, chuckling and shaking his head in admiration. "Only Wilf Brim could manage to be stranded on something like that. It should be *most* interesting to discover how he did it this time."

Chapter 64

. . .I.F.S. Barfluer

U.S.S. *WASP*, IN THE SARGASSO SEA,   40 TRIAD, 52017
                                          18 DECEMBER, 1965

Half pushed along by Barbousse, Brim arrived at the flight deck ahead of Captain Hartley and Nadia Tissuard. By now the great chords coming from the sky had reached heroic proportions, and a shadow was obscuring light from the nearby star. Looking up, Brim found himself shocked by the immense bulk descending about three c'lenyts off to port, obviously slowing to match the forward speed of the *Wasp*. Slim and shaped like a colossal needle, the immense hull carried four sleek superstructures equally spaced around its circumference, each mounting three long-barrel, 1800-mmi disruptors fore and aft. Dazed by the spectacle, Brim recalled reading those disruptors were rated at a destruction range of more than a light year. Then he gasped as he glanced across the *Wasp's* deck to the vast gravity indentation the great starship was causing in the water. Clearly, whoever was at the helm was being extremely prudent; a quarter c'lenyt closer, and the *Wasp* would be drawn into the maelstrom and be destroyed.

"What is *that*?" Schirra and Hartley demanded together.

"It's a battlecruiser," Tissuard explained.

"Must be a mile long," Schirra said, clearly awestruck.

"Just *short* of a mile," Tissuard corrected. "About five thousand of your *feet*.'

Hartley was about to speak, when the great chords lapsed into silence and a voice boomed out from the immense ship, "**We come in peace to rescue Lord Wilf Ansor Brim!**"

Brim—still dressed in his LifeGlobe jump suit—felt his face burn as everyone stopped what he or she was doing and stared at him. He grimaced and shrugged. "Guess that's me," he mumbled.

Again the great voice thundered out of the heavens, **"We come in peace to rescue Lord Wilf Ansor Brim!"** Moments later this was followed by, **"If you are visible on deck, M'Lord, please show yourself by waving to us."**

Brim shut his eyes and smiled ruefully. *Of course,* he thought, *the voice was familiar because it was Toby Moulding!* He waved both arms and imagined the droll Admiral standing on the bridge of the great battlecruiser and chuckling. Coming to attention, he threw his best military salute toward the battlecruiser.

"Thank you, Lord Brim," the great voice boomed, **"We are ready to take you aboard whenever you desire,".**

Brim saluted again, then felt a hand on his sleeve.

"Er, L-lord Brim," Hartley interrupted gently, "our President asks to speak to you personally."

"I'd be honored," Brim stumbled in the native language, "but I cannot speak your language."

"I'll translate," Tissuard said quickly, and took the phone from the Captain. She spoke a few words into the phone; Brim recognized the terms *Tissuard* and *Brim*, but nothing else.

Suddenly, Tissuard put hand had over the microphone and grimaced with eyes wide open. "Voot's Beard," she exclaimed, "he has such a thick accent he doesn't sound anything like the others we've met."

"Could you understand *anything*"? Brim demanded.

"Oh yes—the usual garbage," Tissuard replied. "'Welcome to the *Wasp* and speaking for his country, he wants you to know they are honored that you are his guest."

"Well isn't that nice?" Brim said with a smile. "Guess we're supposed to forget all about the armed guards and the brig, right?" Beside him, Barbousse stifled a laugh with some difficulty.

"You *really* don't want me to say that, do you?" Tissuard admonished.

"No," Brim relented. "I think I'm past that, now. Tell him we're grateful to be aboard his ship and give thanks for offering shelter until rescue came from our own Fleet."

"Much better," Tissuard said and began translating Brim's thoughts. At some length, she turned away from the phone. "President Johnson wants to know how long we will be staying on the planet," she said.

Brim chuckled. "Tell him we'll be on his ship just long enough for the *slowest* of us to reach *Four Sixes* at a dead run."

"Wilf!"

"All right. Tell him we need a few moments for some special good byes, then we must be off quickly, as we are tying up a major unit of out Imperial Fleet. Otherwise, we would love to stay and explore his beautiful planet. Great gorksroar, eh?"

"By Voot's Beard," Tissuard replied. "Not bad for a simple Helmsman."

"Thank you," Brim said with a little bow.

Tissuard rolled her eyes skyward and began translating.

While she was busy, Brim guided Morgan to Schirra. "Please tell Wally that meeting him in orbit is one of the proudest moments of my life," he said.

After Morgan translated, Brim took off his well-worn ring and offered it to an obviously surprised Schirra. "I'm not much for speeches," he said, "but ask Astronaut Schirra if he will accept my ring from the Helmsman's Academy. I have nothing more valuable to offer, but he is as skilled a Helmsman—probably better skilled—than anyone I have encountered, including myself."

"Wilf," Morgan said, eyebrows raised. "Everyone knows how valuable those rings are. Especially yours!"

"This Schirra guy is truly special," Brim said. "I'd love to see him handle a WF-400."

"Wow," Morgan whispered, and translated Brim's words, clearly impressed.

Schirra seemed clearly moved by the gesture. Before he accepted Brim's ring, he took off his own and offered it in trade.

Brim gladly accepted, donned the other's ring before stepping back and saluting.

The man named Schirra matched his salute.

"Good bye, Wally Schirra," Brim said emotionally in the native tongue: *English* it was called, he thought. "Serena, please tell Wally I shall proudly wear this ring for as long as I live."

"Good bye, Wilf Brim," Schirra said in broken Avalonian, followed by more words in his own language.

"Wally says pretty much the same," Tissuard said.

At this point, Tissuard interrupted. "Sorry to bust up this manly ceremony," she said, "but the President asks when you might return to this planet."

Brim thought about this, pursing his lips for a moment. "Please inform President Johnson that such is unlikely," he declared after some thought. "Instead, we shall wait for him and his American brothers to come to us some time in the future—as we are certain they will."

Once Tissuard had translated, Brim added, "Please send our farewells to the Captain and his President," then, nodding to Barbousse, he peered up at the ship's flag streaming proudly from the ship's narrow superstructure. "Something tells me we'll see those stars and stripes again some day," he predicted.

"Maybe not us, Skipper," Barbousse replied, as Tissuard and Morgan joined them. "But your daughter, Hope, probably will."

"Thanks," Brim whispered, then looked up at the streaming flag. "All right, troops," he said. "Let's make this look good, then. Ready?"

"Ready Skipper," the others said in unison.

"Salute!" Brim commanded, and the four Imperials became to first aliens to recognize a flag of planet Earth.

This accomplished, the four started off across the wide deck toward *Four Nines.* "Hey," Brim exclaimed suddenly, "what happened to the starboard Hyperscreens? Looks like the ship's taken a hit."

"Got suckered by one of the natives," Barbousse admitted.

"Huh?"

"Yeah. Thought I'd pretty much knocked the wind out of a native aircraft that attacked us with a missile of some sort. Figured I'd send him on home before I had to kill him, but he pulled the old 'slow-up and fire' routine on me at close range and, well, there it is...."

"Good lesson," Brim said, clapping Barbousse on the back. "Once someone takes a shot at you...."

"...Make sure it's his last," Barbousse recited. "WarFighting 101 at the Helmsman's Academy."

"I take it that was his last shot?"

"*Very* last, Skipper," the Chief said, "but the damage was done to Four Nines. Onrad's going to be furious."

"Onrad never seemed to mind what I did to the ship," Brim said, reassuringly. "Besides, Toby will have the whole thing cleaned up aboard *Barfluer* soon as we get there. If that's the worst we do to His Majesty's personal '400,' we'll all be damned lucky."

Suddenly, Captain Hartley shouted something after them.

"Nadia, what'd he say?" Brim asked.

"He's reminding us we're leaving the LifeGlobe behind," Tissuard replied.

Brim smiled. "Please inform Captain Hartley we bequeath it to his country," he said. "He'll find some interesting technology aboard that might save his race quite a bit of time joining us. The word is *SpinGrav*."

Chapter 65

. . .departure of the aliens

U.S.S. *WASP*, IN THE SARGASSO SEA,   40 TRIAD, 52017
                                            18 DECEMBER, 1965

Tiredly, the four Imperials continued on their way toward *Four Nines*. Barbousse issued a thumbs-up to Baun, and instantly the WF-400 came alive with navigation lights flashing and KA'PPA beacon glowing; the other three Wakefields quickly followed suit.

Upon reaching the little ship, Brim stood aside as first Tissuard, then Morgan, then Barbousse boarded. Brim flashed a last thumbs-up to the Astronauts across the deck before he ascended the ladder and secured the hatch. Noting that Kermis was busy welcoming Morgan, he made his way to the control bridge, where Tissuard and a bright-looking young SubLieutenant were already in the jump seats. Barbousse had seated himself in the right, co-helmsman's recliner and was beginning systems checks when he smiled and peered behind him. "Hey, Baun," he said, "You've got it all checked out!"

"Of course, Chief," the young man said. "We'll need to ask Admiral Moulding for some energy without delay—and perhaps get the Starboard Hyperscreen repaired—but otherwise, she's ready to lift. Oh, and there's a message directly from the Imperial Palace for Lord. Brim," he added.

"Where is it?" Brim asked, surprised.

"Came in the clear," Baun replied, "with a *for-spoken-transmission-only* imprimatur, Lord Brim."

"All right, SubLieutenant," Brim said. "Let's hear it. Somehow I get the idea it's not private."

313

Baun rose to his feet. "The Emperor said—and I quote—" he recited with reddening cheeks, "'Get your ass back here to Avalon on the double, Slacker. After that vacation, I've got a big job for you and the Chief.' It's signed 'O,'"

"That's it?"

"That's the entire message, M'Lord."

Brim had stopped short of the twin helms when he entered the cockpit. Now he stood for a moment in thought. For a long time, he stared out through the forward Hyperscreens, eyes focused elsewhere in both time and space. Only after a long pause did he climb into the left seat and peer over at Barbousse, who was chuckling while he checked the flight controls.

"Hope you feel rested, Skipper," Barbousse said, clearly struggling to keep a straight face.

"Oh, absolutely," Brim growled in faux irritation. "Onrad never gives us civilians a break." Then he sat back and chuckled. "Okay, fun seekers," he said, "let's go over and pay our respects to Toby so he can show off his new toy...."

— o — 0 — o —

Schirra relaxed against a bulkhead with Stafford and the NASA crew, watching the aliens shuffle off toward their space ship. A little apart from the group, Hartley stood almost at attention providing a running radio-commentary for President Johnson.

No mistaking: the Aliens looked tired; Schirra was, too. When the four approached their ship, a hatch opened and someone inside lowered a ladder. Schirra smiled to himself. If this were Science Fiction, the ladder would have descended automatically. Some things never changed, he supposed with a chuckle.

These aliens made *big* machines, he considered; the *little* one here was big as the old ELCO 83-foot PT boats he remembered as a kid. He closed his eyes wondering what it must be to fly something like that, then shook his head. *All in good time* he reminded himself, *all in good time....*

314

His gaze wandered some miles beyond the ordered clutter of the flight deck to where the colossal Starship silently coasted along, matching speed with *Wasp* and pushing a cavity in the sea that could contain at least *five* aircraft carriers of her class. What a couple of days these had been! And the alien named Brim—*Lord* Brim, no less—had seemed so impressed by his simple rendezvous with Gemini VII. He laughed to himself. *Well,* he thought, *his little Gemini spacecraft might not be much in comparison with what Aliens flew, but by golly, it was one Hell of a start in the way of catching up!*

Daylight didn't last very long at this short end of the year; already the sky was darkening. As Schirra watched, one by one, lights in what he guessed were the cockpits of the alien craft dimmed. Promptly, a stuttering growl come from the all-black ship, sending up a shimmering, sparkling cloud from its right-hand nacelle as, a thunderous chord from a pipe organ sounded. A second growl followed in quick succession from the left nacelle, producing its own sparkling cloud and triumphant chord—music to Schirra's ears.

As the three other ships also started up, their sounds settled into a synchronized thunder, and when the Astronaut reflexively glanced at the ring Brim had swapped with him, the winged comet attached to the blue stone was glowing! Absently, he wondered what the worn runes surrounding the stone meant, then smiled, guessing that Brim would be wondering what his ring meant, too.

One by one, the vehicles rose gently, retracting their tiny landing pods as they slid sideways out over the water, tilting sharply to starboard. Dipping their wings, they sped off, toward the great starship, to disappear like small birds into an open port in the top superstructure.

Presently, the great, triumphant chord from a thousand pipe organs returned: softly at first, then increasing as the colossus began to rise until its cavity in the sea was replaced by the normal, rolling white caps of the Caribbean Sea. It hovered there for a few cycles more before every loudspeaker on the *Wasp* broadcast a short message in English:

May stars light all thy paths, Star Travelers.

Then the great ship gradually pulled ahead, gathering speed at an impossible rate until its colossal bulk disappeared completely among the first stars appearing in the tropical winter sky.

While the others froze in place, transfixed by the passage of the great starship, Wally Schirra took a step forward and saluted. *Keep checkin' six, Star Travelers,* he thought with a determined smile. *We'll be on your tail before ya' even know it!*

Chapter 66

. . .revelations

Brim walked aft for a break in *Four Nines'* tiny Wardroom. As he stepped through the hatch, Tissuard and Morgan were sitting on a couch across from him, intently playing Cre'el. Pouring himself a mug of cvc'eese, Brim could stand the silence no more. "All right, you two," he grumbled, "I want to know what's going on."

The women look up, surprised. "What do you mean: 'what's *going on*?'" Tissuard demanded.

". . .Between you two."

Before Tissuard could answer, Morgan raised her hand. "I'll tell him, Nadia," she said. "I appreciate your silence, but it's time he learns the truth."

"You sure?" Tissuard demanded with a raised eyebrow.

"I'm sure," Morgan said. "Remember: I haven't committed any crime."

"*This* time," Tissuard corrected with a grimace.

"So who can prove there were *other* times?" Morgan asked with a little shrug.

"*Now*, what are you two talking about?" Brim demanded.

"About my profession," Morgan said.

"Your *profession*, Serena? I didn't know you were a professional. What is it you *do*?"

"Wilf, Dear," Morgan said, reaching across the table to grasp Brim's arm. "I kill people."

"You *kill* people*?*"

"It's how I make my living," Morgan replied modestly.

"Nadia, is she on the level?"

"*Quite* on the level, Wilf," Tissuard assured him. "In fact, Serena here is rather famous among her, er, professional colleagues."

"You're an *assassin*, Serena?"

"That's only *one* word for it," Morgan replied calmly. "After all, a girl has to make a decent *living*."

"An assassin," Brim repeated, shaking his head. "Good grief, I'd never have suspected."

"That's part of what makes me a success," Morgan said modestly.

"But for Xaxt' sake, Serena, you simply don't *look* like an assassin."

"Really?" Morgan asked with a smile. "And what, pray tell, *does* an assassin look like?"

Brim stopped short. "Well," he started, then narrowed his eyes. "Is it possible, Serena Morgan, an assassin might disguise herself as an old woman?"

Morgan's face broke into a little smile. "Quite possible, Wilf," she assured him.

"Great Voot," Brim swore quietly, "so you were aboard *Purple Abagail* as an assassin?"

"Only reason you'd fine me on a broken-down rust bucket like that," Morgan said quietly. "Normally, I travel in style."

"Who were you after?"

"I was after *you*, Wilf," she said. "Surely, you *must* have guessed."

Brim considered her words for a considerable time. "No," he admitted some embarrassment, "I really didn't. How come I'm still alive, then?"

"After you saved my life, I couldn't harm you under any circumstances," she explained. "That changed the rules."

"The rules?" Brim asked, completely confused by now.

"Once you saved my life, I could not take yours—at least not until I could save yours again." She shrugged, "But you got so far ahead in the saving business, I simply had to give up."

"Voot's greasy Beard," Brim whispered as a chill ran along his spine. "So the little old kitchen lady was going to kill me?"

"Oh yes, she was," Serena confessed. "You'd never have known what hit you."

Brim shivered again. "I believe that, Serena," he said. "Guess the loss of *Purple Abagail* was as lucky for me as it was unlucky for everyone else."

"Including me," Serena said with as little smile. "The man who hired me contracted to pay a great deal for my services. All I have now is the deposit."

"Might I inquire as to whom that was?" Brim asked.

"Sure," Serena said. "His name is Case, and he certainly had taken a *big* dislike to you."

"*Barny* Case?"

"That's his name," Serena said.

"Holy thraggling Voot!" Brim exclaimed. "Why would Case want *me* dead?"

"A question I never asked," Serena declared. "His checks cleared; that was the extent of my interest."

Stunned by the tiny woman's admission, Brim shook his head. "So why should I believe you won't try to earn the remainder," he demanded.

"Probably I should answer," Tissuard interrupted. "As a sister Lampsonite, I took care of that eventuality when we first met."

"Okay," Brim agreed, "I'm willing to believe nearly anything at this juncture. What did you do?"

"I merely warned Serena should she harm you in any way—accidentally or purposely—I should personally devote my life to causing her death in the most painful manner possible. Of course, now, I know that wasn't necessary"

"You recognized her as an assassin? How?"

"Back home," Tissuard explained, "Serena is a well known, er, *businesswoman*. I recognized her immediately."

"You'd seen her before?"

"No; I recognized her thoughts—the moment she recognized mine."

"How?"

319

"Wilf," Morgan interrupted gently, "Nadia and I are both members of the Lampsonite killing professions. I'm military; she works alone, but we are both in the business of killing."

"I always thought Lampsonites are *healers*."

"*Mostly* correct," Tissuard said with a momentary glance at Morgan.

"…But there are exceptions to every *always*," Morgan finished for her. "We are simply two of *them*."

Chapter 67

. . .back home

High in Lake Mersin's Civilian Traffic Control tower, Controller Seyess Inhardt had been watching and listening for the ebony 400 known a *Four Nines*. When it appeared on the INBOUND board, he signed himself out for the lavatory and stepped onto the viewing ledge, peering Lightward into the arrival stream. Presently, he sighted the sleek little ship—in formation with three others, this time—and whisked out his HoloPhone to picture its arrival.

He waited until his camera could accurately record the astroplane's tail number, took the picture, then placed a call to an assigned destination. As always, the display was blank, but the voice was the same he had heard since he started reporting the movements of this vehicle whenever it appeared at the Lake. Suddenly, he felt a presence behind him, and his HoloPhone display came alive with the image of a cloaked, almost-skeletal face in the rectus of shock—at which time the image froze. Seyess made a desperate attempt to pocket the 'Phone, but his arms were abruptly pinned behind him.

"Enough, Inhardt," a gentle voice whispered in his ear. "This should end your days as a rather sorry agent."

"W-who *are* you?" Seyess demanded as he felt cold handcuffs encircle his wrists.

"My name is not at all important," the gentle voice informed him, "but be informed that I work for His Majesty's Secret Service—and you, Mister Seyess, are presently under arrest. "

— o — 0 — o —

As Brim taxied along the cluttered canal toward TopLine, he noticed that the ebony 400 was no longer drawing curious looks from the untidy warehouses and businesses lining the ancient walls. "Nobody watching today, Chief," he said. "I fear we're getting to be old-hat around here."

"Considering we're leading three other WF-400s," Barbousse commented, "I'd say we've become downright boring."

"Uh oh," Brim mumbled. "Do you see what I see ahead?"

Barbousse shifted in his seat, peered around the next curve in the canal, then grimaced. "I think I'd better take back those words about us being boring. Have you ever seen so many limousines pulled up at old TopLine?"

"If I had, I'd never admit it," Brim said. "What *will* the neighbors think?"

"Probably the whole den of thieves headed for the hills today," Barbousse said with a chuckle.

"Ya' know, Chief," Brim suggested, "if we turn this ship around right now, we could probably avoid what's coming."

"If we weren't so low on energy, that would be one great idea," Barbousse agreed with a bleak look.

"Yeah," Brim said in faux resignation, "there *is* the little problem of energy. Well then, I guess we've faced worse together, haven't we?"

"This time, Skipper, "Barbousse said, "I'm making no bets."

Brim checked the aft view to make certain he'd left ample room for the other three astroplanes, then deftly walked *Four Nines* to a gentle landing at the sea wall, where she was immediately swarmed by a dozen ratings who prepared the ship for her lift inside the shop. "Finished with 'Gravs, Chief," he said.

"Gravs off," Barbousse seconded.

The two old friends sat in silence for a moment, each lost in his own thoughts. Finally, Brim broke the silence. "Lets go face reality, Chief," he said.

"Reality?" Barbousse responded, climbing from his recliner. "I'm beginning to really *dislike* this stuff called reality...."

— o — 0 — o —

Captain Nadia Tissuard, I.F.S., waved a hurried good bye to Wilf
Brim, who was escorted to one of the black limousine skimmers the
moment his boot touched the pavement. Nearby, her own limo was
waiting to take her back to her bender, but she had at least one more
loose end to secure—and very little time to do it. "Serena," she said,
"I'm sure you know why those two Secret Service types are walking
this way."

"I have a pretty good idea," Morgan replied coolly. "Nothing
much I can do but see this all through. After all, I *have* committed no
crime on this trip."

"Good," Tissuard said. "Just stick to your story and I think you'll
glide right through any troublesome interviews. Now, how are you
fixed for credits?"

Morgan smiled. "I'm a bit insolvent right now, but I won't be
after I get to a Bankomat."

"Here, take this," Tissuard said, placing a hefty roll of credits in
Morgan's hand. "Just in case that Bankomat doesn't show up for a
while."

Morgan's eyes widened. "T-that's really kind of you, Nadia," she
said, "especially since you know who I am."

Tissuard held up a warning hand to the two agents who had nearly
reached them, then pointed to the Captain's stripes on her Fleet Cloak.
The pair stopped in their tracks. "Keep this in mind, Sister, she
continued in a half whisper. We professionals must stick together—
always."

"I'll keep in touch, Nadia," the tiny woman promised. "Especially
now I owe *you* a favor. We Lampsonites never forget our debts." She
then flicked a little salute and turned to the Government agents.
"Gentlemen," she called out, "take me where you will!"

Afterward, Tissuard made her way to Barbousse's side. "Well,
Chief," she said, hugging his massive arm, "another Wilf Brim
adventure finished, and we're all survived again—including Wilf."

"Absolutely, Cap'm," Barbousse said with a warm smile, "but this
one was pretty close—a lot closer than I like. If it hadn't been for
Admiral Moulding, we might still be back there on the carrier, playing

Cre'el with no cards." He shook his head for a moment. "We've got to get him back in a Fleet Cloak before he kills himself."

"...And drags us all with him." Tissuard added with a chuckle.

"...That too," Barbousse agreed rolling his eyes heavenward, "But I don't think the Emperor is going to put up with the Skipper's predicament much longer. He needs Brim in the thick of the action—not sidelined the way he's been since that fake court martial."

"Chief," Tissuard said, touching Barbousse's arm, "you know if there's anything I can do to help, I'll be there."

"You certainly proved that when you arrived here at TopLine."

"Xaxt if I did," Tissuard laughed. "I damn near killed those two Government bozos who 'kidnapped' me."

"Unfortunate, that," Barbousse said. "But when Onrad's in a hurry, he's usually in a *big* hurry."

"It all turned out well—only thing that counts," Tissuard said. Then, standing on tiptoe to plant a long kiss on Barbousse's cheek, she made for her Limousine, finding herself considerably relieved to find the men who came to pick her up weren't the ones who had dropped her off previously. Nevertheless, it was *much* more than obvious they were treating her as if she were a live hand grenade. Made her smile all the way back to her bender.

Chapter 68

. . .do keep in touch

AVALON/ASTURIUS, AVALON CITY, TOPLINE SPC&R, 1
TETRAD, 52016

Waving to Tissuard's departing limousine Barbousse made his way back to *Four Nines*, which been moved to an inside lift and was being polished like a black gem. Inside, SubLieutenant Baun was seated in the tiny wardroom, reading a technical manual on his HoloPad.

"Hello, SubLieutenant," Barbousse said, taking a seat on the opposite side of the table. "What's new?"

"Don't ask me, Chief," Baun replied with a grin. "SubLieutenants are 'way at the far end of the info channel. How about you? Got any word about what's next?"

"Nothing yet," Barbousse admitted, "but we've still have ourselves an important assignment."

"Oh," Baun replied. "What's that?"

"Do you have any idea whose personal astroplane this is?"

Baun frowned, and he shrugged. "The Imperial Fleet's, I suppose" he said. "Never really thought about it."

"This one doesn't belong to the Fleet," Barbousse said quietly. "*Four Nines* is *privately* owned."

"You're kidding, Chief! Civilians can't own warships like this, can they?"

"Does the civilian name *Onrad* sound familiar?" Barbousse asked.

"Like in '*Emperor Onrad, Grand Galactic Emperor, Prince of the Reggio Star Cluster, and Rightful Protector of the Heavens?*'" Baun gasped in surprise.

"That's the man," Barbousse assured him. "Now do you understand why we still have important assignments?"

"Ya' think we should grab some polishing rags and go outside to help?"

Barbousse laughed. "No," he said with a chuckle. "Everybody's got a job, we don't want to take theirs away from them do we?"

"Absolutely not, Chief," Baun said.

"Then you get back to your technical manual, Lieutenant," Barbousse advised, "...while I go forward and get a few Metacycles' bunk time. One thing I've learned over the years is when you're working with the Skipper *or* The Emperor, action is never far away...."

— o — 0 — o —

"Admiral Calhoun will see you now, M'Lord," the Admiral's secretary-of-the-day announced cheerfully.

Brim nodded and touched the ENTRY panel of Calhoun's great oak door. As it swung open, Grand Admiral Baxter Calhoun, Supreme Commander of the Imperial Fleet rose from his desk and indicated a pair of magnificent, high-backed armchairs. "Sit ye down, Wilf," the Admiral said with a great smile. "I want t' hear aboot tha' 'Vacation' Onrad's sae steamed aboot."

"If he knew what an adventure it all turned out to be, the Emperor would be jealous," Brim replied.

"Faith, Brim," Calhoun said, "Ony' you wud come up wi' a comment luik tha'."

"Well, it really was," Brim protested.

"Then tell me a' aboot it," Calhoun ordered, rolling his eyes.

— o — 0 — o —

Nearly a metacycle—and two mugs of cvc'eese—later, Calhoun shook his head, settled back in his chair, and laughed. "Weel, Wilf," he said, "I've got to admit, it does sound luik quite an adventure—except for havin' your life in imminent danger much o' the time."

"As stated, Admiral, I wouldn't have missed the adventure for anything. And bcforc old *Purple Abagail* got hcrsclf blown up, I took some pretty good mental notes for making our merchantmen safer in wartime."

"I'm certain ye did, Brim," Calhoun said. "We'll want those recorded soon as there's time. Right now, however, I need to fill ye in aboot a number o' events tha' hae' transpired since ye left on your ill-fated mission."

"Hmm," Brim mused, "I had a feeling there was plenty of catching up to do."

"Probably that feelin' began when ye' learned your beautiful traveling companion war hired to murder ye'. I assume ye know aboot that by now."

"I do, Cal," Brim replied, "Serena Morgan indicated that this last incident—if it was an incident at all—was funded by Barny Case."

"What d' ye mean, '*If* it war an incident at all?'"

"Well, Admiral," Brim said with a smile, "Morgan committed no crime at all, did she?"

"Brim," Calhoun replied with a grin, "ye niver could resist a well-turned ankle, could ye?"

"Well, no, I'll admit that," Brim acknowledged. "But you should have seen her when I met her, She was a wizened old woman until she got aboard the LifeGlobe."

"Guid at disguises, eh?"

"A lot better than, 'good,' Cal."

"Whatever," Calhoun said with a shrug. "Sounds as if ye don't intend to press charges, then."

"For *what*, Admiral?" Brim asked, innocently as he could.

Calhoun held up a hand. "I understand, Brim," he said. "I HoloPhoned Tissuard while ye were on your way here. She warned me ye weren't about to mak any trouble for Morgan."

"I couldn't, Admiral," Brim replied with a grin. "We actually saved each other's lives too often."

"Also wha' Tissuard told me," the Admiral said, standing dismissively. "At any rate, there's a lot more to this than meets the eye, Brim—an' it ties in with tha' Met Station incident at the Bright Triad of Eli, too."

Brim rose to accept the Admiral's hand. "I guess I'm about to learn about the whole thing," he said.

"Ye'll find a man waiting in my outer office who will take ye o'er to Tazmir Adam's office at the IMI campus, where ye wull put a stamp o' approval on your friend Morgan's release. Ye'll be glad to know her cooperation hae' put the finishing touches to an investigation that's gone on far too long."

"An *investigation*?" Brim asked. "I'm all ears."

"I shall be, too," Calhoun said, as Brim walked to the door. "Once you and Tazmir have cleared up the last ugly details."

Brim smiled and tossed off a military salute.

"Ye'll want to get some practice salutin' like tha', Lord Brim," Calhoun called with a peculiar smile as he settled into the chair behind his desk. "Do keep in touch."

Chapter 69

. . .departures

AVALON/ASTURIUS, AVALON CITY, THE IMPERIAL PALACE,
1 TETRAD, 52017

At the IMI campus, Brim found himself immediately escorted to Tazmir Adam's lobby where the first person he encountered was Serena Morgan, delicately sipping a cup of cvc'eese and looking fresh as if she'd come from a spa. "Hey," he said. "Hoped I might see you again here."

Morgan giggled. "To tell the truth, I was rather hoping the same about you."

"'Great minds…,'" Brim quipped. "Is everything okay with you?"

"Depends on *you*, my one-time victim," Morgan said with a winsome smile. "Once more, I'm entirely in your hands."

"Mmmmm," Brim whispered, "wouldn't mind *that* at all, but perhaps Doctor Adam might object if we started something interesting here and now?"

"Regrettably, that will have to wait until next time, Lover," Morgan returned, batting her eyelashes. "Right now—as you Xaxtdamn well know—you could put me away forever."

"For what?" Brim replied with a look of faux consternation. "You have done no wrong I know of."

"Glad you feel that way," Morgan said, then glanced at the door to Adam's inner office suite. "Ever met this guy Adam?"

"Of course," Brim replied, "…a number of times—very likable, and utterly *brilliant*."

"Handsome devil, too," she said under her breath with a little giggle.

"Should I be jealous?" Brim asked with faux concern.

"Wilf Brim," she said, looking him directly in the eyes, "in that particular area of endeavor, you need be jealous of *no one*."

Brim felt his cheeks begin to burn, and was about to comment further, when the door to Adam's office opened and the tall Director stepped into the lounge, offering his hand.

"Admiral Brim," he said, "I have rarely been more pleased to see anyone in my life. For a while, we weren't sure you were coming back from your latest adventure!"

"Not sure if I'd have made it this time except from Ms. Morgan here, Doctor," Brim said, shaking the Director's hand. "Without her, I might still be back there on the primitive planet they call 'Earth.'"

"Not to put too fine a point on it, Admiral," Adam said, "but is it true Ms. Morgan made no threatening moves toward your person?"

"Voot's Beard, no, Doctor!" Brim explained. "She actually saved my life—didn't you, Serena?"

"More like we saved each other's lives," Morgan seconded.

"Ah, glad to hear it, Admiral," Adam said. "For a while, there were a number of nefarious activities that *could* be linked to Ms. Morgan here."

"Serena? Nefarious activities?" Brim exclaimed in mock surprise.

"Well," Adam continued with a little smile, "there certainly *were* nefarious activities afoot recently—incidentally conducted by two well known citizens."

"Who—aside from Barny Case?" Brim asked.

"You *have* been out of circulation for some time," Adam commented.

"Guess so," Brim said, shaking his head. "What happened?"

"Well, for starters," Adam said, "these baddies were both involved in attempts on *your* life."

"My *life*?"

"Absolutely," Adam assured him, "...and some of their activities—toward *you*—might have *incidentally* pointed to Ms. Morgan, here."

Brim glanced at Morgan, who made an innocent little smile and shrugged. "Who were these guys, Doctor?" he demanded.

"Oh, you know them both," Adam declared. "Couple of seriously bad customers named Tal Confisse Trafford and Lord Daniel Cranwell."

"Voot's beard," Brim swore in astonishment. "I haven't heard a thing about those two big shots being in trouble. Which one was murdered?"

"Trafford," Adam replied. "…by his son, no less."

"Didn't know Trafford even a son," Brim commented. "What happened?"

"Whole thing went down aboard Trafford's yacht," Adam declared. "Seems both Trafford and Cranwell had been playing games under the table with the League. To make a long story short, Cranwell blew the lid off their schemes when he clumsily transferred some large funds that came to the attention of your friends Marston and Zinnkin. They provided their information to my organization, and we were on our way to pick them up when the two of them tried to take off in *Princess Megan* for Arelida, one of the pleasure planets in neutral territory."

"But the murder?"

"Happened when the yacht's Captain refused to lift off without clearance," Adam explained. "Trafford put a blaster to the Captain's head, then, evidently, Trafford's son put a blaster to his *Dad's* head."

Brim grimaced. "Guess the Son pulled his trigger first, then?"

"He did."

"What happened then?"

"The son—a weird one known as, 'Covall the Wraith'—managed to escape overboard before the police boats arrived. We've had no sign from him since."

"Wow," Brim remarked. "I assume, then, Cranwell was taken alive."

"Oh yes.," Adman assured him. "He is now in custody of the Imperial Secret Police."

"And none of this has affected General Trafford's career?"

Adam smiled coldly. "Oh, be assured General Trafford's career is still completely intact," he said. "But without her father's influence, General Hagbutt has recently placed her in charge of Salvage operations somewhere on the other side of the planet."

"No comment, Doctor," Brim said. Then he frowned. "So where does all this leave Ms. Morgan, here?"

"Ah yes," Adam continued, "Well, since you vouch for her *innocence* of attempts to bring physical harm to your person, I think we can release her whenever she's ready to go."

"How does that sound to you, Serena?" Brim asked.

Morgan smiled—a little sadly, Brim thought. "Yes," she said. "It's time to be on my way."

"I'm certain your visit here could not have been pleasant, Ms. Morgan," Adam offered, "but I hope we have made you comfortable, at least."

"Doctor Adam," Morgan said with sincere mien, "you have indeed done everything you could to ensure my comfort. I owe you many thanks."

Adam smiled. "The person you owe, Ms. Morgan,—as if you didn't know it yourself—is Captain Tissuard." He chuckled. "She had you legally cleared even before you arrived here. After her call, we needed only Admiral Brim's word—to cover the Ministry's collective rear ends—and you were free to go."

"No matter who is responsible for what," Morgan said quietly, "I thank you, Doctor Adam, for whatever paths you've taken in this affair—but perhaps more for those you *haven't*."

Adam smiled and made a little bow. "You honor me, Madame, as well as my Ministry. It is now *I* who thanks *you*." Then, glancing at his timepiece, he looked at Brim. "Admiral," he said, "I have another appointment. Would you do me the honor of escorting Ms. Morgan to the front entrance? A skimmer awaits her orders."

"My pleasure, Doctor," Brim said, rising, "but Chief Barbousse can pick both of us up since I believe I'm also concluded my business here and should get myself back to TopLine and see to the ship."

Adam laughed. "You are correct about your business here, Admiral," he said, "but others have more immediate plans for your presence. Chief Barbousse has orders for delivering you to a far different location."

Brim raised an eyebrow. "?"

"It's my belief that *you*, Admiral Brim, are due at the Palace within the Metacycle." He extended his hand to Brim. "Good to have caught up with you, again, Admiral," he said.

"Likewise, Doctor."

Adam bent to kiss Morgan's hand, then Brim led her to the elevator bay. "That seemed to go well, Serena," he said.

Morgan smiled. "Wilf," she said, "I'm quite fortunate to have made friends with you and Captain Tissuard."

Brim thought for a few moments while the elevator descended in its serpentine path to the main lobby. "Seems to me, both Nadia and I are also pretty fortunate to have become friends with you, Serena," he said. "I think we've all grown a little with our shared experiences."

Suddenly, they were in the lobby. Ahead through the double-glass doors, he could see Barbousse in the Phantom-III as well as the government van waiting for Morgan. "Guess this is it, Serena," he said, taking her hands. "Shall I ever see you again?"

"Depends on you, Wilf Brim," she replied, almost as if she'd expected his question. "Do you *want* to see me again?"

Brim looked deeply into the tiny woman's eyes. "Yes I do, Serena," he said with a fervor that surprised even himself.

"Then you will, my once and future lover," she said. "Count on it." Suddenly, she stood on her tiptoes, pulled his fact to hers, and kissed him on the lips. "Now, I must go before I make a fool of myself," she gasped, releasing him and hurrying through the double-door airlock, whose panels slid open as if they had been waiting for her exit.

Before Brim could utter a word, she had climbed into the Government van, and—somehow forewarned—he stopped short of the double doors until her chauffeur had driven off. Something told him this brave, intelligent, and incredibly deadly woman was a great deal more special to him than he'd had any idea—and it would be *she* who continued their relationship on her own terms and in her own time. The one thing he did know—and counted on—was there *would* be another time. Only after her van had cleared the security gate, did he walk slowly to the sleek Phantom-III, where Barbousse was holding a door open for him, grinning.

Chapter 70

. . .the emperor's new clothes

AVALON/ASTURIUS, AVALON CITY, THE IMPERIAL PALACE,
1 TETRAD, 52017

While Barbousse drove along the Palace's famed serpentine parkway, Brim noticed they were passing a number of parked Imperial Fleet and Army vehicles—including a huge Rill Limousine skimmer from the Sodeskayan Embassy—with little knots of uniformed chauffeurs smoking and watching the Phantom-III pass with some interest. "Big military stuff going on here this evening," he said. "Wonder if we should have gone to a rear entrance?"

"Don't think so, Skipper. My orders were to drive under the main portico."

"That's all?"

"All I got."

"Okay, Chief," Brim said, "but I sure hope somebody didn't screw up and issue us somebody else's orders. This looks like some sort of celebration."

"Yeah, it does, doesn't it?" Barbousse replied. "Well, I'm for at least showing up as ordered. We're even on time for a change—and the worst they can do is tell us to go home."

Soon, it was too late to turn back. Past the next curve of the Serpentine was the Palace Marque, beneath which a crowd of liveried Pages and Secret Servicemen appeared to be waiting. As Barbousse pulled to a stop, a uniformed officer motioned him to open his window.

"Are we in the right entrance, Officer?" Barbousse asked.

"Absolutely, Master Chief Barbousse," the officer replied. "Please allow me to park the Phantom while you accompany Lord Brim inside."

"Okay with you about the Phantom, Skipper?"

"No argument from me, Chief. We're clearly outnumbered."

At the same moment, a liveried page opened the rear right door for Brim. "Lord Brim," the man said, "Will you and Master Chief Warrant Officer Barbousse please follow me inside?"

"Um…, all right," Brim mumbled, glancing at Barbousse who gave a little shrug as he hurried around the back of the skimmer. "Lead the way."

Over the years, Brim had been in many parts of the Imperial Palace, but the auditorium to which he and Barbousse were led was completely unfamiliar. At the entrance, Brim stopped for a moment and peered inside stunned. Emperor Onrad had positioned himself on a small dais before which perhaps 100 individuals were seated—many of whom looked familiar, even from the rear.

Still in the doorway, Brim frowned at Barbousse. "Chief," he growled under his breath, "what do you know about this?"

Barbousse grimaced: "Well, um, Skipper…, you *know* the scuttlebutt grapevine has never failed me."

"Then wha…?" Brim began, but on the moment, Onrad glanced up to where they stood, grinned, and stilled the polite conversation with his deep voice.

"Friends," he boomed out, in a serious mien, "I shall make this short, because we have much to celebrate this evening; however, I feel it is highly important we gather at this moment, especially since our equally busy guest of honor has just arrived. Lord Brim, will you join me at the dais here?"

Sudden applause greeted Brim as the crowd came to its feet and turned his way.

Barbousse placed a reassuring hand on Brim's shoulder. "Go get your Fleet Cloak back, Skipper," he whispered.

"My what?"

"The Fleet Cloak these idiots owe you, Skipper. *You know*…."

"I know nothing of the sort, Chief."

"Well, ya' do now," Barbousse said with a little smile and gently started Brim toward the dais.

"Thanks, Chief," Brim returned as—mastering many emotions—he made his way down the aisle, more aware with every step the audience was made up of friends and associates whom he had known throughout his career in the Imperial Fleet.

Stepping to the dais, he bowed to Onrad, then turned to face the audience.

"Hear me, Imperials," Onrad boomed, again quieting the applause and sending the audience to its collective seats. "I am using this occasion to announce an important stride we are taking to speed our ultimate victory in this war with Nergol Triannic and his minions. It is a personnel action...." He was forced to pause for more applause. "...This is a action most of you have been anticipating for nearly two years—and I intend to carry it out immediately. Lord Brim," he said without delay, "I am personally ordering you back into the Imperial Fleet as of today, with advancement in grade from Rear Admiral to Vice Admiral. Grand Admiral Calhoun will administer your oath immediately."

At this, a grinning Grand Admiral Calhoun stepped from the wings carrying a Fleet Cloak over his arm. "All right, Brim," he said under his breath, "ye should na hae lost this in the first place, guid friend."

"T-thanks, Cal," Brim gulped in return. "Almost can't believe this is happening..."

"Weel, let's mak it authentic, then, Admiral," Calhoun muttered, stepping behind Brim and placing the cloak over his shoulders.

— o — 0 — o —

From then on, Brim scarcely remembered reciting the Imperial Fleet Oath or the words of greeting by Onrad or the handshakes or the wild applause. The reception afterward was a friendly blur of faces from his career in and out of The Imperial Fleet.

As Barbousse drove him home in the Phantom, the memories most clear in his mind were the Grand Admiral's final words: "Ye'll be a-shippin' off to Sodeskaya soon as ye can assemble yer staff an' get ye briefed on yer new job."

"Ready for Sodeskaya, Chief?" Brim asked absently.

Barbousse laughed. "As long as they still issue heated battle suits and long johns, I'm ready for anything this war throws at us."

With that, Vice Admiral (Lord) Wilf Ansor Brim, Imperial Fleet, relaxed in his new Fleet Cloak and quickly fell asleep in the back seat....

THE END

(. . .for the nonce)

Epilogue

. . .to ice, to snow. . .

AVALON/ASTURIUS, AVALON CITY, 19 TETRAD, 52017

Dressed alike in soiled coveralls, Vice Admiral Wilf Brim and Master Chief Warrant Officer Utrillo Barbousse relaxed at a table in the crowded Sail and Cannon Tavern. Just another frenetic day preparing to move Brim's new office of Strategic Military Operations to the G.F.S.S.

"Big operation," Brim sighed. "Still rather spend our time flying and fighting instead of playing politics."

"Wouldn't worry about that, Skipper," Barbousse advised, "Every time we've wound up with the Sodeskayans, we've been in the thick of it."

"Would you want it any other way, Chief?" Brim asked with a chuckle.

"Try me when we're twice our ages," Barbousse said, taking a draught of meem. "Until then, can't see wasting m' life in any better way."

"Hey," Brim exclaimed, "isn't that young SubLieutenant Baun in mufti coming through the door with.... Why, that blonde on his arm looks familiar!"

"You bet she's familiar," Barbousse, said, pushing back his chair to nab two empty seats from a nearby table. "That's Ann Hunt with him!"

"Over here, you two!" Brim called out.

Grinning, Baun and Hunt pushed their way through the noisy crowd and took the seats Barbousse offered—with Hunt *somehow* squashed tightly between Brim and The Chief.

341

"Ann!" Brim exclaimed—mysterious perfume tickling his nose. "What brings you to Avalon? Another report to Admiral Calhoun?"

Hunt laughed. "Not quite, Admiral Brim," she said. "I've had both a transfer *and* a promotion."

"Whoa!" Brim exclaimed. "Congratulations, *Captain* Hunt! Who do you work for now?"

"Well, at some level: *you*, Admiral," she said with a little smile. "I've been placed in charge of insuring new material coming from Carescria reaches Sodeskayan ports in the most effective manner. I'm now *your* DTOU, only in reverse."

"Waiter!" Barbousse exclaimed. "Meem all around, then!"

Suddenly, against his better instincts, Brim asked, "Hey What about the young Admiral who didn't like talking to civilians?"

Hunt shrugged sadly and pursed her lips for a long moment. "The truth is, he left me for someone who could better enhance his career."

"Ouch," Brim said with a wince.

"It happens, she said wistfully."

"I'm certainly sorry to hear that," Brim lied. "How did you find about the job opening here?"

"Strange," Hunt said. "One day, a notification for *this* job appeared in my mail—at the same time another Commander became available who could more than fill my position as DTOU at Gantaclar. Almost as if the whole thing had been *arranged*."

"Then we got *really* lucky," Brim said, glancing sideways at Barbousse—who was doing all he could to appear as if he had noticed something *fascinating* about the tavern's ceiling.

"And how did you two manage to end up *here* tonight, Lieutenant Baun?" Brim asked with a frown.

Baun shrugged. "Kind of an accident, Skipper," he said. "The Personnel Office called, asking me to meet a senior officer at the Military terminal, and it turned out to be Captain Hunt."

"I see," Brim continued. "And...?"

"Well, wouldn't have been polite to just drop her off at the VOQ, so I brought her along."

"And how did you know we would be here?" Brim asked.

"After watching you and the Chief work all day, where *else* would I think you'd you end up? Have you two had a look at yourselves in a mirror?"

Barbousse chuckled. "Poor Captain Hunt," he said, "What a first impression of her new co-workers."

"Begging the Chief's pardon," Baun quipped, "but she *really* wanted to come. She let me know."

"I did," Hunt said with a little blush. "After my ride back to Gantaclar in the WF-400, I figured I'd already met a good cross section of the people who would be here. I wasn't worried about fitting in."

Then, pointing to the door, Baun exclaimed, "Uh oh here comes more of the crew."

At this, Barbousse stood and instantly snagged a whole table—complete with chairs—nearly out from under a uniformed Commodore and his guests. Moments later, Nero Lu, Warrant Officers Kermis and Treble, and Chief Boson Greg Steele joined the table. "I understand you're buying drinks, Chief," Steele shouted to Barbousse.

"Well..., guess I am now," the big man said, laughing good naturedly while he signaled the waiter again.

"*And,*" Steele continued, "did any of you hear who was murdered this today?"

"Um.... Anybody we know?" Barbousse asked.

"How about Barny Case?" Steele replied.

"*Barny Case?*" Brim demanded as everyone at the table fell silent.

"Yeah," Steel responded. "Heard it on my way over here. The guy didn't show up at work this morning, but since he rarely showed up at his office on time, nobody went looking for him until late this afternoon. They found him at his home; evidently, someone cut his throat from ear to ear."

Barbousse met Brim's eyes. "Before you ask, Skipper," he half-whispered from the side of his mouth, "you know more than I do about the matter. All I heard was Morgan's liner departed around mid-day for the Lampson Provinces."

Brim pursed his lips and nodded. "Poor Barny. He probably never saw it coming."

343

"Well," Barbousse replied, "that was probably a blessing. I imagine Serena made it painless as she could—if, of course, she had anything to do with it."

Brim glanced down at Ann Hunt—his arm now solidly affixed around her shoulders. She was talking across the table with Kermis about Sodeskaya. "Quite a lady, our Serena," Brim whispered to Barbousse.

"One of a kind," The Chief replied. "What d' you say we simply ignore the whole thing?"

"What a concept!" Brim agreed.

"A concept?" Hunt asked looking up into Brim's eyes. "What Concept?"

"The concept of ignoring unpleasantness unless you can do anything about it," Brim explained with a grin.

"I'll drink to that, Admiral," she said. "Who's buying now? You?"

"Well, if I'm buying, then my name is *Wilf*, not *Admiral,*" Brim stated firmly.

"Never *heard* of an Admiral Brim, Mister Wilf," Hunt replied with a little smile, "—and won't, at least until morning, when I have to report in."

During the next half metacycle, more or less, Grand Admiral Calhoun arrived at the tavern door in company with a heavy-set, bearded gentleman who had an extraordinary likeness to Emperor Onrad—and an elderly Sodeskayan Bear with a gray muzzle. Afterward, the party grew in earnest—although the tavern's customers seemed to have been replaced with Secret Service men and drinks had abruptly become free.

It was quite late when everyone joined voices in a song many had learned years in the past:

> To Ice,
> to snow,
> to Sodeskaya we go....

Somewhat later, Brim discovered to his great pleasure that—among other delights—Ann Hunt had the most beautiful feet he had ever encountered....

WILF BRIM GLOSSARY
. . .for *The Turning Tide*

a

A'zurn: A galactic domain of flighted beings—now occupied by
 Nergol Triannic's League of Dark Stars.

Adam, Tazmir: Improbably professorial Imperial Intelligence Chief.

Agnords: Special-forces commandoes from the League of Dark Stars.

Anak, Kabul: Grand Admiral of the League of Dark Stars.

AnGrail: A device (like an Roman/Fascist *fasces*) carried before the
 Emperor that serves as an icon of authority.

Asturius: (the Golden Triad) consists of three stars—a "tri-star"—
 around which circle the five planets of greater Avalon.

Atalanta: Great port city on the planet Haelic orbiting the star Hador.

Atalantan: One whose home is Atalanta

Aunkayr: Final, humiliating retreat from three watery planets orbiting
 the Effer'wyckean star Aunkayr by General Hagbutt's battered
 Imperial Expeditionary Forces during the early days of the
 Second Great War

AutoHelm: "Autopilot"

Avalonian: One whose home is Avalon

Astroplane: comparatively small, fast starship, analogue: airplane.

b

Barfluer, I.F.S.: Newest, most powerful battlecruiser of the Imperial
 Fleet.

Battlecruiser: Large "cruiser killer" type starships (analog: fast
 battleships)

Baun, Sub Lieutenant, I.F. Recent graduate from The Helmsman's
 Academy.

Barbousse, Utrillo: Master Chief Warrant Officer, I.F. (said to closely resemble American actor Vin Diesel, born Mark Sinclair Vincent; July 18, 1967).

Beardsmore: a section of Avalon City, Avalon/Asturius.

Bender: Benders are starships that can render themselves invisible by literally bending all electromagnetic waves of the spectrum around their hulls without otherwise altering their path. The technique required a data system so capable that it could track particles at the subatomic level, processing—in real time—terabits of information for every square milli-iral of hull surface. Such a system, for a ship even the size of an escort vessel, required unheard-of computing capacity and dynamic energy that might easily power a full-sized battleship.

BKAEW: A an object-detection system that uses KA'PPA waves to determine the range, bearing, direction, and speed of both moving and fixed objects in galactic space.

Borodov, Anastas Alexi, Grand Duke (Doctor), Sodeskayan Bear, master of vast baronial estates in the deeply wooded lake country outside the capital city of "holy" Gromcow on the G.F.S.S. "Mother" Planet of Ostra/Sodeskaya itself.

Bright Triad of Eli: small, intensely bright star within a few hundred Standard Light Years of Carescria. It has captured two large asteroids that reflect the star's brilliance so well the whole thing seems like a triad.

Brim, Wilf Ansor, Rear Admiral (RADM), (Lord), I.F. (said to resemble George Peppard, Jr., American film and television actor, October 1, 1928 – May 8, 1994).

Burtis: Carescrian planet.

C

C'lenyt: See Helmsman Linear Units

Caer Landria: Important port on the planet Burtis/Celeron in the province of Carescria.

Ca'omba: Plant that bears Ca'omba fruits.

Carescria: Vast star system from which Wilf Brim and Baxter Calhoun hail. a Provence of Onrad's Empire. Carescria might be—or have been—the most maligned portion of the Empire, but even Emperors drink Carescrian cvc'eese and ride in ships made of Hullmetal from Carescrian asteroid mines.

Chambre: Port on Dorches/Orlena in the Carescrian star system.

CIGAs: Members of the Congress for Intra-Galactic Accord, a powerful, secretly League-backed organization opposing war; specifically: those who participated in antiwar demonstrations that put the Empire at risk following the Treaty of Garak (52000: a self-serving treaty by Nergol Triannic that ended the previous, "Great" war).

COMM: Variously used term for Communications gear.

Confisse: Imperial title.

Covall: Known as Covall the Wraith, bastard son of Count Trafford, this chance product of random debauchery was treated like some mongrel hound; however, the man's unholy aptitude for finance always made him useful enough to keep alive

Cranwell: Lord Daniel Cranwell, Imperial Minister of Commerce and blood relative of powerful Count Tal Confisse.

Camarge: Type of spiced cigarette

Cre'el: Card game reminiscent of poker with "resources" and Tomers.

Cvc'eese: Thick, hot, and sweet drink similar to coffee.

d

Decad: See Helmsman Dates

Diad: See Helmsman Dates

Dorches/Orlena: The planet of Dorches orbiting the Carescrian star Orlena.

Droshcat: A mammoth feline native to many of the Sodeskayan planets, often used as draft animals.

DTOU: Director of Transport Operations Underway

e

Effer'wyck: Proud and powerful dominion with more than ten thousand Standard Years of history.

Effer'wyck, Princess Margot: Her Serene Majesty, Princess Margot of the Effer'wyck Dominions and Baroness (Grand Duchess) of the Torond. Wilf Brim's first real love. Since the night she and Brim met in I.F.S. *Truculent's* wardroom that night some 21 years previously, she had married *two* husbands: the second of whom she truly loved. To the first husband, Rogan LaKarn, she bore a son, who was now lost to her. A victim of TimeWeed, she saw her entire being stolen and ravaged, along with her pride and integrity. In her own words, "Margot Effer'wyck died during those years, For a long time, only Cameron Delacroix believed in me. He truly loved me in spite of what I had become. He searched much of the galaxy before he found a healer for me—gave up all thought of fortune while we traveled among the stars in *Golden Bird*. He left me with a healing family in the Lampson Provinces." Recently, Effer'wyck has surfaced back in Avalon.

Elidean: *I.F.S. Queen Elidean*: A class of Starship Battleship

Emithrnéy/Bax: General Megan Trafford's failure to destroy the Bax-Emithrnéy Gravity docks during Operation EPPEID resulted in a politically-motivated Court Martial in which when Count Tal Confisse's daughter General Megan Trafford lost control of the situation and managed to transfer her guilt to Wilf Brim—Admiral Brim at the time—that cost Brim his commission in the Imperial Fleet and beloved Fleet Cloak.

Eppeid: City on Emithrnéy/Bax in the Effer'wyckean Star Kingdom

Eyren: Nabob Mustafa Eyren, Nabob of occupied Fluvanna.

g

G.F.S.S.: Grand Federation of Sodeskayan States.

Gallsworthy: Bosporus Park Gallsworthy. First surfaced in Brim's life as Principal Helmsman aboard his first ship, I.F.S. *Truculent*. Once considered the Fleet's greatest starship driver, he'd risen to the level of Vice Admiral and Chief of Defense Command, one of the highest offices in the Fleet, with a permanent position on Emperor Onrad's War Cabinet

Gantaclar: Gantaclar Harbor, Imperial Province Of Carescria, Linfarne/Navron

Gemini: Project Gemini was the second NASA human spaceflight program; it was conducted between projects Mercury and Apollo, with ten manned flights occurring in 1965 and 1966. <http://en.wikipedia.org/wiki/Gemini_space_program>

Gemini-6A: Gemini VI-A was a 1965 manned United States spaceflight in NASA's Gemini program that achieved the first manned rendezvous with another spacecraft: its sister Gemini 7. <http://en.wikipedia.org/wiki/Gemini_6A>

Gemini-7: Gemini VII was a 1965 manned spaceflight in NASA's Gemini program. The crew spent nearly 13 2/3 days in space for a total of 206 orbits, and were joined on orbit by the Gemini-6A flight that performed the first rendezvous maneuver of manned spacecraft. <http://en.wikipedia.org/wiki/Gemini_7>

Gilruth: Robert Rowe Gilruth: (1913–2000), an American aviation and space pioneer. <http://en.wikipedia.org/wiki/Robert_R._Gilruth>

Gimmas: the planet of the sprawling Gimmas/Haefdon star base

Gontor: huge asteroid fairly bristling with anti-space disruptors transformed under the command of Admiral Wilf Brim from an ancient wreck to a modern space bastion that now fairly bristled with anti-space disruptors—as well as wrecked Leaguer starships. Below the surface an even more impressive transformation had manifested itself. The once-dark and airless corridors, assembly rooms, warehouses, and barracks now teemed with activity. Colossal, vault-like hangars were jammed with landing craft of every type-including whole chambers filled with a new class of landing craft, called LSCs, designed specifically to carry battle crawlers. If nothing else had been gained from the debacle of Operation Eppeid, it was the importance of large concentrations of heavy armor with massive disruptors firing horizontally (instead of vertically against sites specially hardened against attack from overhead) to support invading troops on the ground.

Gradgroat-Norchelite: one of the many religious sects throughout the Home Galaxy.

Gradygroats: Gradgroat-Norchelite believers

Grand Achtite Canal: an important canal within the city limits of Avalon City, Avalon/Asturius.

Grav: common term for SpinGrav, a hypo-light means of propulsion.

Grobermann, Zoguard, League Minister of State

Gorksroar: Untrue, as in "Horse Hockey"

Gratzl: a small, deer-like animal found in the wilds of Sodeskayan planets.

h

Haelic/Hador: Planet on which the great starport of Atalanta is located.

Haefdon: The dying star of Gimmas/Haefdon.

Hagbutt: General in the Imperial Army.

Hasselblad: a top-of-the-line still camera used by NASA in the '60s.

Helmsman Dates:

The Standard Imperial Calendar in use throughout most of the Home Galaxy is based upon the Avalonian local calendar and consists of four-hundred-day years, divided into ten months: *Unad, Diad, Triad, Tetrad, Pentad, Hexad, Heptad, Octad, Nonad,* and *Decad,* each with 40 days, grouped into four, ten-

---

day weeks. Dates are expressed either as <day>/<year>, as in 131/52013, or <day> <month>, <year>, as in 11 Triad, 52013.

Helmsman Linear Units:
Mmi - One thousandth of an iral.
Thumb = One Tenth the length of an "average" human foot.
Iral = Derived from ancient measurements of an "average" human foot.
C'lenyt = 5,500 irals.

Helmsman Planet-Naming convention
Planets are named for the astronomical object (typically a *star*) around the which they rotate as in
<Planet name>/<Star name> = Avalon/Asturius

Helmsman Surface Directions:
Lightward = Facing planetary rotation.
Nightward = Opposite direction from planetary rotation.
Boreal = Left-hand planetary pole, facing *Lightward.*
Austral = Right-hand planetary pole, facing *Lightward.*

Helmsman Time-of-Day Designations:
Time of day throughout the Home galaxy is based upon the Avalonian local day and is fixed by six , four-metacycle "Watches:" *Dawn* (0:4), *Morning*(5:8), *Brightness*(9:12), *Evening*(13/1:16/4), *Twilight*(17/5:20/8), and *Night*(21/9:24/12).

These are adjusted to local time, whenever possible; however, where local rotation time is either too short or too long, partial or multiple Standard Days are implemented. Time of day is normally written as:
<watch initial>:<metacycle>:<cycle>:<click>,truncated as desired. Example: D:3:45 or B:00:15.

Verbally, time of day is expressed by speaking the watch name followed optionally by, "plus " and a one, two, or three-metacycle offset toward the next watch . This may optionally be followed by, "and" with a one to forty-nine-cycle offset toward the next watch. Examples: Dawn plus one and twenty-five, Evening and forty, Twilight plus three.

In casual speech, the use of "and a half" indicates twenty-five cycles past a metacycle, as in, "Dawn and a half," or "Dawn plus three and a half."

One Standard Day anywhere in the galaxy is based on the six-watch Avalonian Day

Helmsman Time Measurement Units:

Click = 1.5 x human eye blink☐

Microclick = .001 click☐

Cycle = 50 clicks ☐

Metacycle = 50 Cycles

☐NOTE: "Standard" day, week, month, year designations are based on those on the planet Avalon/Asturius.

Standard Day = 24 Metacycles☐

Standard Week = 10 Standard days☐

Month = 40 Standard days, or 4 Standard Weeks☐

Standard Year = 400 Standard Days,☐ or 40 Standard Weeks, or 10 Standard Months.

Helmsman Units of Mass

Stoneweight = 1/2000 of a Milston.☐☐

Milston = Mass of approximately one Standard Mill Stone (see Imperial Museum, Avalon/Asturius).

Helmsmanship: Art and science of piloting starships.

HoloMap: Holographic map.

HoloPhone: Holographic display on a personal phone.

Holophotos: Holographic photographs.

Hullmetal: Collapsium from which starships are routinely constructed.

Hunt, Ann: Commander, I.F. Slim, attractive blonde . During moment Brim met her glance, he caught the cosmopolitan warmth of someone whose keen intellect had seen and appreciated much of the Known Universe. He also detected the barest hint of perfume, forbidden by military code. He was drawn to her immediately—strongly—but he had no idea why.

HyperLight: Travel at faster-than-LightSpeed velocity.

Hyperscreen: Controlled-crystal windows that provide "normal" views outside a starship when the vehicle is traveling faster than LightSpeed.
Hyperspeed: Travel at a velocity faster than the speed of light.
HyperTorp: Torpedo capable of traveling greater than the speed of light

i

I.F.S.: Acronym for "Imperial Fleet Starship"
Inhardt: Seyess: tall, gray-bearded Tower controller at Lake Mersin
Intragalactic = Within the Home Galaxy.
Iral: See Helmsman Linear Units
IVG: Imperial Volunteer Group.

k

KA'PPA: Instantaneous, Universe-wide communication
Karlsson: A type of extra-bright floodlight.
Kelton: Lake Kelton, a lake on Linfarne/Navron, Imperial Provence of Carescria
Knez = Emperor of Sodeskaya.
Korbu: Small star-planet system invaded and occupied by The League of Dark Stars.
Krasni-Peych: "KPOCHBL-II3TY" a galaxy-famous Star-Drive manufacturer and research center, located only a short drive outside Gromcow

1

LaKarn: Rogan, became Grand Duke of the Torond when his mother, Honorotha was deposed in 52008. Married Margo Effer'wyck, who bore him a son.

Lamintir: Small, star nation occupied by the League of Dark Stars.

Lampson Provinces: a planet system whose inhabitants have a natural ability to translate from listening to emotions, not words. Contemporary has no idea how it works. Lampsonites are born with the power."

Lampsonite: one who hails from the Lampson Provinces

LifeGlobe: globe-shaped vehicle carried aboard starships in case of accident. These vehicles are provided with a SpinGrav anti-gravity engine sufficiently powerful to bring the boat to manageable velocities below LightSpeed. Heir databases can find habitation for nearly any creatures that might be aboard.

LightSpeed: the speed of light. 186,000 c'lenyts per click

Lightward: see Helmsman Surface Directions, above.

Linfarne: a planet of the star Navron in the Imperial Provence of Carescria.

Logish: Quality standard of Meem, a fermented fruit drink of the Logus Vine. "Logish" may be applied to "Meem" only when the Meem is of the very highest quality.

LPM: a measure of velocity expressed in Light Years per Metacycle.

Magor: the capital city of The Fluvannian planets on Ordu/Ephial.

Marston, Porterfield: Portly financial wizard who manages Lord Brim's vast holdings.

Meem: Meem, a fermented fruit drink of the Logus Vine.

MET Station: The Space Transportation Safety Establishment established a MET station on The Bright Triad of Ely's larger

asteroid to monitor gravity storms passing toward Greater
Avalon from the galactic center.

Moulding: Rear Admiral Tobias Moulding, I.F, long-time, close friend
of Wilf Brim.

Metacycle: See Helmsman Time Measurement Units

Milston: see Helmsman Units of Mass

mu'occo: a type of Atalantan cigarette.

n

Navron: Star within in the Imperial Provence of Carescria.

Nergol: see Triannic, below

Nightward: see Helmsman Surface Directions, above.

Nonad: see Helmsman Dates, above.

o

Octad: see Helmsman Dates, above.

Onrad: Emperor, Onrad V, Grand Galactic Emperor, Prince of the
Reggio Star Cluster, and Rightful Protector of the Heavens

Ornwald: *Ornwald* "girls" are special prostitutes who dress in the
abbreviated green dresses of their singular profession. They
congregate in the Ornwald section of Avalon city.

Ophet: a type of leather.

p

Pidwings: birds at Avalonian Admiralty (equiv = pigeon)

r

Raddisma: The late Chief Consort of Mustafa Erian and mother of Brim's daughter, Hope.

Radiosphere: the sphere of radiation around any space object.

S

Schirra: Walter Marty Schirra, Jr. (March 12, 1923 – May 3, 2007) was an American test pilot, United States Navy officer, and one of the original Mercury 7 astronauts chosen for the Project Mercury, America's effort to put humans in space. He is the only person to fly in all of America's first three space programs (Mercury, Gemini and Apollo). He logged a total of 295 hours and 15 minutes in space. Schirra was the fifth American and the ninth human to ride a rocket into space. He was the first person to go into space three times.

Seyess: Seyess Inhardt, tall, gray-bearded Tower Controller

Sodeskaya: Sprawling star nation that subsumes half the Home Galaxy—largely populated by highly intelligent, Bear-like beings. Also known as the Great Federation of Sodeskayan States.

SpinGrav: a type of Hypo-Light gravity generator used for propulsion to velocities up to the speed of light, where Drive Crystals take over for HyperLight flight.

S.S. *Purple Abagail*, an aging starship.

S.S. Benoath: *S.S. Benoath*, a fast, luxury-liner starship that had been converted into a fast transport shortly after the beginning of hostilities with the League of Dark Stars

Starfury: Graceful, 66-iral-long astroplanes that could top 400 LightSpeed, or 400 Light Years per Standard Metacycle. With a cruising range of 660 light years (1,300 light years in the PR X model) they could tangle with anything the Galaxy could throw at them. They were reduced in size by nearly half from the Mark 1C Starfury "pocket Battle cruisers" that were their immediate ancestors, yet they retained the identical main battery of twelve 406-mmi disruptor cannon and required a crew of only fifteen. In their intended role as short-range interceptors, they were renowned - and feared - throughout the galaxy.

Star Sailor: One who plies the stars.

SubLieutenant: Entry-Level officer in the Imperial Fleet.

Starflight: Travel at HyperLight speeds among the stars.

Starliners: Huge starships plying the star routes of the Home Galaxy, typically at speeds less than 60 LPM.

Starports: Major ports at which starships load and unload.

Starscape: The night sky is a starscape.

t

Tarrott: Capital city of the League of Dark Stars on the planet Dahlem orbiting the trinary star Uadn'aps

Terraforming: the act and art of transforming a planet to coincide with the critical needs of various beings.

TimeWeed: Extremely addictive narcotic, used mostly by upper echelons of The League of Dark Stars.

Tissuard, Nadia: from the Lampson Provinces. Tiny and prematurely gray, her round face, laughing eyes, pug nose, and full, sensuous lips endowed her face with the look of a true pixie. She had a compact figure with largish hands and feet—and a prominent bosom that rarely failed to attract male attention, even when mostly concealed by a Fleet Cloak. Standard Years ago, as Brim's First Lieutenant aboard I.F.S. Starfury during a prewar tour of duty, she had proven herself an exceptional Helmsman who could carry out a myriad of duties with the cheerful willingness of a Gradgroat saint. She was also utterly frank and—off duty—quite extraordinarily sensual. A personal bond had formed between her and Brim, and on more than one occasion they had been at pains to remain on the "safe" side of professionalism. Following her reassignment as captain of the bender I.F.S. *Nord*, however, their friendship had gradually changed to one of a more intimate nature, though Dame Fortune had yet to provide them with opportunity for anything but a few hurried gropings.

TopLine SPC&R: Spacecraft Performance, Customization and Research): a bogus corporation set up by Brim and Barbousse in a warehouse to house a complete Hullmetal machine shop, a shielded Drive maintenance room, overhead lifts, and a Ship Lift suitable for the WF-400.

Torond: Star Kingdom and major ally of The League of Dark Stars.

Triannic, Nergol: Emperor of the league of Dark Stars

Tupolev 128: Tu-28 (NATO reporting name *Fiddler*) was a long-range interceptor aircraft introduced by the Soviet Union in the 1960s. The official designation was Tu-128. It was the largest and heaviest fighter ever in service.
[see: http://en.wikipedia.org/wiki/Tupolev_Tu-28#Specifications_.28Tu-128.29]

Tutti, Nurse: Originally Raddisma's Nurse, upon Raddisma's death, she elected to remain with The Consort's newly-born daughter, Hope, Wilf Brim's only offspring.

U

Unad: See Helmsman Dates, above.

V

Valemont, Claudia: Claudia Valemont-Nesterio, Wilf Brim's long-time (and married) love interest from the great port city of Atalanta on Haelic/Hador.

Vertrucht: Language spoken by citizens of The League of Dark Stars.

Voot: Imaginary, god-like being.

Voshell, Captain, Imperial Fleet., Captain of battlecruiser I.F.S. *Barfluer*.

W

'Wyckean Void: Large rift in the Home Galaxy separating Emperor Onrad's Imperial stars and planets from those of numerous other Star Kingdoms. So named because in many maps, Effer'wyck lies directly opposite the Empire.

WF: Manufacturer designation for astroplane builder Wakefield.

WF-400: Designation of astroplanes newest built by Wakefield. These astroplanes resemble, but are complete redesigns of the WF Type-327.

X

Xaxt: Ancient and little-known god.

Z

Z'tinod: L'rak Z'tinod, League Commander of O-ships (benders).

Zinnkin, Dr., Factovar: Longtime friend of friend of Porterfield Marston from the mysterious World of Forensic Finance.

Zonga'ar: Zonga'ar = space reef "near" Fluvanna where the league has built a great space fortification.

Zortech: Small, inexpensive skimmer often employed by the Imperial Government.

Zukeed: Offensive appellation most often given to another individual.

CPSIA information can be obtained at www.ICGtesting.com
Printed in the USA
BVOW02s0918220114

342671BV00010B/872/P